"When Kinsolving  ... be-ware!"

Commodore John Grimes would have done well to heed this warning. But the evil magic of Kinsolving draws him on, pulling him on a journey through the universes. Is Grimes a swiftly fading literary ghost, doomed to disappearance for the inadvertent theft of a meerschaum pipe? Or, is he a flesh and blood Commodore, sailing the spaceways from world to world, enjoying dangerous voyages to momentary safe ports?

It does not matter what role is the "true John Grimes" for none can protect him from the grasp of Kinsolving's Planet, an abandoned colony which reaches out for man, for the target, John Grimes, who is inexorably sucked toward his final destiny....

Turn this book over for
second complete novel

A. BERTRAM CHANDLER
ALTERNATE ORBITS

ACE BOOKS

A Division of Charter Communications Inc.
1120 Avenue of the Americas
New York, N.Y. 10036

HALL OF FAME

Sonya Grimes was unpacking. Grimes watched her contentedly. She was back at last from her galactic cruise, and the apartment was no longer just a place in which to live after a fashion, in which to eat lonely meals, in which to sleep in a lonely bed. It was, once more, home.

She asked lightly, "And have you been *good* while I've been away?"

"Yes," he replied without hesitation, bending the truth only slightly. There had been that girl on Mellise, of course, but it had all been in the line of duty. A reminiscent grin softened his craggy features. "So good, in fact, that I was given the honorary rank of Admiral on Tharn . . ."

She laughed. "Then I'd better give you something too, my dear. Something I know you'll like . . ." She fell gracefully to her knees beside a suitcase that she had not yet opened, unsnapped and lifted up the lid, plunged a slender hand into a froth of gossamer undergarments. "Ah, here it is. I didn't want it to get broken . . ."

It was a leather case and, although it obviously had been well cared for, it was worn and cracked, was ancient rather than merely old. The Commodore took it carefully from his wife, looked at it with some puzzlement. Its shape was clue enough to what it contained, but Grimes had never guessed that such homely and familiar masculine accessories could ever possess any value other than a strictly utilitarian one.

"Open it!" she urged.

Grimes opened the case, stared in some bewilderment at the meerschaum pipe that was revealed, archaic and fragile in its nest of faded plush.

"There was a little shop in Baker Street," she said, speaking rapidly. "An antique shop. They had this. I knew you'd like it . . ."

"Baker Street . . ." he repeated. "In London? On Earth?"

"Of course, John. And you *know* who lived there . . ."

Yes, thought Grimes. *I know who lived there. And he smoked a pipe, and he wore something called a deerstalker hat. The only trouble is that he never lived at all in real life. Oh Sonya, Sonya, they must have seen you coming. And how much did you pay for . . . this?*

"Think of it," she went on. "Sherlock Holmes's own pipe . . ."

"Fantastic."

"You don't like it?" Neither of them was a true telepath, but each was quick to sense the mood of the other. "You don't like it?"

"I do," he lied. But was it a lie? The thought behind the gift was more important, much more important than the gift itself. "I do," he said, and this time there was no smallest hint of insincerity in his voice. He put the precious pipe down carefully on the coffee table. "But you've brought yourself back, and you're worth more to me than Sherlock Holmes's pipe, or Julius Caesar's bloodstained toga, or King Solomon's mines. Come here, woman!"

"That's an odd-looking weapon you've got, Grimes," remarked Admiral Kravinsky.

The Commodore laughed. "Yes, and there's quite a story attached to it, sir. Sonya bought it for me in London—and you'd think that a woman who holds a commission in the Intelligence Branch of the Survey Service would have more intelligence than to be taken in by phony antiques! This, sir, is alleged to be the actual pipe smoked by the great Sherlock Holmes himself."

"Really?"

"Yes, really. But I'll say this for Sonya, she's got a sense of humor. After I'd explained to her in words of one syllable that Sherlock Holmes was no more than a fictional character she saw the joke, even though it was on her . . ."

"And on you."

"I suppose so. When I think of all the first class London briars that could have been purchased for the same money . . ."

"I'm surprised that you're smoking *that*. After all, a secondhand pipe . . ."

"Sonya's thorough. She took the thing to the nearest forensic laboratory to have it examined. They assured her that it was untouched by human hand—or lip. It's a perfectly good meerschaum, recently manufactured and artificially aged. So she said that she liked to see her husband smoking the most expensive pipe in the Rim Worlds. It's not a bad smoke either . . ."

"Don't drop it," warned the Admiral. "Whatever you do, don't drop it." Then the tolerant smile vanished from his broad, ruddy features. "But I didn't send for you to discuss your filthy smoking habits." He selected a gnarled, black cigar from the box on his desk, lit it. "I've a job for you, Grimes. I've already spoken to Rim Runners' management and arranged for your release for service with the Reserve."

Normally Grimes would have been pleased, but with Sonya just back . . .

"The Federation has a finger in this particular pie as well, Grimes. And as their Commander Sonya Verrill is back in Port Forlorn she may as well go along with you."

Grimes's face cleared.

"And this *will* please you, Commodore. I haven't any warships to spare, and so your beloved *Faraway Quest* will be recommissioned, with you in full command. The selection of personnel will be up to you."

"And what is the job, sir?" asked Grimes.

"A detailed, leisurely investigation of Kinsolving's Planet. We all of us tend to shy away from that ruddy world—but, after all, it is in our back garden. And after those outsiders from Francisco landed there to carry out their odd experiments . . ."

"I was there too," said Grimes.

"Well I bloody well know it. And I had to organize the rescue party. Anyhow, you're our expert on Rim World oddities. Things seem to happen around you rather than to you. If anybody falls through a crack in the continuum the odds are at least a hundred to one that Commodore Grimes, Rim Worlds Naval Reserve, will be lurking somewhere in the background . . ."

"I've been in the foreground too, sir."

"I know, Grimes, I know. But you always survive, and the people with you usually survive. I had no hesitation in recommending you for this . . . survey. Yes, I suppose you could call it that, although what you'll be surveying God knows."

"Which god?" asked Grimes, remembering vividly what had happened to the expedition from Francisco.

"Fill me in," ordered Sonya. "Put me in the picture."

"I wrote to you," said Grimes. "I told you all about it."

"I never received the letter."

7

"It must still be chasing you. Well, you know of Kinsolving's Planet, of course . . ."

"Not as much as I should, my dear. So just make believe that I've just come out to the Rim, and that I was never in the Intelligence Branch of the Survey Service. Start from there."

"You have access to all the official reports, including mine."

"I prefer to hear the story in less formal language. I never did care for officialese."

"Very well, then. Now, Kinsolving's Planet. It's one of the Rim Worlds, and it was colonized at the same time as the others, but the colonization didn't stick. There's something . . . odd about the atmosphere of the place. No, not chemically, or physically. Psychologically. There are all sorts of fancy theories to account for it; one of the more recent is that Kinsolving lies at the intersection of stress lines; that there the very fabric of space and time is stretched almost to bursting; that the boundaries between *then* and *now*, between *here* and *there*, are so thin as to be almost nonexistent. Oh, I know that the same sort of thing has been said often enough about the Rim Worlds in general—but nowhere is the effect so pronounced as on Kinsolving. People just didn't like living on a world where they could never feel sure of *anything*, where there was always the dread at the back of their minds that the Change Winds would reach gale force at any tick of the clock. So, when their suicide rate had risen to an unprecedented level and their nut hatches were crammed to capacity, they got the hell out.

"That was that. And then, a century and a half ago, Galactic Standard, one of the Commission's tramps, *Epsilon Eridani*, made an emergency landing at the spaceport. She had to recalibrate the controls of her Mannschenn Drive and, as you know, that's best done on a planetary surface. It could be that the temporal precession fields set up while this was being done triggered some sort of continuum-warping chain reaction . . . Anyhow, a few of the officers were allowed shore leave, and they decided to explore the famous caves, which were not far distant. In these caves are remarkably well-preserved rock paintings, made by the Stone Age aborigines who once lived on Kinsolving. (What happened to *them*, nobody knows. They just vanished, millennia before the first humans landed.) They returned to their ship

8

in quite a dither, reporting that the paint of some of the pictures of various animals was *wet*.

"The Federation's Survey Service finally got to hear about this and sent a small team of investigators, one of them a very well-qualified young lady from the Rhine Institute. They found the rock paintings without any trouble—and found that a new one had been added, one depicting men in the standard spaceman's rig of that period. While they were standing around marveling they were pounced upon by a horde of cavemen and made prisoner.

"But the Rhine Institute's star graduate was equal to the occasion. Telepathy, teleportation, psychokinesis—you name it, she had it. The party escaped with a prisoner of their own, the artist in person. His name was Raul . . .

"And, back on Earth, Raul became a pet of the Rhine Institute himself. He was a very specialized kind of painter. When he drew an animal, that animal was drawn, in the other sense of the word, to within range of the weapons of the hunters. He was also a telepath, and after the Institute had just about sucked him dry he went to Francisco to become chief psionic radio officer of the Deep Space Communications Station on that world. By this time he'd married the wench who'd captured him and, although he wasn't human, strictly speaking, the genetic engineers were able to make certain modifications to his body so that the union was a fruitful one.

"You've been to Francisco, of course. You know how religion is almost a primary industry on that planet. Raul got religion—and became, of all things, a neo-Calvinist, as did all his family. His great-granddaughter fell from grace with a loud thud and became one of the so-called Blossom People . . ."

"So there's a woman mixed up in it!" commented Sonya.

"Look around, my dear, and you'll find a woman mixed up in almost everything. But where was I? Yes, Clarisse. She rather overdid things—drink, sex, drugs—and was picked up out of the gutter and brought back into the fold. But the neo-Calvinists weren't being charitable. They knew that she had inherited her ancestor's talents, and they knew that certain of the psychedelic drugs amplified these same talents, and so . . ."

"And so?" she echoed.

"And so some perverted genius cooked up a scheme that

even now makes me shudder. The idea was that she should be taken to Kinsolving and there, on a suitable mountain top, invoke by her graphic art and magic the God of the Old Testament, in the pious hope that He would provide for the neo-Calvinists a new edition of the Ten Commandments. That bunch of unspeakable wowsers had to get the permission of the Confederacy, of course, before they could land on Kinsolving—and so my lords and masters decided that Commodore Grimes, Rim Worlds Naval Reserve, should go along as an observer . . ."

"You never tell me anything."

"I wrote to you about it. And it's all in the reports that you, as the senior representative of the Survey Service's Intelligence Branch on the Rim Worlds, should have read by now. Besides, I've hardly had a chance to get a word in edgewise since you came home."

"Never mind that. What happened?"

"They set up shop on top of the mountain that they'd decided was the new Sinai. Clarisse, after the proper preparations, painted a picture of a suitably irate-looking, white-bearded deity . . . The trouble was, of course, that so many of those patriarchal gods looked alike. And the Blossom People's religion is a pantheistic one. Cutting a long and sad story short—what we got wasn't Sinai, but Olympus . . ."

There was a long silence. And then, "If I didn't know you, and if I didn't know from personal experience what odd things do happen out on the Rim, I'd say that you'd missed your vocation, that you should be a writer of fairy stories . . . But you assure me that all this is in the reports?"

"It is. And Clarisse is still on Lorn. She married Mayhew. I was thinking that we might have them round tomorrow evening. And they'll be coming with us in the *Quest*, in any case."

"But what's our expedition supposed to be in aid of?" she demanded. "You're leading it, and I shall be your second-in-command; and two more unlikely people to be involved in any sort of religious research, I can't think of."

The Commodore smiled a little crookedly. "I'll tell you what Kravinsky said to me. 'It boils down to this, Grimes. Both the Confederacy and our big brothers of the Federation think that something should be done about Kinsolving. Nobody is quite sure what. So I'm sending you, with your usual crew of offbeats and misfits, and if you bumble around in your inimitable manner *something* is bound to happen . . .' "

Sonya grinned back at him. "The man could be right," she said.

Finally—the recommissioning of a long laid up vessel takes time, *Faraway Quest*, Commodore John Grimes commanding, lifted slowly from Port Forlorn. She was well-manned; Grimes had selected his crew, both spacefaring personnel and civilian scientists and technicians, with care. The officers of all departments were, like the Commodore himself, naval reservists, specialists in navigation and gunnery and engineering: in ship's biochemistry. And there was the Major of Marines—also, as were his men, a specialist. Grimes hoped that the spaceborne soldiers' services would not be needed, but it was good to have them along, just in case. There was Mayhew, one of the few psionic radio officers still on active service, youthful in appearance but old in years; and Clarisse, really beautiful since her marriage and her breakaway from the neo-Calvinists and their severe rules regarding dress and decorum, her hair styling revealing the pointed ears inherited from her nonhuman ancestor. There were the two fat, jolly men from the Dowser's Guild who, even in this day and age, were shunned by the majority of the scientists. There were men and women whose specialty was the measurement of radiation, others whose field was chemistry, organic and inorganic. There were archeologists, and paleontologists, and . . .

"One more specialist, Grimes," Admiral Kravinsky had growled, "and that old bitch of yours won't be able to lift a millimeter . . ."

But a converted freighter, with all space properly utilized, has quite amazing capacity insofar as the carrying of passengers is concerned.

So she lifted, her inertial drive running sweetly and uncomplainingly, with Grimes himself at the controls, all the old skill flowing back into his fingers, the ship an extension of his fit, stocky body, obedient to his will, as were his officers grouped around him in the control room, each in his own chair with his own bank of instruments before him.

She lifted, accelerating smoothly, soaring up to the low cloud ceiling, and through it, breaking out into the steely sunlight of high altitudes, driving up to the purple sky that soon deepened to black, into the darkness where glimmered

11

the few, faint stars of the Rim, where, rising above the gleaming arc that was the sunlit limb of the planet, glowed the misty ellipsoid that was the Galactic Lens.

Sonya, who had traveled vast distances as a passenger, said quietly, "It's good to see this from a control room again."

"It's always good . . ." said Grimes.

Faraway Quest was clear of the atmosphere now, still lifting, and below them the planet presented the appearance of a huge, mottled ball, an enormous flawed pearl lustrous against the black immensities. She was clear of the Van Allen, and Grimes snapped an order. The Senior Communications Officer spoke quietly into his intercom microphone. "Attention all! Attention all! There will be a short countdown, from ten to zero. The inertial drive will be shut off, after which there will be a period of free fall, with brief lateral accelerations as trajectory is adjusted." He turned to the Commodore. "Ready, sir?"

Grimes studied the chart tank. "Now!" he said.

"Ten . . ." began the officer. "Nine . . ."

Grimes looked to Sonya, raised his heavy eyebrows and shrugged. She shrugged back, and made even this gesture graceful. She knew, as he knew, that all this formality was necessary only because there were so many civilians aboard.

". . . Zero!"

The irregular, throbbing beat of the inertial drive suddenly ceased and there was brief weightlessness and a short silence. Then there was the hum of the maneuvering gyroscopes, rising to a whine, and centrifugal force gently pressed those in Control to the sides of their chairs. Slowly, slowly, the target star, the Kinsolving sun, drifted across the black sky until the glittering spark was centered in the cartwheel sight, wavered, then held steady. The inertial drive came on again, its broken rumble a bass background to the thin, high keening of the ever-precessing rotors of the Mannschenn Drive. Ahead, save for the tiny, iridescent spiral that was the target sun, there was only emptiness. Lorn was to starboard; a vast, writhing planetary amoeba that was dropping back to the quarter, that was dwindling rapidly. And out to port was the Galactic Lens, distorted by the temporal precession field of the Drive to the similitude of a Klein flask blown by a drunken glassblower.

Grimes rather wished, as he had often wished before,

that somebody would come up with another way of describing it. He doubted if anybody ever would.

This was a far more pleasant voyage than the one that he had made to Kinsolving in the unhappy *Piety*. To begin with, he had Sonya with him. Second, he was in command, and the ship was being run his way. *Faraway Quest* was no luxury liner, but she was warm, comfortable. Her internal atmosphere carried the scents of women's perfume, of tobacco smoke, of good cooking—not that omnipresent acridity of disinfectant. The snatches of music that drifted through her alleyways from the playmasters in the public rooms were anything and everything from grand opera to the latest pop, never the morbid hymns and psalms in which the neo-Calvinists had specialized. He spoke of this to Clarisse. She grinned and said, "You're not with it, Dad. You're just not with it. By *our* standards this wagon is bitter endsville, just a spaceborne morgue."

He grinned back. "If the best that the Blossom People can do is to resurrect the hip talk of the middle twentieth century, I doubt if you're with it either."

"Every religion," she told him seriously, "uses archaic language in its scriptures and in its rituals." Then she laughed. "I'm not complaining, John. Believe me, I'm not complaining. When I look back to the *Piety*, and Rector Smith and Presbyter Cannan, and that she-dragon of a deaconess, I realize how lucky I am. Of course, I could have been luckier . . ."

"How so?"

"That tall, beautiful redhead of yours could have been left behind."

"To say nothing of that highly capable telepath you're married to."

Her face softened. "I was joking, John. Before I met Ken—before I met him physically, that is—something might have been possible between us. But I'm well content now, and I feel that I owe it all to you. Ken was against our coming on this expedition, but I insisted. I'll do anything I can to aid your . . . researches."

"Even to a repeat performance?"

"Even to a repeat performance."

"I hope it doesn't come to that."

"Frankly, John, so do I."

The voyage was over. *Faraway Quest*, her Mannschenn Drive shut down, her inertial drive ticking over just sufficiently to induce a minimal gravitational field, was falling in orbit about the lonely world, the blue and green mottled sphere hanging there against the blackness. The old charts were out, and the new ones too, made by Grimes himself with the assistance of the officers of *Rim Sword*. "Here," said the Commodore, stabbing a blunt forefinger down onto the paper, "is where the spaceport *was*. There's only a crater there now. Whoever or whatever destroyed *Piety* made a thorough job of it. And here's the city—Enderston it was called—on the east bank of the Weary River . . ."

" 'Where even the weariest river winds somewhere safe to sea . . .' " quoted Sonya. "They must have been a cheerful bunch, those first colonists."

"I've already told you that the very atmosphere of the planet engenders morbidity. And there, on the shore of Darkling Tarn, is what was the Sports Stadium, where *Rim Sword* landed. In the absence of any spaceport facilities it's as good a place as any." He turned from the chart to the big screen upon which a magnification of the planet was presented. "You can see it all there—just to the east of the sunrise terminator. That river, with all the S bends, is the Weary, and that lake which looks like an octopus run over by a streamroller is Darkling Tarn. The city's too overgrown for it to show up at this range."

"You're the boss," said Sonya.

"Yes. So I suppose I'd better do something about something." He turned to his executive officer. "Make it landing stations, Commander Williams."

"Landing stations it is, sir."

The officers went to their acceleration chairs, strapped themselves in. In seconds the intercom speakers were blatting, "Secure all for landing stations! Secure all for landing stations! All idlers to their quarters!" And then the maneuvering gyroscopes hummed and whined as the ship was tilted relative to the planet until the surface was directly beneath her. The sounding rockets were discharged as she began her descent, each of them releasing a parachute flare in the upper atmosphere, each of them emitting a long, long streamer of white smoke.

Faraway Quest dropped steadily—not too fast and not too slow. Grimes made allowance for drift and, as the first of the flares was swept west by a jet stream, he applied lateral thrust. Down she dropped, and down, almost falling free, but always under the full control of her master. The picture of the surface on the target screen expanded. The city could be seen now, a huddle of ruins on the river bank, and beside the lake there was the oval of the Stadium, *Eau de Nil* in the midst of the indigo of the older growth. The last of the flares to have been fired was still burning down there, the column of smoke rising almost vertically. The brush among which it had fallen was slowly smoldering.

Grimes shivered. The feeling of *déjà vu* was chillingly uncanny. But he had seen this before. He had been here before—and, save for the different choice of landing site, circumstances had been almost exactly duplicated, even to that luckily unenthusiastic bush fire. And again there was the sensation that supernal forces—malign or beneficent?—were mustering to resist the landing of the ship.

But she was down at last.

There was the gentlest of shocks, the faintest of creakings, the softest sighing of the shock absorbers as the great mass of the vessel settled in her tripodal landing gear. She was down. "Finished with engines!" said Grimes softly. Telegraph bells jangled, and the inertial drive generators muttered to themselves and then were still. She was down, and the soughing of the fans intensified the silence.

Grimes turned in his swivel chair, looked toward the distant mountain peak, the black, truncated cone sharp against the blue sky. "Sinai," Presbyter Cannan had named it. "Olympus," Grimes had called it on his new charts. It was there that the neo-Calvinists had attempted to invoke Jehovah, and there that the old gods of the Greek pantheon had made their disastrous appearance. Grimes hoped that he would never have to set foot upon that mountain top again.

He was not first off the ship; after all, this was no newly discovered planet, this was not a historic first landing of Man. The honor fell to the Major of Marines, who marched smartly down the ramp at the head of his clattering column of space soldiers. He barked orders and the detachment broke up into its component parts, fanning out from the landing site, trampling through the bushes. From somewhere came a sharp rattle of machine-pistol fire. The Commodore was not concerned. He said, "There'll be fresh pork or rabbit

15

on the table in the Marines' mess tonight. Or pigburger or rabbitburger if the man who fired was too enthusiastic."

"Pigs? Rabbits?" inquired Sonya.

"Descendants of the livestock brought here by the original colonists. They—the pigs, probably—seem to have wiped out most of the indigenous fauna. And, come to that, the hens and the sheep and the cattle." He lit his pipe. "They were, I suppose, the two species best fitted to survive. The pigs with their intelligence, the rabbits with their ability to go underground and to breed . . . like rabbits."

She said, "I could do with some fresh air after weeks of the tinned variety. What's good enough for pigs and rabbits and Marines is good enough for me."

"Just as well that the gallant Major didn't hear you say that. Commander Williams!"

"Sir!" replied the burly Executive Officer.

"Shore leave is in order, as long as a full working watch —and that includes the manning of weaponry—is left aboard the ship at all times. And every party of boffins is to be accompanied by at least one officer or one Marine other rank, armed. Nobody is to go down the ramp without checking out or without wearing his personal transceiver. Apart from that, we'll make this a day of general relaxation. After all, there are no physical dangers on this world. As for the other kind—I doubt if the Federation's Grand Fleet could cope with them."

"Good-oh, Skipper," replied Williams.

Grimes glared at him, then laughed. "I wondered how long it would be before the veneer of your last drill in the Reserve wore off. Anyhow, those are the orders—and just try to remember now and again that this is an auxiliary cruiser of the Rim Worlds Navy, not your beloved *Rim Mamelute*." He closed on a formal note. "The ship is yours, sir, until my return."

"The ship is mine, sir, until your return."

Then Grimes and Sonya went down to their quarters, replaced their light uniform sandals with knee-high boots, strapped on their wrist transceivers, buckled on the belts from which depended their holstered hand weapons. The Commodore was sure that these would never be required but, as leader of the expedition, he could not break the orders that he had issued. It was, he already knew, warm outside; the slate gray shorts and shirts that he and his wife were wearing would be adequate.

They made their way down to the after airlock, checked out with the officer on gangway duty, walked slowly down the ramp. The fresh air was good, and the last traces of smoke from the now dead fire added a pleasant tang to it. The light of the sun, past its meridian and now dropping slowly to the west, was warm on the exposed portions of their bodies. (*I made much better time down than Rector Smith did in his* Piety, thought Grimes smugly. It had been late afternoon when that ship had landed.) And yet there was a chill in the air—psychological rather than physical. There was a chill in the air, and with the scent of green growing things there was a hint of corruption.

Sonya shivered. "There's something . . . wrong," she stated.

"That's why we're here," Grimes told her.

They were met by the Major. He was returning to the ship, seven of his men behind him. Four of them carried the bodies of two large boars, slung on branches; the others were loaded down with rabbits. The young officer saluted cheerfully. "Enemy beaten off, sir, with heavy casualties."

"So I see, Major. But this is more than a hunting party, you know."

"I know, sir. I've set alarms all around the field so that we shall all be alerted if anything large and dangerous approaches."

"Good."

Grimes and Sonya walked on, picking their way with care over the tangle of tough vines, making their slow way toward what had once been the Stadium's grandstand, now a terraced, artificial hillock overgrown with flowering creepers. They saw the two dowsers, stumbling about happily with their gleaming divining rods in their hands, trailed by a bored-looking junior officer. They passed a party of the more orthodox scientists setting up a piece of apparatus that looked like a miniature radio telescope. They met Mayhew and Clarisse.

"Do *you* feel it?" demanded the Psionic Radio Officer. "Do *you* feel it, sir? None of these others seem to."

"Yes, I feel it. And so does Sonya."

"Like something that has been waiting for us for a long time. Like something getting ready to pounce. But it's not sure that it has the strength anymore . . ."

"Yes . . . I thought myself that the ominous atmosphere wasn't quite so pronounced as when I was here last. What do you think, Clarisse? You were here too."

"I'm not as scared as I was then, John. But there are reasons for that."

"It's pronounced enough for me," said Sonya.

"It's here still," admitted Grimes. "But it could be fading. It could be that this planet has been at the very focus of . . . forces, and now the focus is shifting." He laughed. "We shan't be at all popular if, after our masters have sent us here at enormous expense, nothing happens."

"Frankly," said Clarisse, "I hope nothing does."

Nothing did.

Day followed day, and the parties of scientists spread out from around the landing site, on foot and in *Faraway Quest's* pinnaces. The archeologists grubbed happily in kitchen middens that they discovered on the banks of the lake and the river, penetrated the caves and photographed the famous paintings in a wide range of illuminations. Nothing new was found in the middens, no evidence that would throw any light at all on the disappearance of the aboriginal race. The rock paintings were just rock paintings, the pigments dry and ancient. The dowsers dowsed, and discovered deposits of metals that would be valuable if the planet were ever recolonized, and found oil, and mapped the meanderings of underground streams in desert areas. The other specialists plotted and measured and calculated—and found nothing that could not have been found on any Earth-type planet.

"At least," said Grimes, "we've proven that this world is suitable for resettlement." He, with Sonya and Clarisse and Mayhew, was sitting over after dinner coffee in his comfortable day cabin. "All hands are really enjoying a marvelous outdoor holiday."

"Except us," said Sonya in a somber voice.

"There's a reason for that, my dear. You're sensitive to my moods, as I am to yours. And I had such a scare thrown into me when I was here last that I could never feel at ease on this planet. And Clarisse was more frightened than I was—and with good reason!—and all the time she was in telepathic touch with Mayhew."

"I still say that there's something wrong," insisted Mayhew. "I still say that we should be absolutely sure before we put in a report recommending another attempt at colonization."

Grimes looked at Clarisse. "Would you be willing to repeat that experiment?" he asked.

She replied without hesitation. "Yes. I was going to suggest it. I've talked it over with Ken. And I feel that if I try to call those old gods, rather than the deity of the neo-Calvinists, the results might be better. It could be that it is in their interests that this world be peopled again—this time with potential worshippers."

"Like your Blossom People," said Mayhew, unmaliciously.

"Yes. Like the Blossom People. After all, the slogan *Make Love, Not War*, would appeal to Aphrodite if not to Ares . . ."

Grimes laughed, but without real humor. "All right, Clarisse. We'll arrange it for tomorrow night. And we'll have all hands out of the ship and well scattered just in case Zeus is too handy with his thunderbolts again. Williams has been getting too fat and lazy; it'll do him good to have a job of organization thrown suddenly onto his lap . . ."

Williams enjoyed himself; things had been altogether too quiet for his taste. And then, with the ship quiet and deserted, Grimes, with Sonya and Clarisse and Mayhew, and with a full dozen of assorted scientists, boarded one of the pinnaces, in which the necessary materials had already been stowed.

It was just before sunset when they landed on the smooth, windswept plateau that was the summit of the mountain. A thin, icy wind swept into the little cabin as the door opened. One by one, Grimes in the lead, the members of the party clambered down on to the bare, barren rock, the last ones to emerge handing down the equipment before making their own exits. There was an easel, as before, a floodlight, pots of paint, brushes. There were cameras, still and cinematographic, one of which would transmit a television picture to receivers on the plain below the mountain. There were sound recorders.

Silently, slowly, Mayhew and his wife walked to the center of the plateau, accompanied by Grimes and Sonya, carrying what she would be using. Grimes set up the easel, with its stretched black canvas, and the powerful floodlight. Sonya placed the painting materials at its foot. Mayhew, his thin face pale and anxious, lifted the heavy cloak from

19

Clarisse's shoulders. She stood there as she had stood before, naked save for the brief, rough kilt of animal hide, her arms crossed over her full breasts for warmth rather than from modesty. She looked, thought Grimes (again) as her remote ancestresses on this very world must have looked, was about to practice the magic that they had practiced. Mayhew had produced from a pocket a little bottle and a tiny glass—the psychedelic drug. He filled the glass, held it out to her. "Drink this, my dear," he ordered gently.

She took it from him, drained it, threw it down. It shattered with a crystalline crash, surprisingly loud in spite of the wind. "Your bare feet . . ." muttered Mayhew. He squatted down, carefully picking up the glittering fragments. She did not appear to see what he was doing, stood like a statue when he, on his feet again, laid his free hand on her bare shoulder in an attempted gesture of reassurance and . . . farewell?

He whispered to Grimes, his voice taut with strain and worry, "I can't get through to her. Somebody, something's got hold of her . . ."

The three of them walked back to where the scientists were standing by the pinnace, their recording apparatus set up and ready. And suddenly the sun was gone, and there was only the glare of the floodlight, in which Clarisse was standing. Overhead was the almost empty black sky with its sparse scatter of dim stars, and low to the east was the arc of misty luminescence that was the slowly rising Galactic Lens. The wind could have been blowing straight from intergalactic space.

Conditions were almost the same as they had been on the previous occasion. Almost. It was the human element that was different. This time those on the mountain top were skeptics and earnest inquirers, not true believers. But the feeling of almost unendurable tension was the same.

Hesitantly, Clarisse stooped to the clutter of materials at her feet. She selected a brush. She dipped it into one of the pots, then straightened. With swift, sure strokes she began to paint.

But it was wrong, Grimes realized. It was all wrong. It was white paint that she had used before; this time she was applying a bright, fluorescent pigment to the canvas. A figure was taking shape—that of a tall, slender man in red tights, with a pointed beard, a mocking smile . . . A man?

But men do not have neat little goatlike horns growing from their heads; neither do they have long, lissome tails ending in a barbed point . . .

A god?

Pan, perhaps.

No, not Pan. Pan never looked like that.

There was a dreadful crack of lightning close at hand, too close at hand, but the flash was not blue white but a dull, unnatural crimson. There was a choking, sulphurous stench. And then *he* was standing there, laughing; amid the roiling clouds of black smoke, laughing.

Grimes heard one of the scientists almost scream, "What the devil . . . ?"

And the devil advanced, still laughing, his very white and very sharp teeth flashing. His surprisingly elegant right hand stretched out to rest on the Commodore's wrist. "You are under arrest," he said. "And I must warn you that anything you say will be taken down and may be used as evidence."

"By what authority?" Grimes heard Sonya cry. "By what . . .?"

And then there was darkness deeper than that between the universes, and absolute silence.

How long did the journey last? An eternity, or a fraction of a microsecond? It could have been either.

There was light again; not bright, but dim and misty. There was light, and there was solidity underfoot—and there was still the pressure of that restraining hand on his wrist. Grimes looked down—he was reluctant to look up—and saw what looked like a marble pavement. At last he allowed his eyes slowly to elevate. There were the slim, pointed red shoes, inches from his own. There were the slender yet muscular legs in their skintight scarlet hose. There were the elaborately puffed trunks. There was the scarlet, gold-trimmed doublet . . . Suddenly Grimes felt less frightened. This was the Mephistopheles of fancy dress balls, and of opera, rather than a real and living embodiment of unutterable evil. But when he came to the face his assurance began to ebb. There was a reckless handsomeness, but there was power, too much power, power that would be used recklessly and selfishly.

Behind Grimes a very English voice was saying, "We must congratulate our friend on his speedy arrest, Watson."

A deeper voice replied, "Yes, yes, my dear Holmes. But are we sure that we have the right man? After all, to judge by his uniform, he's an officer, and presumably a gentleman . . ."

Mephistopheles laughed sneeringly. "Well I know the villainies of which so-called gentlemen are capable. But I have carried out my part of the bargain and now I shall return to my own place; it's too infernally cold here for comfort."

There was a flash of dull crimson light, the stench of burning sulphur, and he was gone.

"Turn around, fellow, and let us look at you," ordered the first English voice.

Slowly Grimes turned, and what he saw was no surprise to him. There was the tall man with aquiline features, wearing peculiar garments that he knew were a Norfolk jacket, an Inverness cape and a deerstalker cap. There was the short, stout man with the walrus moustache, formally clad, even to black frock coat and gleaming top hat.

Grimes looked at them, and they looked at him.

Then, "Hand it over, sir," ordered the tall man. "Hand it over, and I shall prefer no charges."

"Hand what over?" asked Grimes, bewildered.

"My pipe, of course."

Silently the Commodore drew the leather case from his pocket, placed it in the outstretched hand.

"A remarkable piece of deduction, my dear Holmes," huffed the stout man. "It baffles me how you did it."

"Elementary, my dear Watson. It should be obvious, even to you, that a crime, any crime, cannot take place in the three dimensions of space only. The additional factor, the fourth dimension, time, must always be taken into account. I reasoned that the thief must be somebody living so far in our future that our fictional origin will be forgotten. Then I enlisted the aid of the London branch of the Baker Street Irregulars—those fellows are always absurdly flattered when I condescend to share their dreams! Through them I maintained a round the clock watch on the antique shop that stands where our lodgings used to be. At last it was reported to me that my pipe had been purchased by a red-haired young lady of striking appearance. I learned, too— once again through the invaluable Irregulars—that she was the wife of one Commodore Grimes, of the Rim Worlds Naval Reserve, and would shortly be returning to her husband, who was resident in a city called Port Forlorn, on a planet called Lorn, one of the Rim Worlds. These Rim Worlds are outside our ambit, but I was able to persuade that learned colleague of yours who dabbles in magic to persuade his . . . er . . . colleague, Mephistopheles to place his services at my disposal. Between us we were able to lay a very subtle psychological trap on yet another planet, one with the unlikely name of Kinsolving . . ." Holmes opened the case, took out the pipe, looked at it, sniffed it. His face darkened. "Sir, have you been *smoking* this?"

"Yes," admitted Grimes.

Watson intervened. "It will be a simple matter, Holmes, to sterilize it. Just a jet of steam from a boiling kettle, back in our lodgings . . ."

"Very well, Watson. Let us proceed with the purification rites forthwith."

The two men walked rapidly away, their forms becoming indistinct in the mist. Grimes heard Watson say, "And when I chronicle this case, I shall call it 'The Adventure of the Missing Meerschaum . . .' "

And what about "The Case of the Kidnapped Commodore"? wondered Grimes. But before he could start in pursuit of the great detective and his friend another figure had appeared, blocking his way.

He, too, was English, most respectably dressed in the style of the early twentieth century, in black jacket and trousers with a gray waistcoat, a stiff white collar and a black necktie. He was inclined to stoutness, but the ladies of the servants' hall must often have referred to him—but never in his dignified hearing—as "a fine figure of a man."

He raised his bowler hat, and Grimes had sufficient presence of mind to bring the edge of his right hand to the peak of his cap to return the salute. He said, his voice deferential but far from servile, "Welcome aboard, sir." He contrived to enclose the words between quotation marks.

"Er . . . Thank you."

"Perhaps, sir, you will accompany me. I am the only member of my profession in this place, and so it has become my duty—and my pleasure, sir—to welcome new arrivals and to arrange for their accommodation."

"That's very good of you, er . . ."

"Jeeves, sir. At your service. This way, Commodore—I take

23

it that the braid on your epaulettes still has the same significance as in my time—if you please."

"Where are you taking me?"

"I took the liberty, sir, of arranging for your accommodation at the Senior Service Club. There are other naval gentlemen in residence. There is Admiral—Lord Hornblower, that is. You must have heard of him. And there is Commander Bond—a very likable young gentleman, but not quite my idea of what a naval officer should be. And . . ." a flicker of distaste crossed Jeeves's plump face . . . "a certain Lieutenant Commander Queeg, who somehow appointed himself club secretary. He even tried to have Captain Ahab evicted from the premises. How did he put it?" Jeeves's voice acquired a nasal twang. " 'How can I run a taut ship with that damned whaling skipper stomping around the decks on his peg leg? He'll be putting that pet whale of his in the swimming bath next. I kid you not.' But the Admiral—he's president; although old Captain Noah is the senior member he's really not much interested in anything—asked my advice. So Commander Bond was ordered to act as a one-man press gang—a form of activity for which he seemed well qualified—and, after Captain Ahab had been pressed into the King's service he was promptly commissioned by Lord Hornblower. As an officer of the Royal Navy he was really more entitled to Club membership—it's a very British institution—than Commander Queeg . . ."

"Very ingenious," commented Grimes.

"I am always happy to oblige, sir." Jeeves raised his hat to a tall woman who had appeared out of the mist, a striking brunette, barefooted, wearing a long white nightgown. "Good morning, Your Ladyship."

She ignored him but concentrated on Grimes. She glared at him from slightly mad, dark eyes, and all the time her hands were making peculiar wringing motions. "Ye havena brought any decent soap wi' ye?" she demanded.

"Soap, madam?"

"Aye, soap, ye lackwitted Sassenach!"

"I'm afraid not. If I'd known that I was coming here . . ."

The woman brushed past him, muttering, "Will *nothing* wash these white hands?"

"I have tried to help her, sir," said Jeeves, "But I can only do so much. After all, I am not a qualified psychiatrist. But many of the guests in this establishment are more odd than otherwise." He gestured toward a break in the mist, through which Grimes glimpsed lush greenery, vivid flowers, a veritable jungle. And surely that was the coughing roar of a lion, followed by the shrill chattering of disturbed tropical birds . . . "Lord Greystoke lives there, sir, with his wife, the Lady Jane. They have a house in a big tree, and they consort with *apes* . . . And the people next door, in the next estate—like an English woodland, it is—live in a gamekeeper's cottage. A Mr. Mellors and a Lady Constance Chatterley. You would think that with their mutual love of nature the two couples would be on *very* friendly terms. But no. Lady Chatterley said to me once when I mentioned it—it was when I had invited her and Mr. Mellors to my quarters for a real English afternoon tea, and we were discussing the Greystokes—'The only nature I'm interested in, Jeeves, is *human* nature.' " Again he raised his hat. "Good morning, Colonel."

"Who was that?" asked Grimes, staring after the figure in the fringed buckskin shirt, with a revolver slung at each hip.

"Colonel William Cody, sir. I feel sorry for the gentleman. You see, he isn't really one of us. As well as living an actual life on the printed page he was also a flesh and blood person. As I understand it, a New York publishing house of his time commissioned a writer to produce a series of stories about the Wild West, and this writer, instead of creating a character, used one who was already in existence in the flesh and blood world, calling him Buffalo Bill. And this, you will understand, makes him, insofar as *we* are concerned, illegitimate. But he is not the only one. There are the Greek ladies and gentlemen—Helen, and Cassandra, and Odysseus, and Achilles, and Oedipus . . . And others. And, of course, there is the Prince, although His Highness claims that he was cribbed from an earlier work of fiction and not from what the flesh and blood people call real life."

"So I'm not real?" demanded Grimes.

"But you are, sir, otherwise you could never have come here. You are, like the rest of us, a creation, a product of the imagination of some gifted writer." He stopped suddenly, and Grimes stopped with him. "But, sir, are you an *enduring* product?" He walked around the Commodore like a tailor inspecting the fit and cut of a new uniform. "This is indeed unfortunate, sir. Already I detect a hint of insubstantiality . . ." He paused, turned to face a newcomer, bowed. "Good morning, Your Highness."

The tall, thin, pale man in formfitting black, with the white lace at throat and cuffs, did not reply to the salutation. Instead he said in a sonorous voice, "To be or not to be, that is the question . . ."

"Too right," agreed Grimes.

The Prince of Denmark looked down at the age-mottled skull that he held in his right hand. "Alas, poor Yorick, I knew him well . . ." He stared at the Commodore. "But you I do not know." He turned on his heel, strode away.

"Good night, sweet Prince," said Grimes bitterly.

"Do not mind His Highness," said Jeeves. "He has a sardonic sense of humor."

"Maybe he has. But you must have had other . . . characters here who were not, as you put it, enduring products. What happened to them?"

"They . . . faded, sir. There was a young man dressed up in old woman's clothing who called himself 'Charley's Aunt.' He lasted quite a few years, Earth Time, but he's vanished now. And there have been many gentlemen like yourself, spacemen. None of them lasted long."

"But what happens to them? To *us*?"

"I cannot say, sir. When the last book in which you appeared has crumbled into dust, when your last reader has gone to wherever the flesh and blood people go, what then?"

"There must be *some* way," muttered Grimes. Then, aloud "All right. I'm scared. I admit it. But my own case is different. All you others came here, I suppose, after the death of your authors. You're immortality—perhaps—for the men who created you. But I was brought here before my time. I was the victim of a plot cooked up—and what more unlikely fellow conspirators could there ever be!—by Sherlock Holmes and Dr. Faustus. And Mephistopheles."

Jeeves laughed quietly. "I knew that Mr. Holmes had lost his pipe. I offered to assist him in its recovery; but he, of course, was too proud to accept my humble services. He always likes to do things his own way. And you, sir, I take it, are the innocent victim."

"You can say that again. I was shanghaied away from my own universe to this . . . limbo . . ."

"We prefer, sir, to call it the Hall of Fame."

"And I'm not the only victim. Back there I've a wife, and a ship . . . I must get back to them."

"I appreciate your anxiety, sir, and I admit that there could be need for haste. Time is measured differently here than elsewhere, sir, and already you are becoming quite diaphanous . . ."

Grimes held out his hand, looked at it. He could see the marble flooring through skin and flesh and blood and bone.

"Hurry, sir," urged Jeeves.

They hurried. Nonetheless, Grimes retained a confused memory of their nightmarish gallop. Men and women stopped to stare at them; and some of them Grimes recognized; and some were hauntingly familiar; and a very few struck no chords in his memory whatsoever. There were occasional rifts in the eddying mists to afford fleeting glimpses of buildings, and, like the clothing of the people, the architecture was of all historical periods. Turreted Camelot, its towers aflutter with gay pennons, they sped by; and beyond its walls was a barren and dusty plain whereon a solitary knight, a scarecrow figure astride a skeletal horse, tilted at windmills. Then there was Sherwood Forest, where the outlaws in Lincoln green paused in their archery practice to cheer on the two runners.

And for a while there was the shambling monstrosity that lurched along beside them, keeping pace, like a large, unlovely dog trying to make friends. Grimes glanced at this giant, who seemed to have been put together from not quite matching parts pilfered from the graveyard, then looked hastily away, sickened by the sight of him and by the charnel stench that emanated from the crudely humanoid form. Then there was the other monster, the handsome man in nineteenth century dress finery who hovered above them on black bat's wings. Jeeves, who did not suffer from lack of wind, muttered something uncomplimentary about Eastern European aristocracy.

At last there loomed before them the house that was their destination. All high gables it was, and oak beams, with narrow, diamond-paned windows. Set high on the stout, iron-bound door was the black, iron knocker—metal cast in the form of an inverted crucifix. Jeeves reached for it, rapped smartly.

Slowly the door creaked open. An old, graybearded man

27

peered out at them suspiciously. He was dressed in a rusty black robe upon which cabalistic symbols gleamed with a dull luster and a tall, conical, black hat. His blue eyes were so faded as to be almost white.

He demanded querulously, "Who disturbs my rest?"

"It is I, Jeeves, Herr Doktor . . ."

"And this other? This . . . phantasm?"

"The innocent victim, Dr. Faustus, of the peculiar machinations set in motion by yourself and Mr. Holmes."

"What is done cannot be undone." He glared at Grimes, through Grimes. "And do *you* cry, 'Oh, Lord, put back Thy Universe, and give me back my yesterday'?"

"I have done so," whispered Grimes. "As who has not?"

"*I* cannot help you." The door was starting to close.

But Jeeves had inserted a stout, highly polished shoe into the narrowing opening. "Do not forget that *I* have helped you, Dr. Faustus. Have I not sent patients to you?" He added nastily, "Although Achilles still limps, and Oedipus still chases after older women . . ."

"My name is Faustus, not Freud," grumbled the old man.

"Furthermore," continued Jeeves, "both you and your partner rely upon me for the supply of the luxuries that were unavailable in your own day and age."

The door opened abruptly. "Come in!" snarled the old doctor.

Inside it was dark, the only light coming from a brazier over which a cauldron bubbled. The room was a large one, but it was so cluttered with a fantastic miscellany of objects that it was hard to move without fouling something. Grimes ducked hastily to avoid striking his head on a stuffed crocodile that hung from the low ceiling, then almost tripped over a beautiful—but woefully inaccurate—celestial globe that stood on the stone floor. He would have tripped had his body been solid, but his shadowy leg passed through the obstacle with no more than the faintest hint of resistance.

Grumbling, the old man shuffled to a bench littered with the apparatus of alchemy. "Chalk . . ." he muttered, "for the pentagram . . . Where did I put it? And the sulphur candles . . ."

"There's no time for that, Doctor. Can't you see? This gentlemen needs help urgently."

"But *He* will not like it if I do not observe protocol."

"*He* won't like it if he has to go thirsty from now on."

"Very well, very well. But I warn you—*He* will be bad tempered."

Dr. Faustus tottered to a low table upon which stood a large, stuffed owl. He lifted the bird, which was hollow, revealing a jarringly anachronistic telephone. He handed the owl to Jeeves, who regarded it with some distaste, then took the handset from its rest, punched a number.

"Yes," he croaked into the instrument. "At once." There was a pause. "Yes, I know that you always insist that the proper procedure be followed, but Mr. Jeeves says that this is urgent." There was another pause. "You'd better come, unless you want to do without your brandy and cigars . . ."

This time there was no thunder, no crimson lightning, no clouds of black, sulphurous smoke. But Mephistopheles was standing there, his arms folded over his muscular chest, scowling down at Grimes. "Yes?" he demanded shortly. "Yes, my man?"

The Commodore, his voice a barely audible whisper, said, "Take me back to where I belong."

The Commodore stepped silently forward, peered over the writer's shoulder. He read, *He was standing in a ship's cabin. The carpeted deck swayed and lurched under his feet* . . . Then the carpeted deck lurched really heavily. Grimes put out a hand, to the back of the other man's chair, to steady himself.

The writer started violently, exclaimed, "What the hell!" He twisted in his seat, stared at Grimes. His pipe fell from his mouth, clattered to the deck. "No . . ." he said slowly. "No. It can't be. Go away."

"I wish that I could," Grimes told him.

"Then why the hell don't you?"

"You, sir, should know the answer to that question," said Grimes, reasonably enough. He looked curiously at the other man, his . . . creator? His . . . parent? But there was no physical resemblance to himself. He, Grimes, was short and stocky, and his ears were his most prominent facial feature. The writer was tall, with normal enough ears, but too much nose.

"You, sir, should know the answer to that question," repeated Grimes.

"I'm sorry, Commodore, but I don't. Not yet, anyhow."

Then, in a tone of forced cheerfulness, "But this is only a silly dream. It must be."

"It's not, Captain." The man's gold-braided epaulettes and the uniform cap, with the scrambled egg on its peak, hanging on a hook just inside the curtained door made this a safe enough guess. "It's not, Captain. Pinch yourself."

"Damn it! That hurt."

"Good. Do you mind if I sit down?" Carefully, Grimes eased himself on to the settee that ran along one bulkhead of the day cabin. He feared at first that he was going to sink through the cushion, but it had substance (or he had substance) and supported him, although only just. He shut his eyes for a moment, trying to dispel the faintness that was creeping over him. It was the result of shock, he realized, of shock and of disappointment. He had expected to find himself aboard his own ship, the old, familiar, tried and trusted *Faraway Quest*, to be welcomed back by his wife. But where was he now? *When* was he? On Earth, the mother world of humankind? Aboard some sort of surface vessel?

The writer answered the unspoken questions. He said, "I'll put you in the picture, Commodore. You're aboard the good ship *Kantara*, which same plies between Melbourne and the port of Macquarie, on the wild west coast of Tasmania. We load pyritic ore in Macquarie for Melbourne, and make the return trip (as we are doing now) in ballast. I doubt very much if you have anything like this trade in your day and age, sir. Macquarie's one of those places that you can't get into when you're outside, and that you can't get out of when you're inside. To begin with, the tides are absolutely unpredictable, and it's safe to work the entrance—it's called Hell's Gates, by the way—only at slack water. If you tried to come in against a seven knot ebb you'd be in trouble! And the Inner Bar and the Outer Bar are always silting up, and with strong north westerlies—which we've been having—Outer Bar breaks badly. I've been riding out a howling westerly gale, keeping well to seaward, as I just don't like being caught on a lee shore in a small, underpowered and underballasted ship. But the wind's backed to the south'ard and is moderating, and the glass is rising, and all the weather reports and forecasts look good. So I'm standing in from my last observed position—P.M. star sights—until I'm just inside the extreme range of Cape Sorell light, and then I'll just stand off and on until daylight, keeping within easy reach of the port. Come the dawn, I'll have a natter with the harbor master on the radio telephone, and as soon as he's able to convince me that conditions are favorable I'll rush in."

"Why bother with the extreme range of the light?" asked Grimes, becoming interested in spite of all his troubles. "You have radar, don't you?"

"I do. I have radar and echo sounder. But my radar gets old and tired after only a few hours' operation, and my echo sounder's on the blink. I've nothing against electronic gadgetry *as long as it can be relied upon*. At the moment, mine can't be." The writer laughed. "But this is crazy. To sit here discussing navigation with a navigator from the distant future! I hope that none of my officers comes in to find me carrying on a conversation with myself!"

"I'm real, Captain. And I'm here. And I think that you should do something about getting me back to where I belong."

"What can *I* do, Commodore? People have said, more than once, that my stories just *happen*. And that's true, you know. Furthermore, I've always given *you* a free hand. Time and time again I've had to make plot changes because you've insisted on going your own way."

"So you can't help me . . ."

"I wish that I could. Believe me, I wish that I could. Do you think that I want to be haunted by you for the rest of my life?"

"There could be a way . . ." whispered Grimes. *Yes*, he thought, *there could be a way*. Life in that Hall of Fame would not be at all bad as long as he—*and Sonya*—were assured of the same degree of permanence as the others: Oedipus Rex, Hamlet, Sherlock Holmes, James Bond . . . He said, "I shan't mind a bit going back to that peculiar Elysium you cooked up as long as my status there is better than that of an ephemeral gate crasher. And, of course, I'd like Sonya with me."

"And just how can I arrange that for you, Commodore?"

"Easily, Captain. All you have to do is write a best seller, a series of best sellers."

The other man grinned. "It's a pity you can't meet my wife." He gestured toward a peculiarly two dimensional photograph in a frame over the desk. The auburn-haired woman who looked out at them reminded Grimes of Sonya. "That's what she's always telling me."

There was a sharp buzz from the telephone on the desk. The writer picked up the handset. "Master here."

"Third Officer here, sir," Grimes heard faintly. "I've just picked up Cape Sorell light, at extreme range, right ahead . . ."

"Good, Mr. Tallent. Turn her on to the reciprocal course. Yes, keep her on half speed. I'll be right up."

Grimes followed the shipmaster out of the day cabin, up the narrow companionway to the chartroom, out of the glass-enclosed wheelhouse, then out through a sliding door to the wing of the bridge. The night was clear, and the stars (would he ever see them again as more than lights in the sky?) were bright. Astern was the winking, group-flashing light, an intermittent spark on the far horizon. And then the light itself was gone, only a flash recurring at regular intervals marking its position as the lantern dipped below the planet's curvature.

The captain grunted his satisfaction, then turned to stare forward. There was still quite a sea running, the wave crests faintly phosphorescent in the darkness; there was still a stiff breeze, broad on the port bow, but there was no weight to it. The ship was lifting easily to the swell, the motion not at all uncomfortable. The captain grunted again, went back to the chartroom. Grimes looked over his shoulder as he bent over the chart, noted the range circle with Cape Sorell as its center, the dot on it in the middle of its own tiny, penciled circle with the time—2235—along it, and another, cryptic notation, $\triangle$ 33.5. On the chart, to one side, was a message pad. *Final Gale Warning*, it was headed. "Wind and sea moderating in all areas," read Grimes. "All pressures rising."

The shipmaster was busy now with parallel rulers, pencil and dividers. From the observed position he laid off a course —270° True. With the dividers he stepped off a distance, marked it with a cross and wrote alongside it "0200?" Grimes realized that the officer of the watch had come into the chartroom. He could see the young man, but the young man, it seemed, could not see him.

"Mr. Tallent," said the shipmaster, "we'll stand out to this position, then bring her around to 090 True. All being well, we shall be within comfortable VHF range at daylight, and with any luck at all the Bar will have stopped breaking and we shall have slack water. I'll not write up my night orders yet; I'll see the second officer at midnight before I turn in . . ."

"We should get in tomorrow all right, sir," said the officer.

"Don't be so bloody sure. You can never tell with this bloody place!"

"Good night, sir."

"Good night, Mr. Tallent."

Back in the day cabin, Grimes said, "You can see, Captain, that I have no real existence *here* and *now*. You *must* try to make me real *somewhere*."

"Or somewhen."

"Or somewhen."

"More easily said than done, Commodore. Especially in the existing circumstances. At the moment of writing *I* am master of this little rustbucket. Master under God, as Lloyd's puts it. This ship is my responsibility—and *you* should be able to appreciate that. This evening I was writing just as relaxation, one hand on the keyboard, the other ready to pick up the telephone . . ."

Grimes said, "You take yourself too bloody seriously. This is only a small ship with a small crew on an unimportant trade."

"Nonetheless," the shipmaster told him, "this is *my* ship. And the crew is *my* crew. The trade? That's the Company's worry; but, as Master, it's up to me to see that the ship shows a profit."

"And I'm your responsibility too," Grimes pointed out.

"Are you? As I've already said, Commodore, you've proven yourself able to go your own sweet way in any story that I've written. But if I *am* responsible just bear in mind that I could kill you off as easily as I could swat a fly. More easily. How do you want it? Act of God, the King's enemies, or pirates? Nuclear blast—or a knife between the ribs?"

"You're joking, surely."

"Am I? Has it never occurred to you, Commodore, that a writer gets rather tired of his own pet characters? Sir Arthur Conan Doyle killed off Sherlock Holmes, but had to drag him back to life to please his public. Ian Fleming was becoming more than somewhat browned off with James Bond when he, himself, kicked the bucket . . ."

Grimes looked toward the photograph over the desk. "But you like Sonya," he said.

"I do. She's too good for you."

"Be that as it may. She's part of my world, my time . . ."

"So?"

"Well, I thought . . ."

The telephone buzzed. The shipmaster picked up the handset. "Yes?"

"The wind's freshening, sir, and it's veered to west."

"Put her back on full speed, Mr. Tallent." The captain got up from his chair, went to the aneroid barometer mounted on the bulkhead. He tapped it. The needle jerked in a counterclockwise direction. "Just what I need;" he said. "A bloody secondary."

"What does that mean, Captain?"

"It means, Commodore, that those *Final Gale Warnings* aren't worth the paper that Sparks typed them on. Very often, too often, in these waters the secondary depression is more vicious than the so-called primary."

"What can you do?"

"Stand out. Make offing. Get the hell off this bloody lee shore."

Again the telephone buzzed. "Master here."

"Sir, we've lifted Cape Sorell again . . ."

"Tell the engineers to give her all they've got. I'll be right up."

The ship was lurching, was rolling heavily as she fell away from the wind. She was pounding as her fore part lifted and then slammed back down into the trough. Her screw was racing each time that her stern came clear of the water, and as the propeller lost purchase, so did the rudder. "Sir," complained the helmsman, "the wheel's hard over, but she's not coming back . . ."

"Keep it hard over until she answers," ordered the Master. He was looking into the radar screen. It was not a very good picture. There was spoking, and there was too much clutter. But there, right astern, was the faint outline of the rocky coast, a ragged luminosity. And there were the range circles—and slowly, slowly, the coastline was drifting from the 24 mile to the 20 mile ring. Even Grimes, peering over the other man's shoulder, could appreciate what was happening.

"Mr. Tallent!"

"Sir?"

"Call the Chief Officer. Tell him to flood the afterhold."

"*Flood* the afterhold, sir?"

"You heard me. We have to get the arse down somehow, to give the screw and the rudder some sort of grip on the water."

"Very good, sir."

"She's logging three knots," whispered the Master. "But she's making one knot—*astern*. And that coast is nothing but rocks . . ."

"And flooding the hold will help?" asked Grimes.

"It'd better. It's all I can do."

They went back out to the wing of the bridge, struggling to retain their balance as the wind hit them. Cape Sorell light was brightly visible again, right astern, and even to the naked eye it had lifted well clear of the sea horizon. A shadowy figure joined them there—the Chief Officer, decided Grimes.

"I've got two fire hoses running into the hold, sir. What depth of water do you wont?"

"I want 100 tons. Go below and work it out roughly."

"What if the ceiling lifts?"

"Let it lift. Put in your hundred tons."

"Very good, sir."

Another officer came onto the bridge—big, burly, bearded. This must be, realized Grimes, the midnight change of watch. "Keep her as she's going, sir?" he asked.

"Yes. Keep her as she's going, Mr. Mackenzie. She'll be steering better once we get some weight in aft, and racing less. But you might tell the engineers to put on the second steering motor . . ."

"Will do, sir."

The shipmaster made his way back into the wheelhouse, staggering a little as the vessel lurched in the heavy swell. He went to the radar unit, looked down into the screen with Grimes peering over his shoulder. Right astern, the ragged outline of Cape Sorell was touching the twenty mile ring. Slowly the range decreased—slowly, but inexorably.

The Chief Officer was back. "About two foot six should do it, sir."

"Make it that . . ."

Then, gradually, the range was opening again. The range

was opening, and the frequent heavy vibrations caused by the racing screw were becoming less. The wind was still shrieking in from the westward, whipping the crests off the seas, splattering them against the wheelhouse windows in shrapnel bursts of spray, but the ship was steering again, keeping her nose into it, clawing away from the rocks that had claimed, over the years, too many victims.

Grimes followed the Master down to the afterdeck, stood with him as he looked down a trunkway into the flooded hold. Swirling in the filthy water were the timbers of the hold ceiling, crashing against the bulkheads fore and aft, splintering themselves against frames and brackets and the hold ladders, self-destroying battering rams driven by the force of the ship's pitching and rolling. There would be damage, even Grimes could see that. There would be damage—and, inevitably, the writing of reports with carbon copies every which way.

Grimes knew this, and he should have had more sense than to attempt to bring up the subject again of his own, private worries.

He said, "This hold flooding seems to have worked . . ."

"Yes."

"Then perhaps, Captain, you could spare the time to discuss the question of returning me to my own place and period . . ."

". . . off!" snarled the shipmaster. "I've more important things on my plate than your troubles. . . . Off!"

The screaming wind took hold of Grimes, whirling him away into the darkness. But, before he was gone, he heard the Chief Officer ask his captain, "Who was that sir? I thought I saw somebody standing there with you, a stranger in an odd-looking uniform . . ."

"Just a figment of the imagination, Mr. Briggs. Just a figment of the imagination."

He was standing in his own day cabin, aboard *Faraway Quest*. He was staring at Sonya, and she, her face white under the auburn hair, was staring at him.

"John! You're back!"

"Yes."

"I've been holding the ship, here on Kinsolving, but our lords and masters have been putting the pressure on us to return . . ."

"It wouldn't have mattered," Grimes told her.

"Why not?"

"Because wherever *you* are, that's where I belong."

He was sitting in his day cabin, trying to relax over a stiff drink. He had brought his ship into port, scurrying in during a lull between two depressions, pumping out after ballast to compensate for the weight of water in the flooded hold, clearing the Bar without touching. He was overtired and knew that sleep was out of the question. But there was nothing for him to do; his Chief Officer was capably overseeing the pumping out of the flooded compartment and would, as soon as possible, put the necessary repairs in hand.

He thought, *I might as well finish that bloody story.*

He inserted paper into his typewriter, refueled and lit his pipe, began to write. As the final words shaped themselves on the white sheet he looked up at the photograph of the red-haired woman over his desk. *Because wherever you are, that's where I belong . . .*

"And I hope you're satisfied, you cantankerous old bastard," he muttered.

"And it all actually happened . . ." murmured Admiral Kravinsky, indicating the thick report that lay on his desk.

"I . . . I suppose so . . ." said Grimes uncertainly.

"You should know, man. You were there."

"But *where* was *there?*"

"Don't go all metaphysical on me, Grimes." The Admiral selected a gnarled cheroot from the box before him, lit it. In self-defense the Commodore filled and ignited a battered briar pipe. He regretted, he realized, having lost that meerschaum during his last adventure.

Kravinsky regarded the swirling clouds of acrid blue smoke thoughtfully. He said at last, "It was rummy, all the same. Very rummy."

"You're telling *me*," concurred Grimes.

"I think that we shall be leaving Kinsolving severely alone for quite a while. I don't like this business about our just being a figment of the imagination or an imagination of the figment or whatever . . ."

"*You* don't like it . . ." muttered Grimes.

"All right, all right, my heart fair bleeds for you. Satisfied? And now, Admiral, I have a job for you that should be right up your alley."

"Admiral? Have I been promoted, sir?"

"That'd be the sunny Friday! But, Grimes, I seem to remember that you're an honorary admiral in the Tharn Navy, and that same Navy consists of seagoing surface vessels. The rank, meaningless though it is, should be useful to you when we send you to Aquarius."

"The rank's not meaningless, sir," protested Grimes.

"So much the better, then. On your way, Admiral. Weigh anchor, splice the main brace, heave the lead or whatever it is you seafaring types do when you get under way."

"It should be interesting," said Grimes.

"With you around to complicate matters, it's bound to be."

THE SISTER SHIPS

CAPTAIN JOHN GRIMES stood impassively in the port wing of his bridge as his ship, the round-the-world tramp *Sonya Winneck*, slid gently in toward her berth. But although his stocky body was immobile his brain was active. He was gauging speed, distances, the effect of the tide. His engines were stopped, but the vessel still seemed to be carrying too much way. He was stemming the ebb, but, according to the Port Directions there was sometimes—not always—an eddy, a counter current along this line of wharfage. In any case, it would be a tight fit. Ahead of him was *Iron Baron*, one of the steel trade ships: a huge, beamy brute with gigantic deck cranes almost capable of lifting her by her own bootstraps. In the berth astern was the Lone Star Line's *Orionic*, with even more beam to her than the *Baron*.

"Port!" ordered Grimes. "Hard over!"

"Hard a port, sir!" replied the quartermaster.

Sonya Winneck was accosting the wharf at a fairly steep angle now, her stem aimed at a bollard just abaft *Iron Baron*'s stern. Grimes lifted his mouth whistle to his lips, blew one short, sharp blast. From the fo'c'sle head came the rattle of chain cable as the starboard anchor was let go, then one stroke of the bell to signal that the first shackle was in the pipe.

Grimes looked aft. *Sonya Winneck*'s quarter was now clear of *Orionic*'s bows. "Midships! Slow astern!"

He heard the replies of the man at the wheel and the Third Officer. He felt the vibration as the reversed screw bit into the water. But would slow astern be enough? He was about to order half astern, then realized that this was what he was getting, if not more. The transverse thrust of the screw threw *Sonya Winneck*'s stern to port even as her headway was killed. Already a heaving line was ashore forward, and snaking after it the first of the mooring lines. Aft, the Second Mate was ready to get his first line ashore.

"Stop her," ordered Grimes. "That will do the wheel, thank you."

On fo'c'sle head and poop the self-tensioning winches were

39

whining. Grimes, looking down from the bridge wing to the marker flag on the wharf, saw that he was exactly in position. He made the traditional "arms crossed above the head" gesture—*Make her fast as she is*—to the Chief Officer forward, the Second Officer aft. Then he walked slowly into the wheelhouse. The Third Officer was still standing by the engine control pedestal.

"Finished with engines, Mr. Denham," said Grimes coldly.

"Finished with engines, sir." The young man put the lever to that position. There was a jangling of bells drifting up from below.

"Mr. Denham . . ."

"Sir?" The officer's voice was an almost inaudible squeak. He looked frightened, and, thought Grimes, well he might be.

"Mr. Denham, I am well aware that in your opinion I'm an outsider who should never have been appointed to command of this vessel. I am well aware, too, that in your opinion, at least, your local knowledge far surpasses mine. Even so, I shall be obliged if you will carry out my orders, although you will still have the right, the obligation, in fact, to query them—but not when I'm in the middle of berthing the bloody ship!" Grimes simmered down. "For your information, Mr. Denham, even I realized that slow astern would not be sufficient. I was about to order more stern power, then saw that you had taken matters into your own possibly capable but definitely unqualified hands."

"But, sir . . ."

Grimes's prominent ears had reddened.

"There are no 'buts.' "

"But, sir, I *tried* to put her to slow astern. The lever jerked out of my hand to full."

"Thank you, Mr. Denham," said Grimes at last. He knew that the young man was not lying. "You'd better see the Engineer, or the Electrician, and get those controls fixed. The next time they might do the wrong thing, instead of the right one."

He went through the chartroom and then down to his quarters. Sonya, who had watched the berthing from the lower bridge, was there waiting for him. She got up from her chair as he entered the day cabin and stood there, tall and slim and graceful. Her right hand snapped up to the widow's peak of her shining auburn hair.

She said, "I salute you, Cap'n. A masterly piece of ship handling."

"Mphm," grunted Grimes.

"But, John, it was like something out of one of your own books." She went to the case on the bulkhead in which were both privately owned volumes and those considered by the Winneck Line to be fit and proper reading for its masters. From the Company's shelf she lifted *The Inter-Island Steamer Express*, by John Grimes. She read aloud, ". . . These captains, maintaining their timetables and berthing and unberthing their big, seagoing passenger ferries in the most appalling weather conditions, were, without doubt, among the world's finest ship handlers . . ."

"The weather conditions this morning aren't appalling," said Grimes. "In any case, that was on Earth. This is Aquarius."

Aquarius, as its name implies, is a watery world.

It lies in toward the center from the Rim Worlds, fifty or so light-years to the galactic east of the Shakespearean Sector. It is Earth-type insofar as gravitation, atmosphere and climate are concerned, but geographically is dissimilar to the "home planet." There are no great land masses; there are only chains of islands: some large, some small, some no more than fly specks on even a medium scale chart. In this respect it is like Mellise, one of the planets of the Eastern Circuit. Unlike Mellise, it possesses no indigenous intelligent life. Men colonized it during the Second Expansion—and, as was the case with most Second Expansion colonizations, it was discovery and settlement by chance rather than by design. Time and time again it happened, that disastrous, often tragic sequence of events. The magnetic storm, the gaussjammer thrown light millennia off course, her pile dead and the hungry emergency diesels gulping precious hydrocarbons to feed power to the Ehrenhaft generators, the long plunge into and through the Unknown; the desperate search for a world, any world, that would sustain human life . . .

Lode Messenger stumbled upon Aquarius and made a safe landing in the vicinity of the North Magnetic Pole. Like all the later ships of her period she carried a stock of fertilized ova, human and animal, a wide variety of plant seeds and an extensive technical library. (Even when the gaussjammers were on regular runs, as *Lode Messenger* had been, there was always the possibility that their people would finish up as founders of a new colony.) When the planet was re-discovered by Commodore Shakespeare, during his voyage of exploration out toward the Rim, the settlement was already well established. With the Third Expansion it accepted its quota of immigrants, but insisted that all newcomers work for a probationary period in the merchant or fishing fleets before, if they so wished, taking up employment ashore. Somebody once said that if you wanted to emigrate to Aquarius you had to hold at least an "Able-bodied seaman's" papers. This is not quite true, but it is not far from the truth. It has also been said that Aquarians have an inborn dislike and distrust of spaceships but love seagoing ships. This is true.

Grimes, although not an immigrant, was a seaman of sorts. He was on the planet by invitation, having been asked by its rulers—the Havenmaster and the Master Wardens—to write a history of the colony. For that he was well qualified, being acknowledged as the leading maritime historian, specializing in Terran marine history, in the Rim Worlds. His books: *The Inter-Island Steamer Express, The Flag Of The Southern Cross, The Western Ocean Greyhounds, Times of Transition*—had sold especially well on Aquarius, although in the worlds of the Rim Confederacy they were to be found mainly only in libraries, and in very few libraries at that.

And Commodore Grimes, Rim Worlds Naval Reserve, Master Astronaut, was more than just a writer about the sea. He held the rank of admiral—honorary, but salt water admiral nonetheless—in the Ausiphalian Navy, on Tharn. Captain Thornton, the Havenmaster, had said, "Legally speaking, that commission of yours entitles you to a Certificate of Competency as a Master Mariner. Then you can sail in command of one of our ships, to get the real feel of life at sea."

"I'm not altogether happy about it, Tom," Grimes had objected, not too strongly.

"I'm the boss here," Thornton assured him. "And, in any case, I'm not turning you loose until you've been through crash courses in navigation, seamanship, meteorology, cargo stowage and stability."

"I'm tempted . . ." Grimes had admitted.

"Tempted?" scoffed Sonya. "He's just dying to strut his

bridge like the ancient mariners he's always writing about. His only regret will be that you Aquarians didn't re-create the days of sail while you were about it."

"Now and again I regret it myself," admitted the Havenmaster. "Fore and aft rig, a diesel auxiliary, electrical deck machinery—there'd be something quite fast enough for some of our trades and economical to boot. But I'm well known as an enemy of progress—progress for its own sake, that is."

"A man after my own heart," said Grimes.

"You're just a pair of reactionaries," Sonya had told them.

I suppose I am a reactionary, Grimes had thought. But he enjoyed this world. It was efficiently run, but it was always recognized that there are things more important than efficiency. There was automation up to a certain point, but up to that certain point only. (But the Havenmaster had admitted that he was fighting a rearguard action to try to keep control of the ships in the hands of the seamen officers . . .) There was a love of and a respect for the sea. It was understandable. From the first beginnings of the colony these people had grown up on a watery world, and the books in their technical library most in demand had been those on shipbuilding, seamanship and navigation. Aquarius was poor in radioactives but rich in mineral oil, so the physicists had never been able, as they have on so many worlds, to take charge. The steam engine and the diesel engine were still the prime movers, even in the air, where the big passenger-carrying airships did the work that on other planets is performed by jet planes and rockets.

The surface ships were, by modern standards, archaic. Very few of them ran to bow thrusters—and those only ferries, cargo and passenger, to whom the strict adherence to a timetable was of paramount importance, whose masters could not afford to make a leisurely job of backing into a roll-on-roll-off berth and therefore required the additional maneuvering aid. There was some containerization, but it was not carried to extremes, it being recognized that the personnel of the cargo carriers were entitled to leisure time in port. Self-tensioning winches and, for cargo handling, cranes rather than derricks cut down the number of hands required on deck, and engine rooms were almost fully automated, with bridge control for arrival and departure maneuvers.

There were electronic navigational aids aplenty—radar, echometer, loran, shoran, an inertial system, position fixing by artificial satellite—but these the Havenmaster frowned upon, as did most of the senior shipmasters. He quoted from Grimes's own book, *Times Of Transition*, "The electronic wizards of the day, who were not seamen, failed to realize that a competent navigator, armed only with sextant, chronometer and ephemeris, together with a reasonably accurate log, can always fix the position of his ship with reasonable accuracy provided that there is an occasional break in the clouds for an identifiable celestial body to shine through. Such a navigator is never at the mercy of a single fuse . . ."

"And that, John, is what I'm trying to avoid," said Thornton. "Unless we're careful our ships will be officered by mere button pushers, incapable of running a series of P/Ls. Unluckily, not all the Master Wardens think as I do. Too many of them are engineers, and businessmen—and in my experience such people have far less sales resistance than we simple sailors."

"And what pups have they been sold?" asked Grimes.

"One that's a real bitch from my viewpoint, and probably from yours. You've heard of Elektra?"

"Yes," broke in Sonya. "Carinthian Sector. Third Expansion colonization." She grinned a little unkindly. "It's a planet where the minimum qualification for immigration is a doctorate in one of the sciences, preferably physics. But they have to let in occasional chemists, biologists and the like to keep the dump habitable."

"And they have quite a few, now, with degrees in salesmanship," went on the Havenmaster. "One of them was here a few years back."

"And he sold you this female pup," said Grimes.

"He did that. The Purcell Navigator. It's named, I suppose, after its inventor. It's a sealed box, with the gods know what sort of mess of memory fields and the like inside it. It's hooked up to all the ship's electronic navigational gear: gyro compass, radar, echometer, loran, shoran . . . Just name a pie and it's got a finger in it. Or a tentacle. It knows just where the ship is at any given second. If you ask it nicely it might condescend to tell you."

"You don't like it," said Grimes.

"I don't like it. To begin with, some of the shipowners—and this is a private enterprise planet, remember—feel that now the bridge can be automated to the same extent as the engine room, with just one man, the Master, in charge, snoring his head off on the chartroom settee and being awakened by an alarm bell just in time to rub the sleep out of his eyes and take his ship into port. But that's not the worst of it. Now the Institute of Marine Engineers is saying, 'If navigation is only a matter of pushing buttons, we're at least as well qualified as deck officers.' "

"I've heard that often enough," said Grimes. "Even in space."

"Does anybody know how these Purcell Navigators work?" asked Sonya.

"No. One of the terms of sale is that they must be installed by technicians from the world of manufacture, Elektra. Another is that they must not, repeat not, be tampered with in any way. As a matter of fact the Chief Electrician of the Carrington Yard did try to find out what made one tick. He was lucky to lose only a hand."

"It seems," said Grimes, "that I came here just in time."

"What do you mean, John?"

"Well, I shall be able to enjoy the last of the old days, the good old days, on Aquarius, and I shall have the material for a few more chapters to my *Times Of Transition*."

"He likes being morbid," said Sonya. "Almost as much as he likes being reactionary."

"Mphm," grunted Grimes. "Old-fashioned sounds better."

He got up from his chair, walked soundlessly over the carpeted floor to the bookshelves that formed a space divider in the huge, circular room that was called the Havenmaster's Lookout. He stared at the rows of books, most of them old (but in recent printings), only a few of them new. And they were *real* books, all of them, not spools of microfilm. There were the standard works on the old arts of the seaman, hopelessly out of date on most worlds, but not (yet) on this one. Brown, Nicholl, Norie, Riesenberg . . . Lecky . . . Thomas . . . And the chronicles of the ancient explorers and navigators: Hakluyt, Dampier, Cook, Flinders, Bligh . . . Then there were the novels: Conrad (of course), McFee, Monsarrat, Herman Wouk, Forester . . . Grimes's hand went out to Melville's *Moby Dick,* and he remembered that odd Hall of Fame to which he had been whisked from the mountaintop on Kinsolving, and felt regret that he had not been able to meet Lieutenant Commander Queeg, Admiral Hornblower and Captain Ahab. (Were there any white whales in the Aquarian seas?)

He turned, saw that his wife and Captain Thornton had risen from their own seats, were standing staring out through the huge window that formed the entire outer wall of the Lookout that, in its turn, was the top level of the two thousand foot high Havenmaster's Control Tower. Above it was only the mast from which sprouted antennae, radar scanners, anemometers and the like, that was topped by the powerful, group-flashing Steep Island light.

Grimes walked slowly to join Sonya and his host, gazed out through the clear glass into the darkness. At regular intervals the beam of the light, a sword of misty radiance, swept overhead. Far to the south, a loom of luminescence on the distant sea horizon, was Port Stellar, and to east and west, fainter still, were other hazy luminosities, island cities, island states. Almost directly below was a great passenger liner, from this height no more than a gaudy, glittering insect crawling over the black carpet of the sea.

In spite of the insulation, the soundproofing, the thin, high whine of the wind was evident.

Sonya shivered. "The winds of change are blowing," she whispered.

"A seaman should be able to cope with the wind," said the Havenmaster. Then, to Grimes, "I wonder how you'll cope, John? I've arranged for you to take over *Sonya Winneck* at Port Stellar tomorrow."

"I'll get by," said Grimes.

"He always does," said Sonya. "Somehow."

Grimes fell in love with *Sonya Winneck* from the very start. She was, of course, his first sea command; nonetheless, she made an immediate appeal to the eye, even to the eye of one who, for all his admiral's commission, had very little practical knowledge of oceangoing ships. The lady was a tramp, but the tramp was also a lady.

Five hundred feet long overall, she was, with a seventy-foot beam. Bridge and funnel—the latter scarlet, with a black top and two narrow black bands—were amidships. Her upperworks and deck cranes were white, her hull green with a yellow ribbon. The boot-topping was red.

There is more to a ship than outward appearance, however. And Grimes, himself a shipmaster of long standing, knew this as well as the most seasoned master mariner on the oceans of Aquarius. But she had, he discovered, a fair turn of speed, her diesel-electric drive pushing her through the water at a good twenty knots. She was single screw, with a right-handed propeller. Her wheelhouse and chartroom reminded him almost of the spaceships that he was accustomed to command, but the electronic gadgetry was not unfamiliar to him after the sessions he had put in on the various simulators in the Havenmaster's Control Tower. The only thing that he did not like was the Purcell Navigator squatting like a sinister octopus in its own cage abaft the chartroom. Oh, well, he would make sure that his young gentlemen had no truck with the electronic monster. He hoped.

"I don't like it either," said the tall, skinny, morose Captain Harrell, whom Grimes was relieving. "But it works. Even I have to admit that. It works."

Then Harrell led Grimes down to the big, comfortable day cabin where the two wives—Mrs. Harrell very dumpy and mousy alongside the slender Sonya—were waiting. The Harrells' baggage, packed and ready to be carried ashore, was against one bulkhead. On a table stood bottles and glasses, a bowl of cracked ice. The officers came in then, neat in their slate gray shirt-and-shorts uniforms, their black, gold-braided shoulderboards, to say good-bye to their old captain, to greet their new one. There was Wilcox, Chief Officer, a burly, blond young (but not too young) giant. There was Andersen, the Second, another giant, but red-haired. There was Viccini, the Third, slight and dark. And Jones, the Engineer, a fat, bald man who could have been any age, came up to be introduced, and with him he brought Mary Hales, the Electrician, a fragile, silver-headed little girl who looked incapable of changing a fuse. Finally there came Sally Fielding, Stewardess-Purser, plump and motherly.

Glasses were charged. "Well, Captain," began Harrell. "Or should I say Commodore, or Admiral?"

"Captain," Grimes told him.

"Well, Captain, your name's on the Register and the Articles. You've signed the Receipt for Items Handed Over. You've a good ship, and a good team of officers. Happy sailing!"

"Happy sailing," everybody repeated.

"Thank you, Captain," replied Grimes. "And I'm sure that we all wish you an enjoyable leave."

"And how are you spending it, Mrs. Harrell?" asked Sonya.

"We've a yacht," the other woman told her. "Most of the time we shall be cruising around the Coral Sea."

"A busman's holiday," commented Grimes.

"Not at all," Harrell told him, grinning for the first time. "There'll just be the two of us, so there'll be no crew problems. And no electronic gadgetry to get in my hair either."

"Happy sailing," said Grimes, raising his glass.

"Happy sailing," they all said again.

And it was happy sailing at first.

It did not take Grimes long to find his feet, his sea legs. "After all," he said to Sonya, "a ship is a ship is a ship . . ." He had been afraid at first that his officers and crew would resent him, an outsider appointed to command with no probationary period in the junior grades—but there hung about him the spurious glamour of that honorary admiral's commission, and his reputation as a maritime historian earned him respect. *Sonya Winneck's* people knew that he was on Aquarius to do a job, a useful job, and that his sailing as master of her was part of it.

Sonya enjoyed herself too. She made friends with the other women aboard: with Mary Hales, with Sally Fielding, with the darkly opulent Vanessa Wilcox, who had joined just before departure from Port Stellar, with Tessa and Teena, the Assistant Stewardesses, with the massive Jemima Brown who was queen of the beautifully mechanized galley. This shipboard life—*surface* shipboard life—was all so new to her, in spite of its inevitable resemblances to life aboard a spaceship. There was so much to see, so much to inquire into . . .

The weather was fine, mainly, with warm days and nights with just sufficient chill to provide a pleasant contrast. Grimes played with the sextant he had purchased in Port Stellar, became skilled in its use, taking altitude after altitude of the sun, of the planet's two moons, of such stars, planets and artificial satellites as were visible at morning and evening twilight. His officers watched with a certain amusement as he plotted position after position on the working chart, congratulated him when these coincided with those for the same times shown on the chart that was displayed on the screen of the Purcell Navigator. And they, he was pleased to note, tended to ignore that contraption, consulting it only when there was a wide variance between positions taken by two observers.

A shipmaster, however, is more than a navigator. Pilotage was not compulsory for the majority of the ports visited by *Sonya Winneck*, although in each one of them pilots were available. Grimes had taken a pilot sailing from Port Stellar, but after the six-day run between that harbor and Tallisport decided to try to berth the ship himself. After all, he had spent hours in the simulator and, since joining his ship, had read Ardley's *Harbor Pilotage* from cover to cover.

This book, a standard, Terran, twentieth century work on the handling and mooring of ships, had been given him by the Havenmaster, who had said, "You should find this useful, John. Ardley was one of *the* authorities of his time. One thing I like about him—he says that anchors are there to be used. For maneuvering, I mean . . ." He laughed, then added, "But don't go making too much of a habit of it. It annoys chief officers!"

And so, having made a careful study of the large scale chart, the plan and the "sailing directions," Grimes stood in to Tallisport shortly after sunrise. The wheel was manned, the engines on stand by. According to the Tide Tables it was just two hours after first high water, which meant that *Sonya Winneck* would be stemming the ebb on her way in. (But, Wilcox had told him, complications were bound to crop up in this river harbor. All wharfage was on the western bank of the river, on the starboard hand entering—and to berth starboard side to is to risk damage in a vessel with a right-handed single screw, especially when the master is an inexperienced ship handler. Sometimes, however, an eddy, a countercurrent, set strongly along the line of wharfage, giving the effect of flood tide. If this eddy were running— and, only visual observation when approaching the berth would confirm this or not—Grimes would be able to bring the ship's head to starboard, letting go the starboard anchor to stub her around, and then ease her alongside, port side to, with the anchor still on the bottom.)

Grimes stood into Tallisport. With his naked eye he could now see the Main Leads, two white towers, nicely in line. He told the Harbor Quartermaster to steer for them, to keep them right ahead. Yes, and there was the breakwater to port, with its red beacon . . . The red beacon was abeam now, and *Sonya Winneck* was sweeping into the harbor in fine style.

"Hadn't you better reduce speed, sir?" suggested the Third Officer.

"Mphm. Thank you, Mr. Viccini. Better make it slow—no, dead slow."

"Dead slow, sir."

The rhythmic thudding of the diesel generators was unchanged, but there was a subtle diminution of vibration as the propeller revolutions decreased. The Main Leads were still ahead, but coming abeam to starboard were the two white obelisks that were the Leads into the Swinging Basin. "Port ten degrees," ordered Grimes. Would it be enough? Then he saw the ship's head swinging easily, heard the clicking of the gyro repeater. "Midships. Steady!"

He went out to the starboard wing of the bridge, looked aft. The Swinging Basin Leads were coming into line astern nicely. "Steady as you go!" he called.

Now *Sonya Winneck* was creeping up the last navigable reach of the river. To starboard was the line of wharfage, and behind it the clumps of greenery, spangled with blossoms like jewels, the white-walled houses, all clean and bright in the morning sun. But Grimes had no eye for scenery; he was too new to the game. Through his binoculars he studied the quay at which he was to berth, the furthest up river. Beyond it was a mess of dredging equipment, all part and parcel of the port expansion plan. Which side to would it be? He had still to make up his mind.

"Sir," said the Third Officer.

"Yes?"

"It doesn't look as though the eddy, the countercurrent is running, sir."

"What makes you think that, Mr. Viccini?"

The young man pointed to the small craft—a yacht, two fishing vessels—past which they were sliding. Their upstream moorings were bar taut, their downstream lines hanging in bights. "Mphm," grunted Grimes. So it was ebb all over the river. He made up his mind. "Tell the Chief and Second Officers it will be starboard side to. Tell Mr. Wilcox to have his port anchor ready."

He came to starboard, lined the ship's head up on the up river end of the wharf. With his mouth whistle he blew one short, sharp blast. The chain cable of the port anchor rattled out through the pipe, the grip of the flukes in the mud acted as a brake. *Sonya Winneck* was still making way, but with the ebb against her and the drag of the anchor she was almost stopped.

This, thought Grimes, *is easy,* as he nosed in toward his berth.

But there was an eddy after all, and as soon as the ship was well inside it she was swept upstream toward the dredges, buoys and pipelines. "Hard a-starboard!" Grimes ordered. The anchor was still holding, luckily, and it acted as a fulcrum, checking the upstream motion of the stem while the stern was free to swing. The vessel was broadside on to the line of the river now, still approaching the wharf, but head on.

"Swing her, sir," suggested Viccini. "Get a headline ashore and tell the linesmen to run it to the down river end of the berth . . ."

Yes, thought Grimes, *it'll work. It'd better . . .*

A heaving line snaked ashore from the fo'c'sle head, was caught by one of the waiting linesmen. He and another man ran with it to the post indicated by the Chief Officer. Then the self-tensioning winch, whining, took the weight. Belatedly Grimes thought that he had better stop the engines, had better go astern before the ship's stem crashed through the wharf stringer. But the order had been anticipated. *A good lad, Viccini . . .* he thought. *But he'd better not make a habit of this sort of thing.*

Now *Sonya Winneck*'s bows were being pulled downriver against the countercurrent, her stem still only a few feet from the stringer, the stern swinging in easily. "Stop her," Grimes ordered. She was alongside now, with the very gentlest of impacts, and the leading hand of the mooring gang was shouting up that she was in position.

Grimes filled and lit his pipe. "Make fast fore and aft," he said. "That'll do the wheel. Finished with engines." And then, "Mr. Viccini, I appreciate your help. Don't get me wrong, I like an officer to show initiative. But I think you should try to remember there's only one Master on the bridge."

"But, sir . . ."

"That's all right, Mr. Viccini. You did the right things,

51

and I appreciate it. I'll try to do the right things myself in future."

Probably the Third Officer would have made a full explanation to Grimes during the day, but as soon as the gangway was out the Winneck Line's local agent came aboard with the mail, and among it was a letter saying that Viccini was to be paid off to commence his annual leave and would be relieved that morning by a Mr. Denham.

Sonya Winneck continued her steady, round-the-planet progress, rarely straying north or south of the tropics. The met. screen in the chartroom rarely showed indications of disturbed weather conditions, and when it did these were invariably hundreds of miles from the ship's track. It was, Mr. Wilcox said to Grimes, the sort of weather you sign on for. The days and the nights passed pleasantly. At sea, there was sunbathing, swimming in the ship's pool that, when inflated, occupied all the foredeck between the forward and after cranes of the main hatch, deck golf and, in the evenings, a variety of games or a wide selection of programs on the playmasters installed throughout the accommodation. In port, the day's business over, there was so much to see, so much to do. There was *real* swimming from sunwashed, golden beaches, and surfing; and now and again Grimes was able to hire a small sailing yacht for the day and found this sport much more enjoyable than on the lakes of Lorn, where there was wind enough but it was always bitter. There were the waterfront taverns—and both Grimes and Sonya loved seafood. The Terran lobster, prawn, oyster and herring had all done well in the Aquarian seas, and there were the local delicacies: the sand crawlers, which were something like Earth's trilobites must have been, the butterfly fish and the sea steaks.

It was, for both of them, a holiday, but for Sonya it was a holiday that palled in time. It was all right for Grimes; he had his navigation to play with, his pilotage and, when he got around to it, research to carry out on the projected history and a chapter or so of it to write. His wife, however, was becoming bored.

It was a longish run between Lynnhaven and Port Johnson, all of seven days. During it Sonya found stacks of magazines in one of the lockers in the ship's office, back numbers of the *Merchant Shipping Journal*, dating back for years. She brought a pile of them up to the master's day cabin. She said, "These could be useful to you, John." Grimes picked one up, leafed through it. "Mphm. All rather *dry* stuff. At the moment I'm trying to get the essential *feel* of this planet."

"But they're full of information."

"So's a dictionary."

She said, "Suppose I go through them, making notes of anything that might be useful to you . . ."

"That," he told her, "is very sweet of you, Sonya."

She made a grimace at him, then settled down with the supply of factual reading matter. Everything was there: specifications of new tonnage, sales, breakings up, wrecks, strandings, collisions, courts of inquiry. These latter were of interest to her. She could see how, time and time again, the unfortunate Master was given only seconds to decide what to do, while learned judges, counsel and marine assessors had weeks to decide what should have been done. And then, as she read on, nagging hints of some sort of pattern began to form in her mind, her trained mind. After all, she had been an intelligence officer, and a good one, in the Federation's Survey Service.

It seemed to her that the Winneck Line ships were getting into more than their fair share of trouble, with Lone Star Line running a close second. She knew little about the Lone Star Line, although she had seen their ships often enough in various' ports and, with Grimes, had been a guest aboard a few of them for drinks and meals. They were well-run, well-maintained vessels. She could speak with more authority regarding the Winneck Line; *Sonya Winneck* was typical of their newer tonnage. There wasn't the same spit and polish as in the Lone Star, but there was a very real efficiency.

She read again the details of one of the collision cases. *Olga Winneck* had been bound up the Great Muddy River to Steelport, *Suzanne Winneck* had been outbound. The ships had passed each other—or had attempted to pass each other —in Collier's Reach, the navigable channel in that locality being both deep and wide. Suddenly *Olga Winneck* had taken a sheer to port and, in spite of the efforts of both Masters to avert collision, had struck *Suzanne Winneck* on her port quarter, holing her so badly that she was obliged to return to dock for repairs.

There was the transcription of evidence:

Mr. Younghusband (counsel for Havenmaster's Office): Can you tell me, Mr. Margolies, what orders were given by Captain Hazzard?

Mr. Margolies (Third Officer of *Olga Winneck*): Yes, sir. The Master ordered, "Hard a-starboard! Stop engines! Full astern!"

Mr. Younghusband: And were these orders carried out?

Mr. Margolies: Of course. I at once put the controls to full astern.

Mr. Younghusband: And what about the wheel? Quartermasters have been known to put the helm the wrong way, especially in an emergency.

Mr. Margolies: The quartermaster put the wheel hard to starboard.

Mr. Younghusband: And did you look at the rudder indicator? It has been suggested that steering gear failure was a cause of the collision.

Mr. Margolies: Yes, I looked. The pointer was hard over to starboard.

And so it went on. It was established finally that both Masters had done all the right things, although Captain Hazzard should have realized that a delay was inevitable when switching directly from full ahead to full astern. It was thought that a tidal eddy had been responsible for the collision. The court recommended that ships passing in Collier's Reach keep each well to their own sides of the channel, also that speed be reduced.

That was one case. There were others, and Sonya made notes, drew up tables. There had been collisions in narrow channels and in the open sea. Some had been in clear weather, some in conditions of reduced visibility. The causes were various: tidal eddies, steering gear failure, radar breakdown and, inevitably, errors of judgment. And the Winneck Line and the Lone Star Line were having more than their fair share of marine casualties . . . It was odd, she thought. Odd. There was something rotten in the state of Aquarius.

She asked Grimes if she could browse through the ship's files of correspondence. He said, "Of course. They aren't top secret." She found the one labeled *Damage Reports*. It wasn't especially bulky. But its contents were interesting.

"Sir, (she read)

I regret to have to report that whilst berthing this

morning at No.3 Inner East, Port Kantor, the stem of the vessel came into heavy contact with the starboard side of the Lone Star Line's *Canopic*. Damage to *Sonya Winneck* was superficial only—please see enclosed sketch—but that to the other ship was considerable and, I am informed by *Canopic*'s master, will necessitate dry-docking.

I entered the harbor at 0545 hrs., standing in on the Main Leads. When clear of the breakwaters I reduced to dead slow and altered course to port, steering for the shore end of No.3 Jetty. Visibility was good, wind was ENE at about 10 knots, tidal influence, it being just after low water slack, was negligible.

When my bridge was just abeam of *Canopic*'s stern, however, *Sonya Winneck* took a sudden sheer to port. I at once ordered a hard a-starboard, stopped the engines and ordered full astern. Also I signaled to the Chief Officer to let go the starboard anchor, but unfortunately it jammed in the pipe, and was released too late to have any effect. In spite of the application of full starboard rudder and full stern power, contact occurred at 0555 hrs.

It is possible that I underestimated the force of the wind while standing in to my berth, but, even so, find it hard to account for the sudden sheer to port . . ."

But *Sonya Winneck* was sometimes at the receiving end. "Sir,

I have to report that this afternoon, at 1327 hrs., the vessel was struck by the Company's *Elizabeth Winneck*, which same was proceeding down river, bound for sea. Unfortunately, it being Saturday afternoon, with no work in progress, no officers were on deck at the time of the contact, and the Company's gangway watchman was at his place of duty, at the head of the gangway, on the inshore side of the vessel.

Damage, fortunately, was not extensive and all above the waterline. My Chief Officer's report is enclosed herewith. No doubt you will be hearing from Captain Pardoe of *Elizabeth Winneck* . . ."

There were several more letters, some going into great detail, others composed on the good old principle of "least said, soonest mended." With two exceptions the other ships concerned were units of either the Winneck or the Lone Star fleets. One of the exceptions was the contact with *Iron Duchess*. On that occasion Captain Harrell, Grimes's predecessor, had been trying to berth his ship during a howling gale. The other occasion was a collision with a ferry steamer in Carrington Harbor, with fortunately no loss of life.

So, Sonya wondered, just what was the connection between the Winneck Line and the Lone Star Line? She borrowed from the Chief Officer's office the bulky *Aquarian Registry* in which was listed comprehensive details of all the commercial shipping of the planet. Against the name of each ship were the lines of information: tonnage, gross, net and deadweight; propulsion; speed; length overall, length between posts, breadth . . . And builders.

She looked up her namesake first. She had been built by the Carrington State Dockyard. She looked up *Canopic*. Her builders were Varley's Dockyard, in Steelport. She looked up *Elizabeth Winneck*—another Varley's job. So it went on. The majority of the collisions had occurred between ships constructed at those two yards.

And what about the contact that her husband, Grimes, had so narrowly averted, that time coming into Newhaven? What was the name of the ship that he had almost (but not quite) hit? *Orionic* . . . She looked it up. Carrington State Dockyard. She murmured, "All us Carrington girls must stick together . . ."

"What was that?" demanded Grimes, looking up from his book.

"Just a thought," she told him. "Just a passing thought."

"Mphm."

"Do ships *really* have personalities?" she asked.

He grinned. "Spacemen and seamen like to kid themselves that they do. Look at it this way. You're bringing a ship in —a spaceship or a surface ship—and you've failed to allow for *all* the factors affecting her handling. Your landing or berthing isn't up to your usual standard. But you kid yourself, and your officers that it wasn't *your* fault. You say, 'She was a proper little bitch, wasn't she? Wouldn't do a thing right . . .' But *you* were the one who wasn't doing a thing right."

She said, "I've handled ships too."

"I know, my dear. I've seen you do it. Your landing technique is a little too flashy for my taste."

"Never mind that now. I'm talking about surface ships. Is there any reason to believe, John, that two ships built to the same design, but in different yards, would have conflicting personalities?"

Grimes was starting to get annoyed with his wife. "Damn it all," he expostulated, "spacemen's superstitions are bad enough! But I'm surprised that you, of all people, should pay any heed to seamen's superstitions."

"But are they superstitions? Couldn't a machine absorb, somehow, something of the personalities of the people who built it, the people who handle it?"

"Hogwash," said Grimes.

"If that's the way you feel about it . . ." She slumped in her deep chair, struck a cigarillo on her thumbnail, put it to her mouth, looked at her husband through the wreathing smoke. "All right. Before you get back to your precious research, what do the initials P N mean?"

"In what context?"

Sonya nudged with a slim, sandaled foot the bulky *Aquarian Registry*, which lay open on the deck in front of her. "It's printed against the names of some of the ships, the newer ships—but only those built by the Carrington State Dock-yard or Varley's."

"P . . . N . . ." muttered Grimes. "P . . . N . . . ? We can ask the Mate, I suppose . . ."

"But you don't like to," she scoffed. "You're the Captain, you know everything."

"Almost everything," he qualified smugly. The ship lurched suddenly, and Grimes knew the reason. When last he had been on the bridge he had been slightly perturbed by the chart presented in the met. screen, televised from one of the weather satellites. Ahead of *Sonya Winneck* was a deepening depression, almost stationary. He had considered altering course to try to avoid it—but, after all, he had a big, powerful ship under his feet, well found, stoutly constructed. And, he had thought, he would not like to be remembered on this world as a fair weather sailor. Even so, he saw in his mind's eye that chart—the crowded isobars, the wind arrows with their clockwise circulation. Now the heavy swell running outward from the center, like ripples from a pebble dropped into a pond, was beginning to make itself felt. He looked at the aneroid barometer on the bulk-head. The needle had fallen ten millibars since he had last set the pointer, two hours ago.

He said, "I fear we're in for a dirty night."

She said, "It's what you're paid for."

He grunted, got up from his chair, went up to the bridge by the inside companionway to the chartroom. He looked at the instruments over the chart table. According to the Chernikeeff Log, speed through the water had already dropped by half a knot. The barograph showed a fairly steep fall in pressure. The met. screen, set for the area through which the ship was passing, showed a chart almost identical with the one that he had last seen.

He went out to the bridge. The sky was mainly overcast now, with the larger of the two Aquarian moons, almost full, showing fitfully through ragged breaks in the cloud. There was high altitude wind, although it had yet to be felt at sea level. But the swell seemed to be increasing.

Young Mr. Denham, the Third Officer, came across from the wing of the bridge. He said, rather too cheerfully, "Looks like a blow, sir."

"We can't expect fine weather all the time," Grimes told him. He stood with his legs well apart, braced against the motion of the ship. He wondered if he would be seasick, then consoled himself with the thought that both the actual Lord Nelson and the fictional Lord Hornblower had been afflicted by this malady.

Mr. Denham—since Grimes had torn that strip off him regarding the unauthorized engine movements he had tended to overcompensate—went on chirpily, "At this time of the year, sir, the revolving storms in these waters are unpredictable. In theory the center should be traveling east, away from us, but in practice it's liable to do anything."

"Oh?"

"Yes, sir. I remember one when I was in the old *Sally—Sara Winneck*, that is. Captain Tregenza tried to outmaneuver it; we had a pile of deck cargo that trip, teak logs from Port Mandalay. But it was almost as though it had a brain of its own. Finally it sat right on top of us and matched speed and course, no matter which way we steered. We lost all the cargo off the foredeck, and the wheelhouse windows were smashed in . . ."

Cheerful little swine . . . thought Grimes. He stared ahead into the intermittently moonlit night, at the long swell that was coming in at an angle to the ship's course. *Sonya Winneck*'s bows lifted then dipped, plunging into and through the moving dune of water. They lifted again, and a white

58

cascade poured aft from the break of the fo'c'sle, spangled with jewels of luminescence. Grimes said, "Anyhow, we have no deck cargo this trip."

"No, sir."

He remained on the bridge a while longer. There was nothing that he could do, and he knew it. The ship was far from unseaworthy, capable of riding out a hurricane. There was ample sea room; the Low Grenadines were many miles to the north of her track. And yet he felt uneasy, could not shake off a nagging premonition. Something, he somehow knew, was cooking. But what, when and where?

At last he grunted, "You know where to find me if you want me. Good night, Mr. Denham."

"Good night, sir."

Back in his quarters his uneasiness persisted. He told Sonya that he would sleep on the settee in his day cabin, so as to be more readily available in the event of any emergency. She did not argue with him; she, too, felt a growing tension in the air. It could have been that she was sensitive to his moods but, she told him, she didn't think so. She quoted, *"By the pricking of my thumbs something wicked this way comes."*

He laughed. "A tropical revolving storm is not wicked, my dear. Like any other manifestation of the forces of nature it is neither good nor evil."

She repeated, "Something wicked this way comes."

They said good night then, and she retired to the bedroom and he disposed himself comfortably on the settee. He was rather surprised that sleep was not long in coming.

But he did not enjoy his slumber for more than a couple of hours. A particularly violent lurch awakened him, almost pitched him off his couch. He switched on a light, looked at the aneroid barometer. The needle was down another twenty millibars. And, in spite of the well-insulated plating of the accommodation, he could hear the wind, both hear and feel the crash of the heavy water on deck. He thrust his feet into his sandals and, clad only in his shorts (Master's privilege) went up to the bridge. He found the Second Officer—it was now the middle watch—in the wheelhouse, looking ahead through the big clear view screen. Grimes joined him. When his eyes became accustomed to the semi-darkness he could see that the wind was broad on the starboard bow; he could see, too, that with each gust it was veering, working gradually around from southeast to south. *Southern Hemisphere*, he thought. *Clockwise circulation, and the low barometer on my left hand* . . . Now that he had something to work on he might as well avoid the center with its confused, heavy seas. "Bring her round to starboard easily," he told the Second Officer. "Bring wind and sea ahead."

"Wind and sea ahead, sir." The officer went to the controls of the autopilot. Grimes watched the bows swinging slowly, then said, "That should do, Mr. Andersen."

"Course one three five now, sir."

Grimes went back into the chartroom, looked down at the chart, busied himself briefly with parallel rulers and dividers. He grunted his satisfaction. This new course took him even further clear of the Low Grenadines, that chain of rocky islets that were little more than reefs. There was nothing to worry about.

He was aware that Sonya was standing behind him; there was a hint of her perfume, the awareness of her proximity. He said without turning around, "Passengers not allowed on the bridge."

She asked, "Where are we?"

He indicated with the points of the dividers the penciled cross of the position, the new course line extending from it. "I'm more or less, not quite heaving to. But she's easier on this heading, and it pulls her away from the eye of the storm."

She said, "There's a lot to be said for spaceships. They don't pitch and roll. When you're in your virtuous couch you're not slung out of it."

"We take what comes," he told her.

"We haven't much option, have we?"

Then they went below again, and she made coffee, and they talked for awhile, and eventually Grimes settled down to another installment of his broken night's sleep.

The next time he awakened it was by the insistent buzzing of the bridge telephone, which was in his bedroom. He rolled off the settee, stumbled through the curtained doorway. Sonya, looking rather hostile, lifted the instrument off its rest, handed it to him.

"Master here," said Grimes into the mouthpiece.

"Second Officer, sir. There's a Mayday . . ."

"I'll be right up."

The Second Mate was in the chartroom, plotting positions on the chart. He straightened as Grimes came in, turned to speak to him. "It's *Iron Warrior,* sir. One of their big bulk carriers. She's broken down, lying in the trough, and her cargo's shifted. Zinc concentrates."

"Not good. Where is she?"

The young man stood away from the chart so that Grimes could see, indicated the other ship's position with the point of a pencil. "Here, sir. Just twenty miles south of the Low Grenadines. And she reports a southerly gale, the same as we're getting."

"Not good," said Grimes again. "Not good at all. She'll be making leeway, drifting . . ." Swiftly he measured the distance between *Sonya Winneck*'s last recorded position—electronic navigation had its good points!—and that given by the disabled ship. One hundred and fifty nautical miles . . . And *Sonya Winneck* would have to turn, putting the wind right aft. With her high superstructure this should mean a marked increase of speed . . . Suppose she made twenty knots over the ground . . . Twenty into one hundred and fifty . . . Seven and a half hours . . . He looked at the chartroom clock. Oh three thirty . . .

"Put your standby man on the wheel, Mr. Andersen," he ordered. "I'm bringing her round manually."

He went out into the wheelhouse. Both moons were down, but the sky had cleared. Overhead the scattered stars were bright; and bright, too, were the living stars thrown aloft and back in the sheets of spray each time that the ship's prow crashed down to meet the racing seas. Grimes stood there, waiting, hoping for a lull, however brief. He glanced behind him, saw that the wheel was manned and that Andersen was standing beside the helmsman.

He looked ahead again. It seemed to him that the pitching of the ship was a little less pronounced, that sea and swell were a little less steep. "Port," he ordered. "Easily, easily . . ." He heard the clicking of the gyro-repeater as the ship's head started to come round. And then he saw it, broad on the starboard bow, a towering cliff of water, white capped, a freak sea. "Hard a-port!" Grimes shouted. "Hard over!"

She responded beautifully, and the clicking of the repeater was almost one continuous note. She responded beautifully, but not quite fast enough. The crest of the dreadful sea was overhanging the bridge now, poised to fall and smash. Still she turned, and then she heeled far over to port, flinging Grimes and the Second Officer and the helmsman into an untidy huddle on that side of the wheelhouse. She shuddered as the tons of angry water crashed down to to her poop, surged forward along her decks, even onto the bridge itself. There was a banging and clattering of loose gear, cries and screams from below. But miraculously she steadied, righted herself, surging forward with only a not very violent pitching motion.

Somehow Grimes got to his feet, disentangling himself from the other two men. He staggered to the untended wheel, grasped the spokes. He looked at the repeater card. Three two oh . . . Carefully he applied starboard rudder, brought the lubber's line to the course that had been laid off on the chart, three three five. He saw that Andersen and the seaman had recovered their footing, were standing by awaiting further orders.

"Put her back on automatic," he told the Second Officer. "On this course." He relinquished the wheel as soon as this had been done. "Then take your watch with you and make rounds through the accommodation. Let me know if anybody's been hurt."

"Who the hell's rocking the bloody boat?" It was Wilcox, the Chief Officer. Then, as he saw Grimes by the binnacle, "Sorry, sir."

"It's an emergency, Mr. Wilcox. A Mayday call. *Iron Warrior*, broken down and drifting on to the Low Grenadines. We're going to her assistance."

"What time do you estimate that we shall reach her, Captain?"

"About eleven hundred hours."

"I'd better start getting things ready," replied the Mate.

Grimes went back into the chartroom, to the transceiver that had been switched on as soon as the auto-alarm had been actuated by the Mayday call. "*Sonya Winneck* to Ocean Control, Area Five," he said.

"Ocean Control to *Sonya Winneck*. I receive you. Pass your message."

"I am now proceeding to the assistance of *Iron Warrior*. Estimated time of visual contact ten thirty hours, Zone Plus Seven."

"Thank you, *Sonya Winneck*. *Pleiadic* cannot be in the vicinity until thirteen hundred hours at the earliest. Please use Channel Six when working *Iron Warrior*. Call me on Sixteen to keep me informed. Over."

He switched to Channel Six. "*Sonya Winneck* to *Iron Warrior* . . ."

"*Iron Warrior* here, *Sonya Winneck*." The other Captain's voice, was, perhaps, a little too calm.

"How are things with you, *Iron Warrior?*"

"Bloody awful, to be frank. A twenty degree list, and my boats and rafts smashed on the weather side. Estimated rate of drift, two knots."

"I should be with you in seven hours," said Grimes. "I shall try to take you in tow."

"We'll have everything ready, Captain."

"Good. We shall be seeing you shortly. Over and standing by."

Wilcox had come into the chartroom. He said, "Everybody's been informed, sir. The Chief reckons that he can squeeze out another half knot."

"Anybody hurt when she went over?"

"Only minor lacerations and contusions, sir."

"Such as this," announced Sonya, who had joined the others in the chartroom, putting a cautious hand up to the beginnings of a black eye. "But it's in a good cause."

Iron Warrior was not a pretty sight.

She lay wallowing in a welter of white water, like a dying sea beast. The seas broke over her rust-colored hull in great explosions of spray, but now and again, during brief lulls, the extent of the damage that she had sustained could be made out. She was a typical bulk carrier, with all the accommodation aft, with only a stumpy mast right forward and her mainmast growing out of her funnel, and no cargo gear but for one crane on the poop for ship's stores and the like. That crane, Grimes could see through his binoculars, was a twisted tangle of wreckage. That would explain why the *Warrior*'s Captain had not used oil to minimize the effect of breaking waves; probably the entrance to the storerooms was blocked. And there must be some other reason why it had not been possible to pump diesel fuel overside—even though a mineral oil is not as effective as vegetable or animal oil it is better than nothing. The side of the bridge seemed to be stove in, and under the boat davits dangled a mess of fiberglass splinters.

Beyond her—and not far beyond her, a mere three miles —was the black, jagged spine of Devlin's Islet, dead to leeward. It seemed more alive, somehow, than the stricken ship, looked like a great, malevolent sea monster creeping nearer and ever nearer through the boiling surf toward its dying prey.

Grimes was using oil, a thin trickle of it from his scuppers, wads of waste soaked in it thrown overside to leeward. Luckily there had been plenty of it in *Sonya Winneck*'s storerooms—fish oil for the preservation of exposed wire ropes, a heavy vegetable oil for the treatment of wooden decks and brightwork. It was beginning to have effect; the thin, glistening surface film was a skin over the water between the two ships, an integument that contained the sea, forcing some semblance of form upon it. The swell was still there— heavy, too heavy—but the waves were no longer breaking, their violence suppressed.

Aft, Andersen and his men were standing by the rocket gun. The heavy insurance wire was already flaked out ready for running, its inboard end taken not only around both pairs of bitts—these, in a ship with self-tensioning winches, were rarely used for mooring, but there was always the possibility of a tow—but also around the poop house. The sisal messenger was coiled down handy to the line-throwing apparatus.

On the bridge, Grimes conned his ship. She was creeping along parallel to *Iron Warrior* now, at reduced speed. She was making too much leeway for Grimes's taste; unless he was careful there would be two wrecks instead of only one. Too, with the swell broad on the beam *Sonya Winneck* was rolling heavily, so much so that accurate shooting would be impossible. But the necessary maneuvers had been worked out in advance. At the right moment Grimes would come hard to port, presenting his stern to the *Iron Warrior*. Andersen would loose off his rocket, aiming for a point just abaft the break of the other ship's fo'c'sle head, where men were already standing by. They would grab the light, nylon rocket line, use it to pull aboard the heavier messenger, use that to drag the end of the towing wire aboard, shackling it to the port anchor cable. After that, it would be plain sailing (Grimes hoped). He would come ahead slowly, slowly, taking the weight gently, trying to avoid the imposition of overmuch strain on either vessel. Slowly but surely he would pull the wounded *Warrior* away from the hostile fortifications. (*Come off it, Grimes,* he told himself sternly. *Don't be so bloody literary.*)

"Hard a-port!" he ordered.

"Hard a-port, sir!" The clicking of the repeater was audible above the shrieking of the wind.

"Ease her . . . Midships . . . Steady! Steady as you go!"

Sonya Winneck hung there, her stern a bare two cables from the side of *Iron Warrior*. Grimes thought, *I cut that rather too close. But at this range it'll be impossible for Andersen to miss.* To the Third Officer, at the radar, he called, "Are we opening the range?"

"Slowly, sir."

It was time that Andersen got his rocket away. The ship was not pitching too badly; firing at just the right moment should not be difficult. As long as the missile passed over the target it would be a successful shot. Grimes went out to the wing of the bridge to watch. The air scoop dodger deflected the wind, throwing it up and over, so it was not too uncomfortable away from the wheelhouse.

Andersen fired—and at precisely the wrong moment the ship's head fell off heavily to starboard. The rocket streaked through the air, arcing high, a brief orange flare against the gray, ragged clouds, a streamer of white smoke, and behind it the fluorescent yellow filament of the nylon line. Inevitably it missed, finally splashing to the sea well forward of and beyond *Iron Warrior*'s bows.

Grimes didn't see it drop. He stormed into the wheelhouse, bawled at the helmsman, "What the hell do you think you're playing at?"

"It's the wheel, sir," The man's voice was frightened. "It turned in my hands. I can't budge it!"

The ship was coming round still, turning all the time to starboard. The gale force wind and her own engines were driving her down on to the helpless *Warrior*. "Stop her!" ordered Grimes. "Full astern!"

Denham was still at the radar, so Wilcox jumped to the engine controls. He slammed the lever hard over to the after position. Still the ship was making headway—but, at last slowing. She stopped at last, her stem scant feet from *Iron Warrior*'s exposed side. Grimes could see the white faces of her people as they stared at him, as they watched, in horrified disbelief, this rescuer turned assassin.

Sonya Winneck was backing away now, her stern coming up into the wind. She was backing away, but reluctantly. Wilcox shouted, "Denham, come and give me a hand! I can't keep this bloody handle down!"

Grimes dragged his attention away from the ship he had so nearly rammed to what was happening on his own bridge. Both the Chief and Third Officer—and Wilcox was a big, strong man—were having to exert all their strength to keep the metal lever in its astern position. It was jerking, forcing itself up against their hands.

Sonya—who until now had been keeping well out of the way—grabbed him by the arm. "Tell the Chief to put the engine controls on manual!" she screamed. "I know what's happening!"

"What's happening?"

"No time now to tell you. Just put her on manual, and get Lecky up here!"

Grimes went to the telephone, rang down to the engineroom. "Manual control, your end, Mr. Jones," he ordered. "Keep her on full astern until I order otherwise. And send Miss Hales up to the bridge. At once."

Thankfully, Wilcox and Denham released their painful grip on the bridge control lever. On the console the revolution indicator still showed maximum stern power. Ahead, the distance between the two ships was fast diminishing. From the VHF transceiver came a frightened voice, "What's happening, *Sonya Winneck?* What's happening?"

"Tell him," said Grimes to Denham, "that we're having trouble with our bridge controls. We'll get a line aboard as soon as we can."

Wilcox, watching the indicator, yelled, "She's stopped! The bitch is coming ahead again!"

Sonya said urgently, "There's only one thing to do, John. Shut off the Purcell Navigator. *Iron Warrior* has P N against her name in the Registry—and she was built by Varley's." She turned to Mary Hales, who had just come onto the bridge. "Mary, switch off that bloody tin brain, or pull fuses, or something—*but kill it!*"

The pretty little blonde was no longer so pretty. On one side of her head the hair was charred and frizzled, and her smooth face was marred by an angry burn. "We've been trying to," she gasped. "The Chief and I. It won't let us."

"She's coming astern again," announced Wilcox. "She's . . . No, she's stopped . . ."

"Watch her, Mr. Wilcox," ordered Grimes. He ran with his wife and the Electrician to the house abaft the chartroom in which the Purcell Navigator lived. It squatted there sullenly on its four stumpy legs, the dials set around its spherical body glaring at them like eyes. From its underside ran armored cables, some thick and some thin—that one leading aft and down must be the main power supply, the ones leading into the wheelhouse and chartroom would be connected to various controls and navigational equipment. On the after bulkhead of the house was a switchboard and fuse box. Mary Hales went straight to this, put out her hand to the main switch. There was a sudden, intense violet flare, a sharp crackling, the tang of overheated metal. The girl staggered back, her blistered hands covering her eyes. "That's what happened to the engineroom switchboard!" she wailed. "It's welded itself in the *On* position!" Then, using language more seamanlike than ladylike, she threw herself at the fuse box. She was too late—but perhaps this was as well. Had she got the lid open she would have been blinded.

Still cursing softly, she grabbed a spanner from her belt. Her intention was obvious; she would unscrew the retaining nut holding the main supply lead firmly in its socket. But an invisible force yanked the tool out of her hand, threw it out of the open door.

Grimes watched, helpless. Then he heard Sonya snarling, "Do something. *Do* something, damn you!" She thrust something into his right hand. He looked down at it. It was the big fire ax from its rack in the chartroom. He got both hands about the haft, tried to swing up the head of the weapon, staggered as the magnetic fields which now were the machine's main defense tugged at it. But he lifted the ax somehow, brought it crashing down—and missed his own right foot by a millimeter. Again he raised the ax, straining with all his strength, and again struck at the thick cable. The ship lurched heavily, deflecting his aim, and, fantastically, the magnetic deflection brought the head back to its target. The armored cable writhed away from the blow, but not in time, not enough. The keen edge bit home, in a coruscation of violet sparks. And Mary Hales, with a smaller ax that she had found somewhere, was chopping away, sobbing and cursing; and Sonya was jabbing with a heavy screwdriver at the thing's "eyes"—and so, at last, it died.

And so it died, damaged beyond its built-in powers of self-regeneration. (Mary Hales made sure of that.) And so Grimes was able to get a line aboard *Iron Warrior*, and the *Warrior's* people got the towing wire shackled onto their anchor cable, and slowly, slowly but surely, the crippled ship was dragged to safety, away from the avidly waiting fangs and talons of Devlin's Islet; the rocky teeth and claws that, when the tow finally commenced, had been less than half a mile distant.

The Purcell Navigator was dead, and its last flares of energy had destroyed or damaged much more than itself. The gyro-compass and the autopilot were inoperative (but the ship had a magnetic compass and hand steering). Loran and radar were burned out, inertial navigator and echometer were beyond repair, even the Chernikeeff Log was useless. But Grimes was not worried. He had sextant, chronometer, ephemeris and tables—and the great navigators of Earth's past had circled their globe with much less in the way of equipment. In the extremely unlikely event of his not knowing where he was he could always ask *Iron Warrior* for a fix—but he did not think that he would have to do so.

He did, however, urge the *Warrior's* Master to put his own Purcell Navigator out of commission, explaining why in some detail. Then he went to the house abaft the chartroom where, under the direction of Mary Hales, Wilcox and his men were loosening the holding down bolts, disconnecting the cables that had not already been cut. (There might still be a flicker of life in the thing, some capability of self-repair.) He watched happily as the Mate and three brawny ratings lifted the spherical casing from the deck, staggered with it out the door.

"What shall we do with it, sir?" asked the Mate.

"Give it a buoyancy test," ordered Grimes. He followed the men to the side rail of the bridge, watched as they tipped it over. It sank without a trace.

Grimes was relieved of his command in Longhaven, after the successful completion of the tow, and flown back to Steep Island, accompanied by Sonya. Neither he nor his wife felt very strong when they boarded the airship—the crews of both *Sonya Winneck* and *Iron Warrior* had united in laying on a farewell party more enthusiastic than restrained. ("You *must* be glad to see the back of us," Sonya had remarked at one stage of the proceedings.) Even so, old and tired as he was feeling, Grimes had insisted on seeing the airship's captain so as to be assured that the craft was not fitted with a Purcell Navigator. Then, he and his wife went to their cabin and collapsed into their bunks.

Steep Island, although not officially an airport, had a mooring mast, so a direct flight was possible. When the time came for Grimes and Sonya to disembark they were feeling better and, in fact, had been able to put the finishing touches to their report.

Captain Thornton, the Havenmaster, welcomed them warmly but was obviously anxious to hear what they had to tell him. In minutes only they were all seated in the Havenmaster's Lookout and Thornton was listening intently as they talked.

When they were finished, he smiled grimly. "This is good enough," he said. "It's good enough even for the Council of Master Wardens. I shall issue orders that those infernal machines are to be rendered inoperative in every ship fitted with them, and that no more are to be put aboard any Aquarian vessel. Then we make arrangements to ship them all back to where they came from."

Grimes was surprised, and said so. He was used to having his recommendations adopted eventually, but in most cases there was a lot of argument first.

Thornton laughed. "What you've said is what I've been saying, John, for months. But nobody listens to me. I'm just a reactionary old shellback. But you, sir, as well as being a well-known maritime historian, have also one foot—at least—in what to us is still the future. You're a master astronaut, you hold the rank of commodore in the Space Navy of your Confederacy. They'll listen to you, when they won't listen to me."

"It's Sonya they should listen to," Grimes said. "She's a spacewoman *and* an intelligence officer. She tied the loose ends together."

"But it was all so obvious," she said smugly. "Two yards, and two yards only, on this planet licensed to fit the Purcell Navigator: Varley's and the Carrington State Dockyard. Two . . . sororities? Yes, two sororities of ships, the Varley Sisterhood and the Carrington Sisterhood, each hating the other. Limited intelligence, but, somehow, a strong, built-in spite, and also a strong sense of self-preservation. That much, I think, was intended by those electronic geniuses on Elektra —and possibly more, but I'll come to that later.

"Anyhow, if a Carrington sister saw a chance of taking a swipe at a Varley sister without much risk of damage to herself she'd take it. And *vice versa*. Hence all the collisions, and all the minor berthing accidents. Now and again, of course, the sense of self-preservation worked to everybody's benefit . . ." She smiled at her husband rather too sweetly. "I know of at least one bungled berthing where everything, almost miraculously, came right in the end . . ."

"But what's behind it all?" asked the Havenmaster. "You're the Intelligence Officer. Is it, do you think, intentional on somebody's part?"

"I don't know, Tom. I'd have to snoop around on Elecktra to find out, and I doubt if the Elektrans would let me. But try this idea on for size . . . What if the Elektrans want to make Aquarius absolutely dependent upon them?"

"It could be . . ." mused Thornton. "It could be . . ." He went up, walked to the bookshelves, took out a book, opened it. It was Grimes's own *Times Of Transition*. The Havenmaster leafed through it to find the right place. He read aloud, " 'And so was engendered a most unseamanlike breed of navigator, competent enough technicians whose working tools were screwdrivers and voltmeters rather than sextants and chronometers. Of them it could never be said *Every hair a ropeyarn, every fingernail a marlinespike, every drop of blood pure Stockholm tar*. They were servants to rather than masters of their machines, and ever they were at the mercy of a single fuse . . .' " He shut the book with a slam. He said, "It can't happen here."

"Famous last words," scoffed Sonya, but her voice was serious.

"It mustn't happen here," said Grimes.

THE MAN WHO SAILED THE SKY

IT WAS FORTUNATE, Sonya always said, that the Federation Survey Service's *Star Pioneer* dropped down to Port Stellar, on Aquarius, when she did. Had not transport back to the Rim Worlds, although it was by a roundabout route, become available it is quite possible that her husband would have become a naturalized Aquarian citizen. Seafaring is no more (and no less) a religion than spacefaring; be that as it may, John Grimes, Master Astronaut, Commodore of the Rim Confederacy's Naval Reserve, Honorary Admiral of the Ausiphalian Navy and, lately, Master Mariner, was exhibiting all the zeal of the new convert. For some months he had sailed in command of an Aquarian merchantman and, although his real job was to find out the cause of the rapidly increasing number of marine casualties, he had made it plain that insofar as his own ship was concerned he was no mere figurehead. Although (or because) only at sea a dog watch, he was taking great pride in his navigation, his seamanship, his pilotage and his ship handling.

"Damn it all," he grumbled to Sonya, "if our lords and masters wanted us back they'd send a ship for us. I know that *Rim Eland* isn't due here for another six weeks, on her normal commercial voyage—but what's wrong with giving the Navy a spot of deep space training? The Admiralty could send a corvette . . ."

"You aren't all that important, John."

"I suppose not. I'm only the Officer Commanding the Naval Reserve, and the Astronautical Superintendent of Rim Runners . . . Oh, well—if *they* don't want me, there're some people who do."

"What do you mean?" she asked sharply.

"Tom told me that my Master Mariner's Certificate of Competency and my Pilotage Exemption Certificates are valid for all time. He told me, too, that the Winneck Line will give me another appointment as soon as I ask for it. There's just one condition . . ."

"Which is?"

"That we take out naturalization papers."

"No," she told him. "No, repeat, capitalize, underscore no."

"Why not, my dear?"

"Because this world is the bitter end. I always thought that the Rim Worlds were bad enough, but I put up with them for your sake and, in any case, they've been improving enormously over the past few years. But Aquarius . . . It's way back in the twentieth century!"

"That's its charm."

"For you, perhaps. Don't get me wrong. I enjoyed our voyage in *Sonya Winneck*—but it was no more than a holiday cruise . . ."

"An odd sort of holiday."

"You enjoyed it too. But after not too long a time you'd find the life of a seafaring commercial shipmaster even more boring than that of a spacefaring one. Do you want to be stuck on the surface of one planet for the rest of your life?"

"But there's more variety of experience at sea than there is in space . . ."

Before she could reply there was a tap on the door. "Enter!" called Grimes.

Captain Thornton, the Havenmaster of Aquarius, came into the suite. He looked inquiringly at his guests. "Am I interrupting something?" he asked.

"You are, Tom," Sonya told him. "But you're welcome to join the argument, even though it will be the two of you against me. John's talking of settling down on Aquarius to continue his seafaring career."

"He could do worse," said Thornton.

Sonya glared at the two men, at the tall, lean, silver-haired ruler of Aquarius, at her stocky, rugged husband whose prominent ears, already flushing, were a thermometer of his rising temper. Grimes, looking at her, had the temerity to smile slightly, appreciatively. Like the majority of auburn-haired women she was at her most attractive when about to blow her top.

"What are you grinning at, you big ape?" she demanded.

"You."

Before she could explode Thornton hastily intervened. He said, "I came in with some news that should interest you, both of you. I've just got the buzz that the Federation's *Star Pioneer* is putting in to Port Stellar. I know that you used to be in the Survey Service, John, and that Sonya still holds

72

a Reserve commission, and it could be that you'll be meeting some old shipmates . . ."

"Doubtful," said Grimes. "The Survey Service has a very large fleet, and it's many years since I resigned . . ."

"Since you were asked to resign," remarked Sonya.

"You were still in your cradle, so you know nothing about the circumstances. But there might be some people aboard that Sonya would know."

"We shall soon find out. I have to throw a party for the Captain and officers—and you, of course, will be among the guests."

Grimes knew none of *Star Pioneer*'s officers, but Sonya was acquainted with Commander James Farrell, the survey ship's captain. How well acquainted? Grimes felt a twinge of jealousy as he watched them chatting animatedly, then strolled over to the buffet for another generous helping of the excellent chowder. There he was engaged in conversation by two of the *Pioneer*'s junior lieutenants. "You know, sir," said one of them, "your name's quite a legend in the Service . . ."

"Indeed?" Grimes felt flattered.

The other young man laughed—and Grimes did not feel quite so smug. "Yes, sir. Any piece of insubordination—justifiable insubordination, of course—is referred to as 'doing a Grimes . . . '"

"Indeed?" The Commodore's voice was cold.

The first young man hastened to make amends. "But I've heard very senior officers, admirals and commodores, say that you should never have been allowed to resign . . ."

Grimes was not mollified. "*Allowed* to resign? It was a matter of choice, *my* choice. Furthermore . . ." And then he became aware that Sonya, with Commander Farrell in tow, was making her way toward him through the crowd. She was smiling happily. Grimes groaned inwardly. He knew that smile.

"John," she said, "I've good news."

"Tell me."

"Jimmy, here, says that I'm entitled to a free passage in his ship."

"Oh."

"I haven't finished. The Survey Service Regulations have been modified since *your* time. The spouses of commissioned officers, even those on the Reserve List, are also entitled to a free passage if suitable accommodation is available. *Star Pioneer* has ample passenger accommodation, and she will be making a courtesy call at Port Forlorn after her tour of the Carlotti Beacon Stations in this sector of space . . ."

"We shall be delighted to have you aboard, sir," said Farrell.

"Thank you," replied Grimes. He had already decided that he did not much care for the young Commander who, with his close-cropped sandy hair, his pug nose and his disingenuous blue eyes, was altogether too much the idealized Space Scout of the recruiting posters. "Thank you. I'll think about it."

"We'll think about it," said Sonya.

"There's no mad rush, sir," Farrell told him, with a flash of white, even teeth. "But it should be an interesting trip. Glebe, Parramatta, Wyong and Esquel . . ."

Yes, admitted Grimes to himself, *it could be interesting.* Like Aquarius, Glebe, Parramatta and Wyong were rediscovered Lost Colonies, settled originally by the lodejammers of the New Australia Squadron. Esquel was peopled by a more or less humanoid race that, like the Grollons, had achieved the beginnings of a technological civilization. Grimes had read about these worlds, but had never visited them. And then, through the open windows of the hall, drifted the harsh, salty smell of the sea, the thunderous murmur of the breakers against the cliff far below.

I can think about it, he thought. *But that's as far as it need go.*

"We'll think about it," Sonya had said—and now she was saying more. "Please yourself, John, but I'm going. You can follow me when *Rim Eland* comes in. If you want to."

"You'll not consider staying here on Aquarius?"

"I've already made myself quite clear on that point. And since you're hankering after a seafaring life so badly it'll be better if you make the break *now*, rather than hang about waiting for the Rim Runners' ship. Another few weeks here and it'll be even harder for you to tear yourself away."

Grimes looked at his wife. "Not with you already on the way home."

She smiled. "That's what I thought. That's why I took Jimmy's offer. He is rather sweet, isn't he?"

"All the more reason why I should accompany you aboard his blasted ship."

She laughed. "The old, old tactics always work, don't they?"

"Jealousy, you mean?" It was his turn to laugh. "Me, jealous of that puppy!"

"Jealous," she insisted, "but not of *him*. Jealous of the Survey Service. You had your love affair with the Service many years ago, and you've gotten over it. You've other mistresses now—Rim Runners and the Rim Worlds Naval Reserve. But I was still in the middle of mine when I came under the fatal spell of your charm. And I've only to say the word and the Service'd have me back; a Reserve Officer can always transfer back to the Active List . . ." She silenced Grimes with an upraised hand. "Let me finish. If I'd taken passage by myself in *Rim Eland* there'd have been no chance at all of my flying the coop. There's so much of *you* in all the Rim Runners' ships. And the Master and his officers would never have let me forget that I was Mrs. Commodore Grimes. Aboard *Star Pioneer*, with you not there, I'd soon revert to being Commander Sonya Verrill . . ."

Slowly, Grimes filled and lit his pipe. Through the wreathing smoke he studied Sonya's face, grave and intent under the gleaming coronal of auburn hair. He knew that she was right. If he persisted in the pursuit of this new love for oceangoing steamships, she could return to her old love for the far-ranging vessels of the Interstellar Federation's military and exploratory arm. They might meet again sometime in the distant future, they might not. And always there would be the knowledge that they were sailing under different flags.

"All right," he said abruptly. "Better tell your boyfriend to get the V.I.P. suite ready."

"I've already told him," she said. She grinned. "Although as a mere Reserve Commander, traveling by myself, I shouldn't have rated it."

The last farewells had been said, not without real regrets on either side, and slowly, the irregular throbbing of her inertial drive drowning the brassy strains of the traditional *Anchors Aweigh*, *Star Pioneer* lifted from the Port Stellar apron. Guests in her control room were Grimes and Sonya. Usually on such occasions the Commodore would be watching the ship handling technique of his host, but today he was not. He was looking down to the watery world fast falling away below. Through borrowed binoculars he was staring down at the slender shape that had just cleared the breakwaters of the Port Stellar seaport, that was proceeding seawards on yet another voyage; and he knew that on her bridge *Sonya Winneck*'s officers would be staring upward at the receding, diminishing ship of space. He sighed, not loudly, but Sonya looked at him with sympathy. That was yet another chapter of his life over, he thought. Never again would he be called upon to exercise the age-old skills of the seaman. But there were worse things than being a spaceman.

He pulled his attention away from the viewport, took an interest in what was going on in the control room. It was all much as he remembered it from his own Survey Service days—dials and gauges and display units, telltale lights, the remote controls for inertial, auxiliary rocket and Mannschenn Drives, the keyboard of the Gunnery Officer's "battle organ." And, apart from the armament accessories, it was very little different from the control room of any modern merchantman.

The people manning it weren't quite the same as merchant officers; and, come to that, weren't quite the same as the officers of the Rim Worlds Navy. There was that little bit of extra smartness in the uniforms, even to the wearing of caps inside the ship. There were the splashes of fruit salad on the left breast of almost every uniform shirt. There was the crispness of the Captain's orders, the almost exaggerated crispness of his officers' responses, with never a departure from standard Naval terminology. This was a taut ship, not unpleasantly taut, but taut nonetheless. (One of Grimes's shortcomings in the Survey Service had been his inability, when in command, to maintain the requisite degree of tension.) Even so, it was pleasant to experience it once again—especially as a passenger, an outsider. Grimes looked at Sonya. She was enjoying it too. Was she enjoying it too much?

Still accelerating, although not uncomfortably, the ship drove through the thin, high wisps of cirrus. Overhead the sky was indigo, below Aquarius was already visibly a sphere, an enormous mottled ball of white and gold and green and blue—mainly blue. Over to the west'ard was what looked like the beginnings of a tropical revolving storm. And who would be caught in it? Grimes wondered. Anybody he knew? In deep space there were no storms to worry about, not now, although in the days of the lodejammers magnetic storms had been an ever-present danger.

"Secure all!" snapped Commander Farrell.

"Hear this! Hear this!" the Executive Officer said sharply into his microphone. "All hands. Secure for free fall. Report."

Another officer began to announce, "Sick Bay—secure. secure. Enlisted men—secure. Hydroponics—secure . . ." It was a long list. Grimes studied the sweep second hand of his wristwatch. By this time a Rim Runners' tramp would be well on her way. Quite possibly, he admitted, with some shocking mess in the galley or on the farm deck. ". . . Mannschenn Drive Room—secure. Inertial drive room—secure. Auxiliary rocket room—secure. All secure, sir."

"All stations secure, sir," the Executive Officer repeated to the Captain.

"Free fall—execute!"

The throb of the inertial drive faltered and died in mid-beat.

"Centrifugal effect—stand by!"

"Centrifugal effect—stand by!"

"Hunting—execute!"

"Hunting—execute!"

The mighty gyroscopes hummed, then whined. Turning about them, the ship swung to find the target star, the distant sun of Glebe, lined it up in the exact center of the Captain's cartwheel sights and then fell away the few degrees necessary to allow for galactic drift.

"Belay gyroscopes!"

"Belay gyroscopes!"

"One gravity acceleration—stand by!"

"One gravity acceleration—stand by!"

"One gravity acceleration—execute!"

"One gravity acceleration—execute!"

The inertial drive came to life again.

"Time distortion—stand by!"

"Time distortion—stand by!"

"Mannschenn Drive—stand by!"

"Mannschenn Drive—stand by!"

"Mannschenn Drive—3 lyps—On!"

"Mannschenn Drive—3 lyps—On!"

There was the familiar thin, high keening of the ever-precessing gyroscopes, the fleeting second (or century) of temporal disorientation, the brief spasm of nausea; and then, ahead, the sparse stars were no longer steely points of light but iridescent, pulsating spirals, and astern the fast diminishing globe of Aquarius could have been a mass of multi-hued, writhing gases. *Star Pioneer* was falling down the dark dimensions, through the warped continuum toward her destination.

And about time, thought Grimes, looking at his watch again. *And about bloody time*.

Glebe, Parramatta, Wyong . . . Pleasant enough planets, with something of the Rim Worlds about them, but with a flavor of their own. Lost Colonies they had been, settled by chance, discovered by the ships of the New Australia Squadron after those hapless lodejammers had been thrown light-years off course by a magnetic storm, named after those same ships. For generations they had developed in their own way, isolated from the rest of the man-colonized galaxy. Their development, Commander Farrell complained, had been more of a retrogression than anything else. Commodore Grimes put forward his opinion, which was that these worlds were what the Rim Worlds should have been, and would have been if too many highly efficient types from the Federation had not been allowed to immigrate.

Sonya took sides in the ensuing argument—the wrong side at that. "The trouble with you, John," she told him, "is that you're just naturally against all progress. That's why you so enjoyed playing at being a twentieth century sailor on Aquarius. That's why you don't squirm, as *we* do, every time that you hear one of these blown away Aussies drawl, 'She'll be right . . .' "

"But it's true, ninety-nine percent of the time." He turned to Farrell. "I know that you and your smart young technicians were appalled at the untidiness of the Carlotti Stations on all three of these planets, at the slovenly bookkeeping and all the rest of it. But the beacons work and work well, even though the beacon keepers are wearing ragged khaki shorts instead of spotless white overalls. And what about the repairs to the one on Glebe? They knew that it'd be months before the spares for which they'd requisitioned trickled down through the Federation's official channels, and so they made do with the materials at hand . . ."

"The strip patched with beaten out oil drums . . ." muttered Farrell. "Insulators contrived from beer bottles . . ."

"But that beacon works, Commander, with no loss of accuracy."

"But it shouldn't," Farrell complained.

Sonya laughed. "This archaic setup appeals to John, Jimmy. I always used to think that the Rim Worlds were his spiritual home—but I was wrong. He's much happier on these New Australian planets, which have all the shortcomings of the Rim but nary a one of the few, the very few good points."

"What good points are you talking about?" demanded Grimes. "Overreliance on machinery is one of them, I suppose. That's what I liked about Aquarius, and what I like about these worlds—the tacit determination that the machine shall be geared to man, not the other way round . . ."

"But," said Sonya. "The contrast. Every time that we step ashore it hits us in the eye. Jimmy's ship, with everything spick and span, every officer and every rating going about his duties at the very peak of efficiency—and this city (if you can call it that) with everybody shambling around at least half-asleep, where things get done after a fashion, if they get done at all. It must be obvious even to an old-fashioned . . . seaman like yourself."

"Aboard a ship," admitted Grimes, "any sort of ship, one has to have some efficiency. But not too much."

The three of them were sitting at a table on the wide veranda of the Digger's Arms, one of the principal hotels in the city of Paddington, the capital (such as it was) of Wyong. There were glasses before them, and a bottle, its outer surface clouded with condensation. Outside the high sun blazed down on the dusty street, but it was pleasant enough where they were, the rustling of the breeze in the leaves of the vines trailing around the veranda posts giving an illusion of coolness, the elaborate iron lace of pillars and railing contributing its own archaic charm.

A man came in from outside, removing his broad-brimmed hat as soon as he was in the shade. His heavy boots were noisy on the polished wooden floor. Farrell and Sonya looked with some disapproval at his sun-faded khaki shirt, the khaki shorts that could have been cleaner and better pressed.

"Mrs. Grimes," he said. "How yer goin'?"

"Fine, thank you, Captain," she replied coldly.

"How's tricks, Commodore?"

"Could be worse," admitted Grimes.

"An' how's the world treatin' you, Commander?"

"I can't complain," answered Farrell, making it sound like a polite lie.

The newcomer—it was Captain Dalby, the Port Master—pulled up a chair to the table and sat down with an audible *thump*. A shirt-sleeved waiter appeared. "Beer, Clarry," ordered Dalby. "A schooner of old. An' bring another coupla bottles for me friends." Then, while the drinks were coming, he said, "Your Number One said I might find you here, Commander."

"If it's anything important you want me for," Farrell told him, "you could have telephoned."

"Yair. Suppose I could. But yer ship'll not be ready ter lift off fer another coupla days, an' I thought the walk'd do me good . . ." He raised the large glass that the waiter had brought to his lips. "Here's lookin' at yer."

Farrell was already on his feet. "If it's anything serious, Captain Dalby, I'd better get back at once."

"Hold yer horses, Commander. There's nothin' you can do till you get there."

"Get *where?*"

"Esquel, o' course."

"What's wrong on Esquel?"

"Don't rightly know." He drank some more beer, taking his time over it. "But a signal just came in from the skipper of the *Epileptic Virgin* that the Esquel beacon's on the blink."

"*Epsilon Virginis,*" corrected Farrell automatically. Then—"But this could be serious . . ."

"Nothin' ter work up a lather over, Commander. It's an unwatched beacon, so there's no need to worry about the safety of human personnel. An' it's not an important one. Any nog who can't find his way through this sector o' space without it ain't fit ter navigate a plastic duck across a bathtub!"

"Even so . . ." began Farrell.

"Sit down and finish your beer," said Grimes.

"Yer a man after me own heart, Commodore," Dalby told him.

"Did the Master of *Epsilon Virginis* have any ideas as to what might have happened?" asked Sonya.

"If he had, Mrs. Grimes, he didn't say so. Mechanical breakdown, earthquake, lightnin'—you name it." He grinned happily at Farrell. "But it suits me down ter the ground that you're here, Commander. If you weren't, I'd have ter take me own maintenance crew to Esquel an' fix the bloody thing meself. I don't like the place, nor its people . . ." He noticed that Sonya was beginning to look at him in a rather hostile manner. "Mind yer, I've nothin' against wogs, as long as they keep ter their own world an' I keep ter mine."

"So you've been on Esquel?" asked Sonya in a friendly enough voice.

"Too right. More'n once. When the beacon was first installed, an' three times fer maintenance. It's too bleedin' hot, for a start. It just ain't a white man's planet. An' the people . . . Little, gibberin' purple monkeys—chatter, chatter, chatter, jabber, jabber, jabber. Fair gets on yer nerves. I s'pose their boss cockies ain't all that bad when yer get ter know 'em—but they know what side their bread's buttered on an' try ter keep in our good books. If they hate our guts they don't show it. But the others—the lower classes I s'pose you'd call 'em—do hate our guts, an' they do show it."

"It often is the way, Captain," said Sonya. "Very often two absolutely dissimilar races are on far friendlier terms than two similar ones. I've never been to Esquel, but I've seen photographs of the natives and they're very like Terran apes or monkeys; and the apes and monkeys are our not so distant cousins. You and your men probably thought of the Esquelians as caricatures in very bad taste of human beings, and they thought of you in the same way."

"Yair. Could be. But I'm glad it's not me that has ter fix the beacon."

"Somebody has to," said Farrell virtuously.

Star Pioneer was on her way once more, driving along the trajectory between Wyong and Esquel, her inertial drive maintaining a normal one standard gravity acceleration, her Mannschenn Drive set for cruising temporal precession rate. Farrell had discussed matters with Grimes and Sonya and with his own senior officers. All agreed that there was no need for urgency; the Esquel beacon was not an essential navigational aid in this sector of space; had it been so it would have been manned.

There was, of course, no communication with the world toward which the ship was bound. The Carlotti beacons are, of course, used for faster-than-light radio communication between distant ships and planets, but the one on Esquel was a direction finding device only. A team of skilled technicians could have made short work of a conversion job, rendering the beacon capable of the transmission and reception of FTL radio signals—but there were no human technicians on Esquel. Yet. Imperialism has long been a dirty word; but the idea persists even though it is never vocalized. The Carlotti beacon on Esquel was the thin end of the wedge, the foot inside the door. Sooner or later the Esquelian rulers would come to rely upon that income derived from the rental of the beacon site, the imports (mainly luxuries) that they could buy with it; and then, not blatantly but most definitely, yet another planet would be absorbed into the Federation's economic empire.

There was conventional radio on Esquel, but *Star Pioneer* would not be able to pick up any messages while her time and space warping interstellar drive was in operation, and not until she was within spitting distance of the planet. There were almost certainly at least a few Esquelian telepaths—but the Survey Service ship was without a psionic radio officer. One should have been carried; one had been carried, in fact, but she had engineered her discharge on Glebe, where she had become wildly enamored of a wealthy grazier. Farrell had let her go; now he was rather wishing that he had not done so.

The *Pioneer* fell down the dark dimensions between the stars, and life aboard her was normal enough. There was no hurry. Unmanned beacons had broken down before, would do so again. Meanwhile there was the pleasant routine of a ship of war in deep space, the regular meals, the card-playing, the chess and what few games of a more physically demanding nature were possible in the rather cramped conditions. Sonya was enjoying it, Grimes was not. He had been too long away from the spit and polish of the Survey Service. And Farrell—unwisely for one in his position—was starting to take sides. Sonya, he not very subtly insinuated, was his breed of cat. Grimes might have been once, but he was no longer. Not only had he resigned from the finest body of astronauts in the galaxy, known or unknown, but he had slammed the door behind him. And as for this craze of his for—of all things!—seamanship . . . Grimes was pained, but not surprised, when Sonya told him, one night, that aboard this ship he was known as the Ancient Mariner.

Ahead, the Esquel sun burgeoned; and then came the day, the hour and the minute when the Mannschenn Drive was shut down and the ship reemerged into the normal continuum. She was still some weeks from Esquel itself, but she was in no hurry—until the first messages started coming in.

Grimes sat with Sonya and Farrell in the control room. He listened to the squeaky voice issuing from the transceiver. "Calling Earth ship . . . Calling any Earth ship . . . Help . . . Help . . . Help . . ."

It went on and on without break, although it was obvious that a succession of operators was working a more or less regular system of reliefs at the microphone. Farrel acknowledged. It would be minutes before the radio waves carrying his voice reached the Esquelian receiver, more minutes for a reply to come back. He said, as they were waiting for this, that he hoped that whoever was making the distress call had more than one transceiver in operation.

Abruptly the gibbering plea for unspecified aid ceased. A new voice came on the speaker. "I talk for Cabarar, High King of Esquel. There has been . . . revolution. We are . . . besieged on Drarg Island. Cannot hold out . . . much longer. Help. You must . . . help."

There was a long silence, broken by Farrell. "Number One," he ordered, "maximum thrust."

"Maximum thrust, sir." Then, into the intercom, "All hands to acceleration couches! Maximum thrust!"

The backs of the control room chairs fell to the horizontal, the leg rests lifted. The irregular beat of the inertial drive quickened, maddening in its noisy nonrhythm. Acceleration stamped frail human bodies deep into the resilient padding of the couches.

I'm getting too old for this sort of thing, thought Grimes. But he retained his keen interest in all that was going on about him. He heard Farrell say, every word an effort, "Pilot . . . Give me . . . data . . . on . . . Drarg . . ."

"Data . . . on . . . Drarg . . . sir . . ." replied the Navigator.

From the corner of his eye Grimes could see the young officer stretched supine on his couch, saw the fingers of his right hand crawling among the buttons in the arm rest like crippled white worms. A screen came into being overhead, a Mercator map of Esquel, with the greens and yellows and browns of sprawling continents, the oceanic blue. The map expanded; it was as though a television camera was falling rapidly to a position roughly in the middle of one of the seas. There was a speck there in the blueness. It expanded, but not to any extent. It was obvious that Drarg was only a very small island.

The map was succeeded by pictorial representations of the beacon station. There were high, rugged cliffs, with the sea foaming angrily through the jagged rocks at the waterline. There was a short, spidery jetty. And, over all, was the slowly rotating antenna of the Carlotti beacon, an ellipsoid Mobius strip that seemed ever on the point of vanishment as it turned about its long axis, stark yet insubstantial against the stormy sky.

Farrell, speaking a little more easily now, said, "There's room on that plateau to land a boat—but to put the ship down is out of the question . . ."

Nobody suggested a landing at the spaceport. It must be in rebel hands; and those same rebels, in all probability, possessed at least a share of Earth-manufactured weapons and would be willing to use them against the Earthmen whose lackeys their rulers had been. *Star Pioneer* was armed, of course—but too active participation in other people's wars is frowned upon.

"You could land on the water," said Grimes. "To leeward of the island."

"I'm not a master mariner, Commodore," Farrell told him rather nastily. "But this is *my* ship, and I'm not hazarding her. We'll orbit about Esquel and send down a boat."

I hope that one boat will be enough, thought Grimes, not without sympathy. *The mess isn't of your making, Jimmy boy, but you'll have to answer the "please explains." And as human beings we have some responsibility for the nongs and drongoes we've been propping up with Terran bayonets—or Terran credits, which have been used to purchase Terran bayonets or their present day equivalent.*

"Whatever his shortcomings," commented Sonya, "High King Cabrarar used his brains. He knew that if the beacon ceased functioning there'd be an investigation . . ."

"And better us to make it," said Farrell, "than Dalby and his bunch of no hopers."

"Why?" asked Grimes coldly.

"We're disciplined, armed . . ."

"And if you'll take my advice, Commander, you'll not be in a hurry to use your arms. The top brass is apt to take a dim view of active intervention in outsiders' private squabbles."

"But Cabrarar . . ."

". . . *was* the Federation's blue-eyed boy. His kingdom now is limited to one, tiny island. I've no doubt that your lords and masters are already considering dickering with whatever new scum comes to the top."

"Sir . . ." One of the officers was trying to break into the conversation.

"Yes, Mr. Penrose?"

"A signal, sir, from Officer Commanding Lindisfarne Base . . ."

The young man crawled slowly and painfully to where his captain was stretched out on the acceleration couch, with a visible effort stretched out the hand holding the flimsy. Farrell took it, managed to maneuver it to where his eyes could focus on it.

After a long pause he read aloud, "Evacuate King Cabrarar and entourage. Otherwise do nothing, repeat nothing, to antagonize new regime on Esquel."

"As I've been saying," commented Grimes. "But at least they're exhibiting some faint flickers of conscience."

Shortly thereafter Farrell ordered a half hour's reduction of acceleration to one G, a break necessary to allow personnel to do whatever they had to do essential to their comfort. Grimes and Sonya—she with some reluctance—left the control room and retired to their own quarters.

Star Pioneer was in orbit about Esquel. Free fall, after the bone-crushing emergency acceleration, was a luxury—but it was not one that Commander Farrell and those making up the landing party were allowed to enjoy for long. Farrell had decided to send down only one boat—the pinnace. There was insufficient level ground on the island for more than one craft to make a safe landing. He had learned from King Cabrarar that the rebels had control of the air, and that their aircraft were equipped with air-to-air missiles. An air-spacecraft hovering, awaiting its turn to land, would be a tempting target—and effective self-defense on its part could easily be the beginnings of a nasty incident.

The deposed monarch and his party comprised three hundred beings, in terms of mass equivalent to two hundred Earthmen. In addition to its crew the pinnace could lift fifty men; so four rescue trips would be necessary. While the evacuation was in process a small party from the ship would remain on the island, deciding what in the way of stores, equipment and documents would be destroyed, what lifted off. Sonya had volunteered to be one of the party, pointing out that she was the only representative of the Intelligence Branch of the Survey Service in the ship, Reserve commission notwithstanding. Too, Esquelian was one of the many languages at her command; some years ago it had been intended that she visit Esquel, at the time of the installation of the Carlotti beacon, but these orders had been canceled when she was sent elsewhere on a more urgent mission. So, even though she had never set foot on the planet, she could make herself understood and—much more important—understand what was being said in her hearing.

Grimes insisted on accompanying his wife. He was an outsider, with no standing—but, as he pointed out to Farrell, this could prove advantageous. He would have more freedom of action than *Star Pioneer*'s people, not being subject to the orders of the distant Flag Officer at Lindisfarne Base. Farrell was inclined to agree with him on this point, then said, "But it still doesn't let *me* off the hook, Commodore. Suppose you shoot somebody who, in the opinion of my lords and masters, shouldn't have been shot . . . And suppose I say, 'But, sir, it was Commodore Grimes, of the Rim Worlds Naval Reserve, who did the shooting . . .' What do *they* say?"

"Why the bloody hell did you let him?" replied Grimes, laughing. "But I promise to restrain my trigger finger, James."

"He's made up his mind to come," Sonya said. "But not to worry. After all his playing at being a merchant sea captain he'll not know one end of a gun from the other . . ."

So, with the landing party aboard, the pinnace broke out of its bay and detached itself from the mother ship. The young lieutenant at the controls was a superb boat handler, driving the craft down to the first tenuous wisps of atmosphere, then decelerating before friction could overheat the skin. Drarg Island was in the sunlit hemisphere, the sky over which was unusually clear—so clear that there was no likelihood of mistaking the smoke from at least two burning cities for natural cloud. Navigation presented no problems. All that the officer had to do was to home on a continuous signal from the transmitter on the island. Grimes would have liked to have played with the bubble sextant and the ephemerides—produced by *Star Pioneer*'s navigator just in case they would be needed—that were part of the boat's equipment, but when he suggested so doing Sonya gave him such a scornful look that he desisted.

There was the island: a slowly expanding speck in the white-flecked sea. And there, a long way to the westward, were two airships, ungainly dirigible balloons. They must have seen the pinnace on her way down, but they made no attempt to intercept; a blimp is not an ideal aircraft in which to practice the *kamikaze* technique. But, remarked Farrell, they would be reporting this Terran intervention to their base. The radio operator found their working frequency and Sonya was able to translate the high-pitched squeakings and gibberings.

"As near as I can render it," she reported, "they're saying, 'The bastard king's bastard friends have come . . .' In the original it's much more picturesque." The operator turned up the gain to get the reply. " 'Keep the bastards under observation,' " said Sonya. Then, " 'Use Code 17A . . .' "

"They can use any code they please," commented Farrell. "With what weaponry there is on this world, the island's impregnable. It'll be more impregnable still after we've landed a few of our toys."

"Never underrate primitive peoples," Grimes told him. He dredged up a maritime historical snippet from his capacious memory. "In one of the wars on Earth—the Sino-Japanese War in the first half of the twentieth century—a modern Japanese destroyer was sent to the bottom by the fire of a concealed battery of primitive muzzle-loading cannon, loaded with old nails, broken bottles and horseshoes for luck . . ."

"Fascinating, Commodore, fascinating," said Farrell. "If you see any muzzle-loaders pointed our way, let me know, will you?"

Sonya laughed unkindly.

Grimes, who had brought two pipes with him, took out and filled and lit the one most badly in need of a clean.

They dropped down almost vertically on to the island, the lieutenant in charge of the pinnace making due allowance for drift. As they got lower they could see that the elliptical Mobius strip that was the antenna of the Carlotti beacon was still, was not rotating about its long axis. Draped around it were rags of fabric streaming to leeward in the stiff breeze. It looked, at first, as though somebody had improvised a wind sock for the benefit of the landing party—and then it was obvious that the fluttering tatters were the remains of a gasbag. A little to one side of the machinery house was a crumpled tangle of wickerwork and more fabric, the wreckage of the gondola of the crashed airship. Some, at least, of the refugees on the island must have come by air.

Landing would have been easy if the Esquelians had bothered to clear away the wreckage. The lieutenant suggested setting the pinnace down on top of it, but Farrell stopped him. Perhaps he was remembering Grimes's story about that thin-skinned Japanese destroyer. He said, "There's metal there, Mr. Smith—the engine, and weapons, perhaps, and other odds and ends. We don't want to go punching holes in ourselves . . ."

So the pinnace hovered for a while, vibrating to the noisy, irregular throb of her inertial drive, while the spidery, purple-furred humanoids on the ground capered and gesticulated. Finally, after Sonya had screamed orders at them through the ship's loudhailer, a party of them dragged the wreckage to the edge of the cliff, succeeded in pushing it over. It plunged untidily down to the rocks far below. There was a brilliant orange flash, a billowing of dirty white brown smoke, a shock wave that rocked the pinnace dangerously. There must have been ammunition of some kind in that heap of debris.

Farrell said nothing. But if looks could have killed, the King, standing aloof from his loyal subjects, distinguishable by the elaborate basketwork of gold and jewels on his little, round head, would have died. Somebody muttered, "Slovenly bastards . . ." Grimes wondered if the rebels were any more efficient than the ruling class they had deposed, decided that they almost certainly must be. It was such a familiar historical pattern.

The pinnace grounded. The noise of the inertial drive faded to an irritable mumble, then ceased. Farrell unbuckled his seat belt, then put on his cap, then got up. Sonya—who was also wearing a uniform for the occasion—did likewise. Somehow, the pair of them conveyed the impression that Grimes had not been invited to the party, but he followed them to the airlock, trying to look like a duly accredited observer from the Rim Worlds Confederacy. The airlock doors, inner and outer, opened. The Commodore sniffed appreciatively the breeze that gusted in, the harsh tang of salt water that is the same on all oceanic worlds. His second sniff was not such a deep one; the air of the island was tainted with the effluvium of too many people cooped up in far too small a space.

The ramp extended. Farrell walked slowly down it, followed by Sonya, followed by Grimes, followed by two ratings with machine pistols at the ready. The King stood a few yards away, watching them, surrounded by his own officers, monkeylike beings on the purple fur of whose bodies gleamed the golden ornaments that were badges of rank.

Stiffly (reluctantly?) Farrell saluted.

Limply the King half raised a six-fingered hand in acknowledgment. The rings on his long fingers sparkled in the afternoon sunlight. He turned to one of the staff, gibbering.

The being faced Farrell, baring yellow teeth as he spoke. "His Majesty say, why you no come earlier?"

"We came as soon as we were able," said Farrell.

There was more gibbering, unintelligible to all save Sonya. Then—"His Majesty say, where *big* ship? When you start bomb cities, kill rebels?"

Farrell turned to face his own people. He said, "Take over, please, Commander Verrill. You know the language. You might be able to explain things more diplomatically than me. You know the orders."

"I know the orders, Commander Farrell," said Sonya. She stepped forward to face the King, speaking fluently and rapidly. Even when delivered by her voice, thought Grimes, this Esquelian language was still ugly, but she took the curse off it.

The King replied to her directly. He was literally hopping from one splayed foot to the other with rage. Spittle sprayed from between his jagged, yellow teeth. The elaborate crown on his head was grotesquely awry. He raised a long, thin arm as though to strike the woman.

Grimes pulled from his pocket the deadly little Minetti automatic that was his favorite firearm. Viciously, Farrell knocked his hand down, whispering, "Hold it, Commodore! Don't forget that we represent the Federation . . ."

"*You* might," snarled Grimes.

But the King had seen the show of weapons; Grimes learned later that the two spacemen had also made threatening gestures with their machine pistols. He let his arm fall to his side. His clawed fingers slowly straightened. At last he spoke again—and the unpleasant gibbering was less high-pitched, less hysterical.

Sonya translated. "His Majesty is . . . disappointed. He feels that he has been . . . betrayed."

"Tell his Majesty," said Farrell, "that my own rulers forbid me to take part in this civil war. But His Majesty and those loyal to him will be transported to a suitable world, where they will want for nothing."

Grimes tried to read the expression on the King's face. Resignation? Misery? It could have been either, or both. Then his attention was attracted by the glint of metal evident in the crowd behind the deposed monarch. He saw that most of the Esquelians were armed, some with vicious-looking swords, others with projectile weapons, archaic in design, but probably effective enough. He doubted if any of the natives would be able to fly the pinnace—but a human pilot might do what he was told with a knife at his throat.

Farrell spoke again. "Tell His Majesty, Commander Verrill, that if he has any ideas about seizing my pinnace he'd better forget 'em. Tell him that those odd-looking antennae poking out from their turrets are laser cannon, and that at the first sign of trouble this plateau will be one big, beautiful barbecue. Tell him to look at that bird, there . . ." he pointed . . . "over to the eastward." He raised his wrist to his mouth, snapped an order into the microphone.

After Sonya finished her translation, everybody looked at the bird—if bird it was. It was a flying creature of some kind, big, with a wide wing span. It was a carrion eater, perhaps, hovering to leeward of the island in the hope of a meal. It died suddenly in a flare of flame, a gout of greasy smoke. A sparse sprinkling of smoldering fragments drifted down to the surface of the sea.

There was an outburst of squealing and gibbering. The Esquelians, with quite advanced armaments of their own at the time of Man's first landing on their world, had never, until now, been treated to a demonstration of the more sophisticated Terran weaponry. But they were people who knew that it is not the *bang* of a firearm that kills.

"His Majesty," said Sonya, "demands that he and his peo-

ple be taken off this island, as soon as possible, if not before."
She grinned. "That last is a rather rough translation, but it
conveys the essential meaning."

"I am happy to obey," replied Farrell. "But he and his
people will have to leave all weapons behind."

There was more argument, and another demonstration of
the pinnace's firepower, and then the evacuation was gotten
under way.

It had been intended, when the beacon was established
on Drarg Island, that the island itself should serve as a base
for some future survey party. The rock was honeycombed
with chambers and tunnels, providing accommodation, should
it be required, for several hundred humans. At the lowest
level of all was the power station, fully automated, generat-
ing electricity for lights and fans as well as for the Carlotti
beacon. The refugees had been able to live there in reasonable comfort—and in considerable squalor. Grimes decided
that, as soon as things quietened down, he would get Sonya to inquire as to whether or not the flush toilet had
been invented on Esquel. In spite of the excellent ventilation system, the stench was appalling.

But it was necessary for Sonya, at least, to go down into
those noisome passages. In spite of the King's protests, Farrell had ordered that no property be lifted from the island;
his orders were to save life, and life only. There were tons,
literally, of gold and precious stones. There were tons of documents. These latter were, of course, of interest, and Sonya
was the only member of *Star Pioneer's* party able to read
them. And so, accompanied by Grimes and two junior officers, she went into the room in which the papers had been
stacked, skimmed through them, committing those that she
thought might be important to microfilm. Now and again,
for the benefit of her helpers, she translated. "This," she
told them, "seems to be the wages sheet, for the palace staff
. . . No less than fourteen cooks, and then fifty odd scullions
and such . . . And a food taster . . . And a wine taster
. . . And, last of all, and the most highly paid of the lot,
a torturer. He got twice what the executioner did . . ." She
passed the sheet to the Ensign who was acting as photog-
rapher, picked up the next one. "H'm. Interesting. This is
the pay list for the Royal Guard. The Kardonar—roughly
equivalent to Colonel—got less than the Third Cook . . ."

"This could be just yet another Colonels' Revolt," commented Grimes. He looked at his watch, which had been adjusted to local time. "Midnight. Time we had a break. This stink is getting me down."

"You can say that again, sir," agreed one of the Ensigns.

"All right," said Sonya at last. "I think we've skimmed the cream down here."

"*Cream?*" asked Grimes sardonically.

They made their way up the winding ramps, through the tunnels with their walls of fused rock, came at last to the surface. The plateau was brightly illumined by the floodlights that Farrell's men had set up. The pinnace was away on a shuttle trip, and only a handful of natives remained, huddling together for warmth in the lee of the beacon machinery house. The King, Grimes noted sardonically, was not among them; obviously he was not one of those captains who are last to leave the sinking ship. He was quite content to let Farrell be his stand in.

The Commander walked slowly to Grimes and Sonya. "How's it going, Commander Verrill?" he asked.

"Well enough," she replied. "We've enough evidence to show that this was a thoroughly corrupt regime."

"Physically, as well as in all the other ways," added Grimes. "This fresh air tastes good! How are you off for deodorants aboard *Star Pioneer*, Commander Farrell?"

"Not as well as I'd like to be, Commodore. But I'll put the bulk of the passengers in deep freeze, so it shouldn't be too bad." He looked up at the sky. "It'll be a while before the pinnace is back. Perhaps, sir, you might like a look at some of the surface craft that these people came out to the island in. There's a half dozen of them at the jetty; rather odd-looking contraptions . . ."

"I'd like to," said Grimes.

Farrell led the way to the edge of the plateau, to a stairway, railed at the seaward edge, running down the cliff face to a sheltered inlet in which was a short pier. Moored untidily alongside this were six sizable boats, and there was enough light from the floods at the cliff top for Grimes to make out details before he and the others commenced their descent.

"Yes, I'd like a closer look," he said. "Steam, I'd say, with those funnels. Paddle steamers. Stern-wheelers. Efficient in smooth water, but not in a seaway . . ."

He led the way down the stairs, his feet clattering on the iron treads. He said, "I'd like a trip in one of those, just to see how they handle . . ."

"Out of the question, Commodore," laughed Farrell.

"I know," said Grimes; as Sonya sneered, "You and your bloody seamanship!"

They stepped from the stairway on to the concrete apron, walked across it to the foot of the jetty. Grimes stopped suddenly, said, "Look!"

"At what?" demanded Sonya.

"At that craft with the red funnel . . . That's smoke, and a wisp of steam . . . She's got steam up . . ."

Farrell's laser pistol was out of its holster, and so was Sonya's. Grimes pulled his own Minetti out of his pocket. Cautiously they advanced along the pier, trying to make as little noise as possible. But the natives who erupted from the tunnel at the base of the cliff were completely noiseless on their broad, bare feet and, without having a chance to use their weapons, to utter more than a strangled shout, the three Terrans went down under a wave of evil-smelling, furry bodies.

Grimes recovered slowly. Something hard had hit him behind the right ear, and he was suffering from a splitting headache. He was, he realized, propped in a sitting posture, his back against a wall of some kind. No, not a wall—a bulkhead. The deck under his buttocks had a gentle rolling motion, and—his head was throbbing in synchronization—there was the steady *chunk, chunk, chunk* of a paddle wheel. Grimes tried to lift his hands to his aching head, discovered that his wrists were bound. So were his ankles.

He heard a familiar voice. "You and your bloody boats!"

He opened his eyes. He turned his head, saw that Sonya was propped up beside him. Her face, in the light of the flickering oil lamp, was pale and drawn. She muttered sardonically, "Welcome aboard, Commodore." Beyond her was Farrell, trussed as were the other two. Nonetheless, he was able to say severely, "This is no time for humor, Commander Verrill."

"But it is, James," she told him sweetly.

"What . . . what happened?" asked Grimes.

"We were jumped, that's what. It seems that a bunch of the loyalists—quote and unquote—suffered a change of mind. They'd sooner take their chances with the rebels than on some strange and terrifying planet . . ."

"Better the devil you know . . ." said Grimes.

"Precisely."

"But where do *we* come in?" asked the Commodore.

"They had to stop us from stopping them from making their getaway," explained Farrell, as though to a mentally retarded child.

"There's more to it than that, James," Sonya told him. "There's a radio telephone of some kind in the compartment forward of this. Battery powered, I suppose. Not that it matters. Our friends have been arranging a rendezvous with a rebel patrol craft. They've made it plain that they're willing to buy their freedom, their lives. And the price is . . ."

"Us," completed Grimes. "What's the current market value of a full Commander in the Survey Service these days, Farrell? I've no doubt that the rebels will wish to show a profit on the deal."

"And how many laser cannon, complete with instruction manuals, is the Confederacy willing to pay for you, Commodore?" asked Commander Farrell.

"Shut up!" snapped Sonya.

The cabin was silent again, save for the creaking of timbers, the faint thudding of the engines, the *chunk, chunk, chunk* of the paddle. And then, audible in spite of the intervening bulkhead, there was the high-pitched gibbering, in bursts, that, in spite of the strange language, carried the sense of *"over," "roger"* and all the rest of the standard radio telephone procedure.

Sonya whispered, "As far as I can gather, hearing only one end of the conversation, the patrol craft has sighted this tub that we're in. We've been told to heave to, to await the boarding party . . ." As she spoke, the engines and the paddle wheel slowed, stopped.

There was comparative silence again. Grimes strained his ears for the noise of an approaching stern-wheeler, but in vain. There was, he realized, a new mechanical sound, but it came from overhead. Then it, too, ceased. He was about to speak when there was a loud *thud* from the deck outside, another, and another . . . There was an outbreak of excited gibbering. Shockingly, there were screams, almost human, and three startlingly loud reports.

Abruptly the cabin door slammed open. Two Esquelians

came in. There was dark, glistening blood on the fur of one of them, but it did not seem to be his own. They grabbed Grimes by the upper arms, dragged him roughly out on deck, jarring his lower spine painfully on the low sill of the door. They left him there, went back in for Sonya, and then Farrell.

Grimes lay where they had dropped him, looking upward. There were lights there, dim, but bright against the black sky, the sparse, faint stars. As his eyes grew accustomed to the darkness he could make out the great, baggy shape of the dirigible balloon, the comparative rigidity of the gondola slung under it. While he was trying to distinguish more details a rope was slipped about his body and he was hoisted aloft, like a sack of potatoes, by a creakingly complaining hand winch.

"And what now, Commodore? What now?" asked Farrell. By his tone of voice he implied, *You've been in far more irregular situations than me . . .*

Grimes chuckled. "To begin with, we thank all the odd gods of the galaxy that real life so very often copies fiction . . ."

Sonya snarled, "What the hell are you nattering about?"

Grimes chuckled again. "How often, in thrillers, have the baddies tied up the goodies and then carelessly left them with something sharp or abrasive to rub their bonds against . . . ?"

"You aren't kidding?" she asked. Then—"And since when have you been a goodie?"

"You'd be surprised . . ." Grimes swore then, briefly and vividly. The sharp edge in the wickerwork of which the airship's car was constructed had nicked his wrist quite painfully. He grunted, "But in fiction it's usually much easier . . ."

He worked on, sawing away with his bound hands, even though his wrists were slippery with blood. He was afraid that one of the airship's crew would come into the cabin to look at the prisoners, but the four Esquelians in the control room at the forward end of the gondola seemed fully occupied with navigation and, presumably, the two who were aft were devoting all their time to the engine of the thing.

Hell! That rope was tough—tougher than the edge against which he was rubbing it, tougher than his skin. Not being able to see what he was doing made it worse. He began to wonder if the first result that he would achieve would be the slitting of an artery. He had never heard of that happening to a fictional hero; but there has to be a first time for everything. Sonya whispered, very real concern in her voice, "John! You're only hurting yourself! Stop it, before you do yourself some real damage!"

"It's dogged as does it!" he replied.

"John! It's not as though they're going to kill us. We're more value to them alive than dead!"

"Could be," he admitted. "But I've heard too many stories about samples from the bodies of kidnap victims being sent to their potential ransomers to speed up negotiations. Our furry friends strike me as being just the kind of businessmen who'd stoop to such a practice!"

"After the way in which they slaughtered the crew of the steamboat," put in Farrell, "I'm inclined to agree with the Commodore."

"The vote is two against one," said Grimes. And then the rope parted.

He brought his hands slowly round in front of him. There was a lamp in the cabin, a dim, incandescent bulb, and by its feeble light he could see that his wrists were in a mess. But the blood was dripping slowly, not spurting. He was in no immediate danger of bleeding to death. And he could work his fingers, although it seemed a long time before repeated flexings and wrigglings rendered them capable of use.

He started on the rope about his ankles then. He muttered something about Chinese bowlines, Portuguese pig knots and unseamanlike bastards in general. He complained, "I can't find an end to work on." Then, with an attempt at humor, "Somebody must have cut it off!"

"Talking of cutting . . ." Sonya's voice had a sharp edge to it. "Talking of cutting, if you can get your paws on to the heel of one of my shoes . . ."

Yes, of course, thought Grimes. Sonya was in uniform, and the uniform of a Survey Service officer contained quite a few concealed weapons. Sophisticated captors would soon have found these, but the Esquelians, to whom clothing was strange, had yet to learn the strange uses to which it could be put. Without overmuch contortion Grimes was able to get his hand around the heel of his wife's left shoe. He twisted, pulled—and was armed with a short but useful knife. To slash through his remaining bonds was a matter of seconds.

The Esquelian came through into the cabin from forward just as Grimes was getting shakily to his feet. He was wearing a belt, and from this belt depended a holster. He was quick neither on the draw nor the uptake, but the Commodore was half crippled by impeded circulation to his ankles and feet. The native got his pistol—a clumsy revolver—out before Grimes was on him. He fired two shots, each of them too close for comfort, one of them almost parting the Commodore's close-cropped hair.

Grimes's intention—he told himself afterward—had been to disable only, to disarm. It was unfortunate, perhaps, that the airship at that moment dived steeply. The Earthman plunged forward in a staggering run, the knife held before him, stabbing deep into the furry chest. The Esquelian screamed shrilly as a disgustingly warm fluid gushed from his body over Grimes's hands, tumbled to the deck. As he fell, Grimes snatched the pistol. He was more at home with firearms than with bladed weapons.

Surprisingly it fitted his hand as though made for him— but there is parallel evolution of artifacts as well as of life forms. Holding it, almost stumbling over the body of the dead native, Grimes continued his forward progress, coming into the control cabin. It was light in there, wide windows admitting the morning twilight. Gibbering, the three Esquelians deserted their controls. One of them had a pistol, the other two snatched knives from a handy rack. Grimes fired, coldly and deliberately. The one with the revolver was his first target, then the nearer of the knife wielders, then his mate. At this range, even with an unfamiliar weapon with a stiff action, a man who in his younger days had been a small arms specialist could hardly miss. Grimes did not, even though he had to shoot one of the airmen twice, even though the last convulsive stab of a broad-bladed knife missed his foot by a millimeter.

He did not know whether or not the gun that he had been using was empty; he did not bother to check. Stooping, he quickly snatched up the one dropped by the dead pilot. It had never been fired. He turned, ran back into the cabin. He was just in time. One of the engineers was just about to bring a heavy spanner crashing down on Sonya's head but was thrown back by the heavy slug that smashed his own skull.

Saying nothing, Grimes carried on aft. The other engineer was dead already, killed by the first wild shot of the encounter. Grimes thought at first that the loud dripping noise was being made by his blood. But it was not. It came from the fuel tank, which had been pierced by a stray bullet. Before Grimes could do anything about it, the steam turbine ground to a halt.

The sun was up. It was a fine morning, calm insofar as those in the disabled airship were concerned, although the whitecaps on the sea were evidence of a strong breeze. To port was the coastline: rugged cliffs, orange beaches, blue green vegetation inland, a sizable city far to the south'ard. It was receding quite rapidly as the aircraft, broadside on to the offshore wind, scudded to leeward.

The bodies of the airmen had been dragged into the cabin in which the Terrans had been imprisoned. Farrell and Sonya had wanted to throw them overside, but Grimes had talked them out of it. From his historical researches he knew something—not much, but something—about the handling of lighter-than-air flying machines. Until he had familiarized himself with the controls of this brute, he had no intention of dumping ballast.

He had succeeded in fixing the ship's position. In the control room there was a binnacle, and there were sight vanes on the compass. There were charts, and presumably the one that had been in use at the time of the escape was the one that covered this section of coast. The compass was strange; it was divided into 400 degrees, not 360. The latitude and longitude divisions on the chart were strange, too, but it wasn't hard to work out that the Esquelians worked on 100 minutes to a degree, 100 degrees to a right angle. There was a certain lack of logic involved—human beings, with their five-fingered hands, have a passion for reckoning things in twelves. The Esquelians, six-fingered, seemed to prefer reckoning by tens. Even so, compass, sight vanes and charts were a fine example of the parallel evolution of artifacts.

There was the compass rose, showing the variation (Grimes assumed) between True North and Magnetic North. There was that city to the south. There were two prominent mountain peaks, the mountains being shown by what were obviously contour lines. Grimes laid off his cross bearings, using a roller, ruler and a crayon. The cocked hat was a very small one. After fifteen minutes he did it again. The line between the two fixes coincided with the estimated wind direction. And where would that take them?

Transferring the position to a small scale chart presented no problems. Neither did extending the course line. The only trouble was that it missed the fly speck that represented Drarg Island by at least twenty miles, regarding one minute on the latitude scale as being a mile. Sonya, recruited in her linguistic capacity, confirmed that the (to Grimes) meaningless squiggles alongside the dot on the chart did translate to "Drarg."

The trouble was that the unlucky shot that had immobilized the airship's engines had also immobilized her generator. There were batteries—but they were flat. (During a revolution quite important matters tend to be neglected.) The radio telephone was, in consequence, quite useless. Had there been power it would have been possible to raise the party on the island, to get them to send the pinnace to pick them up when the aircraft was ditched, or, even, to tow them in.

"At least we're drifting away from the land," said Farrell, looking on the bright side. "I don't think that we should be too popular if we came down ashore." He added, rather petulantly, "Apart from anything else, my orders were that there was to be no intervention . . ." He implied that all the killing had been quite unnecessary.

"Self-defense," Grimes told him. "Not intervention. But if you ever make it back to Lindisfarne Base, James, you can tell the Admiral that it was the wicked Rim Worlders who played hell with a big stick."

"We're all in this, Commodore," said Farrell stiffly. "And this expedition is under *my* command, after all."

"This is no time for inessentials," snapped Sonya. She straightened up from the chart, which she had been studying. "As I see it, they'll sight us from the island, and assume that we're just one of the rebel patrol craft. They might try to intercept us, trying to find out what's happened to us. On the other hand . . ."

"On the other hand," contributed Farrell, "my bright Exec

99

does everything by the book. He'll insist on getting direct orders from Lindisfarne before he does *anything*."

"How does this thing work?" asked Sonya. "Can you *do* anything, John? The way that you were talking earlier you conveyed the impression that you knew something about airships."

Grimes prowled through the control compartment like a big cat in a small cupboard. He complained, "If I had power, I could get someplace. This wheel here, abaft the binnacle, is obviously for steering. This other wheel, with what looks like a crude altimeter above it, will be for the altitude coxswain. The first actuates a vertical steering surface, the rudder. The second actuates the horizontal control surfaces, for aerodynamic lift . . ."

"I thought that in an airship you dumped ballast or valved gas if you wanted to go up or down, "said Sonya.

"You can do that, too." Grimes indicated toggled cords that ran down into the control room from above. "These, I *think*, open valves if you pull them. So we can come down." He added grimly, "And we've plenty of ballast to throw out if we want to get upstairs in a hurry."

"Then what's all the bellyaching about?" asked Farrell. "We can control our altitude by either of two ways, and we can steer. If the rudder's not working we can soon fix it."

Grimes looked at him coldly. "Commander Farrell," he said at last, "there is one helluva difference between a free balloon and a dirigible balloon. This brute, with no propulsive power, is a free balloon." He paused while he sought for and found an analogy. "She's like a surface ship, broken down, drifting wherever wind and current take her. The surface ship is part of the current if she has neither sails nor engines. A balloon is part of the wind. We can wiggle our rudder as much as we like and it will have no effect whatsoever . . ." Once again he tried to find a seamanlike analogy —and found something more important. He whispered, "Riverhead . . ."

"*Riverhead?*" echoed Farrell. "What's that, Commodore?"

"Shut up, James," murmured Sonya. "Let the man think."

Grimes was thinking, and remembering. During his spell of command of *Sonya Winneck*, on Aquarius, he had been faced with an occasional knotty problem. One such had been the delivery of a consignment of earth-moving machinery to Riverhead, a new port miles inland—equipment which was to be used for the excavation of a swinging basin off the wharfage. The channel was deep enough—but at its upper end it was not as wide as *Sonya Winneck* was long. However, everything had been arranged nicely. Grimes was to come alongside, discharge his cargo and then, with the aid of a tug, proceed stern first down river until he had room to swing in Carradine's Reach. Unfortunately the tug had suffered a major breakdown so that *Sonya Winneck,* if she waited for the repairs to be completed, would be at least ten days, idle, alongside at the new wharf.

Grimes had decided not to wait and had successfully dredged down river on the ebb.

He said slowly, "Yes, I think we could dredge . . ."

"*Dredge?*" asked Farrell.

Grimes decided that he would explain. People obey orders much more cheerfully when they know that what they are being told to do makes sense. He said, "Yes, I've done it before, but in a surface ship. I had to proceed five miles down a narrow channel, stern first . . ."

"But you had engines?"

"Yes, I had engines, but I didn't use them. I couldn't use them. Very few surface ships, only specialized vessels, will steer when going astern. The rudder, you see, must be in the screw race. You must have that motion of water past and around the rudder from forward to aft . . .

"The dredging technique is simple enough. You put an anchor on the bottom, not enough chain out so that it holds, but just enough so that it acts as a drag, keeping your head up into the current. You're still drifting *with* the current, of course, but not as fast. So the water is sliding past your rudder in the right direction, from forward, so you can steer after a fashion."

"It works?"

"Yes," said Sonya. "It works all right. But with all the ear bashing I got before and after I was inclined to think that John was the only man who'd ever made it work."

"You can do it here?" asked Farrell.

"I think so. It's worth trying."

The hand winch was aft, in the engine compartment. To dismount it would have taken too much time, so Grimes had the rope fall run off it, brought forward and coiled down in the control room. To its end he made fast four large canvas buckets; what they had been used for he did not know, nor ever did know, but they formed an ideal drogue. Farrell, using the spanner that had been the dead engineer's weapon, smashed outward the forward window. It was glass, and not heavy enough to offer much resistance. Grimes told him to make sure that there were no jagged pieces left on the sill to cut the dragline. Then, carefully, he lowered his cluster of buckets down toward the water. The line was not long enough to reach.

Carefully Grimes belayed it to the base of the binnacle, which fitting seemed to be securely mounted. He went back forward, looked out and down. He called back, over his shoulder, "We have to valve gas . . ."

"Which control?" asked Sonya.

"Oh, the middle one, I suppose . . ."

That made sense, he thought. One of the others might have an effect on the airship's trim, or give it a heavy list to port or starboard. *And so*, he told himself, *might this one.*

He was aware of a hissing noise coming from overhead. The airship was dropping rapidly, too rapidly. "That will do!" he ordered sharply.

"The bloody thing's stuck!" he heard Sonya call. Then, "I've got it clear!"

The airship was still falling, and the drogue made its first contact with the waves—close now, too close below—skipping over them. The line tightened with a jerk and the flimsy structure of the gondola creaked in protest. The ship came round head to wind, and an icy gale swept through the broken window. The ship bounced upward and there was a brief period of relative calm, sagged, and once again was subjected to the atmospheric turbulence.

"Ballast!" gasped Grimes, clinging desperately to the sill. It seemed a long time before anything happened, and then the ship soared, lifting the drogue well clear of the water.

"Got rid . . . of one . . . of our late friends . . ." gasped Farrell.

"Justifiable, in the circumstances," conceded Grimes grudgingly. "But before we go any further we have to rig a windscreen . . . I saw some canvas, or what looks like canvas, aft . . ."

"How will you keep a lookout?" asked Farrell.

"The lookout will be kept astern, from the engine compart-

102

ment. That's the way that we shall be going. Now give me a hand to get this hole plugged."

They got the canvas over the empty window frame, lashed it and, with a hammer and nails from the engineroom tool kit, tacked it into place. Grimes hoped that it would hold. He discovered that he could see the surface of the sea quite well from the side windows, so had no worries on that score. Before doing anything else he retrieved the crumpled chart from the corner into which it had blown, spread it out on the desk, made an estimation of the drift since the last observed position, laid off a course for Drarg Island. Once he had the ship under control he would steer a reciprocal of this course, send Sonya right aft to keep a lookout astern, with Farrell stationed amidships to relay information and orders. First of all, however, there was more juggling to be done with gas and ballast.

Grimes descended cautiously, calling instructions to Sonya as he watched the white-crested waves coming up to meet him. The drogue touched surface—and still the ship fell, jerkily, until the buckets bit and held, sinking as they filled. There was a vile draft in the control room as the wind whistled through chinks in the makeshift windshield.

"All right," ordered Grimes. "Man the lookout!"

The others scrambled aft, while the Commodore took the wheel. He knew that he would have to keep the lubber's line steady on a figure that looked like a misshapen, convoluted 7, saw that the ship's head was all of twenty degrees to starboard off this heading. He applied port rudder, was surprised as well as pleased when she came round easily. He risked a sidewise glance at the altimeter. The needle was steady enough—but it could not possibly drop much lower. The instrument had not been designed for wave hopping.

He yelled, hoping that Farrell would be able to hear him, "If you think we're getting too low, dump some more ballast!"

"Will do!" came the reply.

He concentrated on his steering. It was not as easy as he thought it would be. Now and again he had taken the wheel of *Sonya Winneck*, just to get the feel of her—but *her* wheel could be put over with one finger, all the real work being done by the powerful steering motors aft. Here it was a case of Armstrong Patent.

But he kept the lubber's line on the course, his arms aching, his legs trembling, his clothing soaked with perspiration in spite of the freezing draft. He wished that he knew what speed the airship was making. He wanted a drink, badly, and thought longingly of ice-cold water. He wanted a smoke, and was tempted. He thought that the airship was helium filled, was almost certain that she was helium filled, but dared take no risks. But the stem of his cold, empty pipe between his teeth was some small comfort.

Faintly he heard Sonya call out something.

Farrell echoed her. "Land, ho!"

"Where away?" yelled Grimes over his shoulder, his pipe clattering unheeded to the deck.

"Astern! To port! About fifteen degrees!"

Carefully, Grimes brought the ship round to the new course. She held it, almost without attention on his part. There must, he thought, have been a shift of wind.

"As she goes!" came the hail. "Steady as she goes!"

"Steady," grunted Grimes. "Steady . . ."

How much longer? He concentrated on his steering, on the swaying compass card, on the outlandish numerals that seemed to writhe as he watched them. *How much longer?*

He heard Sonya scream, "We're coming in fast! Too low! The cliffs!"

"Ballast!" yelled Grimes.

Farrell had not waited for the order, already had the trap in the cabin deck open, was pushing out another of the dead Esquelians, then another. The deck lifted under Grimes's feet, lifted and tilted, throwing him forward onto his now useless wheel. A violent jerk flung him aft, breaking his grip on the spokes.

After what seemed a very long time he tried to get to his feet. Suddenly Sonya was with him, helping him up, supporting him in his uphill scramble toward the stern of the ship, over decking that canted and swayed uneasily. They stumbled over the dead bodies, skirting the open hatch. Grimes was surprised to see bare rock only a foot or so below the aperture. They came to the engineroom, jumped down through the door to the ground. It was only a short drop.

"We were lucky," said Grimes, assessing the situation. The airship had barely cleared the cliff edge, had been brought up short by its dragline a few feet short of the Carlotti beacon.

"Bloody lucky!" Farrell said. "Some Execs would have opened fire first and waited for orders afterward . . ."

His Executive Officer flushed. "Well, sir, I thought it might be you." He added, tactlessly, "After all, we've heard so many stories about Commodore Grimes . . ."

Farrell was generous. He said, "Excellent airmanship, Commodore."

"Seamanship," corrected Grimes huffily.

Sonya laughed—but it was with him, not at him.

The voyage between Esquel and Tallis, where the King and his entourage were disembarked, was not a pleasant one. Insofar as the Terrans were concerned, the Esquelians stank. Insofar as the Esquelians were concerned, the Terrans stank—and that verb could be used both literally and metaphorically. Commander Farrell thought, oddly enough, that the King should be humbly grateful. The King, not so oddly, was of the opinion that he had been let down, badly, by his allies. Grimes, on one occasion when he allowed himself to be drawn into an argument, made himself unpopular with both sides by saying that the universe would be a far happier place if people did not permit political expediency to influence their choice of friends.

But at last, and none too soon, *Star Pioneer* dropped gently down to her berth between the marker beacons at Tallisport, and the ramp was extended, and, gibbering dejectedly, the Esquelians filed down it to be received by the Terran High Commissioner.

Farrell, watching from a control room viewport, turned to Grimes and Sonya. He said thankfully, "My first order will be 'Clean ship.' And there'll be no shore leave for anybody until it's done."

"And don't economize on the disinfectant, Jimmy," Sonya told him.

THE RUB

Slowly Grimes awakened from his nightmare.

It had been so real, too real, and the worst part of it was always the deep sense of loss. There was that shocking contrast between the dreary life that he was living (in the dream) and the rich and full life that he somehow knew that he should be living. There was his wife—that drab, unimaginative woman with her irritating mannerisms—and that memory of somebody else, somebody whom he had never met, never would meet, somebody elegant and slim, somebody with whom he had far more in common than just the physical side of marriage, somebody who knew books and music and the visual arts and yet evinced a deep appreciation of the peculiar psychology of the spaceman.

Slowly Grimes awakened.

Slowly he realized that he was not in his bedroom in the Base Commander's quarters on Zetland. He listened to the small, comforting noises: the irregular throbbing of the inertial drive, the sobbing of pumps, the soughing of the ventilation system, the thin, high whine of the Mannschenn Drive unit. And there was the soft, steady breathing of the woman in the bed with him. (That other one snored.)

But—such was the impression that his dream had made upon him—he had to be sure. (All cats are gray in the dark.) Without too much fumbling he found the stud of the light switch on his side of the bed. His reading lamp came on. Its light was soft, subdued—but it was enough to wake Sonya.

She looked up at him irritably, her lean face framed by the auburn hair that somehow retained its neatness, its sleekness, even after sleep. She demanded sharply, "What is it, John?"

He said, "I'm sorry. Sorry I woke you, that is. But I had to be sure."

Her face and voice immediately softened. "That dream of yours again?"

"Yes. The worst part of it is knowing that *you* are somewhere, somewhen, but that I shall never meet you."

"But you did." She laughed with him, not at him. "And that's your bad luck."

"My good luck," he corrected.

"*Our* good luck."

"I suppose that we could have done worse . . ." he admitted.

Grimes was awakened again by the soft chiming of the alarm. From his side of the bed he could reach the service hatch in the bulkhead. He opened it, revealing the tray with its silver coffee service.

"The usual?" he asked Sonya, who was making a lazy attempt to sit up in bed.

"Yes, John. You should know by this time."

Grimes poured a cup for his wife—black, unsweetened—then one for himself. He liked sugar, rather too much of it, and cream.

"I shall be rather sorry when this voyage is over," said Sonya. "Jimmy is doing us well. We shouldn't be pampered like this in an *Alpha* Class liner."

"After all, I am a Commodore," said Grimes smugly.

"Not in the Survey Service, you aren't," Sonya told him.

In that dream, that recurring nightmare, Grimes was still an officer in the Federation's Survey Service. But he had never gotten past Commander, and never would. He was passing his days, and would end his days, as commanding officer of an unimportant base on a world that somebody had once described as a planetwide lower middle class suburb.

"Perhaps not," Grimes admitted, "but I pile on enough Gees to be accorded V.I.P. treatment aboard a Survey Service ship."

"*You* do? I was under the impression that it was because of me that Jimmy let us have the V.I.P. suite."

"Not you. You're only a mere Commander, and on the Reserve list at that."

"Don't be so bloody rank conscious!"

She took a swipe at him with her pillow. Grimes cursed as hot coffee splashed onto his bare chest. Then, "I don't know what your precious Jimmy will think when he sees the mess on the sheets."

"He'll not see it—and his laundrobot won't worry about it. Pour yourself some more coffee, and I'll use the bathroom while you're drinking it." Then, as she slid out of the bed, "And go easy on the sugar. You're getting a paunch . . ."

Grimes remembered the fat and slovenly Commander of Zetland Base.

Commander James Farrell, the Captain of *Star Pioneer*, prided himself on running a taut ship. Attendance at every meal was mandatory for his officers. As he and Sonya took their seats at the captain's table, Grimes wondered how Farrell would cope with the reluctance of middle watch keepers aboard merchant vessels to appear at breakfast.

All of *Star Pioneer's* officers were here, in their places, except for those actually on duty. Smartly uniformed messgirls circulated among the tables, taking orders, bringing dishes. Farrell sat, of course, at the head of his own table, with Sonya to his right and Grimes to his left. At the foot of the table was Lieutenant Commander Malleson, the Senior Engineering Officer. There was little to distinguish him from his captain but the badges of rank. There was little to distinguish any of the officers one from the other. They were all tall young men, all with close-cropped hair, all with standardized good looks, each and every one of them a refugee from a Survey Service recruiting poster. *In my young days*, thought Grimes, *there was room for individuality . . .* He smiled to himself. *And where did it get me? Oh you bloody tee, that's where.*

"What's the joke, John?" asked Sonya. "Share it, please."

Grimes's prominent ears reddened. "Just a thought, dear." He was saved by a messgirl, who presented the menu to him. "Nathia juice, please. Ham and eggs—sunny-side up—to follow, with just a hint of French fries. And coffee."

"You keep a good table, Jimmy," Sonya said to Farrell. Then, looking at her husband, "Rather too good, perhaps."

"I'm afraid, Sonya," Farrell told her, "that our meals from now on will be rather lacking in variety. It seems that our Esquelian passengers brought some local virus aboard with 'em. The biologists in the first survey expeditions found nothing at all on Esquel in any way dangerous to human life, so perhaps we didn't take the precautions we should have done when we embarked the King and his followers. Even so, while they were on board their excretory matter was excluded from the ship's closed ecology. But after they were disembarked on Tallis the plumbing wasn't properly disinfected . . ."

Not a very suitable topic of conversation for the breakfast table, thought Grimes, sipping his fruit juice.

"So?" asked Sonya interestedly.

"So there's been a plague running its course in the 'farm.' It's just been the tissue culture vats that have been affected, luckily. We could make do indefinitely on yeasts and algae —but who wants to?" He grinned at Grimes, who was lifting a forkload of yolk-coated ham to his mouth. "Who wants to?"

"Not me, Captain," admitted Grimes.

"Or me, Commodore. The beef's dead, and the pork, and the chicken. The quack says that the lamb's not fit for human consumption. So far the mutton seems to be unaffected, but we can't even be sure of that."

"You'll be able to stock up when we get to Port Forlorn," said Grimes.

"That's a long way off." Farrell looked steadily at Grimes as he buttered a piece of toast. "I've a job for you, Commodore."

"A job for *me*, Commander Farrell?"

"Yes, you, Commodore Grimes. By virtue of your rank you represent the Rim Worlds Confederacy aboard this vessel. Kinsolving's Planet, although no longer colonized, is one of the Rim Worlds. I want to put down there."

"Why?" asked Grimes.

"Correct me if I'm wrong, Commodore, but I understand that the original settlers introduced Earth-type flora and fauna, some of which have not only survived, but flourished. It's not the flora that I'm interested in, of course—but I've heard that there are the descendants of the original rabbits, pigs, cattle and hens running wild there."

"No cattle," Grimes told him. "And no hens. Probably the pigs did for 'em before they could become established."

"Rabbit's a good substitute for chicken," said Farrell.

"Jimmy," reproved Sonya, "I do believe that you like your tummy."

"I do, Sonya, I do," said the young man.

"And so do I," said Lieutenant Commander Malleson, who until now had been eating in dedicated silence.

"But I don't like Kinsolving," grumbled Grimes. "And, in any case, we shall have to get permission to land."

"You will get it, John," said Sonya firmly.

Later that ship's morning, Farrell discussed the proposed landing on Kinsolving with Grimes and Sonya.

"Frankly," he told them, "I'm glad of an excuse to visit the planet. Not so long ago the Survey Service released a report on the three expeditions, starting off with that odd wet paint affair . . ."

"That was over a hundred and fifty years ago," said Grimes.

"Yes. I know. And I know, too, that you've been twice to Kinsolving—the first time as an observer with the neo-Calvinists, the second time in command of your own show . . ."

"And both times," admitted Grimes, "I was scared. Badly."

"You don't frighten easily, Commodore, as well I know. But what actually did happen? The official reports that have been released to the likes of us don't give much away. It was hinted—no more, just hinted—that the neo-Calvinists tried to call up the God of the Old Testament, and raised the entire Greek pantheon instead. And you, sir, attempted to repeat the experiment, and got tangled with a Mephistopheles straight out of Gounod's *Faust*."

"Cutting extraneous cackle," said Grimes, "that's just what did happen."

"What I'm getting at, Commodore, is this. Were your experiences objective or subjective?"

"That first time, Commander, the neo-Calvinists' ship, *Piety*, was destroyed, as well as her pinnaces. Their leaders —the Presbyter, the Rector, the Deaconess and thirteen others, men and women—completely vanished. That was objective enough for anybody. The second time—*I* vanished."

"I can vouch for that," stated Sonya.

"But you came back. Obviously."

"More by luck than judgment." Grimes laughed, without humor. "When you do a deal with the Devil it's as well to read the small print."

"But at no time was there any actual physical harm to anybody."

"There could have been. And we don't know what happened to the neo-Calvinist boss cockies . . ."

"Probably being converted to hedonism on Mount Olympus," said Sonya.

"But we don't know."

Farrell grinned. "And aren't those very words a challenge

to any officer in the Survey Service? You used to be one of us yourself, sir, and Sonya is still on our Reserve list. Kinsolving is almost directly on the track from Tallis to Lorn. I have a perfectly valid excuse to make a landing. And even in these decadent days . . ." He grinned again at the Commodore . . . "my Lords Commissioners do not discourage initiative and zeal on the part of their captains."

Reluctantly, Grimes grinned back. It was becoming evident that Farrell possessed depths of character not apparent on first acquaintance. True, he worked by the book—and had Grimes done so he would have risen to the rank of Admiral in the Survey Service—but he was also capable of reading between the lines. A deviation from his original cruise pattern—the evacuation of the King and his supporters from Esquel—had brought him to within easy reach of Kinsolving; he was making the most of the new circumstances. Fleetingly Grimes wondered if the destruction of the ship's fresh meat supply had been intentional rather than accidental, but dismissed the thought. Not even he, Grimes, had ever done a thing like that.

"Later," said Farrell, "if it's all right with you, sir, we'll go over the official reports, and you can fill in the gaps. But what is it that makes Kinsolving the way it is?"

"Your guess is as good as anybody's, Commander. It's just that the atmosphere is . . . odd. Psychologically odd, not chemically or physically. A terrifying queerness. A sense of impending doom . . . Kinsolving was settled at the same time as the other Rim Worlds. Physically speaking, it's a far more desirable piece of real estate than any of them. But the colonists lost heart. Their suicide rate rose to an abnormal level. Their mental institutions were soon overcrowded. And so on. So they pulled out.

"The reason for it all? There have been many theories. One of the latest is that the Kinsolving system lies at some intersection of . . . of stress lines. Stress lines in *what*? Don't ask me. But the very fabric of the continuum is thin, ragged, and the dividing lines between *then* and *now*, *here* and *there*, *what is* and *what might be* are virtually nonexistent . . ."

"Quite a place," commented Farrell. "But you're willing to visit it a third time, sir?"

"Yes," agreed Grimes after a long pause. "But I'm not prepared to make a third attempt at awakening ancient deities from their well-earned rest. In any case, we lack the . . . I suppose you could call her the medium. She's on Lorn, and even if she were here I doubt if she'd play."

"Good. I'll adjust trajectory for Kinsolving, and then we'll send Carlottigrams to our respective lords and masters requesting permission to land. I don't think that they'll turn it down."

"Unfortunately," said Grimes, but the faint smile that lightened his craggy features belied the word.

Slowly, cautiously Farrell eased *Star Pioneer* down to the sunlit hemisphere of Kinsolving, to a position a little to the west of the morning terminator. Grimes had advised a landing at the site used by the Confederacy's *Rim Sword* and, later, by his own *Faraway Quest*. The destruction of the neo-Calvinists' *Piety* had made the spaceport unusable. This landing place was hard by the deserted city of Enderston, on the shore of the Darkling Tarn. It had been the Sports Stadium.

Conditions were ideal for the landing. The sounding rockets, fired when the ship was descending through the first tenuous fringes of the atmosphere, had revealed a remarkable absence of turbulence. The parachute flares discharged by them at varying altitudes were falling straight down, each trailing its long, unwavering streamer of white smoke.

Grimes and Sonya were in the control room. "There's Enderston," the Commodore said, "on the east bank of the Weary River. We can't see much from this altitude; everything's overgrown. That's the Darkling Tarn . . ." With a ruler that he had picked up he pointed to the amoebalike glimmer of water among the dull green that now was showing up clearly on the big approach screen. "You can't miss it. That fairly well-defined oval of paler green is the Stadium . . ."

The inertial drive throbbed more loudly as Farrell made minor adjustments and then, when the Stadium was in the exact center of the screen, settled down again to its almost inaudible muttering.

At Farrell's curt order they all went to their acceleration chairs, strapped themselves in. Grimes, with the others, watched the expanding picture on the screen. It was all so familiar, too familiar, even to the minor brush fire started by the last of the parachute flares. And, as on the previous two occasions, there was the feeling that supernatural forces were mustering to resist the landing of the ship, to destroy her and all aboard her,

He looked at Farrell. The young Captain's face was pale, strained—and this, after all, was a setting down in almost ideal conditions. There were not, it is true, any ground approach aids. But neither was there wind, or cloud, or clear air turbulence. And Survey Service officers were trained to bring their ships down on worlds with no spaceport facilities.

So Farrell was feeling it too. The knowledge made Grimes less unhappy. *Now you begin to know what it's like, Jimmy boy*, he thought smugly.

But she was down at last.

There was almost no shock at all, and only an almost inaudible complaint from the ship's structure, and a faint sighing of shock absorbers as the great mass of the vessel settled in the cradle of her tripodal landing gear. She was down. "Secure main engines," ordered Farrell at last. Telegraph bells jangled sharply, and the inertial drive generators muttered to themselves and then were still. She was down, and the silence was intensified by the soft soughing of the ventilation fans.

Grimes swiveled in his chair, gazed out through the viewport toward the distant mountain peak, the black, truncated cone hard and sharp against the pale blue sky. "Sinai," Presbyter Cannon had named it. "Olympus," Grimes had labeled it on his new charts of the planetary surface. But that name was no longer apt. On its summit the neo-Calvinists had attempted to invoke Jehovah—and Zeus had answered their call. On its summit Grimes had tried to invoke the gods of the Greek pantheon—and had been snatched into an oddly peopled Limbo by Mephistopheles himself.

This time on Kinsolving the Commodore was going to be cautious. Wild horses—assuming that there were any on this planet, and assuming that they should be possessed by such a strange ambition—would not be able to drag him up to the top of the mountain.

Nonetheless, Grimes did revisit the mountaintop, taken there by the tamed horsepower of *Star Pioneer*'s pinnace rather than by wild horses. Nothing happened. Nothing could happen unless Clarisse, descendant of the long dead

113

artist-magicians, was there to make it happen. There was nothing to see, except the view. All that remained of the two disastrous experiments was a weathered spattering of pigments where the witch girl's easel had stood.

Everybody visited the famous caves, of course, and stared at and photographed the rock paintings, the startlingly life-like depiction of beasts and their hunters. And the paint was dry, and the paintings were old, old, even though some faint hint of their original magic still lingered.

Even so, this was an uneasy world. Men and women never walked alone, were always conscious of something lurking in the greenery, in the ruins. Farrell, reluctant as he was to break the Survey Service's uniform regulations, is-sued strict orders that everybody ashore on any business whatsoever was to wear a bright, scarlet jacket over his other clothing. This was after two hunting parties had opened fire upon each other; luckily nobody was killed, but four men and three women would be in the sick bay for days with bullet wounds.

Grimes said to Farrell, "Don't you think it's time that we were lifting ship, Captain?"

"Not for a while, Commodore. We have to be sure that the new tissue cultures will be successful."

"That's just an excuse."

"All right, it's just an excuse."

"You're waiting for something to happen."

"Yes. Damn it all, Commodore, this sensation of brooding menace is getting me down; it's getting all of us down. But I want to have something definite to report to my Lords Commissioners . . ."

"Don't pay too high a price for that fourth ring on your sleeve, James."

"It's more than promotion that's at stake, sir, although I shall welcome it. It's just that I hate being up against an enemy that I can't see, can't touch. It's just that I want to accomplish something. It's just that I don't want to go slink-ing off like a dog with his tail between his legs."

"The original colony did just that."

"But they . . ." Farrell stopped abruptly.

"I'll finish it for you, James. But they were only civilians. They weren't wearing the Survey Service badge on their caps, Survey Service braid on their sleeves or shoulders. They weren't disciplined. And how long do you think your ship's discipline is going to stand up to the strain, gold braid and brass buttons notwithstanding?"

"For long enough."

Sonya broke in. "This is Jimmy's show, John. He makes the decisions. And I agree with him that we should stay on Kinsolving until we have something to show for our visit."

"Thank you, Sonya," said Farrell. Then, "You must excuse me. I have things to attend to."

When the young man had left their cabin, Sonya turned to her husband. "You're getting too old and cautious, John. Or are you sulking because *you're* not running things?"

"I don't like this world, my dear. I've reasons not to."

"You're letting it get you down. You look as though you haven't slept for a week."

"I haven't. Not to speak of."

"Why didn't you let me know?"

"It's so damned silly. It's that bloody nightmare of mine—you know the one. Every time I shut my eyes it recurs."

"You should have told me."

"I should have done." He got slowly to his feet. "Probably some good, healthy exercise will make me sleep better. A long walk . . ."

"I'll come with you."

She fetched from the wardrobe the scarlet jackets that they had been given. Grimes took from a drawer his deadly little Minetti, put it in one pocket, a spare clip of cartridges in the other. Heavier handguns and miniaturized transceivers they would collect from the duty officer at the airlock.

Within a few minutes they were walking down the ramp to the path that had been hacked and burned and trodden through the encroaching greenery, the trail that led to the ruined city.

It was early afternoon. The sun was still high in the pale sky, but the breeze, what there was of it, was chilly. And the shadows, surely, were darker here than on any other world that Grimes had ever visited, and seemed to possess a life of their own. But that was only imagination.

They walked steadily but carefully, watching where they put their feet, avoiding the vines and brambles that seemed deliberately to try to trip them. On either side of the rough track the vegetation was locked in silent, bitter warfare: indigenous trees and shrubs, importations from Earth and other worlds, and parasites upon parasites. In spite of the overly luxuriant growth the overwheening impression was of death rather than of life, and the most readily identifiable scent on the chill air was that of decay.

They came to the outskirts of the city, picking their way over the tilted slabs of concrete, thrust up and aside by root and trunk, that had once been a road. Once the buildings between which it ran had been drably utilitarian; now the madly proliferating and destructive ivy clothed them in somber, Gothic splendor. An abandoned ground car, the glass of its headlights by some freak of circumstances unobscured, glared at them like a crouching, green-furred beast.

Grimes tried to imagine what this place had been like before its evacuation. Probably it had been very similar to any sizable town on Lorn or Faraway, Ultimo or Thule—architecturally. But there had been one difference, and a very important one. There had been the uncanny atmosphere, that omnipresent premonition of . . . Of . . . ? That fear of the cold and the dark, of the Ultimate Night. Other cities on other worlds had their haunted houses; here every house had been haunted.

He said, "The sooner young Farrell lifts ship off this deserted graveyard, the better."

"At least it's not raining," Sonya told him, with an attempt at cheerfulness.

"Thank the odd gods of the galaxy for one small mercy," grumbled Grimes.

"Talking of odd gods . . ." she said.

"What about them?"

"Sally Veerhausen, the Biochemist, told me that there's a very odd church on a side street that runs off the main drag."

"Oh?"

"Yes. It's to the right, and it's little more than an alley, and you turn into it just before you get to a tall tower with a latticework radio mast still standing on top of it . . ."

"That it there, to the right?"

"Must be. Shall we investigate?"

"What is there to investigate?" he asked.

"Nothing, probably. But I seem to recall a period when you exhibited a passion for what you referred to as freak religions. This could be one to add to your collection."

I doubt it," he told her.

But after a few minutes' careful walking they were turning

off the main street, making their way along an alley between walls overgrown with the ubiquitous ivy that had been brought to the world by some long dead, homesick colonist.

The church was there.

It was only a small building, a masonry cube with its angles somehow and subtly wrong. And it was different from its neighbors. Perhaps the stone, natural or synthetic, from which it had been constructed possessed some quality, physical or chemical, lacking in the building materials in more general use. Its dull gray facade was unmarked by creeper, lichen or moss. Its door, gray like the walls, but of metal, was uncorroded. Over the plain rectangle of the entrance were the embossed letters in some matte black substance—TEMPLE OF THE PRINCIPLE.

Grimes snorted almost inaudibly. Then, "What Principle?" he demanded. "There have been so many."

"Perhaps," said Sonya seriously, "the greatest and most mysterious one of all."

The Golden Way? The greatest, I admit . . ."

"No. Sally got her paws onto such records as still exist—the vaults in the city hall kept their contents quite intact—and found out that there was a cult here that worshipped, or tried to worship, the Uncertainty Principle . . ."

"Mphm. Could have been quite a suitable religion for this world. Inexplicable forces playing hell with anything and everything, so, if you can't lick 'em, join 'em."

"Or get the hell out."

"Or get the hell out. But—who knows?—this freak religion might just have worked. Shall we go inside?"

"Why not?"

The door opened easily, too easily. It was almost as though they had been expected. But this, Grimes told himself, was absurd thinking. The officers from the ship who had found this place must have oiled the hinges. And had they done something about the lighting system too? It should have been dark inside the huge, windowless room, but it was not. The gray, subtly shifting twilight was worse than darkness would have been. It accentuated the wrongness of the angles where wall met wall, ceiling and floor. It seemed to concentrate, in a formless blob of pallid luminescence, over the coffin-shaped altar that stood almost in the middle of the oddly lopsided hall. *Almost* in the middle . . . Its positioning was in keeping with the rest of the warped geometrics of this place.

"I don't like it," said Grimes. "I don't like it at all."

"Neither do I," whispered Sonya.

Yet neither of them made any attempt to retreat to the comparative light and warmth and sanity of the alley outside.

"What rites did they practice?" whispered the Commodore. "What prayers did they chant? And to *what?*"

"I'd rather not find out."

But still they did not withdraw, still, hand in hand, they advanced slowly toward the black altar, the coffin-shaped . . . coffin-shaped? No. Its planes and angles shifted. It was more of a cube. It was more than a cube. It was . . .

Grimes, knew, suddenly, what it was. It was a tesseract. And he knew, too, that he should never have come again to this world. Twice he had visited Kinsolving before, and on the second occasion had become more deeply involved than on the first. Whatever the forces were that ruled this planet, he was becoming more and more attuned to them.

And this was the third time.

"John!" he heard Sonya's distant voice. "*John!*"

He tightened the grasp of his right hand, but the warmth of hers was no longer within it.

"John . . ."

It was no more than a fading whisper.

"John . . ."

"Grmph . . ." He didn't want to wake up. Full awareness would mean maximum appreciation of his nagging headache. His eyes were gummed shut, and he had the impression that small and noisome animals had fought and done other things inside his mouth.

"*John!*"

Blast the woman, he thought.

"*JOHN!*" She was shaking him now.

He flailed out blindly, felt one fist connect with something soft, heard a startled gasp of pain. "Never touch an officer," he enunciated thickly. " 'Gainst regulations."

"You . . . You *hit* me. You brute."

"Own fault."

"Wake up, damn you!"

He got his eyes open somehow, stared blearily at the

118

plump, faded woman in the shabby robe who was staring down at him with distaste.

Who are you? he demanded silently. *Who are you?* The memory of someone slim, sleek and elegant persisted in his befuddled brain. Then—*Where am I? Who am I?*

"You've got a job to do," the woman told him in a voice that was an unpleasant whine. "You'd better get your stinking carcass out of that bed and start doing it. I like to go on eating, even if you don't."

A starvation diet would do you the world of good, he thought. He said, "Coffee."

"Coffee *what?* Where's your manners?"

"Coffee, please."

She left him then, and he rolled out of the rumpled bed. He looked down with distaste at his sagging drinker's paunch, then got to his feet and walked unsteadily to the bathroom. He was surprised at the weakness he felt, the near nausea, the protests of a body allowed to degenerate into a state of general unfitness. It all seemed wrong. Surely he had always taken pride in maintaining himself in good condition.

He stood under the shower, and gradually the mists cleared from his brain. In a little while John Grimes, Officer Commanding the Zetland Base, passed over Commander, would be ready to begin his dreary day.

Nobody quite knew why the Federation maintained a base on Zetland. Once, a long time ago, the planet had been strategically important when it seemed possible that the Federation and the expanding Shaara Empire might clash, but the Treaty of Danzenorg, respected by both cultures, had neatly parceled up the entire galaxy into spheres of influence. True, there were other spacefaring races who belonged neither to the Federation nor the Empire, but their planets were many, many light years distant from Zetland and their trade routes passed nowhere near this world.

There was a base on Zetland. There always had been one; there always would be one. The taxpayer had bottomless pockets. There were spaceport facilities, of a sort. There were repair facilities, also of a sort. There was a Carlotti beacon, which was an absolutely inessential part of the navigational network in this sector of space, and relay station. The whole setup, such as it was, could have been run efficiently by a lieutenant junior grade, with a handful of petty officers and ratings. But a base commander must have scrambled egg on the peak of his cap. The Commander of a base like Zetland is almost invariably on the way up or the way down.

Commander John Grimes was not on the way up.

Nonetheless, he did have that scrambled egg on the peak of his cap. There was also a smear of egg yolk at the corner of his mouth, and a spatter of it on the lapel of his jacket. His enlisted woman driver, waiting for him in the ground car outside the Base Commander's bungalow, looked at him with some distaste—apart from anything else, she had been there for all of twenty minutes—clambered reluctantly out of the vehicle (her legs, noted Grimes, were too thick and more than a little hairy) and threw him a salute that almost, but not quite, qualified as "dumb insolence." Grimes returned it contemptuously. She opened the rear door of the car for him. He got in, thanking her as an afterthought, sagged into the seat. She got back behind the controls, clumsily stirred and prodded the machine into reluctant motion.

It was only a short drive to the military spaceport. The Commander thought, as he had thought many times before, that he should walk to his office rather than ride; the exercise would do him good. But somehow he never felt up to it. He stared unseeingly through the dirty windows. The view was as it always was: flat fields with an occasional low farmhouse, uninteresting machines trudging through the dirt on their caterpillar treads sowing or reaping or fertilizing the proteinuts which were Zetland's only export—and that only to worlds too poverty-stricken to send anything worthwhile in exchange. Ahead was the base—administration buildings, barracks, control tower and the lopsided ellipsoid that was the Carlotti beacon, slowly rotating.

The car rolled over the concrete apron, jerked to a halt outside the control tower. The girl driver got out clumsily, opened the Commander's door. Grimes got out, muttered, "'K you."

She replied sweetly, "It was a pleasure, sir."

Saucy bitch, thought Grimes sourly.

He did not take the elevator to his office on the top level of the tower. Thoughts about his lack of physical fitness had been nagging him all morning. He used the stairs, taking them two at a time at first. He soon had to abandon this practice.

By the time that he reached the door with BASE COM-
MANDER on it in tarnished gilt lettering he was perspiring
and out of breath and his heart was hammering uncomfortably.

Ensign Mavis Davis, his secretary, got up from her desk
as he entered the office. She was a tall woman, and very
plain, and old for her junior rank. She was also highly ef-
ficent, and was one of the few persons on this world whom
Grimes liked.

"Good morning, Commander," she greeted him, a little
too brightly.

"What's good about it?" He scaled his cap in the general
direction of its peg, missed as usual. "Oh, well, it's the only
one we've got."

She said, holding out a message flimsy, "This came in a
few minutes ago . . ."

"Have we declared war on somebody?"

She frowned at him. She was too essentially good a person to regard war as a joking matter. "No. It's from *Draconis*.
She's making an unscheduled call here . . ."

A Constellation Class cruiser, thought Grimes. *Just what
I need* . . . He asked, "When is she due?"

"Eleven hundred hours this morning."

"*What?*" Grimes managed a grin. "The fleet's in port, or
almost in port, and not a whore in the house washed . . ."

"That's not funny, Commander," she said reprovingly.

"Indeed it's not, Mavis," he agreed. Indeed it wasn't. He
thought of the huge cruiser, with all her spit and polish, and
thought of his own, slovenly, planet-based command, with
its cracked, peeling paint, with dusty surfaces everywhere,
with equipment only just working after a fashion, with personnel looking as though they had slept in their uniforms—
as many of them, all too probably, had. He groaned, went
to the robot librarian's console, switched on. "Fleet List," he
said. "*Draconis*. Name of commanding officer."

"Yes, sir." The mechanical voice was tinny, absolutely unhuman. "Captain Francis Delamere, O.G.C., D.C.O., F.M.-
H. . . ." Grimes switched off.

Franky Delamere, he thought. *A lieutenant when I was
a two and a half ringer. A real Space Scout, and without
the brains to come in out of the rain, but a stickler for
regulations. And now he's a four ring captain* . . .

"John . . ." There was sympathy in the Ensign's voice.

"Yes, Mavis?"

She was abruptly businesslike. "We haven't much time, but I issued orders in your name to get the place cleaned up a bit. And the Ground Control approach crew are at their stations, and the beacons should be in position by now . . ."

Grimes went to the wide window. "Yes," he said, looking down at the triangle of intensely bright red lights that had been set out on the gray concrete of the apron, "they are. Thank you."

"Do you wish to monitor G.C.A.?"

"Please."

She touched a switch, and almost immediately there was the sound of a crisply efficient voice. "*Draconis* to Zetland Base. E.T.A., surface contact, still 1100 hours. Is all ready?"

"All ready, *Draconis*," came the reply in accents that were crisp enough.

"Just one small thing, John," said Mavis. She stood very close to him, and with a dampened tissue removed the flecks of egg yolk from the corner of his mouth, from his uniform. "Now, let 'em all come," she declared.

"Let 'em all come," he echoed.

He remembered a historical romance he had read recently. It was about a famous English regiment whose proud epitaph was, *They died with their boots clean.*

Living with your boots clean can be harder.

Draconis was heard long before she was seen, the irregular throb of her inertial drive beating down from beyond the overcast. And then, suddenly, she was below the cloud ceiling, a great, gleaming spindle, the flaring vanes of her landing gear at her stern. Grimes wondered if Francis Delamere were doing his own pilotage; very often the captains of these big ships let their navigating officers handle the controls during an approach. He thought smugly that this was probably the case now; when Delamere had served under Grimes he had been no great shakes as a ship handler.

Whoever was bringing the cruiser down, he was making a good job of it. Just a touch of lateral thrust to compensate for the wind, a steady increase of vertical thrust as altitude diminished, so that what at first had seemed an almost uncontrolled free fall was, at the moment of ground contact, a downward drift as gentle as that of a soap bubble.

She was tall, a shining metallic tower, the control room at

her sharp stem well above the level of Grimes's office. Abruptly her inertial drive was silent. "Eleven oh oh oh seven . . ." announced Mavis Davis.

"Mphm," grunted Grimes.

He retrieved his cap from the floor, let the Ensign, who had found a clothes brush somewhere, brush its crown and peak. He put it on. He said to the girl, "Look after the shop. I have to go visiting." He left his office, took the elevator down to ground level. He was joined by the Base Supply Officer, the Base Medical Officer and the Base Engineering Officer. All three of them, he noted, looked reasonably respectable. Grimes in the lead, they marched out to the ramp that was just being extended from *Draconis's* after airlock.

It was good to be boarding a ship again, thought Grimes, *even one commanded by a man who had once been his junior and who was now his senior.* As he climbed the ramp he threw his shoulders back and sucked in his belly. He returned the salute of the junior officer at the airlock smartly and then, followed by his own officers, strode into the elevator cage. The woman operator needed no instructions; in a very few seconds the party from the base was being ushered into the Captain's day room.

"Ah," said Delamere," "Commander Grimes, isn't it?" He had changed little over the years; his close-cropped hair was touched with gray, but he was as boyishly slim and handsome as ever. The four gold rings gleamed bravely on each sleeve, and the left breast of his uniform was gaudy with ribbons. "Welcome aboard, Commander."

"Thank you, Captain." Grimes had no intention of addressing the other as "sir."

"You're putting on weight, John," said the Specialist Commander who was one of the group of officers behind Delamere.

"Maggie!"

"Commander Lazenby," said the Captain stiffly, "this touching reunion can be deferred until such time as the Base Commander and I have discussed business."

"Aye, aye, sir," snapped Margaret Lazenby, just a little too crisply.

Delamere glared at her, John Grimes looked at her wistfully. *She* hadn't put on weight. She had hardly changed since they had been shipmates in the census ship *Seeker.*

123

Her red hair gleamed under her cap, her figure was as slim and trim as ever. But . . .

But she was not the slender, auburn-haired woman who haunted his dreams.

"Commander Grimes," said Delamere. Then, more loudly, "Commander Grimes!"

"Yes, Captain?"

"Perhaps we can get the introductions over with, and then you and I can get down to business."

"Certainly, Captain. This is Lieutenant Commander Dufay, the Base Medical Officer. Lieutenant Danby, Supplies. Lieutenant Roscoe, Engineering."

Delamere introduced his own people, and then the specialist officers went below, leaving the Captain to conduct business with Grimes.

"A drink, Commander?"

"Please, Captain. Gin, if I may."

"You may. Sit down, Grimes." Delamere poured the drinks, took a chair facing the other. "Down the hatch."

"Down the hatch."

The Captain grinned. "Well, Grimes, I don't seem to have caught you with your pants down. Frankly, I was rather hoping I would . . ."

"What do you mean?"

"I haven't forgotten that bad report you put in on me . . ."

"It was truthful," said Grimes. "You were a lousy ship handler." Then, "By the way, who brought *Draconis* in?"

"None of your business," snapped Delamere, an angry flush on his face. After a second or so he continued. "For your information, Grimes, an economy wave is sweeping the Service. There is a cutting out of deadwood in progress. Certain ships, *Draconis* among them, have been selected by our lords and masters to make the rounds of bases such as this one, and to report upon them. My last call was at Wuggis III. The Base Commander who was in charge is now on the retired list. His G.C.A. was in such a state that I was obliged to use the commercial spaceport."

"How nice for you," commented Grimes.

The Captain ignored this. "I'm giving you fair warning, Commander. You'd better be prepared. For the purposes of this exercise a state of war is deemed to exist. *Draconis* has limped into your base with 75% casualties, including all technical officers. These same technical officers are, even now, arranging a simulation of extensive damage. The Mann-schenn Drive, for example, will require a new governor and will have to have its controls recalibrated. Only one inertial drive unit is functional, and that is held together with spit and string. My laser cannon are burned out. My yeast, algae and tissue culture vats contain only slimy, dead messes utterly unfit for human—or even unhuman—consumption." He laughed. "All the parts that have been removed from machinery and weapons are, of course, securely locked in my storerooms, where your people won't be able to get their greasy paws on them. *You*, Grimes, starting from scratch, using your people, your workshops, starting from scratch, will have to bring *Draconis* back to a state of full fighting efficiency, as soon as possible if not before."

"Then I'd better get cracking," said Grimes. He got to his feet, glanced briefly and regretfully at his almost untouched glass. It was good liquor, far better than any that could be obtained locally—but, even now, he was rather fussy about whom he drank with.

"You'd better," agreed Delamere. "Oh, you haven't finished your drink, Commander."

"Your ship's in such a sorry, simulated state," Grimes told him, "that we'll make believe that you need it yourself."

He forgot to salute on the way out.

"I knew something like this would happen," complained Marian tearfully. "What shall we do, John? What can we do? A commander's pension is not much."

"Too right it isn't." He looked thoughtfully at the half inch of oily gin remaining in his glass, brought it to his mouth and swallowed it, gagging slightly. He reached for the bottle, poured himself another generous shot.

"You drink too much," flared his wife.

"I do," he agreed, looking at her. She was almost passable when alcohol had dimmed the sharp edges of his perception. He murmured:

> *Malt does more than Milton can*
> *To justify God's ways to Man . . ."*

"What?"

"Housman," he explained. "A poet. Twentieth century or thereabouts."

"Poetry!" she sneered contemptuously. "But what are you doing about Captain Delamere? He was such a *nice* young man when he was one of your officers, when we were all happy at Lindisfarne Base . . ."

"Yes, Franky was always good at sucking up to captains' and commodores' and admirals' wives."

"But you must have *done* something to him, John. Couldn't you apologize?"

"Like hell," growled Grimes. "Like adjectival, qualified hell."

"Don't swear at me!"

"I wasn't swearing."

"You were thinking it."

"All right, I was thinking it." He finished his drink, got up, put on his cap. "I'd better get down to the ship to see what sort of mess my butterfly-brained apes are making of her."

"What difference will your being there make?"

"I'm still Commander of this bloody base!" he roared.

He looked back at her briefly as he reached the door, felt a spasm of pity. She was such a mess. She had let herself go. (As he had let himself go.) Only faint traces remained of the attractive Ensign Marian Hall, Supply Branch, whom he, on the rebound, had married. Physically there was no longer any attraction. Mentally there was—nothing. She read only trash, was incapable of intelligent conversation, and could never join Grimes in his favorite pastime of kicking ideas around to see if they yelped. He wondered how things would have worked out if he and Maggie Lazenby had made a go of things. But to have Maggie here, on this world, at this juncture was too much.

He walked to the military spaceport. The night was mild, not unpleasant in spite of the wisps of drizzle that drifted over the flat landscape. Now and again Zetland's twin moons appeared briefly in breaks in the clouds, but their light was faint and pallid in comparison to the glare of the working floods around *Draconis*.

He tramped slowly up the ramp to the airlock, returned the salute of the O.O.D., one of Delamere's men. The elevator was unmanned—but, after all, the ship had suffered heavy simulated casualties, so ratings could not be spared for nonessential duties. He went first to the "Farm." The vats had been cleaned out, but the stink still lingered. The cruiser's Biochemist had carried out his "sabotage under orders" a little too enthusiastically. He exchanged a few words with Lieutenant Commander Dufay, in charge of operations here, then went down a couple of decks to the inertial drive room. He looked at the confusion without understanding it. Roscoe and his artificers had bits and pieces scattered everywhere. It was like a mechanical jigsaw puzzle.

"She'll be right, Commander," said the Engineer Lieutenant. He didn't seem to be convinced by his own words. Grimes certainly wasn't.

"She'd better be right," he said.

Somebody else was using the elevator, so he decided to take the companionway up to Control—he *did* know more than a little about navigational equipment—rather than wait. His journey took him through Officers' Country. He was not altogether surprised when he was accosted by Commander Lazenby.

"Hi, John."

"Hi, Maggie."

"Are you busy?"

He shrugged. "I should be."

"But we haven't seen each other for years. Come into my dogbox for a drink and a yarn. It's all right—the Boy Wonder's being wined and dined by the Governor in Zeehan City."

"He might have told me."

"Why should he? In any case, he's on the Simulated Casualty List. He's probably awarded himself a posthumous Grand Galactic Cross."

"With golden comets."

"And a platinum spiral nebula." She laughed. "Come in, John. Take the weight off your feet." The door to her day cabin opened for her. "This is Liberty Hall. You can spit on the mat and call the cat a bastard."

"You haven't changed, Maggie," he said ruefully, looking at her. "I wish . . ."

She finished it for him. "You wish that you'd married me instead of that little commissioned grocer's clerk. But you were always rather scared of me, John, weren't you? You were afraid that you, a spacehound pure and simple, wouldn't be able to cope with me, a qualified ethologist. But as an ethologist I could have seen to it that things worked out for us."

She sat down on her settee, crossing her slim, sleek legs. Her thin, intelligent face under the red hair was serious.

He looked at her wistfully. He murmured—and it was as much a question as a statement—"It's too late now."

"Yes. It's too late. You've changed too much. You did the wrong thing, John. You should have resigned after that court martial. You could have gone out to the Rim Worlds to make a fresh start."

"I wanted to, Maggie. But Marian—she's incurably Terran. She made it quite plain that she'd not go out to live among the horrid, rough colonials. As far as she's concerned, everywhere there's a Survey Service Base there's a little bit of Old Earth, with society neatly stratified. Mrs. Commander is just a cut above Mrs. Lieutenant Commander, and so on down." He fumbled for his pipe, filled and lit it. "She had the idea, too, that My Lords Commissioners would one day forgive me and that she'd finish up as Mrs. Admiral Grimes . . ."

"My heart fair bleeds for you both," she said drily. "But mix us drinks, John. You'll find the wherewithal in that locker."

"For you?"

"The same as always. BVG, with just a touch of lime."

There was a hologram over the grog locker, a little, brightly glowing window onto another, happier world. It was a beach scene: golden sand, creamy surf, blue sea and sky, and the golden brown bodies of the naked men and women.

Grimes asked, "Do you still spend your long leaves on Arcadia, Maggie?"

"Too right I do. It's the only possible planet for an ethologist who takes the 'Back To Nature' slogan seriously."

"You look happy enough in this hologram . . ." Grimes inspected the three-dimensional picture more closely. "*Who is that with you?*"

"Peter Cowley. He's a Senior Biochemist with Trans-Galactic Clippers."

"No. Not *him*. The woman."

She got up to come to stand beside him. "Oh, her. That's Sonya Verrill. Yet another of the Commanders with whom the Survey Service is infested. She's Intelligence. Do you know her?"

Grimes stared at the depiction of the nude woman. She was like Maggie Lazenby in many ways, her figure, her coloring, her facial features, could almost have been her sister. He looked more closely. There should be a mole on her left hip. There was.

"Do you know her?" asked Maggie again.

"Yes . . . No . . ."

"Make your mind up."

I don't know her, thought Grimes. *I have never met her. But I have dreamed about her. I thought it was Maggie in my dreams, a somehow different Maggie, but she hasn't a mole anywhere on her body . . .*

He said, "No, I don't know her. But she *is* like you, isn't she?"

"I can't see any resemblance. You know, she was almost going to call here; she's sculling around this neck of the woods in one of those little, fully automated armed yachts. Some hush-hush Intelligence deal. But when she heard that this was one of the Boy Wonder's ports of call she decided to play by herself somewhere."

"Has *he* met her?" asked Grimes, feeling absurdly jealous.

"Yes. They do not, repeat not, like each other."

"Then there must be some good in her," said Grimes, with a quite irrational surge of relief.

"Never mind her. What about me? I'm thirsty."

"All right, all right," said Grimes, mixing the drinks.

When he got home Marian was waiting up for him.

"You've been drinking," she accused him.

"And so, to coin a phrase, what?"

"I don't mind that so much. But you've been with that . . . bitch, that Maggie Lazenby."

"I had a couple of drinks with her, that was all."

"Don't lie to me!"

"I'm not lying."

No, he wasn't lying. Maggie, in her woman's way, had offered him more than a drink, but he had turned it down. Even now he was not sure why he had done so. Or he was sure, but would not admit it to himself. It was all so crazy, so utterly crazy. He had been loyal to a woman whom he had never met, whose hologram he had seen for the first time, in Maggie's day cabin.

"After all I've done for you, and you going sniffing around that carroty alley cat. You're no good, you're just no good. You never were, and you never will be . . ."

Grimes brushed past her, into the living room, the Service

severity of which had been marred by his wife's tasteless attempts at interior decoration.

"Say something, damn you! Say something, you waster. Haven't you even the guts to defend yourself?"

The telephone buzzed urgently. Grimes went to it, flipped down the switch. The screen came alive and the plain, almost ugly face of Mavis Davis looked out at him. "Commander, there's an emergency . . ."

"Yes?" *And what was it? Had his fumbling repair squads wreaked some irreparable damage upon the cruiser? He'd better start packing his bags.*

"A Mayday."

"Who?" he demanded. "Where?"

"The armed yacht *Grebe.* In solar orbit between Zetland and Freiad." She rattled off coordinates. "Meteor swarm. Extensive hull and machinery damage. Loss of atmosphere. Orbit decaying."

"Mavis, send a car for me. At once."

"Wilco, Commander."

"And what can *you* do?" his wife sneered. "Captain Delamere's got a cruiser and hundreds of really efficient men and women. What have *you* got?"

"Out of my way!" he snarled.

"John! You can't go. I forbid you!" She clung to his sleeve but, brutally, he shook her off. She followed him for a little way as he strode out of the house, along the dark road, then gave up. "John!" she called. "John!"

The lights of the car were ahead, approaching rapidly. It passed him, turned, braked. Mavis Davis was driving. He got in beside her.

She said, as she restarted the vehicle. "*Husky?*"

Of course, it had to be the base's space tug *Husky.* Delamere's cruiser was out of commission and the tug at the civilian spaceport was, Grimes knew, undergoing annual survey. *Husky* was the only ship on Zetland capable of getting upstairs in a hurry.

And she was Grimes's toy, his pet. She was more than a toy, much more. In her he could feel the satisfaction of real command, or symbiosis with his ship. She was the only piece of equipment on the base in absolutely first class condition—and Grimes and Mavis, working with their own hands, had kept her so. She was referred to as "the Old Man's private yacht."

"I told Petty Officer Willis to warm her up," said Mavis. "Good girl."

"Can . . . Can I come with you?"

"I'd like you to." She was a clerical officer, trained as such, but she should have been an engineer. She possessed the inborn skills, the talents and a keen mathematical mind. Often she had accompanied Grimes on his short jaunts outside the atmosphere. "You know the little bitch better than anybody else on the base."

"Thank you, John."

The car screamed on to the apron, circled the great, useless, floodlit hulk of *Draconis. Husky* was in her own berth, tucked away behind the workshops, a dull metal ovoid standing in her tripodal landing gear like a gray egg in an eggcup. A circle of yellow light marked her airlock door.

As the car stopped Grimes heard a noise in the sky. It was a jet, coming in fast. The shriek of its exhaust varied in pitch as its turret drive was used first to brake and then to ease the aircraft to a vertical touchdown. The aircraft slammed to the concrete just a few feet from the car.

A man jumped out of the cabin, confronted Grimes. It was Delamere, still in his mess dress, starched white linen, black bow tie, tinkling miniatures and all.

"Is she ready?" he demanded.

"Yes, Captain. I'll have her up and away as soon as the airlock's sealed."

"You aren't taking her up, Grimes. I am." Delamere grinned whitely. "Life's been a little too dull lately."

"Like hell you're taking her up, Delamere. This is *my* base, and *my* tug."

"And *I* am your superior officer, Grimes. You'd better not forget it."

"You're not likely to let me, are you? But this is a rescue operation—and *I* know how to handle a ship."

"Out of my way, you insolent bastard!"

Grimes swung clumsily, but with all his weight behind the blow, and the weight of all the years of misery and frustration. Delamere wasn't as fit as he looked. Grimes's fist sank deep into his midriff, under the black silk cummerbund. The air was expelled from the Captain's lungs in an explosive *oof!* He sat down hard and abruptly. He gasped something about striking a superior officer, about mutiny.

"Willis," Grimes called to the Petty Officer, who had appeared in the airlock, "drag the Captain clear of the blast area. I'm going to use the auxiliary rockets. And keep clear yourself."

"But, sir . . ."

"You don't want to be up with me on a charge of mutiny. Get out of here, and take the Captain with you. That goes for you too, Mavis."

"Like hell it does!"

Grimes paused briefly. He could manage the tug single-handed, but with rescue operations involved it would be asking for trouble. He grabbed Mavis by her bony shoulder. "Scream!" he whispered. "I'm dragging you aboard by force!"

She screamed, shrieked, "Let go of me!" From where Delamere was sprawled the struggle would look convincing enough. And then they were in the airlock, and as the door shut Grimes saw that Willis already had Delamere well clear. The Commander hurried up to the little control room while Mavis went to the engines. He plumped down into the pilot's chair and, as he strapped himself in, cast an experienced eye over the telltale lights. REACTION DRIVE —READY. INERTIAL DRIVE—READY. MANNSCHENN DRIVE—STAND BY.

His fingers found the firing studs in the arm of his chair. He said into the microphone hanging before him, "Secure all. Secure all for blast off."

Mavis's voice came in reply. "All secure, Captain."

"Then—*blast!*" almost shouted Grimes.

He pressed the button, and *Husky* screamed upstairs like a bat out of hell.

There was only one person aboard the crippled *Grebe*, a woman. Her voice was faint, almost incoherent. She was in her suit, she said. She had a broken arm, and possible internal injuries. She thought that she would be able to ship a new air bottle when the one in use was exhausted . . .

"Can you actuate your Carlotti transceiver?" demanded Grimes urgently.

"I . . . I think so . . ."

"Try. I'm going to switch to Mannschenn Drive. I'll home on your Carlotti."

"Mannschenn Drive?" asked Mavis, who had come up to Control.

"Yes. I want to be there in minutes, not days, and the

Mannschenn Drive's the only way. I know it's risky, but . . ."

It *was* risky, to operate the Drive in a planetary system with its tangle of gravitational and magnetic fields, but it had to be done. Grimes jockeyed the free-falling *Husky* around on her gyroscope, lining her up on the faint signals from the survivor's suit radio. He started the Drive. There was the usual second or so of disorientation in space and time, and then, astern of them, Zetland assumed the appearance of a writhing, convoluted ball of luminous gas, and ahead and to starboard the sun became an iridescent spiral. Grimes paid no attention. He heard the faint voice from his own Carlotti speaker—"Carlotti *on*."

"Can you fix it so that it sends a continuous note? Turn up the gain . . ."

"Wilco."

A faint, continuous squeal came from the speaker.

Good. Grimes watched the quivering antenna of his Carlotti direction finder and communicator, the ellipsoid Mobius strip that was rotating slowly about its long axis. He restarted the inertial drive and then, with lateral thrust, using the antenna as a compass needle, headed the tug directly for the distant wreck. He pushed the inertial drive control to full ahead. The irregular throbbing shook the little ship. "Mavis," he said, "see if you can coax a few more revs out of the bone shaker . . ."

"I'll try," she told him, and was gone.

A fresh voice came from the speaker. It was Delamere. "Grimes. Captain Delamere calling ex-Commander Grimes. Do you read me?"

"Loud and clear, Delamere. Get off the air. I'm busy."

"Grimes, I order you to return at once. Ensign Davis, I authorize you to use force if necessary to overcome the mutineer and to assume command of *Husky*."

Grimes watched the antenna. It showed a continual drift of the target in a three o'clock direction. The wreck was in orbit, of course. He would have to allow for that. He did so, applying just the right amount of lateral thrust.

"Grimes! Ensign Davis! Do you hear me?"

Damn the man. So far the antenna was keeping lined up on the signal from the disabled *Grebe*, but with the base transmitting at full power it was liable to topple at any second.

"Grimes! Ensign Davis!"

"Grimes here. I can't give any orders, but I can appeal to those of you in the Carlotti room. This is a rescue operation. I'm homing on *Grebe*'s Carlotti beacon. There's a woman out there, in the wreck, and she can't last much longer. Please get off the air, and stay off."

He was never to know what happened, but he thought he heard the sound of a scuffle. He thought he heard a voice—Maggie's voice—whisper, "Pull the fuse!"

He transferred his attention to the spherical tank of the mass proximity indicator. Yes, there it was, a tiny, glowing spark, barely visible. It was drifting fast in toward the center of the globe. Too fast? Not really. For a collision to occur, two vessels must occupy the same space at the same time, and as long as *Husky*'s Mannschenn Drive was operating she was in a time of her own. But—talking of time—he didn't want to waste any. "Mavis," he said into the intercom mike, "when I put her on full astern I *want* full astern. No half measures."

"You'll get it," she assured him.

The spark was brighter now, crossing one concentric ring after another. Grimes adjusted the scale of the indicator, pushing the target back to the outermost circle. Still it drove in. Grimes adjusted the scale again, and again, and once more. Target spark merged with the bead of luminosity that represented *Husky*. For a microsecond there was an uncanny sensation of merging—not of ships, but of two personalities. "Mannschenn Drive—off!" snapped Grimes, executing his order. "Inertial drive—full astern!"

The ship shuddered, striving to tear herself apart. Colors sagged down the spectrum as the ever-precessing gyroscopes of the Mannschenn Drive were braked to a halt—but outside the viewports the stars, vibrating madly, still looked as they had done while the drive was in operation.

"Stop all!" muttered Grimes, jerking the lever to its central position.

And there, scant feet away, rotating slowly about some cockeyed axis, was the torn, buckled hull of the space yacht *Grebe*.

Mavis Davis came up to Control while Grimes was putting on his suit. She was bleeding slightly from an abrasion on her forehead. Like many another plain woman she was beautiful in conditions of emotional and physical stress. Before she lowered the helmet onto his shoulder she kissed him. It was a brief contact, but surprisingly warm. Grimes wished that it could have been longer.

She said, "Good-bye. It's been nice knowing you, John."

"What the hell's this, Mavis?"

She grinned lopsidedly. "I have my fey moments—especially when somebody is playing silly buggers with the Mannschenn Drive . . ." Then she was securing the helmet and further speech was impossible.

Grimes collected what tools he would require on his way down to the airlock. When the outer door opened he found that he could almost step across to *Grebe*. He pushed himself away from his own little ship, made contact with the hull of the other with the magnetic soles of his boots and palms of his gloves. He clambered over her like a clumsy, four-legged spider. He soon discovered that it would be impossible to open *Grebe*'s airlock door. But it didn't matter. A few feet away from it was a hole large enough for him to crawl through.

He said into his helmet microphone, "I'm here."

The faint voice that replied, at long last, held an oddly familiar astringent quality. "And about time."

"I came as quickly as I could. Where are you?"

"In the control room."

Grimes made his way forward, using cutting torch and crowbar when he had to. When he found her she was in the pilot's chair, held there by the seat belt. Moving feebly, she contrived to swivel to look at him. *Husky*'s floods were on, glaring through the viewports, but her face, inside the helmet, was in shadow.

She said, "I hate to have to admit it, but you're right, John."

"What do you mean?"

"What you always say when you deliver yourself of one of your diatribes against automation. 'Never put yourself at the mercy of a single fuse.' My meteor shield might as well have not been there, and by the time the alarm sounded it was too late to do anything . . ."

He was beside her now, holding her, cursing the heavy suits that were between them.

"Sonya, I've got to get you out of here. Aboard *Husky*." He fumbled with the strap that held her.

"Too . . . late." She coughed, and the sound of it, telling

of fluid-filled lungs, was terrifying. "Too . . . late. I hung on as long . . . as I could. Start . . . Mannschenn Drive. Should be some . . . power . . . in batteries . . ."

"Sonya! I'm getting you out of here!"

"No. No! Start . . . Drive . . ."

But he persisted in trying to unstrap her. Summoning her last reserves of strength she pushed him away. He lost contact with the deck, drifted away from her. He clutched at something—a lever?—that moved in his hand.

He did not hear the Drive starting; there was no air in the ship to carry the sound. But he felt the vibration as its rotors stirred into life, was aware that the harsh light of *Husky*'s floods had deepened from white to a sullen red. Around him, around Sonya, the universe lost its substance. But he was solid still, as she was, and her hand was firm in his.

And . . .

She was saying, "We found each other again. We found each other again . . ."

Grimes looked at her, looked at her a long time, dreadfully afraid that she would vanish. He held her hand tightly. Then, but cautiously, he stared around him at the temple. It seemed to have lost its alien magic. It was just a large, featureless room with the dimensions of a cube. On the floor, annoyingly off center, was a block of black stone in the shape of a coffin.

He said, "That dream . . . If it was a dream . . ."

She said, "There is a fourth rate Survey Service Base on Zetland . . ."

He said, "The last I heard of Delamere he'd been kicked upstairs to become a deskbound commodore . . ."

She said, "Damn your silly dream. Forget about it."

"I'll try," he promised. And then, unbidden, familiar words formed themselves in his mind. He said them aloud:

"To sleep, perchance to dream . . .
Ay, there's the rub . . ."

Something about the emphasis he used made her ask, "What's the rub, John?"

"What *is* the dream? *That* or *this*?"

"What does it matter?" she asked practically. "We just make the best of what we've got." Then, as they walked out of the drab temple, "Damn! My ribs are still hurting!"

The World's Best
Award-Winning Science Fiction
Comes from Ace

Commodore John Grimes was finally getting his space wings back. On his old ship, *Faraway Quest*, Grimes was to venture forth to the very Rim of the known worlds, seeking . . . The Outsider.

"The Outsiders' Ship . . . is a storehouse of science and technology . . . we, and the Federation, and the Shaara Empire, and probably quite a few more, have sent expeditions. Every one has ended disastrously."

So, it is out to the Rim and find The Outsider. But the mystery ship is not always easy to find. And other worlds, too, yearn for the treasures of the alien technology. What Commodore Grimes finds at the Rim, and what finds him there, sends him racing through time tracks, surrounded by enemies and temporary friends, trying endlessly to discover the secret and dangers of . . . The Outsider.

Turn this book over for
second complete novel

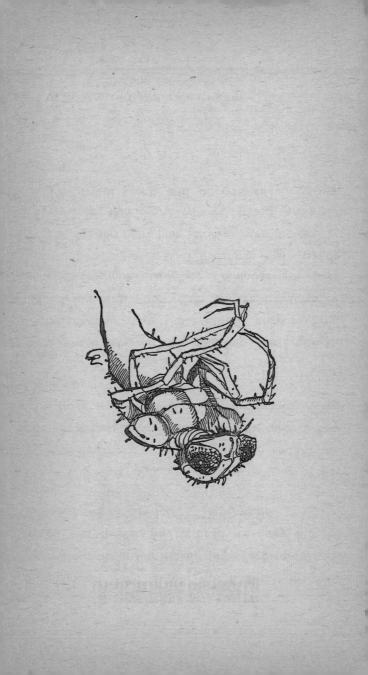

A. BERTRAM CHANDLER
THE DARK DIMENSIONS

ACE BOOKS

A Division of Charter Communications Inc.
1120 Avenue of the Americas
New York, N. Y.   10036

I

"I've another job for you, Grimes," said Admiral Kravitz.

"Mphm," grunted Commodore Grimes, Rim Worlds Naval Reserve, "sir." He regarded the portly flag officer with something less than enthusiasm. There had been a time, not so very long ago, when he had welcomed being dragged away from his rather boring civilian duties as Rim Runners' astronautical superintendent, but increasingly of late he had come to appreciate a relatively quiet, uneventful life. Younger men than he could fare the starways, he was happy to remain a desk-sitting space commodore.

"Rim Runners are granting you indefinite leave of absence," went on Kravitz.

"They would," grumbled Grimes.

"On full pay."

Grimes' manner brightened slightly. "And I'll be drawing my commodore's pay and allowances from the Admiralty, of course?"

"Of course. You are back on the active list as and from 0000 hours this very day."

"We can always use the extra money . . ." murmured Grimes.

Kravitz looked shocked. "I never knew that you were so mercenary, Grimes."

"You do now, sir." The Commodore grinned briefly, then once again looked rather apprehensive. "But it's not Kinsolving's Planet again, is it?"

The Admiral laughed. "I can understand your being more than somewhat allergic to that peculiar world."

Grimes chuckled grimly. "I think it's allergic to me, sir. Three times I've landed there, and each time was unlucky; the third time unluckiest of all."

"I've read your reports. But set your mind at rest. It's not Kinsolving."

"Then where?"

"The Outsider."

"The Outsider . . ." repeated Grimes slowly. How many times since the discovery of that alien construction out beyond the Galactic Rim had he urged that he be allowed to take *Faraway Quest* to make his own investigation? He had lost count. Always his proposals had been turned down. Always he could not be spared or was required more urgently elsewhere. Too, it was obvious that the Confederacy was scared of the thing, even though it swam in space that came under Rim Worlds' jurisdiction. The Federation was scared of it, too. "Let well enough alone," was the attitude of both governments.

"The Outsider . . ." said Grimes again. "I was beginning to think that it occupied top place on the list of untouchables. Why the sudden revival of interest?"

"We have learned," Kravitz told him, "from reliable sources, that the Waldegren destroyer *Adler* is on her way out to the . . . *thing*. I needn't tell you that the Duchy of Waldegren is making a comeback, or that Federation policy is that Waldegren will never be allowed to build its fleet up to the old level. But sophisticated weaponry can give a small navy superiority over a large one.

"The Outsiders' Ship, as we all know, is a storehouse of science and technology thousands—millions, perhaps—of years in advance of our own. *Your* Captain Calver got his paws on to some of it, but passed nothing of interest on to us before he flew the coop. Since then we, and the Federation, and the Shaara Empire, and probably quite a few more, have sent expeditions. Every one has ended disastrously. It is possible, probable, even, that this Waldegren effort will end disastrously. But we can't be sure.

"It should not take long to recommission your *Faraway Quest*. She's only just back from the Fleet Maneuvers, at which she was present as an auxiliary cruiser. . . ."

"I know," said Grimes. "I should have been in command of her."

"But you weren't. For all your early life in the Federation's Survey Service, for all your rank in our Naval Reserve, you don't make a good naval officer. You're too damned independent. You like to be left alone to play in your own little corner. But—I grant you this—whatever sort of mess you fall into you always come up smelling of roses."

"Thank you, sir," said Grimes stiffly.

Kravitz chuckled. "It's true, isn't it? Anyhow, you should

be on the spot, showing the flag, before *Adler* blows in. You'll be minding the shop. Play it by ear, as you always do. And while you're about it, you might try to find out something useful about The Outsider."

"Is that all?" asked Grimes.

"For the time being, yes. Oh, personnel for *Faraway Quest*. . . . You've a free hand. Make up the crew you think you'll need from whatever officers are available, Regulars or Reservists. The Federation has intimated that it'd like an observer along. I think I'm right in saying that Commodore Verrill still holds a reserve commission in the Intelligence Branch of their Survey Service. . . ."

"She does, sir. And she'd be very annoyed if she wasn't allowed to come along for the ride."

"I can well imagine. And now we'll browse through The Outsider files and try to put you in the picture."

He pressed a button under his desk, and a smartly uniformed W.R.W.N. officer came in, carrying a half dozen bulky folders that she put on the Admiral's desk. She was followed by two male petty officers who set up screen, projector and tape recorders.

Kravitz opened the first folder. "It all started," he said, "with Commander Maudsley of the Federation Survey Service's Intelligence Branch. . . ."

II

"It all started," said Grimes, "with Commander Maudsley of the Federation Survey Service's Intelligence Branch. . . ."

As soon as he had spoken the words he regretted them. Sonya, his wife, had known Maudsley well. They had been more, much more, than merely fellow officers in the same service. Grimes looked at her anxiously, the reddening of his prominent ears betraying his embarrassment. But her strong, fine-featured face under the high-piled, glossy, auburn hair was expressionless. All that she said, coldly, was, "Why bring that up, John?"

He told her. "You know the story. Mayhew knows the story. I know the story. But Clarisse doesn't. And as she's to be one of my key officers on this expedition it's essential that she be put in the picture."

"I can get it all from Ken," said Clarisse Mayhew.

"Not in such detail," stated Sonya. "We have to admit that my ever-loving husband has always been up to the eyebrows in whatever's happened on the Rim."

"You haven't done so badly yourself," Grimes told her, breaking the tension, returning the smile that flickered briefly over her face.

"One thing that I *like* about the Rim Worlds," murmured Clarisse, "is that the oddest things always seem to be happening. Life was never like this on Francisco. But go on, please, John."

"Mphm," grunted Grimes. "Talking is thirsty work."

He raised a hand, and on silent wheels a robot servitor rolled into the comfortable lounge room. Most people who could afford such luxuries preferred humanoid automatons and called them by human names, but not Grimes. He always said, and always would say, that it was essential that machines be kept in their proper place. The thing that had answered his summons was obviously just a machine, no more than a cylindrical tank on a tricycle carriage with two cranelike arms. It stood there impassively waiting for their orders, and then from a hatch in its body produced a tankard of cold beer for Grimes, Waverley Scotch and soda for Mayhew, iced Rigellian dragon's milk for the ladies.

"Here's to all of us," said Grimes, sipping appreciatively. He looked over the rim of his glass at his guests—at Mayhew, tall, gangling, deceptively youthful and fragile in appearance, at Clarisse, attractively plump in face and figure, her rich brown hair hanging down to waist level. On Francisco, the world of her birth, she had been one of the so-called Blossom People, and still looked the part.

"Get on with it, John," said Sonya after sampling her own drink.

"Very well. It all started, as I've already said, with Commander Maudsley. As well as being a fully qualified astronaut, he was an Intelligence Officer. . . ."

"It didn't start with Maudsley," said Sonya sharply. "No-one knows *when* it started."

"Oh, all right. I'll go back a few more years in time. It was suspected for quite a long while that there was *something out there*. Many years ago, long before the Rim Worlds seceded from the Federation, Faraway was a penal

8

colony of sorts. The Survey Service actually manned a ship with the sweepings of the jails and sent her out to find that . . . *something*. What happened to her is not known to this day. After we'd established our own Confederacy, the Federation's Survey Service was still snooping around the Rim—and Maudsley, passing himself off as the master of a star tramp called *Polar Queen*, did quite a lot of work out there. So far as we know he was the first *human* spaceman to set eyes on the Outsiders' Ship. Shortly thereafter he crashed his own vessel coming in to a landing at Port Farewell on Faraway. He was the only survivor. After that he stayed out there. He served in a few of our Rim Runners' ships, but he was practically unemployable. We didn't know then that he was a Survey Service Commander, Intelligence Branch at that, but it wouldn't have made any difference. He finished up as mate of a ship called, funnily enough, *The Outsider*. Her master, Captain Calver, had been master in our employ, but he and his officers made a pile of money out of the salvage of the T.G. Clipper *Thermopylae* and invested it in an obsolescent Epsilon Class tramp, going into business as shipowners. To comply with regulations, Calver had to ship a chief officer with at least a Chief Pilot's Certificate—and Maudsley was the only one that he could find on Nova Caledon.

"Maudsley was hitting the bottle, almost drinking himself to death. (Forgive me, Sonya, but that's the way that it was.) He talked in his drunken delirium. He talked about the Outsiders' Ship, the finding of which had somehow wrecked his life. Then he committed suicide. . . ."

Grimes paused, looking at his wife. Her face was expressionless. He went on, "For quite a while after that Calver got by in his *Outsider*. Toward the finish, Sonya was his chief officer—she holds her Master Astronaut's papers, as you know. Trade on the Rim was expanding faster than Rim Runners' fleet and there was plenty of cargo for an independent operator. But, eventually, times got bad for Calver. Rim Runners had sufficient tonnage for all requirements, and a small, one ship company just couldn't compete. It was then that he and his co-owners remembered Maudsley's story, and decided to find the Ship From Outside for themselves. They knew that there was something out beyond the Rim that could make them impossibly rich.

They had Maudsley's sailing directions, such as they were. The Confederacy evinced some slight interest in the matter, and I was able to help out with the loan of a Mass Proximity Indicator—which, in those days, was a *very* expensive hunk of equipment. Even the Federation chipped in. As *you* know, my dear.

"Calver found the Outsiders' Ship. He and his people boarded . . . her? . . . it? A ship? A robot intelligence? A quarantine station? Who knows? But they found the thing. They boarded it. But I'll let Calver speak for himself. This is a recording of the report he made to me."

Grimes switched on the small recorder that was standing ready on the coffee table. He hated himself for raising so many ghosts from Sonya's past—she and Calver had been lovers, he knew—but these ghosts were bound to have been raised during the expedition. Her face was stony, expressionless, as the once familiar voice issued from the little machine.

"Did you ever read a twentieth century Terran author called Wells? He's recommended reading in the 'Fathers of the Future' course they have at most schools. Anyhow, there's one of his stories, a fantasy, called *A Vision Of Judgment.* Wells imagined a Judgment Day, with all living and all who have ever lived called by the Last Trump to face their Maker, to be tried and punished for their sins or, perhaps, to be rewarded for their good deeds. Everyone has his session of Hell as his naked soul stands in full view of the multitude while the Recording Angel recites the long, long catalog of petty acts of meanness and spite. . . . All the trivial (but not so trivial) shabby things, all the things in which even the most perverted nature could never take pride, and even the spectacular wrongdoings made to look shabby and trivial. . . .

"It was left there, the Outsiders' Ship, out beyond the Rim, in the hope that with the development of interstellar flight techniques it would be discovered. It was left there, in the far outer reaches of this galaxy, to test the fitness of its discoverers to use the treasures of science and technology that it contains, to build ships capable of making the Big Crossing. We passed the test without cracking . . . quite. Had we cracked there is little doubt that we should have been bundled off the premises as unceremoniously as Maudsley must have been, bundled outside with memories

of fear and of horror, and of loss, and with some sort of posthypnotic inhibition to stop us from ever talking about it. It's possible, of course, that some of Maudsley's crew did pass the test—but they died with *Polar Queen*.

"The test . . . yes, it's ingenious, and amazingly simple. It's . . . it's a mirror that's held up to you in which you see . . . everything. Yes, *everything*. Things that you've forgotten, and things that you've wished for years that you could forget. After all, a man can meet any alien monster without fear, without hate, after he has met and faced and accepted the most horrible monster of all. . . .

"Himself."

Grimes switched off, then busied himself refueling and lighting his pipe. He said, through the acrid smoke cloud, "Calver came back, as you've gathered, and then he and his engineers did a few odd things to his ship's Mannschenn Drive, and then they all pushed off to . . . ? Your guess is as good as mine. To the next galaxy but three? The general impression was that they had some sort of intergalactic drive. Calver was decent enough to leave me a pile of things—notes and diagrams and calculations. Unfortunately I'm no engineer. . . ."

"You can say that again!" interjected Sonya.

Grimes ignored this. "Our own bright boys tried to make something of them. They actually rebuilt a Mannschenn Drive unit as allegedly specified, but it just won't work. Literally. Every moving part has absolute freedom to move on bearings that are practically frictionless, but . . ." He grinned. "Mayhew reckons that the thing won't work unless its operator is approved by it. Frankly, I can't approve of a *machine* that thinks it has the right to approve or disapprove of *me!*"

"That's only my theory, John," put in Mayhew.

"But you believe it, don't you? Where was I? Oh, yes. After the Calver affair there was quite a flurry of interest in the Outsiders' Ship. The Federation, with our permission, sent *Starfinder* to nose around. She located quite a few derelicts in the vicinity—a Shaara ship, an odd vessel that must have belonged to some incredibly ancient culture, a Dring cruiser. Then she became a derelict herself. When her Carlotti transmissions suddenly stopped we sent *Rim Culverin* to investigate. The *Culverin*'s captain reported that he had boarded *Starfinder* and found all hands very

11

dead; a few had been shot and the rest wiped out by a lethal gas in the air circulation system. Whether or not any of *Starfinder*'s people boarded the Outsiders' Ship we don't know. Probably some, at least, did. *Rim Culverin* was ordered not to investigate The Outsider but to tow *Starfinder* in to Lorn. She did just that. Then our big brothers of the Federation tried again, this time with a Constellation Class cruiser, *Orion. Orion* blew up with no survivors. *Rim Carronade* was with her and saw it happen. *Orion* had put quite a large boarding party onto—or into—the Outsiders' Ship, and it was after their return to their own vessel that the big bang happened. *Rim Carronade* was damaged herself, with quite a few casualties, and returned to Lorn.

"All of you here know me. I'm not one of those people who say, in a revoltingly pious voice, that there are some things that we are not meant to know. For years I've been wanting to take my own expedition out to investigate that hunk of alien ironmongery. I've got my chance at last—and I'm just a little scared.

"And I'm damn glad that I shall have all of you with me."

III

She was an old ship, was *Faraway Quest,* but in first class condition. She had started life as an Epsilon Class tramp, one of those sturdy workhorses of the Federation's Interstellar Transport Commission. Sold to Rim Runners during the days when practically all of the tonnage out on the Rim was at best secondhand, she had been converted into a survey ship. In her, Grimes had discovered and explored the worlds of the Eastern Circuit: Tharn, Mellise, Grollor and Stree. In her he had made the first contact with the antimatter systems to the galactic west.

After secession, the setting up of the Rim Worlds Confederacy, she had been subject to further conversion, this time being fitted out as an auxiliary cruiser. Even though the Rim Worlds Navy now possessed a sizable fleet built to its own specifications, this was still her official status. Nonetheless, Commodore Grimes regarded her as *his* ship.

As Admiral Kravitz had told him, she was practically ready to lift off at once to where The Outsider drifted

in the intergalactic nothingness. She was almost fully stored. Her "farm" was in a flourishing state; her tissue culture, yeast and algae tanks were well stocked and healthy. Main and auxiliary machinery were almost fresh from thorough overhaul. Sundry weaponry had been mounted so that she could play her part in the fleet maneuvers, and this Grimes decided to retain. He liked to think of himself as a man of peace these days but was willing to admit that it is much easier to be peaceful behind laser projections and rocket batteries than in an unarmed ship.

The selection of personnel for the expedition posed no great problems. Billy Williams, normally skipper of the deep space tug *Rim Mamelute*, was available. On more than one occasion he had served as Grimes' second-in-command. James Carnaby, second officer with Rim Runners and an outstandingly competent navigator, had just come off leave and was awaiting reappointment. Like Williams, he held a commission in the Reserve, as did Hendrikson, another Rim Runners' second officer, just paid off from *Rim Griffon*. There was Davis, an engineer whom Grimes knew quite well and liked, and who was qualified in all three Drives: Mannschenn, inertial and reaction. There was Sparky Daniels, currently officer in charge of the Port Forlorn Carlotti Station but who frequently pined for a deep space appointment. And there was Major Dalzell of the Rim Worlds Marines. Grimes had heard good reports of this young space soldier and, on being introduced to him, had liked him at once.

There was what Grimes described as a brain trust of buffoons from the University of Lorn. There was a team of technicians.

There was an officer of the Intelligence Branch of the Federation's Survey Service—just along, as she said, "to see how the poor live." This, of course, was Commander Sonya Verrill, otherwise Mrs. Grimes, who, in spite of her marriage to a Rim Worlder, had retained both her Federation citizenship and her Survey Service commission.

There were the psionicists—Ken Mayhew, one of the last of the psionic communications officers, and Clarisse, his wife. He was a highly trained and qualified telepath. She, born on Francisco, was a descendant of that caveman artist from the remote past who, somehow, on Kinsolving's Planet, had been dragged through time to what was, to him, the

far future. Like her ancestor, Clarisse was an artist. Like him, she was a specialist. Inborn in her was the talent to lure victims to the hunter's snare. Twice, on Kinsolving itself, she had exercised this talent—and on each occasion the hunters had become the victims.

The work of preparing the ship for her voyage went well and swiftly. There was little to be done, actually, save for the rearranging of her accommodations for the personnel that she was to carry, the conversion of a few of her compartments into laboratories for the scientists. Toward the end of the refit Grimes was wishing that on that long ago day when the Rim Worlds had decided that they should have their own survey ship somebody had put up a convincing case for the purchase of an obsolescent Alpha Class liner! Not that there was anything wrong with *Faraway Quest*—save for her relative smallness. And it was not only the civilians who demanded space and yet more space. Officer Hendrikson—who, as a Reserve officer had specialized in gunnery—sulked hard when he was told that he could not have the recreation rooms as magazines for his missiles. (Dr. Druthen, leader of the scientists, was already sulking because he had not been allowed to take them over as workshops.)

Grimes knew that he could not hasten matters, but he chafed at every delay. As long as the *Quest* was sitting on her pad in Port Forlorn far too many people were getting into every act. Once she was up and outward bound he would be king of his own little spaceborne castle, an absolute monarch. Admiral Kravitz had made it clear to him that he would be on his own, that he was to act as he saw fit. It was a game in which he was to make up the rules as he went along.

It was a game that Grimes had always enjoyed playing.

IV

Faraway Quest lifted from Port Forlorn without ceremony; it could have been no more than the routine departure of a Rim Runners' freighter. Grimes had the controls; he loved ship handling and knew, without false modesty, that he was a better than average practitioner of this

14

art. In the control room with him were Sonya, Billy Williams, Carnaby, Hendrikson and Sparky Daniels. Also there, as a guest, was Dr. Druthen. Grimes already did not like Druthen. The physicist was a fat slug of a man, always with an oily sheen of perspiration over his hairless skin, always with an annoyingly supercilious manner. He sat there, a silent sneer embodied. Had he been a crew member he would have faced a charge of dumb insolence.

Daniels was at the NST transceiver, a little man who looked as though he had been assembled from odds and ends of wire, highly charged wire at that. Williams—bulky, blue-jowled, with shaggy black hair—lounged in the co-pilot's seat. He slumped there at ease, but his big hands were ready to slam down on his controls at a microsecond's notice. Slim, yellow-haired, a little too conventionally handsome, Carnaby was stationed at the radar with Hendrikson, also blond but bearded and burly, looking as though he should have been wearing a horned helmet, ready to take over if necessary. He managed to convey the impression that fire control was his real job, not navigation.

And Sonya conveyed the impression that she was just along as an observer. She was slim and beautiful in her Survey Service uniform, with the micro-skirt that would have been frowned upon by the rather frumpish senior female officers of the Confederacy's Navy. She was a distracting influence, decided Grimes. Luckily he knew her well; even so he would find it hard to keep his attention on the controls.

"Mphm," he grunted. Then, "Commander Williams?"

"All stations secured for lift-off, Skipper. All drives on Stand By."

"Mr. Daniels, request clearance, please."

"*Faraway Quest* to Tower. *Faraway Quest* to tower. Request clearance for departure. Over."

The voice of the Aerospace Control officer came in reply. "Tower to *Faraway Quest*. You have clearance." Then, in far less impersonal accents, "Good questing!"

Grimes grunted, keeping his face expressionless. He said into his intercom microphone, "Count down for lift-off. Over to you, Commander Williams."

"Ten . . ." intoned Williams. "Nine . . . Eight . . ."

"A touching ritual," muttered Dr. Druthen. Grimes glared at him but said nothing.

"Five . . . Four . . ."

The Commodore's glance swept the control room, missing nothing. His eyes lingered longer than they should have done on Sonya's knees and exposed thighs.

"Zero!"

At the touch of Grimes' finger on the button the inertial drive grumbled into life. The ship quivered, but seemed reluctant to leave the pad. *I should have been expecting this*, he thought. *The last time I took this little bitch out I wasn't inflicted with this excess tonnage of personnel. . . .* He applied more pressure, feeling and hearing the faint *clicks* as the next two stages were brought into operation. The irregular beat of the drive was suddenly louder.

"Negative contact, sir," stated Carnaby. "Lifting . . . lifting. . . ."

Grimes did not need to look at the instruments. He was flying by the seat of his pants. He could feel the additional weight on his buttocks as acceleration, gentle though it was, augmented gravity. He did not bother to correct lateral drift when the wind caught *Faraway Quest* as soon as she was out of the lee of the spaceport buildings. It did not really matter at which point she emerged from the upper atmosphere of the planet.

Up she climbed, and up, and the drab, gray landscape with the drab, gray city was spread beneath her, and the drab, gray cloud ceiling was heavy over the transparent dome of the control room. Up she climbed and up and beyond the dome; outside the viewports there was only the formless, swirling fog of the overcast.

Up she climbed—and suddenly, the steely Lorn sun broke through, and the dome darkened in compensation to near opacity.

Up she climbed. . . .

"Commodore," asked Druthen in his unpleasantly high-pitched voice, "isn't it time that you set course or trajectory or whatever you call it?"

"No," snapped Grimes. Then, trying to make his voice pleasant or, at least, less unpleasant, "I usually wait until I'm clear of the Van Allen."

"Oh. Surely in this day and age that would not be necessary."

"It's the way that I was brought up," grunted Grimes. He scowled at Sonya, who had assumed her maddeningly

superior expression. He snapped at Carnaby, "Let me know as soon as we're clear of the radiation belt, will you?"

The sun, dimmed by polarization, was still directly ahead, directly overhead from the viewpoint of those in the control room, in the very nose of the ship. To either side now there was almost unrelieved blackness, the ultimate night in which swam the few, faint, far nebulosities of the Rim sky; the distant, unreachable island universes. Below, huge in the after vision screen, was the pearly gray sphere that was Lorn. Below, too, was the misty Galactic Lens.

"All clear, sir," said Carnaby quietly.

"Good. Commander Williams, make the usual announcements."

"Attention, please," Williams said. "Attention, please. Stand by for free fall. Stand by for free fall. Stand by for centrifugal effects."

Grimes cut the drive. He was amused to note that, in spite of the ample warning, Druthen had not secured his seat belt. He remarked mildly, "I thought that you'd have been ready for free fall, Doctor."

The physicist snarled wordlessly, managed to clip the strap about his flabby corpulence. Grimes returned his full attention to the controls. Directional gyroscopes rumbled, hummed and whined as the ship was turned about her short axis. The Lorn sun drifted from its directly ahead position to a point well abaft the *Quest's* beam. The cartwheel sight set in the ship's stem was centered on . . . nothingness. Broad on the bow was the Lens, with a very few bright stars, the suns of the Rim Worlds, lonely in the blackness beyond its edge.

Williams looked toward Grimes inquiringly. The Commodore nodded.

"Attention, please," Williams said. "Stand by for resumption of acceleration. Stand by for initiation of Mannschenn Drive."

Grimes watched the accelerometer as he restarted the engines. He let acceleration build up to a steady one G, no more, no less. He switched on the Mannschenn Drive. Deep in the bowels of the ship the gleaming complexity of gyroscopes began to move, to turn, to precess, building up speed. Faster spun the rotors and faster and their song was a thin, high keening on the very verge of audibility.

And as they spun they precessed, tumbling out of the frame of the continuum, falling down and through the dark dimensions, pulling the vessel and all aboard her with them.

The Commodore visualized the working of the uncanny machines—as he always did. It helped to take his mind off the initial effects: the sagging of all colors down the spectrum, the wavering insubstantiality of the forms, the outlines of everything and everybody, the distortion of all the senses, the frightening feeling of *déjà vu*. He said, making a rather feeble joke of it, "This is where we came in."

The others might be paid to laugh at their commanding officer's witticisms, but Dr. Druthen made it plain that he was not. He looked at Grimes, all irritated and irritating inquiry. "Came in *where?*" he demanded.

Sonya laughed without being paid for it.

Grimes glared at his wife, then said patiently to the scientist, "Just a figure of speech, Doctor."

"Oh. I would have thought that 'this is where we are going out' would have been more apt." Druthen stared out through the viewport, to the distorted Galactic Lens. Grimes, seeing what he was looking at, thought of making his usual remark about a Klein flask blown by a drunken glassblower, then thought better of it. He found it hard to cope with people who had too literal minds.

"And talking of going out," went on Druthen, "why aren't we going out?"

"What do you mean, Doctor?"

"Correct me if I'm wrong, Commodore, but I always understood that the Outsiders' Ship lay some fifty light years out beyond the outermost Rim sun. I'm not a spaceman, but even I can see that we are, at the moment, just circumnavigating the fringe of the galaxy."

Grimes sighed. He said, "Finding The Outsider is like trying to find a tiny needle in one helluva big haystack. At the moment we are, as you have said, circumnavigating the Lens. When we have run the correct distance we shall have the Lead Stars in line or almost in line. I shall bring the Leads astern, and run out on them for fifty light years. *Then* I shall run a search pattern. . . ."

Druthen snorted. What he said next revealed that he must have acquainted himself very well with Grimes' history, his past record. He said sardonically, "What a *seaman-*

like like way of doing it, Commodore. But, of course, you're an honorary admiral of the surface Navy on Tharn, and your Master Mariner's Certificate is valid for the oceans of Aquarius. I would have thought, in my layman's innocence, that somebody would have laid a marker buoy, complete with Carlotti beacon, off The Outsider years ago."

"Somebody did," Grimes told him tersely. "No less than three somebodies did. According to last reports those buoys are still there, but none of them is functioning as a Carlotti transmitter. None of them ever did function for longer than three days, Galactic Standard."

"Steady on trajectory, Skipper," announced Williams.

"Thank you, Commander. Set normal deep space watches," replied Grimes. Slowly he unbuckled himself from his chair. It was customary for the captain of a ship, at this juncture, to invite any important passengers to his quarters for an ice-breaking drink or two. He supposed that Druthen was a passenger of sorts—he had signed no Articles of Agreement—and, as leader of the scientific team he was important enough. Too important.

"Will you join me in a quiet drink before dinner, Doctor?" Grimes asked.

"Too right," replied Druthen, licking his thick lips.

Sonya's eyebrows lifted, although her fine-featured face showed no expression.

V

Druthen drank gin, straight, from a large glass. Sonya sipped a weak Scotch and soda. Grimes drank gin, but with plenty of ice and a touch of bitters. Druthen managed to convey the impression of being more at home in the Commodore's day cabin than its rightful occupants. He talked down at Grimes and Sonya. It was obvious that he considered himself to be the real leader of the expedition, with the astronautical personnel along only as coach drivers.

Patronizingly he said, "Your trouble, Grimes, is that you're too old fashioned. You don't move with the times. I really believe that you'd have been happy in the days of wooden ships and iron men."

"You can say that again," agreed Grimes. He was

pleased to note that Sonya was not taking sides against him, as she usually did when the conversation got on to these lines. He went on, "Then, the shipmaster wasn't at the mercy of his technicians to the extent that he is now."

"And you really believe that . . ." Druthen's pale eyebrows were almost invisible against the unhealthy pallor of his skin, but it was obvious that they had been raised. "But why, my dear Grimes, must you persist in this passion for the archaic? To take just one glaring example—the invention and subsequent development of the Carlotti deep space communications system should have put every over glamorized but unreliable psionic communications officer out of a job. And yet I was amazed to discover that you carry a representative of that peculiar breed aboard this very vessel."

"Ken Mayhew—Commander Mayhew—is an old friend and shipmate. . . ."

"Sentiment, Grimes. Sentiment."

"Let me finish, Druthen." Grimes was childishly pleased to note that the physicist had been offended by the omission of his title. "Let me finish. Commander Mayhew is outstanding in his own field. As long as I have him on board, as well as the Carlotti gadgetry, I shall never be at the mercy of a single fuse. Throughout this voyage he will be in continuous touch, waking and sleeping, with his juniors at the PC Station at Port Forlorn. Too. . . ." But Grimes suddenly decided not to come out with what he had been going to say.

"Go on, Commodore."

I always like to keep at least one ace up my sleeve thought Grimes. He said nothing further about Mayhew's abilities, but went on, "Too, it's just possible that we shall be able to make use of his wife's talents."

Druthen laughed sneeringly. "What sort of outfit *is* this? A telepath and a ghost raiser considered essential to the success of a *scientific* expedition." He raised a pudgy hand. "Hear me out. I've done my homework, Grimes. I've read the reports written by you and about you. I know that you experienced some odd hallucinations on Kinsolving's Planet—but surely you can distinguish between the objective and the subjective. Or can't you?"

"He can," put in Sonya. "And I can. I was there too, one of the times."

"And on the second occasion," said Grimes nastily, "we had a scad of scientists along."

"Agreed," remarked Druthen smugly. "But second-raters, all of them. On the first occasion—correct me if I'm wrong—it was an expedition organized by a group of religious fanatics. On the third occasion there was, with the Commodore and you, Mrs. Grimes, a shipload of fellow spacemen and—women. So. . . ."

Grimes managed to keep his temper. "So it all never happened, Doctor?"

"That is my opinion, Commodore." He refilled his glass without invitation. "Frankly, I maintain that *this* expedition should have been under the command of a hardheaded scientist rather than a spaceman who has shown himself to be as superstitious as the old-time seamen regarding whom he is such an expert."

Grimes grinned mirthlessly. "But I am in command, Doctor."

"That is quite obvious. For example, this wasting of time by running to bring your famous Lead Stars in line rather than steering directly for the last reported position of The Outsider."

Grimes laughed. "As long as I'm in command, Dr. Druthen, things will be done my way. But I will tell you why I'm doing things this way. The Outsider . . . wobbles. Unpredictably. Sometimes it is this side of the Leads, sometimes the other. Sometimes it is further in, toward the Rim, sometimes it is further out. In the unlikely event of its being in the vicinity of the position at which I shall bring the Lead Stars in line it will be within the detection range of several planet-based observatories. It just might be there, but the chances are that it will not be. So I stand out, and out, until I've run my distance, and then if I've picked up nothing on the mass proximity indicator I just cruise around in circles, through an ever expanding volume of space. Quite simple, really."

"Simple!" snorted Druthen. He muttered something about people who must have learned their navigation in Noah's Ark. He splashed more gin into his glass. Grimes was pleased to see that the bottle was empty.

Sonya made a major production of consulting her wristwatch. She said, "It's time that we got dressed for dinner."

Surlily, Druthen took the hint. He finished his drink, got

up clumsily. "Thank you, Commodore. Thank you, Mrs. Grimes. I suppose I'd better freshen up myself. No, you needn't come with me. I can find my own way down."

When the door had shut behind him Grimes looked at Sonya, and she looked at him. Grimes demanded, of nobody in particular, "What have I done to deserve this?"

"Plenty," she told him. Then, "Pour me a drink, a stiff one. I just didn't want to be accused of setting that bastard a bad example."

He complied. "I don't think that anybody could possibly."

She laughed. "You're right." Then, "But don't underestimate him, John. He wasn't the only one doing his homework before we lifted off. I did, too, while you were getting the ship ready. I was able to get my paws on his dossier. To begin with, he's brilliant. Not quite a genius—although he likes to think that he is—but not far from it. He is also notorious for being completely lacking in the social graces."

"You can say that again!"

"But . . . and it's an interesting 'but.' But this he turns to his advantage. When he wants to pick anybody's brains he goes out of his way to annoy them—and, as like as not, they spill far more beans than they would do normally."

"Mphm," grunted Grimes, feeling smugly pleased with himself. "Mphm."

"He resents all authority. . . ."

"Doesn't he just!"

"He feels that he has not received his just due."

"Who doesn't? But since when was this a just universe?"

"In short, he's dangerous."

"Aren't we all in this rustbucket? Aren't we all?" he refilled his glass from the whiskey bottle. "Here's tae us. What's like us? De'il a yin!"

"And thank all the odd gods of the galaxy for *that*," she riposted.

VI

The run out to the departure position was uneventful and reasonably pleasant. It could have been more pleasant; spacemen welcome company aboard their ships whom they

can impress with their shop talk. But the scientists and technicians each had their own mess and, obedient to Druthen, kept themselves to themselves. It could have been unpleasant, Grimes conceded, if Druthen had forced his company upon Sonya and himself. He was content to let well enough alone.

Meanwhile, he could and did enjoy the society of Mayhew and Clarisse, of Billy Williams, of young Major Dalzell, of the other officers. But during the drink and talk sessions it was hard to keep the conversation away from the purpose of their expedition, from the findings and the fates of earlier expeditions.

Why had Calver been successful (if he had been successful)? Why had those before him and after him met disaster? "There's only one way to find out, Skipper," Williams had said cheerfully. "We'll just have to see what happens to *us!* And if you're around, the fat always gets pulled out of the fire somehow!"

"There has to be a first time for everything," Grimes told his second in command with grim humor. "There'll be a first time when the fat won't be pulled out of the fire."

"She'll be right," Williams told him. "Mark my words, Skipper. She'll be right."

And all of them studied the sailing directions, such as they were, until they knew them by heart. "Put Macbeth and Kinsolving's sun in line," the long dead Maudsley had told somebody. "Put Macbeth and Kinsolving's sun in line, and keep them so. That's the way that we came back. Fifty light years, and all hands choking on the stink of frying lubricating oil from the Mannschenn Drive. . . ." And for fifty light years Calver had run, but with the Lead Stars in line astern. He had logged the distance, but had found nothing. He had initiated a search pattern, and at last he had been successful. Those following him had not experienced the same difficulties—but each successive ship had been fitted with an improved model of the mass proximity indicator. Calver's instrument had been no more than a prototype, capable of detection at only short ranges.

On the ship sped, running the Rim, and Carnaby checked and rechecked the fixes that he got from the Carlotti beacons set along the very edge of the galaxy. They were not very accurate fixes; the navigational aids had been posi-

tioned to assist vessels running under Mannschenn Drive from known world to known world, not a ship out where no ship, normally, had any business to be. But Carnaby was a good navigator, possessing the valuable quality of intuition. He could look at a spider's web of intersecting lines and mutter, "That can't be right." He could look at another one and say, "That could be right." Now and again he would state, "This *is* right."

He said firmly, "This *is* right."

Grimes and Williams were with him in the control room. The Commodore did not hesitate. "All right, Commander Williams," he ordered. "You know the drill."

Williams spoke into the most convenient intercom microphone. "Attention, attention. All bridge officers to Control. All hands stand by for shutdown of Mannschenn Drive, free fall and centrifugal effects." Throughout the ship the alarm bells that he had actuated were ringing.

Sonya came in, followed by Hendrikson and Daniels. Each of them went to a chair, strapped himself securely. Druthen came in, bobbing up through the hatch like some pantomime monster. His normally pale face was flushed. He sputtered, "What is the meaning of this, Commodore? We were in the middle of a most important experiment."

"And we, Doctor, are in the middle of a most important piece of navigation."

"There should have been warning."

"There was warning. Three hours ago the announcement was made that the adjustment of trajectory would be at about this time."

"Sir, we shall overrun . . ." warned Carnaby.

"Get into a chair, Druthen!" snapped Grimes.

The scientist, moving surprisingly fast for one of his build, complied, sat there glowering.

"Inertial drive—off!" Grimes ordered.

"Inertial drive—off!" repeated Williams.

The irregular throbbing slowed, ceased. There were weightlessness and loss of spacial orientation.

"Mannschenn Drive—off!"

Down in the Mannschenn Drive room the spinning, precessing gyroscopes slowed to a halt, their thin, high whine dropped to a low humming, a rumble, then was silenced. Sight and hearing were distorted; the time sense was twisted. Grimes heard Sonya whisper, "Odd, very odd. This is the

first time I've seen double. Is it *me*, or is something wrong with the Drive?"

"Did you see double?" asked Carnaby, with professional interest. "*I* didn't, Commander Verrill."

She laughed shakily. "It must have been a manifestation of wishful thinking, or something. It was only my husband, the Commodore, that I saw two of. . . ." She was recovering fast. "And did you see two of *me*, John?"

"One is ample," he replied.

But he had not seen even one of her. The woman who, briefly, had occupied Sonya's seat had not been Sonya, although it was somebody who once had been as familiar to him as Sonya was now.

"I would have thought," commented Druthen, "that you people would have been accustomed by now to the psychological effects of changing rates of temporal precession."

"It's just that we haven't lost our sense of wonder, Doctor," Grimes told him.

He looked out through the viewport. The Lens was there, looking as it should look when viewed in the normal continuum, a glowing ellipsoid against the absolute blackness. Visible against the pearly mistiness were the Rim Suns, sparks upon the face of the haze. Carnaby was busy with his instruments. "Yes," he muttered, "that's Kinsolving all right. Its spectral type can't be confused with anything else . . . Macbeth must be obscured, directly in line with it . . . yes. . . ."

"Set trajectory, Mr. Carnaby?" asked Grimes.

"Yes, sir. You may set trajectory."

"Good." Grimes gave the orders decisively. *Faraway Quest* turned on her directional gyroscopes until the Kinsolving sun was directly astern. Inertial and Mannschenn Drives were restarted. She was on her way.

"I saw two of you again, John," said Sonya in a peculiarly flat voice.

Druthen laughed sneeringly.

And Grimes asked himself silently, *Why did I see her?*

VII

Ever since the first ships, captains have had their confidants. Usually this role is played by a senior officer, but very rarely is it the second-in-command. Ship's doctors, with their almost priestly status, have enjoyed—and still do so enjoy—the status of privileged listeners. But it was not *Faraway Quest*'s doctor whose company Grimes sought when he wished to talk things out. It was Mayhew.

Grimes sat with the psionic communications officer in the cabin that had been put to use as the ship's Psionic Communications Station. As a general rule PCOs used their own living quarters for this purpose, but PCOs did not often carry their wives with them. On this voyage Mayhew was accompanied by Clarisse. Clarisse did not think that the psionic amplifier—the so-called "dog's brain in aspic"—was a pleasant thing to have in plain view all the time, to live with and to sleep with. So Lassie—the name by which Mayhew called his disembodied pet—was banished to a spare cabin that was little more than a dogbox anyhow.

Those wrinkled masses of cerebral tissue suspended in their transparent tanks of nutrient solution gave most people the horrors, and the Commodore was no exception. As he talked with Mayhew he was careful not to look at Lassie. It was hard, in these cramped quarters, to avoid doing so.

"We're on the last leg, Ken," he remarked.

"Yes, John."

"Have you picked anything up from anybody—or anything?"

"I've told Lassie to keep her telepathic ears skinned for any indication that the Waldegren destroyer is in the vicinity. So far—nothing."

"Mphm. Of course, she mightn't have any telepaths on board. Let's face it, Ken, you're one of the last of a dying breed."

"We aren't quite extinct, John, as well you know. Too, everybody transmits telepathically, to a greater or lesser extent. People like myself and Clarisse are, essentially, trained, selective receivers."

"I know." Grimes cleared his throat. "You must have been receiving quite a few things from the personnel of this vessel. . . ."

Mayhew laughed. "I can guess what's coming next. But, as I've told you on quite a few past occasions, I'm bound by my oath of secrecy. We just don't pry, John. If we did pry—and if it became known, as it certainly would—we'd find ourselves the most popular guests at a lynching party. And, in any case, it's not done."

"Not even when the safety of the ship is involved?"

"The old, old argument. All power corrupts, and absolute power corrupts absolutely. I'll not be a party to your corruption."

But Grimes was persistent. "Even when you're not actually prying you must pick a few things up, without trying to, without meaning to. . . ."

"Well, yes. But it's just—how shall I put it?—background noise. Here's a good analogy for you, and one that you'll understand. After all, you're the Rim Worlds' own authority on Terran sea transport from Noah's Ark to the dawn of the Space Age. Think of the early days of radio—or wireless telegraphy as it was then called. Telegraphy, not telephony. Messages tapped out in Morse code, with dots and dashes. There'd be one of the old time Sparkses on watch, his earphones clamped over his head, listening. He'd hear the crash and crackle of static; he'd hear relatively close stations booming in, and thin, mosquito voices of distant ones. But—the only one that he'd actually hear would be the one that he wanted to hear."

"Go on."

"It's like that with Clarisse and myself. We hear a horrid jumble of thoughts all the time but ignore them. But if there were the faintest whisper from the Waldegren ship or from The Outsider we'd do our damnedest to read it loud and clear."

"Yes, I see. But. . . ."

"Something's worrying you, John."

"You don't have to be a telepath to realize that."

Mayhew scowled. "Unless you can convince me that the ship—or anybody aboard her—is in danger I'll not pry."

"Not even on me?"

"With your permission I might. But what seems to be

27

the trouble? Tell me out loud. I'll not put on my thought-reading act unless I have to."

"It was during the alteration of trajectory. You know as well as any of us that there are all kinds of odd psychological effects when the Mannschenn Drive is stopped or restarted."

"Too right."

"This time they were odder than usual. To two of us, at least. To Sonya and myself."

"Go on."

"Sonya . . . saw two of me. No, she wasn't seeing double. There was only one of anybody and anything else in the control room."

"Interesting. I'd have thought that one of you would be ample. And what did you see?"

"Whom did I see, you should have said. I was looking at Sonya. But it was not Sonya whom I saw. Years ago I knew a woman called Maggie Lazenby. She was a specialist officer in the Survey Service, an ethologist, with a doctorate in that science, and commander's rank. Very similar to Sonya in appearance. She married a bloke called Mike Carshalton. He's ad admiral now, I believe."

"Local girl makes good. If she'd married you she'd only be Mrs. Commodore—and a commodore of the Reserve at that."

"I *like* being a commodore of the Reserve. I don't think I'd like being an admiral. But—it was all rather oddish. . . ."

Mayhew laughed. "You, of all people, should be used to the odd things that happen out on the Rim. Don't tell me that you've forgotten the Wild Ghost Chase, in this very ship!"

"Hardly. It was during that when Sonya and I decided to get hitched. But I just don't like these odd things happening at this time."

"Getting choosy in your old age."

"Who's old? But what I'm driving at is this. There's some sort of tie-in with the Outsiders' Ship and Kinsolving's Planet. After all, this business of the Lead Stars—Macbeth and Kinsolving in line. Kinsolving—*and* Macbeth. Years ago, long before our time, there was that odd business on one of the Macbeth planets. A ship from nowhere, old, derelict. A gift horse for the colonists, who didn't look the gift horse in the mouth carefully enough. It came from no-

where and it went back to nowhere—with a few hundred men and women aboard."

"Yes. I've read the story."

"So . . ." murmured Grimes softly.

"So what?"

"I was hoping you'd have some sort of a clue."

"I only work here, John."

"But you're a sensitive."

"A selective sensitive. Do you think it would help if I . . . pried?"

"Go ahead. It's my mind."

"Then . . . relax. Just relax. Don't think of anything in particular. . . ."

Grimes tried to relax. He found that he was looking at that obscenely named animal brain in the transparent container. He tried to look elsewhere, but couldn't. And *it* was aware of him. A dim, wavering image formed in his mind—that of a large, furry dog of indeterminate breed, a friendly dog, but a timid one. What was in his mind's eye was far better than what was in his physical eye, and he was grateful for it. He saw his hand go out and down to pat, to stroke the visionary dog. He saw the plumed tail waving.

Maggie had liked dogs with a sentimentality rare in one qualified in her science. Maggie would like this dog—if she were here. But she was not. She was who knew how many light years distant, and probably very happy as an admiral's lady. But what of all the other Maggies? What of the Maggie whom he had met again, briefly, in that other universe, the doorway into which he had stumbled through on Kinsolving's Planet? How many universes were there—and how many Maggies?

He was jerked back to reality with a start.

Mayhew's voice was coldly censorious. He said, "I wish that you hadn't asked me to do this, John. It's time you realized how bloody lucky you are."

"Eh, what?"

"Lucky I said—and mean. Lucky being married to Sonya. *Her* temporal precession hallucination was just *you*, in duplicate. Yours was an old flame. You're still hankering after her."

"Some men are naturally monogamous, Ken. . . ."

"And some, like you, are not." He laughed. "Oh, well, it takes all sorts to make a universe. Forgive me if I sounded

shocked, but I'd always thought of you and Sonya as being as close as it's possible for two nontelepaths to be. Even a mind reader can be wrong."

"Why shouldn't a man have bread *and* cake?" asked Grimes reasonably. "But the odd part is that Sonya and Maggie are as alike as two slices from the same loaf. They'd pass for sisters. Almost as twin sisters."

Mayhew allowed himself to smile. "I suppose you're in love with a type, John, rather than a person. Oh, well."

Grimes changed the subject. "And how do you find our scientific passengers? Dr. Druthen, I'm sure, regards you and Clarisse as sort of commissioned tea cup readers."

"He would. But that's one mind, John, that I wouldn't care to pry into. The man just oozes bigotry. He's a second-rater, and although he'd hate to admit it, he knows it. That accounts for his attitude toward the universe in general. He has this driving ambition to be on top, no matter what the cost to other people."

"And you haven't pried?"

"No. I have not pried. But every trained telepath is something of a psychologist—not that one needs to be one to figure out what makes a man like Druthen tick."

"Mphm." Slowly Grimes filled and lit his pipe. "Well, thanks, Ken. There're one or two things I'd like to check in Control. I'll see you later."

He let himself out of the little cabin and then, by way of the axial shaft, made his way to the control room. He chatted there for a while with Billy Williams, then went to his own quarters to join Sonya for a drink or two before dinner.

"Why are you looking at me like that?" she asked him.

"There are times," he told her, "when I realize how lucky I am."

VIII

There were times—rather more frequent than he cared to admit—when Grimes was lucky. This was one of them. Part of his luck, perhaps, was in having a really outstanding navigator aboard his ship. Carnaby's last captain had said of him, "He could find a black cat in a coal mine at mid-

night in three seconds flat." This was not far from the truth.

There had been no need whatsoever for *Faraway Quest* to run a wearisome search pattern after the fifty light year plunge outward from the Lead Stars. Carnaby had applied this course correction and that course correction, each time a matter of seconds rather than of minutes or degrees, had played a complicated game of three dimensional—or four dimensional, even—noughts and crosses in the plotting tank, had overworked the ship's computer to such an extent that Williams had said to Grimes, "If the bloody thing had a *real* brain it would go on strike!"

And then the mass proximity indicator had picked up a target just inside its one light year maximum range. Almost directly ahead it was, a tiny spark, a minute bead on the thin, glowing filament that was the extrapolated trajectory. It was time to slow down, although there was no danger of collision. Two solid bodies cannot occupy the same space at the same time—but when one of those solid bodies is proceeding under Mannschenn Drive it is in a time of its own.

Grimes took over personally as the range closed. The tiny spark in the screen slowly expanded to a globe, luminescent, with other tiny sparks in orbit about it. There could be no doubt as to what it was.

The Mannschenn Drive was shut down and *Faraway Quest* proceeded cautiously under inertial drive only, a run of about twelve hours at one G acceleration. The Commodore stayed in Control, smoking, drinking coffee, nibbling an occasional sandwich. His officers, their control room watches completed, stayed on with him. Sonya was there, of course, and so were Mayhew and Clarisse. Major Dalzell was there for most of the time, and even Druthen, uninvited, came up.

The Outsiders' Ship was within radar range now, it and the derelicts circling it. It was within radar range and it could be seen visually at last, a tiny, not very bright star in the blackness where no star had any right to be. The powerful telescope was trained on it, adjusted, and its picture glowed on the forward vision screen. It was. . . . There was only one word for it. It was fantastic. It shone with a light of its own, a cold luminosity, bright but not harsh. It was not a ship so much as a castle out of some

31

old fairy tale, with towers and turrets, cupolas and minarets and gables and buttresses. It should have looked absurd, but it did not. It should have looked grotesque, and it did, but for all the grotesquerie it was somehow . . . right. Its proportions were the only possible proportions.

Grimes stared at the picture, the somehow frightening picture, as did the others. He felt Sonya's hand tighten on his shoulder. The very humanness of the gesture helped him, brought him back to the prosaic reality of the control room of his own ship. There were things to be done.

"Mr. Carnaby," he snapped, "let me have the elements of a stable orbit about this . . . *thing*. Mr. Hendrikson, see if you can ascertain how many derelicts there are in this vicinity. Plot their orbits."

"And have the weaponry in a state of readiness, sir?" asked Hendrikson hopefully.

"Use your tracking system for plotting those orbits," Grimes told him coldly. "It can be used for other things besides gunnery, you know."

Daniels, the radio officer, had not waited for specific orders. He was dividing his attention between the normal space time equipment and the Carlotti transceiver. He reported to Grimes: "I think there's the faintest whisper on the Carlotti, sir. I have it on broad band, but I'll try to get a bearing."

Grimes looked at the pilot antenna, at the elipsoid Mobius strip rotating about its long axis and quivering, hunting, on its universal mount. There was something there, *something*, but it didn't know quite where. He was about to get up from his chair to join Daniels at the communications equipment when, to his annoyance, Druthen remarked, "So you got us here, Commodore." The tone of his voice implied more than mild surprise.

"Yes. I got us here. Excuse me, I'm busy. . . ."

"Sir. . . ." It was the navigator.

"Yes, Mr. Carnaby?"

"All ready, sir. But we'd better not bring her in closer than a couple of miles. That *thing* has the mass of a planetoid."

"Mphm." Carnaby was exaggerating, of course. It was one of his failings. Even so . . . an artificial gravitational field? A distortion of the framework of space itself?

"Sir, I think I have something . . ." broke in Daniels.

"Commander Williams, take over the pilotage, please. Be careful not to run into any of the derelicts that Mr. Hendrikson is using for his make-believe target practice!"

"Good-oh, Skipper."

Grimes unsnapped his seat belt, strode swiftly to the vacant chair beside Daniels, buckled himself in just as the inertial drive was stopped and the ship went into free fall. He saw that the pilot antenna had stopped hunting, was now steady on a relative bearing almost dead astern of *Faraway Quest*, a bearing that slowly changed as Williams began to put the ship into her orbit.

Yes, he could hear a whisper, no more than a faint, faraway muttering, even though the volume control was turned full on. He could not distinguish the words. He did not think that the speaker was using Standard English. He regretted, as he had done before, that he was and always had been so distressingly monolingual.

"New German, I think . . ." Daniels said slowly.

"Sonya," called Grimes, "see if you can get the drift of this!"

But when she joined her husband and Daniels the set was silent again. Perhaps, thought Grimes, Mayhew might be able to pick something up. It was not necessary for him to say it aloud.

"Yes, sir," the telepath almost whispered, "there *is* something, somebody. No, it's not the Waldegren warship you're expecting. . . . It's . . . it's. . . ."

"Damn it all, Commander, who the hell is it?" demanded Grimes.

Mayhew's voice, as he replied, held reproof. "You've broken the very tenuous contact that I'd just begun to make."

"Sorry. But do your best, Commander Mayhew."

"I'm . . . trying. . . ."

"Orbit established, Skipper," reported Williams.

"No dangerous approach to any of the other orbits, sir," reported Carnaby and Hendrikson, speaking as one.

"Yes, yes. Commander Mayhew?"

"I'm trying . . . to try." Mayhew's expression was both very faraway and more than a little pained. "But . . . so much interference. There's somebody we know . . . and there are strangers. . . ."

"Are they in these derelicts? Aboard The Outsider?"

33

"No, sir. If they were close, I should know. But they are distant still. But please, please try not to interrupt any more. . . ."

"Let him go into his trance and get on with the clairvoyance," sneered Druthen.

"Shut up, Doctor! Do you want to be ordered out of Control?" snarled Grimes.

The scientist subsided.

"Please . . ." pleaded Mayhew.

Then there was silence in the control room, broken only by the sibilant whisperings of such machines as, with the ship now in free falling orbit, were still in operation. The soughing of fans, the whining of generators, the very occasional sharp click of a relay. . . .

"Metzenther . . ." muttered Mayhew.

Grimes and Sonya exchanged glances. They were the only two, apart from the psionic communications officer, to whom the name meant anything.

"Trialanne. . . ." He was vocalizing his thoughts for Grimes' benefit. "Metzenther, Trialanne. . . . Where are you bound?" He seemed to find the answer amusing. "No, *we* haven't any company yet, apart from a half dozen or so derelict ships. . . . Be seeing you. . . . Or shall we . . . ? *I* wouldn't know, I'm not a physicist or a mathematician. . . . And can *you* pick up anybody else . . . ? We think we heard a Waldegren ship on our Carlotti. . . . And *I* got the faintest mutter from somebody else. . . . No, not a telepath, just unconscious broadcasting. . . . A servant of some empire or other. . . . Not *yours*, by any chance . . . ? No . . . ?"

"And are we to have the pleasure of meeting that big, blonde cow again?" demanded Sonya coldly.

"She was quite attractive, in a hefty sort of way," Grimes told her.

"You *would* think so."

Mayhew grinned. "I rather think, Commander Verrill, that we shall shortly experience the pleasure of renewing our acquaintance with the ex-Empress Irene, and Captain Trafford, and all the rest of *Wanderer*'s people."

"But they're on a different time track," said Sonya. "And thank all the odd gods of the galaxy for that!"

"Mphm," grunted Grimes. "Mphm." He gestured toward the viewport through which the Outsiders' Ship was clearly

visible. "But here, I think, is where all the time tracks converge."

"I hope you're wrong," said Sonya. "I hope you're wrong. But I'm rather afraid that you're not."

"He's not," confirmed Mayhew.

IX

"Mphm." Grimes made a major production of filling and lighting his foul pipe. "How long before your odd friends get here, Commander Mayhew?"

"*My* friends, sir?"

"Yes. Your friends. Metzenther and his ever-loving. You telepaths always seem to stick together." Grimes grinned. "Frankly, I regarded that ex-Empress woman and her bunch of Imperial Navy throwouts as a pain in the arse. . . ."

Mayhew grinned back. "They thought about you and Commander Verrill in rather the same way."

"Good. But when do they get here?"

The psionic communications officer shut his eyes, concentrated. He said slowly, "In about three hours fifteen minutes Standard."

"That gives us time . . . Commander Williams, I think you'll find one or two Confederate ensigns in the flag locker. You'll want one with wire stiffening, and a pole with a magnetic base. We'll plant our colors on the . . . The Outsider. I doubt if the legality of the claim will be recognized in a court of interstellar law, but it will give us some sort of talking point.

"Meanwhile, probably quite a few of you are wondering what this is all about. *You* know, Commander Williams, and Mayhew knows, but none of the rest of you will have heard the full story. It'll be as well if I put you in the picture." He turned to Williams. "You'd better get your flag planting under way, Commander, just in case Mayhew's ETA is out. And could you lend Commander Williams a couple or three hands for the job, Major Dalzell? And Mr. Daniels, I shall want everything I say put through on the intercom. Thank you."

Williams and Dalzell left the control room. Grimes cleared his throat. He said into the microphone that Daniels

handed him, "Attention, all hands. Attention, all hands. This is important. You will all have seen, in the public information screens, our objective, the Outsiders' Ship. Most of you will have realized that we are now in orbit about it. Shortly you will see a landing party jetting off from this vessel toward The Outsider. They will be planting a flag on it. The reason for this is that we shall soon be having company. This will not be the Waldegren warship that we have been expecting—although she, probably, will be along before very long.

"A few years ago," Grimes continued, "I was instructed to take *Faraway Quest* out to investigate some strange, drifting wreckage—wreckage that, obviously, had not originated in *this* universe. It was the remains of a lifeboat that had belonged to a ship called *Star Scout,* and this *Star Scout* had been a unit of the Imperial Navy. The only empire that *we* know is the Empire of Waverley, and its navy is officially called the Imperial Jacobean Navy. So. . . .

"So we were stooging around, trying to find a few further clues, when this ship, quite literally, appeared from nowhere. Her name was *Wanderer.* She was quite heavily armed, the equivalent to one of our destroyers, but she was privately owned. She had been the yacht of the Empress Irene. She was still owned by the ex-Empress Irene, who was married to her Captain. She carried only a small crew—this Irene woman was mate, as well as owner; a Mr. Tallentire, who had been a gunnery officer in the Imperial Navy was second mate, and his wife, Susanna, had been lady-in-waiting to the Empress, and was now radio-officer-cum-purser. The psionic communications officer was —and still is—a Mr. Metzenther, almost the double of *our* Commander Mayhew. This Metzenther had—has—an Iralian wife called Trialanne. We don't have any Iralians on this time track. They were all wiped out by a plague. Bronheim was the engineer. He, too, had an Iralian wife— Denelleen. . . ."

"Not now he doesn't," Mayhew said soberly. "I've been catching up on past history with Metzenther. Do you mind if I take over, sir?"

"Go ahead, Commander."

"Mayhew speaking. As you all will, by this time, have gathered, I am in psionic touch with the yacht *Wanderer.* She was thrown, somehow, on to this time track when

she attempted the passage of the Horsehead Nebula. She was pursued by two New Iralian cruisers—the New Iralians being insurgents. She was carrying Iralian passengers, some of whom were in sympathy with the rebels. With our help she shook off pursuit, and then tried to get back into her own universe by running back through the Nebula. She was overtaken, but came out on top in the running fight. But the rebels among the passengers tried to take over the ship. Denelleen was one of them. . . . Anyhow, the mutineers were defeated. And that's about all."

"That was *then*," said Grimes. "What are these people doing here *now?*"

"You may remember, sir," Mayhew told him, "that when we last met them they were on charter to an organization called GLASS—Galactic League Against Supression and Slavery. They're still on charter to GLASS. GLASS has the idea that the science and technology in the Outsiders' Ship will be useful to them in their work."

"So *they*: the ex-Empress, GLASS and all the rest of 'em have an Outsiders' Ship in *their* universe. So—as I've already guessed—it's not a different one, but the same one as we have. So the time tracks meet and mingle right here." The Commodore laughed. "Who else shall we meet, I wonder. . . ."

Sonya said flatly, "Williams has planted the flag."

"And so we, more or less legally, own *it*," said Grimes. He added softly, "Unless *it* owns us."

"Rubbish!" sneered Druthen.

Grimes ignored the man.

X

"I just might," suggested Daniels diffidently, "be able to establish Carlotti contact with *Wanderer*. I think that the time tracks will almost have converged by now."

"Mphm," grunted Grimes, giving thought to the possibility. Technologically his universe and the universe of the ex-Empress Irene were almost twins. At the time of his previous encounter with the so-called yacht she had possessed Carlotti equipment almost identical to his own. "Mphm." Then, "No, Mr. Daniels. Concentrate on that

Waldegren destroyer. She's our main worry." He looked out through the viewport and was relieved to see that Williams and the two marines, silvery figures trailing luminous blue exhausts, were almost back to the ship.

"Looks like being quite a party," commented Sonya. "The big, fat blonde, Irene, with her playmates, *and* our dear friends from Waldegren. . . ."

"No friends of mine," growled Grimes. "I was at the Battle of Dartura. . . . Remember?"

"Long before my time, dearie," she commented.

"Commodore! Sir!" broke in Carnaby. "A target, on the radar!"

"Not one of the derelicts, Mr. Carnaby?"

"No. It just appeared out of nothingness. It's closing on us, fast."

"Mr. Hendrikson—all weapons to bear. Do not open fire without orders. Mr. Daniels, try to establish contact. Commander Mayhew—is it *Wanderer?*"

"No, sir."

"Then who the hell . . . or *what* the hell . . . ?"

"Locked on, sir," reported Hendrikson.

"Good."

"Range still closing, but less rapidly. We should have her visually in a few seconds." said Carnaby.

"Thank you. Commander Williams, the telescope."

"Aye, aye, Skipper!"

"No contact, sir," murmured Daniels. "But I *can* hear the Waldegren ship again. She's still distant."

"I've got her in the telescope," drawled Williams. "Odd looking bitch . . . she's on the screen now, if you care to take a butcher's."

Grimes took a "butcher's hook," reflecting that life was already sufficiently complicated without his second-in-command's rhyming slang. The strange ship was there, exactly in the center of the circle of blackness, a silver moth pinned against the backdrop of the night. As she approached, her image expanded rapidly. She was a gleaming disc—but, Grimes realized, he was looking at her head on—from which sprouted a complexity of antennae. And then, slowly, she turned, presenting her profile. Apart from that veritable forest of metallic rods she was not unlike the Survey Service courier that had been Grimes' first command long ago, so very long ago, one of the so-called "flying darning

needles." As yet she had made no hostile move. But, assuming that she was alien, captained by a nonhuman or, even, by a nonhumanoid, would a hostile move be recognized as such before it was too late?

Grimes flashed a glance at Hendrikson, hushed intently over his console. *He* was ready; possibly rather too ready. He looked back at the screen. He thought, he was almost sure, that the lines of the strange vessel showed a human sense of proportion. He snapped at Daniels, "Haven't you raised her yet?"

"I'm . . . I'm trying sir. I've tried every frequency known to civilized Man, and a few that aren't. . . . Ah! Got it!"

There was a babble of sound from the speaker of the NST transceiver. Alien gibberings? No. . . . It sounded more like human speech, but horridly distorted, garbled.

Daniels spoke very slowly and distinctly into his microphone. "Rim Worlds Confederacy's cruiser *Faraway Quest* to unknown vessel. *Faraway Quest* to unknown vessel. Come in, please. Come in, please. Over."

In reply came the meaningless gabble.

Daniels was patient, carefully adjusting his tuning. "*Faraway Quest* to unknown vessel. Please identify yourself. Please identify yourself. Over."

"A shi? A shi?"

What ship? What ship? It could be, thought Grimes.

"A shi? A shi? Dringle na puss. Gleeble."

Tickle my puss? Hardly.

"We'll try visual," said Grimes. "Pass me the key, will you? I don't think that my Morse is too rusty."

Williams passed him the Morse key on its long lead. Grimes took it in his right hand, his thumb on the button. He sent a series of "A"s, the general calling sign. He assumed that somebody, by this time, would have the *Quest*'s big searchlight trained on the stranger. He kept his attention on the image in the telescope screen.

Yes, he, whoever (or whatever) he was seemed to know Morse. The acknowledgment, the long flash, the Morse "T," was almost blindingly obvious.

"What ship?" sent Grimes. "What ship?"

From the other came a succession of "A"s. Grimes replied with "T." Then, "What ship?" he read. "What ship?"

So . . . so was the stranger repeating parrot fashion, or was he being cagey?

"What ship?" sent Grimes again. "What ship?"

"What ship?" he received.

He sent, not too slowly but carefully, making sure that each word was acknowledged, "Identify yourself, or I open fire."

He grinned when the reply came, "You'd better not."

He said aloud, "Not only human, but our sort of people." He flashed, "This is the Rim Worlds Confederacy's cruiser *Faraway Quest*. You are intruding into our sector of space. Please identify yourself."

"Imperial Navy's armed scout *Vindictive*. Rim Worlds Confederacy's Navy not listed in Jane's. Never heard of Rim Worlds Confederacy. Who the hell are you?"

"Commander Williams," said Grimes, "*Jane's Fighting Ships* is in the computer's library bank. Check *Vindictive*, will you? And the Imperial Navy."

"Will do, Skipper. But the only Imperial Navy *we* have is the Waverley one."

"I know. But check it, anyhow." Again his thumb worked rhythmically on the key. "This is *Faraway Quest*. This is Rim Worlds space. You are intruding."

"You are intruding."

Grimes grinned again, sent, "Can't we talk this over?"

For long seconds there was no reply. Carnaby reported that the stranger was no longer closing the range, was maintaining her distance. Hendrikson announced, unnecessarily, that his weaponry was still in a state of readiness.

Daniels asked, "Can I have the key, sir? If I have a yarn with her radio officer I shall be able to find out what frequencies to use. . . ."

And then *Vindictive* started flashing again. "Request permission to board."

"One man only," Grimes replied.

More time passed. Then, "Please prepare to receive my boat."

Oh, no, thought Grimes. *Oh, no.* The dividing line between a boat and a torpedo is a very narrow one. He was satisfied by now that *Vindictive*'s people were human; but the human race has a long record of viciousness and treachery, far too often actuated by the very highest motives.

"One man in a suit," he sent, "will meet one man in a suit, midway between our two vessels. They will return to

Faraway Quest together. You may close the range between ships to ten miles. Do not forget that all my weapons are trained on you, and that my gunnery officer has a very itchy trigger finger." He said aloud, "And I have a very sore thumb."

"Agreed," sent *Vindictive* at last. "Closing. Please remember that you are a big target."

"Commander Mayhew," asked the Commodore, "can you pick up anything, anything at all, from those people?"

"Faintly . . ." replied the telepath slowly. "Very faintly. I sense suspicion, distrust. They will fire if they think that they are about to be fired upon."

"And so will we. And now—who's for the space walk? Don't all answer at once."

There was no shortage of volunteers, but Mayhew's rather high voice was distinctly heard above the others. "There's only one possible choice, sir. Me. When I get close to whoever *they* send I should be able to read his thoughts more easily. And Clarisse can look after the shop in my absence."

"Mphm. Very well, Ken. Get suited up. And—look after yourself."

"I always have done, John, all the years that you've known me." He said nothing to Clarisse, but it was not necessary. Accompanied by Williams he left the control room.

"Please let me know when you are ready," flashed *Vindictive*.

"Willco," replied Grimes.

XI

"I suppose that it has occurred to you," said Sonya, "that this *Vindictive*, of which no mention is made in *our* version of *Jane's Fighting Ships*, could be from that Irene woman's universe. After all, she is supposed to be a unit of the Imperial Navy."

"The thought had flickered across my mind," admitted Grimes, "even though I'm not, and never have been, an intelligence officer." In spite of the absence of gravity he contrived to lay back in his chair. "We rather gathered,

the last—and the only, so far—time that we met the ex-Empress that her employers, these GLASS people, were regarded by the Imperial Government as more than somewhat of a nuisance. Shit stirrers, if you'll pardon the expression."

"I've heard worse. Continue."

"So it is reasonable to suppose that if GLASS want to get their paws on The Outsider and The Outsider's secrets, the Imperial Navy could be sent out to make sure that they didn't. But. . . ."

"What is your 'but'?"

"But I don't think that *Vindictive* was built by the same technology as Irene's *Wanderer*. *Wanderer*, like *Faraway Quest*, had all sorts of odd lumps and bumps on her hull, but she didn't look like a deep space hedgehog. Too, neither *Wanderer* nor ourselves experienced any trouble in initiating either Carlotti or NST radio telephone hookups."

"H'm. I suppose we could get Clarisse to ask that man Metzenther, aboard *Wanderer*, if they're being followed. Not that you can call it being followed when the pursuer gets there hours before the pursued."

"That, my dear, is very sound tactics, when you can manage it."

Williams' voice came over the intercom. "Commander Mayhew suited up an' in the after airlock."

Then, over the transceiver that was operating on the suit frequencies, Mayhew reported, "All ready, sir."

Grimes flashed the signal to *Vindictive*, read the reply, "The Captain is on his way."

"A do-it-yourself-trust-nobody type," commented the Commodore. "Tell Commander Mayhew to shove off."

He felt a slight twinge of anxiety—but, after all, Mayhew was a spaceman as well as a telepath, and Williams would have given him a thorough briefing. It would be simple enough; just switch on the suit's reaction unit and steer straight for the other ship, keeping eyes skinned for the blinker that would be flashing from *Vindictive*'s captain's helmet. But did this peculiar Empire in some peculiar universe observe the same rules of spacemanship as were observed in Grimes' continuum?

Obviously it did. All the lights of *Vindictive* went out, as had all the lights showing from *Faraway Quest*. This would make it easier for the spacewalkers; each of them

42

now would see only the little, but bright beacon toward which he was steering.

Carnaby had the radar on short range, was tracking both space suited men. He was speaking into the microphone of the transceiver. "That's fine, Commander. Steady. . . . Steady as you go. . . . Better shut off your propulsion. . . . Be ready for a retro-blast. . . ."

Grimes, staring through the viewport, could see the two blinking lights almost as one, so nearly in line were they. Surely Mayhew hadn't much further to go. . . .

"Brake, Commander," came Carnaby's voice. "Brake! Yes, he's braking too. Now . . . just a nudge ahead . . . that's it!"

And from the transceiver's speaker came Mayhew's whisper. "Contact. Contact established. He's tough, Commodore. Hard to get inside. . . . But . . . I can assure you that he intends no treachery."

Grimes took the microphone. "Does he know that you're . . . prying?"

"I don't think so."

"Can he hear you? Me?"

"No, sir. I'm careful that our helmets don't come into contact."

"Good. Go through the motions of searching him for any weapons that he may have outside his suit. Then you can touch helmets and talk to him."

"Very good, sir."

There was a silence that seemed to drag on and on. At last Mayhew said, "Be ready to receive us on board, Commodore."

Williams called up from the after airlock to say that Mayhew and the man from *Vindictive* were aboard, and that he was bringing them up to Control. Grimes found himself wondering what his visitor would be like. He was an officer in the armed forces of an empire—and Empire sounded far more glamorous than Federation or Confederacy. *He's probably got a title,* thought Grimes idly, *and a string of letters after his name half a light year long.* He glanced around his control room, missing nothing. All of his officers were in correct uniform, although some of them were more than a little untidy in appearance. Druthen, of course,

was his usual slovenly self—but he was a mere civilian, a passenger.

Williams came up through the hatch. "Commander Mayhew, Skipper," he announced cheerfully. Mayhew, still suited up but carrying his helmet under his left arm, followed Williams. "And Captain Sir Dominic Flandry, of the Imperial Navy. Sir Dominic, may I present Commodore John Grimes, of the Rim Worlds Naval Reserve?" Commander Williams was plainly enjoying himself.

Grimes looked at Flandry. He was not at all sure if he liked what he saw. The Captain of *Vindictive* was a tall man, and conveyed the impression of slimness even in his bulky spacesuit. The suit itself was gleaming black with gold trimmings. The helmet that Flandry carried tucked under his arm was also black, with a wreath of golden oak leaves on its visor, with, as an ornate badge, a golden eagle with outspread wings gripping a conventionalized planetary globe in its talons. His face was harsh, with a fierce beak of a nose, and the pencil line black moustache over the sensual mouth should have looked foppish—but somehow didn't. The glossy black hair was touched with gray at the temples. The eyes were a pale blue, and very bleak.

"Your servant, Commodore," said Flandry stiffly.

That'll be the sunny Friday when you're any man's servant, thought Grimes. He said, "Good to have you aboard, Captain. Or should I say, 'Sir Dominic'?"

"Either will do, Commodore." Flandry's sharp eyes were flickering around the control room, missing nothing, missing nobody. They lingered for a few seconds on Clarisse —and for longer on Sonya. *Of course,* thought Grimes, *she would be wearing that indecent micro-skirted Federation uniform.* Flandry said, "You carry a mixed crew, Commodore."

"Mphm. Yes. Although the ladies are specialist officers. Mrs. Mayhew. . . ." Clarisse unbuckled herself from her chair, came forward. "This is Captain Flandry, of *Vindictive*. Captain Flandry, this is Mrs. Mayhew, our assistant psionic communications officer . . ."

"Psionic communications? A telepath . . . and I take it that Commander Mayhew, whom you sent out to meet me, is your chief psionic communications officer. . . ."

He looked at Clarisse again, and suddenly she flushed.

Flandry laughed. "Sorry," he said. "Sorry, my dear. I should have had the sense to keep my thoughts under proper control." But he did not sound sorry, and Clarisse, although embarrassed, did not look at all resentful.

"And this is Commander Verrill, of the Federation's Survey Service. She is acting as the Federation's observer on this expedition."

"And not a telepath, I take it," murmured Flandry. He looked as though he were undressing Sonya with his eyes—not that she needed much undressing, thought Grimes, in that apology for a uniform. And he did not like the way that she was looking back at the Imperial captain.

Grimes introduced his other officers, and then Druthen. He said, "And now, Sir Dominic, I suggest that we withdraw to my quarters for discussion. Commander Williams, please accompany us. Commander Mayhew, Mr. Daniels—please let me know at once if either of you hear anything further from *Wanderer* or *Adler*."

"*Wanderer?*" asked Flandry, with a lift of one eyebrow.

"One of yours, possibly. She's the private yacht of the ex-Empress Irene."

"Then *not* one of ours," laughed the other. "We don't have an empress. We never have had an empress. I, sir, have the honor . . ." and he made it sound a dubious honor . . . "of serving His Imperial Majesty Edouard XIV. And this *Adler?*"

"A destroyer sailing under the flag of the Duchy of Waldegren."

"The Duchy of Waldegren? Never heard of it."

The officers were looking at Grimes and his visitor curiously. The Commodore decided that they had better continue their discussion in greater privacy. He said, "This way, please, Sir Dominic."

On the way to his suite he noticed that Flandry did not handle himself very well in free fall. So, probably, *Vindictive* ran to some sort of artificial gravity, and when in orbit her officers did not have to cope with the problems of weightlessness. He decided to get one of his engineers aboard the armed scout if it were at all possible. There must be quite a few technologies aboard her well worth copying.

The sliding door opened as Grimes approached it. He stood to one side, waving the others into his day cabin

ahead of him. Flandry moved clumsily, shuffling his feet, in their magnetically soled boots, on the deck.

Grimes said, "This is Liberty Hall. You can spit on the mat and call the cat a bastard."

Sonya looked at him coldly. "This is the first time I've heard you say that for quite some time, John. I'd hoped you'd forgotten it."

Flandry flashed her a smile. "It *is* a vivid figure of speech, Commander Verrill. Have you known the Commodore for a long time?"

"Yes. I'm married to him."

"Commodore Grimes, have you any *unmarried* ladies among your crew as attractive as the two ladies I have already met?"

"No, I haven't." Then, in a less surly tone of voice, "Sit down, Captain. And perhaps you will take a drink with us. . . ."

"I'll be glad of the drink—but this suit's not made for sitting in. And when in a strange ship, quite possibly a hostile ship, I prefer to keep it on."

"As you please, Captain Flandry. And you'll have to take my word for it that the drinks aren't drugged or poisoned." Grimes pulled himself into his own chair, strapped himself in. Sonya followed suit. Williams was about to do likewise when Grimes told him to look after the refreshments. Efficiently the Commander produced bulbs of the drink required. Flandry asked for Scotch.

"Your health, Captain Sir Dominic!"

"Your health, Commodore Grimes." Again there was that sardonic smile. "But should I, as a loyal servant of His Imperial Majesty, be drinking your health?"

"And why the hell shouldn't you be?" demanded Grimes crustily.

"And why should I, Commodore—if you *are* a commodore. Oh, I'll let you have your rank. Even pirates must have officers."

"Pirates? What the hell are you getting at?"

"Pirates." Flandry's voice was harsh. "Pirates, setting themselves up as petty kings on the fringes of a disintegrating Empire. Laying their grubby paws on Imperial property, even planting their absurd flag on it. Tell me, Commodore Grimes, what genius thought up that black banner with a golden wheel on it? What does it signify?"

Grimes didn't answer the question directly. He snapped, "*Imperial* property? I suppose you're referring to that heap of alien ironmongery that somebody left in *our* back yard. The Outsiders' Ship, as we call it, lies within Rim Worlds' territorial space."

"Does it? And who, or what, are the Rim Worlds? The Outsider, as we call it, was first discovered by Admiral Lord Wolverhelm, who commanded the *Fringe Sweep*."

Grimes eyed Flandry cautiously. He thought, *The bastard's enjoying himself. He's trying to make us lose our tempers.* He said, "Neither the Federation nor the Confederacy runs to 'sirs' and 'lords.' The Empire of Waverley does, of course—but it would never dream of sending an expedition out here without our permission."

"Odd name for a ship—the *Fringe Sweep* . . ." commented Williams.

"That, sir, was the designation of the mission," Flandry told him coldly.

"In any case," put in Sonya, who had been silent for too long, "the Outsiders' Ship was first discovered by Commander Maudsley of the Federation's Survey Service. But the Federation recognizes the territorial rights of the Confederacy."

"Somebody," grinned Flandry, "is going to have a good laugh over this conversation." He lifted a gloved hand to tap the collar of his suit, just below the throat. Grimes thought with no surprise, *A concealed microphone.* "In the unlikely event of my not getting back to my ship, all that's being said is being recorded aboard *Vindictive*. It is also being relayed to our nearest base. My masters will already have come to the conclusion that I have blundered into a nest of pirates. . . ."

"Watch it, mate," growled Williams. "Watch it!"

In a blur of motion Flandry snapped on his helmet. His voice, only slightly distorted, issued from a diaphragm. He said, "This suit, gentlemen—and Commander Verrill—is proof against anything that you can throw at me. Probably I should not survive a nuclear blast—but neither would you. And now, if you will excuse me, I must return to my own vessel. I strongly advise that nobody try to stop me."

Grimes said dryly, "As I recollect it, Captain, the main purpose of this meeting was that we should talk things over.

47

I suppose that you can hear what I'm saying inside that gaudy carapace of yours."

"Of course. Say what you must say."

"Well, Captain Flandry, we haven't talked things over. You've jumped to conclusions, assumed that I'm a pirate king or some such. If I were, I'd not be content with the rank of commodore! It's a wonder that you didn't see that wheel of ours on the black flag as a skull and crossbones! Just try to understand this. As far as *we* are concerned, *you* are the intruder."

"And how can that be, Commodore?"

"Been out on the Rim before, Captain Flandry? Or the Fringe, as you people call it?"

"Nobody comes out here but outlaws."

"And yourself, of course. And that Admiral Lord what's-his-name before you. But we live on the Rim. We *know* that here, at the very edge of the expanding universe, the walls between the alternate time tracks are very thin indeed, at times nonexistent. We have good reason to believe that the Outsiders' Ship has warped the continuum about itself so that this small volume of space is common ground for ships—and people—from all the universes. . . ."

"You tell a good fairy story, Commodore."

The intercom buzzed sharply; then Carnaby's voice came through the speaker. "Commodore, sir, *Wanderer* has just broken through! And Mr. Daniels thinks that *Adler* is very close. She is reporting back to her base in some sort of code."

"Reinforcements, Commodore Grimes?" asked Flandry coldly.

Briefly Grimes was tempted to say yes. But that could have been dangerous. This Flandry, feeling himself to be outnumbered, would be quite capable of ordering his ship to lash out with all weapons like a vicious cornered animal. "No," he said slowly. "No. Just old friends—or acquaintances, rather—and old enemies."

"Commodore, sir!" It was Carnaby again. "Mr. Daniels says there's *another* ship using a Carlotti transmitter!"

"Cor stone me Aunt Fanny up a gum tree!" marveled Williams. "How many *more* are goin' to turn up at the Vicar's flamin' afternoon tea party?"

"So," said Flandry, "we seem to have met at the crossroads of the universe. If you are to be believed, that

is. . . . But I think you will agree that I should return to my own vessel."

"If I were in your shoes I should be saying the same," agreed Grimes. "Commander Williams, escort Captain Flandry to the airlock."

"And how shall I keep in touch—assuming, of course, that I wish to do so? By flashing lamp?"

"Get your radio officer to talk to mine on the blinker. Perhaps, between the pair of them, they'll be able to cook something up."

"I'll tell him now." Grimes could see, through the frontal transparency of Flandry's helmet, the man's lips moving, but he could hear nothing. Then: "Before I go, just one more question. These people in *Wanderer* . . . are they friendly or hostile?"

"They could be either. And, to save you the trouble of asking another question, I haven't a clue as to who or what this other strange ship is."

"If this is the Rim," said Flandry, "you're welcome to it." He bowed stiffly to Sonya. "Although life out here seems to have its compensations."

Then he followed Williams out to the axial shaft.

XII

Grimes and Sonya hurried back to the control room.

As Carnaby had told him, *Wanderer* had arrived. She was hanging there in the blackness, slim, sleek and deadly looking, no more than a couple of cables from *Faraway Quest*. Typical, thought Grimes, of Irene Trafford or the ex-Empress Irene or whatever she called herself these days. But the Commodore, over the years, had become more of a merchant officer than a naval officer in his outlook and just could not see the point of exposing a vessel, any vessel, to unnecessary hazard.

Anyhow, there she was, and close, too close. Grimes thought of actuating his inertial drive to put more distance between himself and the armed yacht—but, damn it all, he was here first. Why should he shift?

The screen of the NST transceiver glowed into life. Colors swirled, coalesced; and then Grimes was looking into

the control room of the other ship. Yes, there was Irene, big and brassy as ever, with the careful touch of nonuniform color, the crimson cravat with the white polka dots, added to her otherwise correct attire. Before she became empress, she had been a tough mate in the Dog Star Line, and this outfit, in Grimes' universe as well as in hers, was notorious for its rough and ready star tramps. She had been mate in the Dog Star Line, and was determined that nobody should ever be allowed to forget it. Beside her sat Benjamin Trafford, officially master of *Wanderer*. The little, wiry, sandy-haired man was as neat and correct as he would have been had he still been serving in the Imperial Navy. And behind them Grimes saw the dark, dapper Tallentire, alert at his fire control console; and with him Susanna: tall, slender and with high-piled and glossy auburn hair. There was Metzenther who, if he shaved off his beard, would be almost the double of Grimes' Mayhew. There was Trialanne, the Iralian woman: frail, willowy, beautiful, looking as though she had been blown from translucent glass by a master craftsman who was also a superb artist.

And there was a stranger, a most undistinguished looking man of medium height, dressed in a drab, gray coverall suit. Normally one would not look at him twice. But in *Wanderer*'s control room he was a sparrow among hawks and drew attention. Grimes decided suddenly, *He's hard and dangerous, whoever he is. . . .*

"Commodore Grimes," said Irene in the voice that was almost a baritone.

"Your servant, ma'am," replied Grimes politely—after all, she had been an empress—while, behind him, Sonya snorted inelegantly.

"Come off it, Commodore. Nature never intended you to be a courtier."

"You can say that again," remarked Sonya quietly.

"Commodore Grimes, may I ask what the hell you and your spaceborne junk heap are doing in *our* universe?"

"I might ask the same question of you, Mrs. Trafford."

"Just because I jumped time tracks once—and that accidentally—you needn't think that I make a habit of it."

"Neither do I," said Grimes flatly. This was not quite true, but Irene and her people would not know this.

"And what's that odd looking ship like a tin sea urchin?

You must know. We saw a man in a spacesuit jetting off from your vessel to her."

"One of yours, isn't she? Her captain says that she's the Imperial Navy's armed scout *Vindictive.*"

"*Not* one of ours," said Trafford firmly. "We *do* have a *Vindictive,* Commodore, but she's a light cruiser. I should know. I've served in her."

"Irene," asked that drab, too ordinary man in a voice that matched his appearance, "would you mind putting me in the picture? Who *are* these people?"

"Mr. Smith," said the big blonde, "allow me to present Commodore Grimes, of the Rim Worlds Naval Reserve. In *his* cockeyed continuum the Rim Worlds are self-governing. And Commander Sonya Verrill, who is also Mrs. Grimes, of the Federation's Survey Service. Their Federation is roughly analogous to our Empire. The only other person I know is Mr. Mayhew, who is *Faraway Quest*'s psionic communications officer.

"And this gentleman, Commodore, is Mr. Smith, managing director of GLASS. We have been chartered by him to lay claim to and to investigate the Outsiders' Ship."

"The Outsiders' Ship," Grimes told her firmly, "is in the territorial space of the Rim Worlds Confederacy. Furthermore, we have planted our flag on it."

"According to Space Law," stated Irene, "the mere planting of a flag is not sufficient for laying claim to any planet, planetoid, satellite or whatever. For a claim to be valid a self-sustaining colony must be established. I doubt very much if you have gone so far as that. In any case, the Outsiders' Ship is within Imperial territorial space."

"And *which* Empire, madam?" demanded a sardonic voice.

Daniels whispered, "I've managed a hookup with *Vindictive,* sir. That was Captain Flandry."

"Who the hell was that?" demanded Irene.

"The captain of *Vindictive,*" Grimes replied. "But let us continue our discussion of the finer points of Space Law. As I see it, that *thing* is neither a planet, a planetoid nor a satellite. It is a derelict. . . ."

"It could be held to be a satellite," insisted Irene. "An artificial satellite. . . ."

"A satellite must have a primary."

"Oh, all right, you bloody space lawyer. It's a derelict.

But have you put a prize crew on board? Have you got a towline fast to it?"

"My flag. . . ."

"You know what you can do with that!"

In the little screen Trafford looked both shocked and embarrassed. Tallentire tried to hide a grin. Smith did not try to hide his.

"Mphm," grunted Grimes disapprovingly; and, "What charming friends you have, Commodore," commented Flandry.

"Acquaintances, Captain," Grimes told him.

"As you wish. But might I suggest, sir, that all three parties convene to discuss matters in a *civilized* fashion?"

"That could be worth considering," admitted Grimes reluctantly.

"And might I urge that we do it as soon as possible, if not before? As yet our three ships haven't opened fire on each other—but who knows what might happen when the other two vessels in the vicinity put in an appearance?"

"He's talking sense," said Sonya.

"*What* other two vessels?" demanded Irene. "We only know of the Waldegren destroyer, *Adler*. Who is the other one?"

"I wish I knew," sighed Grimes.

"Well, Commodore?" snapped Flandry. Grimes was sorry that Daniels had not been able to arrange a visual as well as an audio hookup. He would have liked to have been able to read the other's expression.

"Well, Commodore?" echoed Irene.

"Your place or mine?" asked Grimes, with an attempt at humor.

"Neutral territory," said Flandry. "While all the nattering was going on my first lieutenant sent a boarding party to that odd, dome-shaped derelict about 10 kilometers beyond *Vindictive* from your viewpoint. Its late owners were oxygen breathers, although not human. All its life-support systems were intact, and are now functioning. . . ."

"A Shaara ship," stated Grimes.

"The *Shaara?*" asked Irene and Flandry simultaneously. And then Flandry demanded, "And who the hell are they when they're up and dressed?"

"Never mind," said Grimes. "The Shaara ship will do very nicely."

XIII

The Shaara derelict was a good place for a meeting. The ship was in good order and condition; her interior lighting glowed brightly; her humming fans kept the clean, untainted air in circulation. How long had they been doing so? Not for too long. The mosslike growth in the hydroponics tanks that the Shaara used for atmospheric regeneration was neither running wild nor withering for lack of the organic wastes that were its food. But of her crew: of the Queen-Captain, the Princess-Officers, the Drones, the Workers, there was no sign—not even so much as a dry exoskeleton. The logbook was still on its ledge in the control room; but no human could hope to read that straggling script.

She was a latter day *Mary Celeste*. She was one of several *Mary Celestes* in orbit about The Outsider.

Boats from the three ships had rendezvoused at the airlock of the derelict. Grimes himself had piloted *Faraway Quest's* pinnace. With him he had Sonya and Mayhew. Irene had brought with her Trialanne and Stanley Smith, the man from GLASS. Flandry was accompanied only by a simian young officer, almost as broad as he was tall, whom he introduced as Ensign Bugolsky.

This, of course, was when they were all assembled in the Shaara ship's control room, standing among the equipment and instruments, some familiar (although modified to suit arthropodal claws instead of human hands) and some weirdly alien. There were cradles of flimsy-looking webbing but no seats. As the vessel was in free fall, to stand was no hardship.

Flandry, resplendent in his black and gold space armor, removed his helmet. The others removed theirs. Grimes didn't like the way that the man looked at Irene and Trialanne. He most certainly didn't like the way that the man looked at Sonya. And he disapproved most strongly of the way in which the three women looked at Flandry. Mental undressing can be a two-way process.

"And now," announced Flandry with a wide grin, "I declare this meeting open."

53

"Not so fast, Captain," Grimes told him. "As the senior officer present I feel that that should be my privilege."

"Senior officer? But *I* represent the Imperium."

"*What* Imperium?" demanded Irene nastily.

"Commodore!" Mayhew's usually soft voice was sharp with urgency. "Commodore! Sir!"

Grimes waved him aside. "Later, Commander Mayhew—unless my ship's in danger. She's not? Good. Then let's get this business settled first." He turned to the others. "I'm not overly rank conscious, and I'm insisting on my seniority only because Rim Worlds' sovereignty is involved. To begin with—we are in Rim Confederacy's territorial space. Secondly, I outrank everybody present in this control room. . . ."

"In a pig's arse you do!" flared Irene.

"But I do, madam. I concede that you *were* an empress, but you're not now. Legally speaking you're only the chief officer of *Wanderer*. . . ."

"And the owner of *Wanderer*, Grimes! Which is more than you can say regarding yourself and your precious rust-bucket!"

"And *I* still claim," stated Flandry, "that *Wanderer* and *Faraway Quest* are no better than pirates, attempting to steal Imperial property."

"It's a great pity that GLASS is not operative in *your* universe," said Smith in a flat voice. "But since we are discussing legalities, I feel that I, as the charterer of Mrs. Trafford's vessel, should have some voice in the matter."

"Irene!" Trialanne was trying to gain the attention of the ex-Empress. "Irene!"

"Pipe down, damn you! Can't you see I'm busy?"

"Obviously," said Sonya coldly, "it would be pointless to put it to the vote who should be chairman of this meeting. Everybody is quite convinced that he has a more valid claim than anybody else. I could say—and, come to that, I *do* say—that I represent the Federation, but I have no desire to be yet another complication. . . ."

"But a very charming one," murmured Flandry, flashing that dazzling grin.

"Thank you, Sir Dominic."

"Very charming, and, I feel, highly competent. For the record, I do not recognize the Interstellar Federation. Nonetheless, I feel that Mrs. Grimes—or, if you prefer it,

Commander Verrill—should preside over this meeting. She appears, in spite of her marriage . . ." he made it sound as though he meant "disastrous marriage" . . . "to be the nearest thing we have to a neutral. Will you, then, take charge, Commander Verrill?"

She smiled at him. "Thank you, Sir Dominic. I will." She raised her voice slightly. "To begin with, all of you, this situation calls for straight thinking. We are met together in what is, to all of us, an alien ship. We represent, between us, three different cultures, at least four different governments. But we are all—and I include you, Trialanne —human. . . ."

"So *you* say," growled Irene.

Sonya ignored this, went on. "As an aid to straight thinking, recapitulation will be in order. We are all of us *here,* all of us *now*—that much is obvious. But it should be obvious, too, that The Outsider, the Outsiders' Ship, warps normal space/time. It exists simultaneously in our universe, and in yours, Sir Dominic, and in yours, Irene— and yet it is from outside all our universes. . . ."

Somebody was grabbing Grimes' arm, the pressure evident even through the thick sleeve of his suit. It was Mayhew. The telepath was pointing to the hatch which gave access to the control room from the body of the ship. Through it a helmeted head was rising slowly.

"I—we—were trying to tell you!" muttered Mayhew.

"Tell me *what?*" growled Grimes.

In reply the other shrugged—no easy feat in a space suit —infuriatingly. *Bloody prima donna!* thought Grimes. *But it can't be all that important. Probably somebody from one of the ships with some trivial message.*

"It could be," Sonya was continuing, in a schoolmistress' voice, "that we are all of us here on sufferance. . . ."

The shoulders of the new arrival were now visible, but the faceplate of his helmet was almost opaque. Grimes stared at those armored shoulders. They carried the broad gold stripe of a commodore, the winged wheel of the Rim Worlds Navy. Who the hell could it be? Lannigan? Du-Bois? Why should either of them be sent out here to interfere with him, Grimes? And this interloping commodore had somebody with him, wearing commander's badges of rank, and the stylized star cluster of the Federation. . . .

Sonya's voice trailed off into silence. She had seen the newcomers at last. So had all the others.

The stranger put gloved hands to his helmet, twisted, lifted. He stared at Grimes—and Grimes stared at him. It was long seconds before Grimes recognized him. One is used to seeing one's own face in a mirror, but one spends very little (if any) time studying solidographs of oneself. Dimly, Grimes was aware that the other stranger, standing to one side and a little behind the commodore, had removed her helmet. He didn't really notice her until she spoke.

"This is a surprise, John," said Maggie Lazenby.

Flandry laughed. "Getting back to our original argument —just which of you two gentlemen is the senior?"

XIV

"Mphm," grunted Grimes.

"Mphm," grunted Grimes.

Slowly he opened the pouch at his belt, took from it his tobacco tin and his battered pipe. Carefully he filled the pipe, returned the tin to the pouch, brought out a lighter. He lit the pipe. He squinted at Grimes through the swirl of blue, acrid smoke.

Slowly he opened the pouch at his belt, took from it his tobacco tin and his battered pipe. Carefully he filled the pipe, returned the tin to the pouch, brought out a lighter. He lit the pipe. He squinted at Grimes through the swirl of blue, acrid smoke.

Sonya made a major production of a lung-wracking cough.

Maggie said, "Let the man have his little pleasures—and his aid to cerebration."

Sonya demanded, "What are *you* doing with *him?*"

Maggie replied, "I could ask you the same, duckie."

Grimes demanded, "How the hell did *you* get here?"

Grimes replied, "The same way as you." He gestured toward the nearest hexagonal viewport with the hand that held the pipe.

Grimes stared out into the blackness. There had been three vessels there: Flandry's *Vindictive*, Irene's *Wanderer*, his own *Faraway Quest*. Now there were four. He asked, "And what is the name of *your* ship?"

56

"*Faraway Quest*, of course. She was *Delta Puppis* before the Federation flogged her to us."

"Mphm," grunted Grimes again, feeling a twinge of envy. His *Faraway Quest* was an ex-Epsilon Class tramp. He turned to Mayhew. "You might have kept me better informed, Commander."

"Sir, both Trialanne and I tried to tell you as soon as this other *Faraway Quest* broke through. I couldn't tell you anything before then as she does not carry a psionic communications officer."

"Unfortunately, no," agreed Grimes II. "I tried to convince my masters that a good PCO is worth ten thousand times his weight in Carlotti transceivers—but *they* know best." He added after a pause, "I can never understand this craving to put oneself at the mercy of a single fuse. . . ."

"And how many times have you heard *that* before, Maggie?" asked Sonya.

"I've lost count," said Maggie Lazenby.

"But this question of seniority . . . ?" hinted Flandry, obviously determined to extract the utmost in amusement from the situation.

"*I* am the senior," stated both Grimeses.

"I was here first," said Grimes I.

"Mine is the larger ship," said Grimes II.

Grimes I laughed. "This is bloody absurd, Grimes. Before we get involved in any futile arguments would you mind putting me—us—into your picture?"

"I'll try, Grimes. My masters decided that it was time that somebody took another expedition out to the Outsiders' Ship, and I was given the job. Maggie—you *do* know Maggie, of course . . . ?"

"I do. And so does Sonya."

"And I know Sonya. Quite a family party, isn't it? But where was I? Oh, yes. Maggie, although she's married to me, has retained her Federation citizenship and her commission in the Federation's Survey Service. She's along as an observer for the Federation."

"As Sonya is. But go on."

Grimes II carefully relit his pipe. "Well, we rather suspected that there would be other ships, in addition to the known derelicts, in orbit about The Outsider. But we were certainly surprised to find that one of those other ships, like mine, was named *Faraway Quest*. Your second-in-com-

mand, Commander Williams, was even more surprised. It must have been a shock to him to see my face looking out of the screen when we started nattering over the NST radio. It put him in rather a dither. There he was, conditioned to say, 'Yes, sir; no, sir,' to Commodore Grimes. . . ."

"That doesn't sound like Williams!" said Grimes II.

"Well, as a matter of fact he called me 'Skipper.' But he was in a fine tangle of conflicting loyalties. He suggested that I'd better make contact with you to get things sorted out, and told me where I'd find you. And now, Commodore Grimes, suppose you introduce your friends to me. . . ."

"Certainly, Commodore Grimes," said Grimes who, in a dazed sort of way, was beginning to enjoy himself. "Irene, Trialanne, this, as you see, is Commodore Grimes, who obviously is from a time track not too far divergent from my own. And the lady is Commander Lazenby, of the Federation's Survey Service, and also Mrs. Grimes. Commodore, may I present Mrs. Trafford, who is chief officer *and* owner of the so-called yacht *Wanderer*, and Trialanne, one of her PCOs. Oh, yes, before I forget—Mrs. Trafford is also the ex-Empress Irene."

"I am honored," said Grimes II, with a stiff little bow.

"You bloody well should be," growled Irene.

"And Mr. Smith, the managing director of GLASS, charterer of *Wanderer*. GLASS is an acronym for GALACTIC LEAGUE AGAINST SUPPRESSION and SLAVERY. It is, I imagine, a severe pain in the neck to quite a few governments in Irene's universe. . . ."

"We try to be just that," agreed Smith modestly.

"And this, Commodore, is Captain Sir Dominic Flandry, of the Imperial armed scout *Vindictive*. The young gentleman with him is Ensign Bugolsky."

Flandry smiled, but his eyes were cold, wary. "I am glad to meet you, Commodore. And *you*, Commander Lazenby."

You would be, thought Grimes.

"In one way your arrival, sir, is welcome. Until now I have been inclined to doubt your alter ego's stories of alternate time tracks and all the rest of it. But now . . ." Flandry shrugged. He went on, "You are welcome to join our discussion."

"What discussion?" asked Grimes II.

"As to who can lay claim to The Outsider."

58

"You will agree with me," said Grimes I, "that it lies within Rim Confederacy's territorial space."

"Of course," said Grimes II.

"But *whose* Rim Confederacy?" demanded Flandry and Irene simultaneously. "Yours or his?"

"It's *my* flag that's planted on it," stated Grimes I stubbornly.

"You and your bloody flag!" snarled Irene.

"As I see it," said Grimes II judiciously, "this is a matter to be decided between Commodore Grimes and myself."

"Definitely," said Grimes I.

"We're *surrounded* by the bastards," muttered Irene. Then, to Flandry, "You'll not stand for that, Sir Dominic?"

"*You*," said Sonya, "can fight it out between yourselves which Empire has a claim to ownership."

Flandry flashed a charming smile at Irene. "I really think, ma'am, that we imperialists should stick together."

"GLASS has never approved of imperialism," stated Smith. "In any case, *Wanderer* is on charter to my organization."

"I seem to remember," said Sonya coldly, "that quite some time ago it was decided that I should preside over this meeting. Even though my husband has been duplicated, I have not. Therefore I suggest that we carry on from where we left off."

"And just why were you so honored, Sonya?" asked Maggie curiously.

"Because I, as an officer of the Federation's Survey Service, am the only one who can claim neutral status."

"But I, too, am an officer of the Federation's Survey Service, dearie."

"Commodore Grimes!" Mayhew called excitedly.

Both Grimeses turned to look at him.

"Yes, Commander?" asked Grimes I.

"*Faraway Quest*. . . . She's . . . gone!"

"I was in touch with Clarisse," confirmed Trialanne. "But the contact has been broken."

From Flandry's suit radio came a small, tinny voice. "Captain, sir, *Faraway Quest*, the first *Faraway Quest*, has vanished."

There was no need for Grimes to stare out through the viewport, but he did so. There, hanging in nothingness, were the three ships, three only: *Vindictive*, *Wanderer* and what must be the other *Quest*, the wrong *Quest*.

He turned to look at the elaborately grotesque Outsider with something akin to hatred. "That bloody thing!" he muttered. "That bloody thing!" And he thought, *My ship, my people . . . where are they? Where—or when—has It thrown them?*

The Italian woman said softly, "Commodore, *It* is not responsible. Your vessel's Mannschenn Drive was restarted just before she vanished. So I am told by Mr. Tallentire, aboard *Wanderer*."

"Trialanne! Mayhew! Get in touch with Clarisse. Find out what's happening!"

"Don't you think that I'm bloody well trying already?" snarled Mayhew. "Damn your ship. It's my woman I'm worried about!"

"Sorry, Ken," said Grimes. "I needn't tell you to do your best, and better. . . ."

"Mutiny?" asked Grimes II quietly.

"Be your age, Commodore!" flared Grimes I. "With a handpicked crew, like mine, it's impossible."

"The passengers weren't handpicked, John," Sonya told him somberly. "At least, not by you."

Mayhew, his face white and strained, whispered, "The blame is mine, John. I should have disregarded the Rhine Institute's code of ethics. I should have pried."

"But you didn't. And I didn't order you to. . . ." He looked around him at the faces of the others in the control room. All realized the gravity of the situation.

Grimes II broke the silence. He said, "Much as I hate to leave the Outsiders' Ship to these . . . outsiders, my *Faraway Quest* is at your disposal, Commodore. After all, we may as well keep this in the family."

"Mutiny is a crime," stated Irene. "All law-abiding citizens should combine to capture and to punish the criminals. I am with you. I am sure that I speak for my officers."

"And count me in," said Flandry, not without a touch of regret.

"Thank you," Grimes said. "Thank you. All of you."

"And where," asked Maggie Lazenby, "do we go from here?"

XV

Where did they go from there?

Where had *Faraway Quest* gone?

And where was that Waldegren destroyer, *Adler?*

But the discussion, the consideration of these problems was better than the rather childish squabbling as to who had prior claim to the Outsiders' Ship.

It was decided that Grimes, Sonya and Mayhew should take passage in the second *Faraway Quest,* and that Flandry should accompany them. Flandry's own ship, *Vindictive,* was unsuitable for the pursuit of the original *Quest.* She had faster than light drive, of course, and faster than light deep space communications equipment, but neither of these operated on the principles of the Mannschenn Drive or the Carlotti beacon. She could proceed from Point A to Point B at least as fast as *Faraway Quest* or *Wanderer,* but until she reemerged into normal space/time she would be completely out of touch with them.

Vindictive, therefore, would remain in orbit about The Outsider as a guard ship. Flandry impressed upon her acting captain that he was to counter any hostile move made by *Adler,* should she put in an appearance, without hesitation, but that he was to be careful in his dealings with *Faraway Quest I* should she return. As long as there was any possibility that her rightful crew were still alive, as prisoners, as hostages, their safety must be considered at all times.

All this took time, but not too much time. And then Flandry, with his aide, returned briefly to his own vessel, while Irene and her party made their way back to *Wanderer,* while Grimes I in his pinnace followed his other self, in his pinnace, to *Faraway Quest II.* The stowage of this extra boat in the *Quest's* cargo hold presented no great problems. By the time that it was secured Captain Flandry was alongside, at the airlock, and was being admitted.

And then the control rooms of *Wanderer* and *Faraway Quest* were manned. Grimes sat in one of the spare acceleration chairs, with Mayhew to one side of him and Sonya to the other, and with Flandry beside Sonya. He watched

the other Grimes enviously. *He* still had a ship of his own. He looked curiously at the officers at their stations—and they looked curiously at him and at Sonya and at Flandry. He felt that he almost knew them. Almost certainly their counterparts lived in his continuum; he must have met some of them, however briefly. The communications officer, beside whom Mayhew had taken a seat. . . . Surely that was young Carradine, who held the same rank in Rim Runners in Grimes' universe . . .

Grimes II was giving his orders unhurriedly, decisively; they were acknowledged smartly. In the little screen of the NST transceiver, Captain Trafford in *Wanderer's* control room was doing likewise. Then Trafford said, facing the iconoscope, "All machinery on full stand by, Commodore."

"Thank you, Captain," replied Grimes II, just a fraction of a second before Grimes I could do so. (*I'll have to watch myself,* he thought. *I'm only a passenger. . . .*)

"Execute on the count of zero."

"Aye, aye. Execute on the count of zero."

"Five . . ." intoned Grimes II. "Four . . . Three . . . Two . . . One . . . Zero!"

From below came the high, undulating whine of the Mannschenn Drive, and with it the temporal disorientation, the sense of unreality. Grimes looked at Sonya and asked himself, with wry humor, *How many of me is she seeing now?* The picture of *Wanderer's* control room faded from the NST transceiver screen, was replaced by that in the screen of the Carlotti set. Beyond the viewports the brightly lit *Vindictive* and the distant Shaara derelict faded into invisibility—but the cold-gleaming intricacy of the Outsiders' Ship persisted stubbornly.

It is in every space, thought Grimes. *It is in every time. But how is it that nobody else has ever reported this phenomenon?* He answered his own question. *Dead men and missing men do not tell tales.*

And then, suddenly, things were normal—or as normal as they ever are, as they ever can be while the Drive is in operation.

Flandry looked at Grimes. His face was pale. He said, "So this is your Mannschenn Drive. I think I prefer our Standing Wave."

"You get used to it," Grimes told him.

"Speak for yourself," snapped Sonya.

But Grimes II—after all, this was his ship—was taking charge. "Mr. Carradine," he ordered, "keep your ears skinned for the faintest whisper from *anybody* on the main Carlotti. Grab a bearing if you can. Mr. Danby, let me know if you see even the merest flicker in the MPI. And you, Commander Mayhew, I needn't tell *you* what to do. I'm sorry that this ship doesn't run to a psionic amplifier, but Mr. Metzenther and Trialanne in *Wanderer* have one."

Flandry said something about trying to find a black cat in a coal mine at midnight. Grimes II laughed. "Yes, Captain, that just about sums it up. And once we do find it we may not be much better off. For any physical contact to be made between ships while the Mannschenn Drive is operating there must be exact synchronization of temporal precession rates. There have been devices whereby one vessel can induce synchronization in the Mannschenn Drive unit of another vessel with her own. But most ships today —certainly all warships—are fitted with special governors which make this impossible unless the captain so desires."

"And when do you start accelerating, Commodore? I'm finding all this free fall rather boring."

"As soon as we know where to accelerate to."

Flandry shrugged. The gesture, now that he was out of his space suit and attired in a close-fitting, beautifully tailored, black and gold uniform, was much more effective.

Irritated, Grimes II asked sharply, "And do *you* have any ideas, Captain Flandry?"

"Why, yes. People don't hijack ships just for the fun of it. We don't have any Duchy of Waldegren in *my* universe —but, from what I have gathered, the Waldegrenese are baddies. The people who have seized the *Faraway Quest*, the first *Faraway Quest* that I was aboard, are also baddies. Could this hijacked *Faraway Quest* be making a rendezvous with *Adler?*"

"What do *you* think, Commodore?" asked Grimes II.

"I think that Captain Flandry could be right, Commodore," replied Grimes I.

"Of course I'm right," said Flandry.

"Mphm," grunted Grimes II thoughtfully. He turned to his navigator. "Mr. Danby," he said, "run up a trajectory for Waldegren. We'll just have to assume that she's coming out by the most direct route, the same as we did from *Faraway....*"

"No," Grimes told him. "She's running out on the Leads astern, the same as we did."

"The *Leads?*" demanded Grimes II.

"Yes. Macbeth and the Kinsolving sun in line."

"You have some most peculiar ideas about navigation on *your* time track, Commodore. However, this *Adler* also belongs to your time track, so. . . . All right, Mr. Danby, do as the carbon copy Commodore Grimes says. And Mr. Carradine, inform *Wanderer* of our intentions."

Carbon copy . . . thought Grimes indignantly. But, original or not, this was not his ship. He—or his own version of himself—was not giving the orders. He could only suggest and be thankful that this other Grimes did not seem to be as pigheaded as he, more than once, had been accused of being.

Briefly the Mannschenn Drive was shut down, and the big, directional gyroscopes rumbled, hummed and then whined as the ship turned about her short axis. Directly ahead—overhead from the viewport of those in Control—the dim, misty Galactic Lens swam into view and was almost immediately distorted beyond recognition as the interstellar drive was restarted. The irregular throbbing beat of the inertial drive made itself felt, and there was gravity again, and weight, and up and down.

"Now we're getting someplace," murmured Flandry a little smugly.

Grimes glared at him and was even more annoyed when he saw that Sonya was looking at the Imperial Captain with what could have been admiration.

XVI

It was not a long pursuit, and it ended in stalemate.

Falling through the non-space, non-time between the dimensions were the four ships: *Adler, Wanderer,* both versions of *Faraway Quest.* Trajectories had been matched, in spite of the initial efforts of *Adler* and *Faraway Quest I* to throw off their pursuers; but it was only those two vessels that had synchronized temporal precession rates.

Back toward The Outsider they ran, all four of them, a mismatched squadron. And they would run past their ob-

jective, and go on running, until somebody did something, somehow, to break the deadlock.

Meanwhile, Grimes had learned that his crew was safe, although they were now prisoners. At last, at long last, and with assistance from Metzenther and Trialanne, Mayhew had been able to reestablish his *rapport* with Clarisse. It had not been easy, but after many hours of concentrated effort the three telepaths had been able to drag her mind up out of its drugged sleep to a condition of full awareness. She was able, then, to supply the details of Druthen's take-over of the ship. It had been done with surprising ease, merely by the introduction of an instantaneously anesthetic gas into the air circulatory system. In theory, this should have been impossible. Alarms should have sounded; pumps and fans should have stopped; baffle plates should automatically have sealed off the ducts. But Druthen was a scientist, and his people were scientists and technicians. He had a very well equipped laboratory at his disposal. And, most important of all, Mayhew and Clarisse had obeyed that commandment of the Rhine Institute: Thou shalt not pry into the mind of a shipmate.

"It's no use crying over spilt milk, Ken," Grimes told his psionic communications officer. "At least we know that Clarisse and the others are unhurt. . . ."

"What the hell's the use of having these talents if you don't use 'em?" wondered Flandry, all too audibly.

"Some of us," Grimes told him coldly, "subscribe to ethical codes."

"Don't we all, Commodore? Do unto others as they would do unto you—but do it first!"

"Captain Flandry is right, John," said Sonya.

Yes, thought Grimes, *I suppose the bastard is right. And, come to that, I've tried often enough, and sometimes successfully, to get PCOs to pry for me. . . . Like Spooky Deane, who loved his gin—or my gin. . . . Even so. . . .*

Anyhow, there was now telepathic communication between the two *Faraway Quests,* and communication regarding which neither Druthen nor the captain of *Adler* was aware. Not that it would have worried them much if they had known about it. Clarisse was locked up in the quarters that she had shared with her husband. There was little that she could tell him, and nothing that she could do. She could not communicate with the other prisoners,

who were nontelepaths. She could not even pry into the minds of Druthen and his people—and neither could Mayhew and Metzenther and Trialanne. The scientist had, somehow, succeeded in stimulating Mayhew's psionic amplifier —it could, of course, have been just a side effect of the anesthetic gas that had been used during the take-over—and the continual howling of that hapless, disembodied dog's brain blanketed all stray thoughts. Trained telepaths could punch their signals through the psionic interference, but that was all.

In any case, Druthen was willing enough to talk.

He, fat and slovenly as ever, glowered out at Grimes from the screen of the Carlotti transceiver. Grimes stared back at him, trying to keep his own face emotionless. It was all wrong that he should be looking into his own control room this way, from outside, that he should see the nerve center of his own ship in the hands of strangers, of enemies. With Druthen were two of the scientist's own people, and in the background were three uniformed men: large, blond, obviously officers of the Waldegren Navy.

The senior among them, a full commander by his braid, came to stand beside Dr. Druthen. Druthen seemed to resent this, tried to push the officer out of the field of the iconoscope. He muttered, "Nehmen Sie mal Ihre Latschen weg."

The other replied, "Sie sind zwar dick genug für zwei, aber Sie haben nur für einen Platz gezahlt Rücken Sie weiter."

Sonya laughed. Grimes asked her, "What's the joke?"

"Just that they don't seem to love each other. Druthen told the commander to get his big feet out of his way, and the commander told *him* that even though he's big enough to fill two seats he's only paid for one. . . ."

"Paid?" asked Grimes.

"Obviously. He's bought his way into the Duchy of Waldegren."

"Ja," agreed the Waldegren commander. And then, speaking directly to Grimes, "And you the captain of this ship were? But. . . ." His eyes widened. "*Vich* of you der kapitan vas?"

"I suppose we're twins, of a sort," grinned Grimes I. "The gentleman standing behind me is Commodore Grimes, commanding *Faraway Quest*. And I am Commodore Grimes,

commanding *Faraway Quest*—the *Faraway Quest* aboard which you, sir, are trespassing."

"But I am the captain now," stated Druthen smugly.

Grimes ignored this. He asked coldly, "Where are my people?" (There was no point in letting Druthen and the officers of the prize crew know that he was already fully informed on that subject.)

"Do you want them back?" countered Druthen, with an infuriating expression of deliberate incredulity.

"Yes. And my ship."

Druthen laughed sneeringly. "You don't want much, Commodore. Or should I say, ex-Commodore? Your masters will not be very pleased with you. The ship—*I* keep. Doubtless the Duchy will pay me a fair price for her. The crew. . . . They are useful hostages. You and your allies dare make no hostile move for fear of hurting them." The fat face was suddenly gloating, evil. "And, perhaps, I can use them to persuade you to call off this futile chase. Suppose I have them thrown, one by one, unsuited, out of the airlock . . . ?"

"Herr Doktor!" snapped the commander. "Enough. That I will never countenance. I am an officer, not an executioner."

"Sie glauben wohl Sie sind als Schiffsoffizier was besonderes!"

"Hau'ab!" The commander struck rather than pushed Druthen away from the screen. Those in the control room of *Quest II* watched, fascinated, a brief scuffle in the control room of the other ship. And then the senior officer of the prize crew was addressing them again. "Herr Commodore, my apologies. But I my orders must follow, even when I am told to cooperate with *schwein*. *Aber*, my word I give. I, Erich von Donderberg, promise you that your crew will be treated well as long as I in this ship am."

"Thank you, Commander," said Grimes stiffly.

Druthen, with one eye puffed and almost shut, bleeding from the corner of his mouth, reappeared.

"Officers!" he spat. "Gold-braided nincompoops, survivals from a past age who should have become extinct millennia ago! I'm cutting you off, Grimes. I want the transceiver so that I can call Captain Blumenfeld in *Adler*. There'll be some changes made in the composition of this so-called prize crew!"

The screen went blank.

"What now?" asked Flandry. "You know these Waldegren people. I don't."

"They're naval officers," said Grimes at last. "They're
professional naval officers. They can be ruthless bastards—but
they do, at times, subscribe to a rather antique code of
honor. . . ."

"I concur," said Grimes II.

"Would you mind," asked Grimes I, "passing the recording of this rather odd interview on to *Wanderer?* Irene and
her people may have some comments."

"Certainly, Commodore."

"And you should be able to let us know, Ken, if Druthen
is able to persuade Captain Blumenfeld to let him play the
game his way?"

"I'll try," said Mayhew doubtfully. "I'll try. With Clarisse
alert and with Metzenther and Trialanne to help us. . . .
Yes, I should manage."

"And so," commented Flandry, "we just, all of us, go
on falling through sweet damn' all until somebody con-
descends to make something happen."

"That's the way of it," agreed Grimes.

XVII

They, all of them, went on falling through sweet damn'
all.

They swept past the Outsiders' Ship, which was still dimly visible, although the derelicts in orbit about it were not.
Neither was Flandry's *Vindictive*. The Imperial Captain complained rather bitterly that he was unable to communicate
with his ship. Both Grimeses growled, simultaneously, that
it was the fault of his culture for developing neither psionic
communications nor the Carlotti system. Both Mrs. Grimeses
were inclined to commiserate with Flandry. Relations aboard
Faraway Quest II were becoming strained. Aboard *Wanderer* there were not the same problems. There was only
one of each person, and there were no outsiders.

Out they fell, the four ships, out into the ultimate night.

Druthen and Captain Blumenfeld made an occasional attempt at evasion, which was countered with ease by the
pursuers. Once Blumenfeld, using the Carlotti equipment,

tried to reason with Grimes—either or both of him—and with Irene, who had been hooked into the conversation.

Blumenfeld was an older and stouter version of von Donderberg, and he was more of the politician and less of the space officer. His accent was not so heavy. He appeared in the screens of *Faraway Quest II* and *Wanderer* by himself, a fatherly—grandfatherly, almost—figure, smoking an elaborate pipe with a porcelain bowl. It was a pity that his cold, very cold, blue eyes spoiled the effect.

"Come now, Commodore," he said, "we are both reasonable men. And you, Kaiserin, are a reasonable lady. What do any of us gain by this pointless chase?"

"You gain nothing," Grimes told him. "Furthermore, you are intruding in Rim Worlds' territorial space. I order you, legally, to hand my ship and my personnel back to me, and also Dr. Druthen and his people so that they may be dealt with by our courts. . . ."

"*You* order, Commodore?" asked the other Grimes softly.

"Yes. I order, Commodore. *Faraway Quest I* is mine, and Druthen and his accomplices will be my prisoners."

"Speak up, Commodores," put in Blumenfeld jovially. "Do I detect a slight dissension in your ranks? And you, Kaiserin, do you acknowledge the right of these gentlemen to give orders? And you, Captain Sir Dominic Flandry? What is your view?"

"We'll settle our own differences after you have been disposed of," growled Irene.

"I second that," said Flandry.

Captain Blumenfeld puffed placidly at his pipe. Grimes wondered what tobacco it was that he was smoking. The man seemed to be enjoying it. At last he said, through a wreathing blue cloud, "My patience is not inexhaustible, Commodore. Or Commodores. I am addressing, however, whichever one of you it is who commanded the *Faraway Quest* aboard which I have placed my prize crew. The good Herr Doktor Druthen has made certain proposals to me regarding the prisoners. I was horrified, and told him so, in no uncertain terms. But . . ." There was a great exhalation of smoke. "But . . . I have thought about what he said to me. I still do not like it." He shrugged heavily.

"Nonetheless, my loyalty is to the Duchy, not to citizens of a Confederacy that the Duchy still has not recognized. It may—note that I say 'may,' Commodore, not 'will'

—it may be expedient to use those prisoners as a lever to force a certain degree of compliance from you." Again he shrugged. "I shall not like doing it—assuming, that is, that I am obliged to do it. And I shall not resort to painful or . . . messy methods. Just a simple shooting, to be watched by all of you. And then, after a suitable interval, another. And then, if it is necessary, another." He smiled coldly. "But there is no real urgency. You will be given time to think it over, to talk it over. Three days' subjective time, shall we say? Call me on this frequency. Over. And out."

The screen went blank, but the other screen, that showing *Wanderer's* control room, stayed alive.

"Well?" demanded Irene harshly. "Well?"

"Suppose," said Grimes, "just suppose that I do knuckle under, to get my people back, my ship back. Suppose that I, as the ranking officer of the Rim Worlds Confederacy, do allow him prior rights to The Outsider. . . . What about *you*, and *you*, Commodore Grimes, and *you*, Captain Flandry?"

"I shall abide by your decision, John," said the other Grimes.

"Speaking for the Federation," said Sonya, "I shall be with you."

"You beat me to it," said Maggie Lazenby.

"I'll have to think about it," stated Irene.

"As tour charterer," Smith told her, "I have *some* say. A great deal of say. I sympathize with Commodore Grimes. But it's a matter of evaluation. Are the lives of a handful of people of greater importance than the lives of the millions of oppressed men and women and children who look to GLASS for help?"

"Anybody mind if I shove in my two bits' worth?" asked Flandry. "I owe allegiance neither to the Federation nor to the Confederacy and certainly not to GLASS. I swore an oath of fealty to the Emperor." He looked at Irene's face in the screen, and added, "*My* Emperor. But my sympathies are with the Commodore."

"Thank you, Sir Dominic," said Grimes.

"Wait till you see the bill. Furthermore, sir, I would remind you that you have at your disposal equipment and personnel which I have not. The same applies to you, ma'am. You have your espers. Can't you make full use of them?"

"I would remind you, Sir Dominic," said Mayhew, "that my wife is among the prisoners aboard the *Quest*."

"All the more reason why you should pull your finger out. All of you."

You arrogant bastard, thought Grimes.

"Sir Dominic's talking sense," said Sonya. "*We* have the telepaths. *Adler* hasn't. Furthermore, one of *our* telepaths is aboard *your Quest*, John. There must be something that Clarisse can do to help herself. And the others."

"It's all we can do to get through to her," objected Mayhew. "There's too much interference from Lassie. . . ."

Sonya muttered something about a poodle's brain in aspic. Then she said, "Why don't you silence the bitch? Lassie, I mean. There's three of you here: Metzenther and Trialanne aboard *Wanderer*, and yourself. You told us once—remember?—that thoughts can kill."

"I . . . I couldn't, Sonya. . . ."

"Damn it all!" exploded Grimes. "Do you put that animal brain before your wife? What sort of man are you?"

"But . . . but Lassie's so . . . helpless."

"So is Clarisse, unless we do something to help her—and fast. It is *essential* that she be able to keep us informed as to what Druthen is thinking, and von Donderberg . . . and with that psionic interference snuffed out you should be able to keep us informed as to Captain Blumenfeld's intentions. You must do it, Ken."

"Yes," agreed the telepath slowly. "I . . . must. Metzenther and Trialanne will help. They have already told me that."

"Then go to it," ordered Grimes.

Not for the first time he thought, *They're odd people. Too bloody odd. But I suppose when you live inside your pet's brain, and it lives inside yours, you feel more intensely for and about it than any normal man feels for his dog. . . . There'll be guilt involved, too. . . . You'll blame yourself for its absolute helplessness. . . .*

He watched Mayhew stumbling out of the control room, his features stiff, too stiff. He saw the sympathy on the face of Grimes II, and rather more than a hint of a sneer on that of Flandry.

Grimes II looked at his watch. He said, "There's nothing much that we can do, Commodore, until your Commander

71

Mayhew reports results. I suggest that we all adjourn for dinner."

"An army marches on its stomach," quipped Flandry. "I suppose that the same saying applies to a space navy."

"I've never known John to miss a meal," Sonya told him, "no matter what the circumstances."

Women . . . thought Grimes—both of him.

"You said it," agreed Maggie Lazenby.

XVIII

This was the first proper, sit down meal that anybody had enjoyed for quite a while. Not that Grimes really enjoyed it. He was used to eating at the captain's table—but at the head of the board. To see himself sitting there, a replica of himself, was . . . odd. He derived a certain wry pleasure from the fact that this other Grimes, like himself, was not one to let conversation interfere with the serious business of feeding. He did not think, somehow, that Maggie appreciated this trait any more than Sonya did.

There were five of them at the Commodore's table. Grimes II was at the head of it, of course, with Maggie Lazenby at his right and Sonya at his left. Grimes I sat beside Maggie, and Flandry beside Sonya. The Imperial Captain was a brilliant conversationalist, and the two women were lapping it up. He made his own time track sound so much more glamorous than the time tracks of the two Grimeses—which, in any case, differed only very slightly from each other. He made the two Commodores seem very dull dogs in comparison with his flamboyant, charming self. And, in spite of the nonstop flow of outrageous anecdotes, his plate was clean before any of the others.

The meal, Grimes admitted, was a good one. Grimes II kept an excellent table, and the service, provided by two neatly uniformed little stewardesses, matched the quality of the food. There was wine, of which Grimes II partook sparingly, of which the others partook not so sparingly. Grimes thought, with disapproval, *That man Flandry is gulping it down as though it were lager* . . . then realized that he was doing the same.

At last they were finished, sipping their coffee. Grimes—

both of him—pulled out his pipe. His wife—both of her—objected, saying, "John! You *know* that the airconditioners can't cope with the *stink!*" Flandry, sleek and smug, lit a cigar that one of the stewardesses brought him. The ladies accepted lights from him for their cigarillos.

Grimes, from the head of the table, looked at Grimes with slightly raised eyebrows. He said, "I'm going up to Control, Commodore, to enjoy my pipe in peace. The officer of the watch mightn't like it, but he daren't say so. Coming?"

"Thank you, Commodore."

He (they) excused himself (themselves), got to his (their) feet. Flandry and the wives were enjoying liqueurs with their coffee and hardly noticed their going. Grimes II led the way out of the dining saloon, which, as a public room in a much larger ship, was luxurious in comparison with that aboard *Faraway Quest I*. Indoor plants, the lush, flowering vines of Caribbea twining around every pillar. Holograms, brightly glowing, picture windows opening on to a score of alien worlds. Grimes paused before one that depicted a beach scene on Arcadia. Maggie was an Arcadian. He looked closely to see if she were among the naked, golden-skinned people on the sand and in the surf. But what if she was? He grunted, followed his counterpart into the axial shaft.

The control room seemed bleak and cold after the warm luxury of the dining saloon. The officer of the watch got to his feet as the two Commodores entered, looked doubtfully from one to the other before deciding which one to salute. But he got it right. Outside the viewports was—nothingness. To starboard, Grimes knew, were his own ship and *Adler*, and beyond them was Irene's *Wanderer*—but unless temporal precession rates were synchronized they would remain invisible. One of the Carlotti screens was alive. It showed a bored looking Tallentire slumped in his chair, his fingers busy with some sort of mathematical puzzle.

"Any word from our tame telepaths yet, Mr. Grigsby?" asked Grimes II.

"No, sir. Commander Mayhew did buzz me to tell me that he and the people aboard *Wanderer* are still trying but aren't getting anywhere."

"Mphm." Grimes slumped into an acceleration chair, mo-

tioning to Grimes to follow suit. He (they) filled and lit his (their) pipes. "Mphm."

"There must be a way," said Grimes thoughtfully.

"There always is," agreed Grimes. "The only trouble is finding it."

The two men smoked in companionable silence. Grimes I was almost at ease but knew that he would be properly at ease only aboard his own *Faraway Quest*. He looked around him, noticing all the similarities—and all the differences. From the control room he went down, in his mind, deck by deck. And then . . . and then the idea came to him.

"Commodore," he said, "I think I have it. Do you mind if I borrow your O.O.W.?"

"Help yourself, Commodore. This is Liberty Hall. You can spit on the mat and call the cat a bastard."

Grimes winced. So that was the way it sounded when he said it. He caught the attention of the watch officer. "Mr. Grigsby. . . ."

"Sir?"

"Ask Commander Mayhew to come up here, will you?"

"Aye, aye, sir."

The young man spoke into a telephone, then said, "He's on his way."

"Thank you."

When Mayhew came in the two Commodores were wrapped in a pungent blue haze. "Sir?" asked the telepath doubtfully, looking from one to the other. "Sir?"

"Damn it all, Ken," growled Grimes. "*You* should know which one of us is which."

"There was a sort of . . . mingling."

"Don't go all metaphysical on me. I take it that you've made no headway."

"No. We just can't get through to Lassie. And it takes effort, considerable effort, to maintain Clarisse in a state approaching full awareness."

"But you are getting through to her."

"Yes."

"Good. Now tell me, Ken, *where* is she? Yes, yes—I know bloody well that she's aboard my *Faraway Quest*—but where aboard the *Quest*? In your living quarters—or in your watch room?"

"In . . . in the watch room, sir. She hates Lassie, as you know, but she went to the watch room to maintain better

74

communications when we left the ship to go aboard the Shaara derelict. The watch room is fitted up as a living cabin, and Druthen and his crowd left her there after the take-over."

"That makes things easier, a lot easier. Now, get in touch with your cobbers aboard *Wanderer*. . . ."

"I already am." Mayhew's voice was pained.

"Punch this message through, the three of you. *Stop Lassie's life-support system*."

"You can't mean. . . ."

"I do mean. It's the only way to quiet that helpless hound of yours. With that source of telepathic interference wiped out we might be able to learn something. After all, it's only short range work. You don't need an amplifier."

"But. . . ."

"*Do it!*"

"All right. Sir." Mayhew's face was white and strained. "But you don't understand. If I could do it myself, kill Lassie, I mean, it wouldn't be as bad. Because . . . because Clarisse has always hated Lassie. She'll . . . she'll enjoy it. . . ."

"Good for her," said Grimes brutally. "And have Mr. Metzenther inform Captain Trafford of what's going on."

He visualized Clarisse's slim fingers switching off the tiny pumps that supplied oxygen and nutrient fluid to the tank in which floated that obscenely naked brain—but only a dog's brain—and, suddenly, felt more than a little sick.

He said, "I think I'll go below, Commodore."

"As you please, Commodore," replied Grimes II. "I shall stay up here. There should be information coming through at any time now. If things start happening, this is my place."

"Too right," agreed Grimes. "And there's an old saying about two women in the same kitchen. Two shipmasters in the same control room would be at least as bad."

XIX

He made his way down from the control room to the deck upon which the master's quarters and the V.I.P. suite —in which he and Sonya had been housed—were situated. The general layout was very similar to that of his own

ship. There was no extra accommodation in this compartment; everything was on a larger scale.

Absentmindedly he paused outside the door that had above it, in gold lettering, CAPTAIN. It was ajar. He had started to enter when he realized his error, but too late for him to pull back. He could see through into the bedroom. His wife was there, sitting up in bed, reading. The spectacles that she was wearing enhanced her nakedness.

His wife?

But she might have been.

On another time track she was.

"Come in," she not quite snapped. "Don't dither around outside."

He went in.

She put down her book and looked at him gravely, but there was a quirk at the corners of her mouth. She was very beautiful, and she was . . . different. Her breasts were not so full as Sonya's but were more pointed. Her smooth shoulders were just a little broader.

She said, "Long time no see, John."

He felt a wild, impossible hope, decided to bluff his way out—or in. He asked gruffly, "What the hell do you mean?"

She replied, "Come off it, John. She's put her mark on you, just as I've put my mark on him. Once you were identical, or there was only one of you. That must have been years ago, round about the time that we had the fun and games on Sparta. Remember?"

Grimes remembered. It had been very shortly after the Spartan affair that he and Maggie had split brass rags.

"Furthermore," she went on, "my ever-loving had the decency to buzz down to tell me that he'd be in Control all night, and not to wait up for him. . . ."

"But Sonya. . . ."

"Damn Sonya. Not that I've anything against her, mind you. We've known each other for years and have always been good friends. But if you must know, John, she and I have just enjoyed a girlish natter on the telephone, and she's under the impression that you're sharing *my* John's sleepless vigil."

Get the hell out of here, you lecherous rat! urged the rather priggish censor who inhabited an odd corner of Grimes' brain.

"Don't just stand there," she said.

He sat down at the foot of the wide bed.

"John! Look at me."

He looked. He went on looking. There was so much that he remembered vividly, so much that he had almost forgotten.

"Have I got Denebian leprosy, or something?"

He admitted that she had not. Her skin was sleek, golden gleaming, with the coppery pubic puff in delicious contrast, the pink nipples of her breasts prominent. He thought, *To hell with it. Why not?* He moved slowly toward her. Her wide, red mouth was inviting. He kissed her—for the first time in how many years? He kissed her and went on kissing her, until she managed to get her hands between their upper bodies and push him away.

"Enough . . ." she gasped. "Enough . . . for the time being. Better shut the outer door . . . and snap on the lock. . . ."

He broke away from her reluctantly. He said, "But suppose *he* . . ." he could not bring himself to say the name ". . . comes down from Control. . . ."

"He won't. I know him. I should, by this time. The only thing in his mind will be the safety of his precious ship." She smiled. "And, after all, I am an ethologist, specializing in animal behavior, the human animal included. . . ."

Grimes asked rather stiffly, "I suppose you knew that I would be coming in?"

"I didn't know, duckie, but I'd have been willing to bet on it. The outer door was left ajar on purpose."

"Mphm." Grimes got up, went into the day cabin, shut and locked the door. He returned to the bedroom.

She said, "You look hot. Better take off your shirt."

He took off his shirt. It was a borrowed one, of course. And so was the pair of trousers. So were the shoes. (He had boarded this ship, of course, with only the usual long johns under his space suit.)

Borrowed clothing, a borrowed wife. . . .

But was it adultery?

Grimes grinned. What were the legalities of this situation? Or, come to that, the ethics?

"What the hell are you laughing at?" she demanded.

"Nothing," he told her. "Everything."

She said, "I'll do my best to make this a happy occasion."

It was. There was no guilt, although perhaps there should have been. There was no guilt—after all, Grimes rationalized, he had known Maggie for years; he (or one of him) had been married to her for years. It was a wild, sweet mixture of soothing familiar and the stimulating unfamiliar. It was—right.

They were together on the now rumpled bed, their bodies just touching, each of them savoring a fragrant cigarillo.

Grimes said lazily, "After all that, I'd better have a shower before I leave. I don't suppose I—*he*—will mind if I use his bathroom. . . ."

She said, "There's no hurry. . . ."

And then the telephone buzzed.

She picked up the handset. "Mrs. Grimes . . ." she said drowsily, with simulated drowsiness. "Yes, John. It's me, of course. Maggie. . . . Yes, I *did* lock the door. . . ." She covered the mouthpiece with her hand, whispered, "Get dressed, and *out*. Quickly. I'll try to stall him off." Speaking into the telephone again, "Yes, yes. I know that I'm the Commodore's wife and that nobody would dream of making a pass at me. But have you forgotten that *wolf*, Sir Dominic Flandry, who's aboard at *your* invitation, duckie, is *prowling* around your ship seeking whom he may devour? And you left me all by myself, to sit and *brood*, or whatever it is you do up there in your bloody control room. . . . No, Sir Dominic didn't make a pass at me, but I could tell by the way he was looking at me. . . . All right, then. . . ."

Grimes was dressed, after a fashion. As he walked fast toward the door, he saw that Maggie was punching the buttons for another number on the ship's exchange. She called over her shoulder, "Wait a moment!"

"Sorry. See you later."

He went out into the alleyway. He hesitated outside the door to his own quarters. Dare he face Sonya? It would be obvious, too obvious, what he had been doing, and with whom.

The door opened suddenly—and Grimes was staring at

Flandry, and Flandry was staring at him, staring and smiling knowingly.

"You bastard!" snarled Grimes, swinging wildly. The punch never connected, but Flandry's hand around Grimes' right wrist used the momentum of the blow to bring Grimes sprawling to the deck.

"Gentlemen," said Grimes II coldly. "Gentlemen—if you will pardon my misuse of the word—I permit no brawling aboard my ship."

Grimes I got groggily to his feet assisted by Flandry. They looked silently at the Commodore. He looked at them. He said, "Such conduct I expected from you, Captain Flandry. But as for you, Commodore Grimes, I am both surprised and pained to learn that your time track is apparently more permissive than mine."

At last Grimes felt the beginnings of guilt. In a way it was himself whom he had cuckolded, but that was no excuse. And what hurt was that during this night's lovemaking it had been his own counterpart, himself although not himself, who had been the odd man out. He knew how this other Grimes must be feeling.

He thought, *I wish I were anywhere but here.*

He said, "Believe me, Commodore, I wish I were anywhere but here." Then he grinned incredulously, looking like a clown with that smile on a face besmeared with lip rouge. "And why the hell shouldn't I be?"

"If I had any say in the matter you would be, Commodore. You *and* Captain Sir Dominic Flandry." He made it sound as though the honorific were a word of four letters, not three.

"You just might have your wish, Commodore. Tell me, have you received any reports from Commander Mayhew and the other PCOs?"

"This is no time to. . . ."

"But it is. The success of our mission, the safety of our ships; these matters, surely, are of overriding importance. . . ."

"He's right, you know," said Sonya, who had appeared in the doorway, looking as though butter would not melt in her mouth.

"Shut up!" snapped Grimes. "You keep out of it."

"He's right, you know," said Maggie, cool and unruffled, who had just joined the party.

"Shut up!" snapped Grimes II. "You keep out of it."

"He's right, you know," drawled Flandry.

Grimes II snarled wordlessly. Then, "As a matter of fact, your Mayhew and his mates did get Clarisse to . . . to turn off the amplifier. They're trying to sort out the psionic impressions that they're getting from *Adler* and your *Faraway Quest,* now that the interference has been . . . switched off. I was thinking of calling you to let you know, but there was no urgency, and I thought you needed your sleep. Ha, ha."

"So now we work out a plan of campaign . . ." murmured Grimes I.

"Yes. In the control room. It'll be some time before I feel like setting foot in my own quarters again. And might I suggest that you two officers and gentlemen get yourselves looking like officers, at least, before you come up."

Grimes looked doubtfully at Sonya. Then he turned to Flandry. "Do you mind if I make use of your toilet facilities, Sir Dominic?"

"Be my guest, Commodore." Then, in almost a whisper, "After all, I was yours—and you were his."

Grimes didn't want to laugh, but he did. If looks could have killed he would have died there and then. But women have no sense of humor.

XX

Wanderer and *Faraway Quest II* synchronized temporal precession rates, and *Wanderer* closed with the *Quest,* laying herself almost alongside her. It was a maneuver typical of Irene's spacemanship—or spacewomanship—and when it was over Grimes I looked closely at Grimes II's head to see if his counterpart had acquired any additional gray hairs. He thought wryly, *Probably Maggie and I have put a few there ourselves.* . . . It was essential, however, that the meeting of the leaders be held aboard one of the ships; *Adler* would do her best to monitor a conversation conducted over the Carlotti transceivers.

So there they all were in *Faraway Quest's* control room: the two Grimeses, their wives, Sir Dominic, Irene, Trafford, Smith (inevitably), Mayhew and Metzenther. Somehow Grimes I found himself in the chair.

Slowly and carefully, he filled and lit his pipe. (The other Grimes produced and lit a cigarette. *Subtle*, thought Grimes. *Subtle. I didn't think you had it in you, John . . .*) After he had it going well he said, "All right. I think we can take it as read that our PCOs have silenced the dog, and that they—including, of course, Clarisse—are now doing some snooping into the minds of our mutual enemies. Correct?"

"Correct, sir," answered Mayhew.

"Good. Then report, please, Commander."

The telepath spoke in a toneless voice. "Clarisse is well, although her mind is not yet operating at full capacity. As far as she can determine, as far as we can determine, all the other members of *Faraway Quest*'s crew are unharmed. As yet.

"Insofar as their captors are concerned, we have found it advisable to concentrate on key personnel: Dr. Druthen, Captain Blumenfeld and Commander von Donderberg, who is still the senior prize officer aboard *Quest*. Dr. Druthen is not quite sane. He is ambitious. He thinks that the Duchy of Waldegren will appreciate his brilliance, whereas the Confederacy does not. His mother, who exercised considerable influence over him during his formative years, was an expatriate Waldegrener. Druthen, too, has strong sadistic tendencies. Had it not been for the restraining influence of von Donderberg the lot of the prisoners would have been a sorry one. He is still urging Blumenfeld to use them to blackmail us into giving him a free hand with The Outsider.

"Now, von Donderberg. The impression you gained from that talk with him over the Carlotti radio is a correct one. Like many—although not all—naval officers, he regards himself as a spaceman first and foremost. The prisoners happen to be wearing the wrong uniform, but they, as far as he is concerned, are also spacemen. He hates Druthen, and Druthen hates and despises him.

"Finally, Captain Blumenfeld. Once again, sir, you summed him up rather neatly. He is essentially a politician, with a politician's lack of conscience. He would stand on his mother's grave to get two inches nearer to where he wants to be. As a spaceman he is, at best, merely competent—but the success of this mission would put him at least two steps up the promotion ladder. He would play along with Druth-

en if he thought that he could get away with it, but realizes that maltreatment, or even murder of *Faraway Quest*'s rightful crew could lead to an outbreak of hostilities between the Duchy and the Confederacy. He knows that his government would welcome this rather than otherwise, but fears, as they fear, that the Confederacy's Big Brother might step in. Should he get the 'all clear' from Waldegren—we gained the impression that the Duchy's political experts are hard at work evaluating the possibility of Federation intervention—he will tell Druthen to go ahead.

"Meanwhile, he is hoping that there will be dissension in our ranks. That was why he gave us time to think things over; not long, but long enough." He looked at Smith. "As you know, at least one of us present puts his own interests before the well-being of *Faraway Quest*'s crew."

"Mphm." Grimes puffed thoughtfully at his pipe. Then, "Do you concur, Mr. Metzenther?"

"Yes, Commodore. Commander Mayhew has summarized the findings of all four of us."

"And now you know," said Grimes II, who did not seem to be enjoying his cigarette, "what are you going to do about it? Not that you can do much. You haven't a ship of your own, even though. . . ."

"Even though I'm carrying on as though this were my own ship?" asked Grimes. "In a way, she is. Just as. . ."

"She's not. And neither is Maggie."

"Shut up!" snapped the wife referred to. "Shut up! This is no time to let your personal feelings get in the way of important business."

"You should have thought of that last night," her husband told her.

Flandry laughed.

"Just what has been going on aboard this rustbucket?" asked Irene curiously, looking at Sir Dominic speculatively.

"It's a pity that you weren't here," he told her, while Sonya looked at him nastily.

"Just a slight domestic problem," said Grimes airily.

"Some people's idea of what's *slight* . . ." snarled Grimes II.

"Don't forget that I, too, am an injured party."

Flandry laughed again.

"Please . . ." pleaded Grimes. "Please. We're getting no place at all with this petty squabbling." He turned to May-

hew. "You've given us the general background. It's obvious that we have to do something before Blumenfeld gives Druthen the okay, or before Druthen acts off his own bat. I've already thought of something that we—that Clarisse especially—can do. I take it that there are writing materials in your watch room aboard *my Quest?*"

"Of course."

"And writing materials are also drawing materials. . . ."

"Yes. But to call up some peculiar deities or demons at this juncture could make the situation worse than it is now."

"Who mentioned deities or demons?" Grimes saw that Flandry, Irene and Trafford were looking at him curiously, as were his alter ego and Maggie Lazenby. He said slowly, "I suppose I'd better put you in the picture. Clarisse is more than a mere telepath. She is descended from a caveman artist who, displaced in time, was found on Kinsolving's Planet many years ago. He, it seems, had specialized in painting pictures of various animals which, consequently, were drawn into the hunters' traps. Clarisse inherited his talent. . . ."

"Impossible," said Grimes II flatly.

"Not so, Commodore. I've seen it happen. Ken Mayhew has seen it happen. So has Sonya."

"It's true," she agreed soberly.

"So Clarisse could be a sort of Trojan horse . . ." murmured Flandry.

"You're getting the idea. Of course, there's one snag. Each time that she's . . . performed she's been under the influence of some hallucinogenic drug."

"And the rest of you," sneered Smith.

"No. Most definitely not. The main problem now is to get her suitably high."

"That's no problem," said Mayhew. A great load seemed suddenly to have dropped from his thin shoulders. He had something to do at last—something to help to save Clarisse. "That's no problem. Two telepaths who are married have more, much more in common than any pair of nontelepaths. There is far greater sensitivity, far more . . . sharing than in any common marriage. If *I* get high on anything at all, so will Clarisse. If I go on a trip, so will she."

"Good," murmured Grimes. "Good. So buzz the quack and tell him what you need to put your mind in the proper

83

state. Try to get instructions through to Clarisse. All she has to do is sketch us, one by one, and we'll be with her. . . ." He looked rapidly around the control room. "Not you, Ken. I'm sorry, but you'll be too muzzy with dope. What about you, Mr. Metzenther? Good. And you, Flandry? And myself, and Sonya. . . ."

"Count me in," Irene said gruffly. "I still don't believe it, but if it works I'd like to be in the party."

"And me," said Trafford, although not overenthusiastically. "Tallentire can look after the ship."

Smith did not volunteer.

Maggie Lazenby was about to, Grimes thought, but lapsed into silence as her husband looked at her long and coldly.

And Grimes II said, "I'll not be sorry to see some of you off my vessel and back aboard your own ships."

XXI

This shouldn't be happening, thought Grimes. *Magic—and what else can it be called? in the control room of an interstellar ship. . . .* But this was the Rim, where the laws of nature, although not repealed, were not enforced with any stringency. This was beyond the Rim.

He looked at Mayhew as the telepath regarded dubiously the little glass of some colorless fluid that he was holding. "This," the too jovial ship's doctor had assured him, "will give you hallucinations in glorious technicolor and at least seven dimensions. . . ." Grimes looked at Mayhew, and everybody else looked at Mayhew. The PCO quipped, "Now I know how Socrates must have felt."

"Get on with it, Ken," urged Grimes.

"I'm drinking this muck, not you. All right, then. Down the hatch." He suited the action to the words.

His prominent Adam's apple wobbled as the draught went down. He licked his lips, enunciated slowly, "Not . . . bad. Not . . . too . . . bad." An odd sort of vagueness crept over his face. His eyes went out of focus. He wavered on his feet, groped almost aimlessly for a chair, slumped down into it.

Grimes whispered to Metzenther, "Clarisse—is she ready? Are you and Trialanne standing by to help?"

"Of course, Commodore."

Mayhew said with surprising clarity, "The black lambs of Damballa. But they shouldn't. No."

Never mind the bloody black lambs, thought Grimes testily.

"Clarisse . . ." Mayhew's voice was very soft, almost inaudible. "Clarisse. You shouldn't have killed Lassie."

"Damn Lassie," muttered Grimes.

"A man's best friend is his . . . is his . . . is his . . . ? But the black lambs. And no sheep dog. Yes."

Metzenther looked toward Grimes. He whispered reassuringly, "It'll not be long now, Commodore. She's started on her pictures. And they won't be of black lambs. Black sheep, more likely."

"You can say that again," grunted Grimes II.

Grimes I allowed himself a smile. Let Metzenther enjoy his play on words, and let the other Grimes make what he liked of it. It didn't matter. He would soon be back aboard his own ship. He looked down at the Minetti automatic pistol that he was holding, ready, in his right hand. (Luckily, his counterpart shared his taste in personal weaponry—as in other things.) He, he was sure, would be the first to be pulled aboard the *Quest.* After all, he knew Clarisse, had known her before Mayhew had. He took one last look around at the other members of the boarding party. All were armed. Sonya, Trafford and Metzenther wore holstered laser handguns; and Irene, two ugly looking pistols of .50 caliber. Flandry had something that looked as though it had been dreamed up by an illustrator of juvenile science fiction thrillers.

Grimes remembered the two occasions on which he had seen Clarisse at work. He recalled, vividly, that bare, windswept mountaintop on Kinsolving, with the black sky overhead, the Galactic Lens a misty shimmer low on the horizon. He visualized, without any effort on his part, the floodlit easel with its square of canvas, the pots of pigment, the girl, naked save for a scanty scrap of some animal pelt, working with swift, sure strokes on her brushes.

Sudden doubt assailed him.

Those had been ideal conditions. Would conditions aboard the hijacked *Faraway Quest* be as ideal?

Mayhew seemed to be completely out, sprawled loosely in his chair, his eyes closed, his mouth slack. A thin dribble

of spittle crawled down his chin. Had the telepath taken too much of whatever concoction it was that the doctor had prepared? Was Clarisse similarly unconscious?

Metzenther smiled reassuringly at the Commodore, whispered, "Any time now. . . ."

Flandry, overhearing, snorted his disbelief.

Grimes turned to admonish him, and. . . .

Flandry was gone.

XXII

Flandry was gone.

Grimes wondered why there had been no miniature clap of thunder as the air rushed in to fill the vacuum caused by his abrupt departure. Had the exactly correct volume of atmosphere been teleported from the room in which Clarisse was imprisoned to fill the space that the Imperial Captain had occupied? What did it matter, anyhow? Magic is an art, not a science.

Flandry was gone—and who next?

Grimes was more than a little hurt. He had known Clarisse for years. Sonya had known her for almost as long. And yet she called a stranger to her. She had met Sir Dominic only once; he must have made an impression on her.

He turned to the others. "Well, it seems to be working. But why *him?*"

"Why not?" asked Sonya sweetly. "He's resourceful. He's tough."

"And he's out of *my* hair," added Grimes II. He did not say aloud that he hoped that other people would soon be out of his hair. He did not need to.

Mayhew, still unconscious in his chair, twitched. He looked as though he were having a bad dream.

"Is she all right?" demanded Grimes of Metzenther.

"Yes, Commodore," answered the telepath. "Yes." He looked as though he had been about to say more but had decided against it.

"Can't you tell her to get the rest of us shifted across?"

"I . . . I will try. But you must realize that teleportation is a strain upon the operator."

"Damn it all, this is urgent."

"I know, Commodore. But . . . she will not be hurried."

"Druthen, von Donderberg. . . . Do *they* know that Flandry is aboard the ship?"

"No. And with von Donderberg actually in charge everything—including the prisoners' meals—is very much to timetable. There is little chance that Clarisse and Sir Dominic will be disturbed."

Disturbed? thought Grimes. An odd choice of words. . . .

"You must be patient, Commodore," said Metzenther.

Grimes was never to know if it was his own imagination, or if the telepath had deliberately planted the picture in his mind. But he *knew* what was happening, what had happened. He saw Clarisse, her clothing cast aside the better to emulate her savage forebears, working at the sketch she was making on a signals pad. She saw the picture growing out of her swift, sure stylus strokes, the depiction of Sir Dominic. What subconscious desires had been brought to the surface by the drug that Mayhew had taken, the effects of which he had shared with her?

And then. . . .

And then Flandry was with her.

Flandry, the unprincipled, suddenly confronted with a beautiful, naked, available and willing woman.

If Metzenther had not put thoughts, impressions into Grimes' brain he had read the Commodore's mind. He said, telepathically, "Mayhew will never know. We shall make sure of that."

"But . . . but how can she?" asked Grimes silently.

He got the impression of quiet laughter in reply. "How could you? How could Sonya? How could Maggie? Some of us—even you, Commodore—have regarded this straying into other continuua as a sort of a holiday. A pubic holiday. . . . Forgive me. That just slipped out. And Clarisse has been under strain as much as any of us, more than most of us. What's more natural than that she should greet her deliverer in the age-old manner? Are you jealous, Commodore?"

"Frankly, yes," thought Grimes. He grinned ruefully.

"What the hell do you find so amusing?" asked Sonya sharply.

"Oh, er . . . I was just wondering where Sir Dominic

had finished up. As we both of us know, this talent of Clarisse's is rather . . . unreliable."

"You have an odd sense of humor," she told him. She was beginning to look anxious.

There were no pictures in Grimes' mind now. He was rather thankful for that. But still he did not know how long it would be before Clarisse resumed her magical activities. He knocked his pipe out into one of the large ashtrays that were placed all around the control room. He refilled it. He lit it.

"Please, John," said Clarisse, "not in here. It's dreadfully stuffy."

She was, as he had visualized her, naked. She was standing at the desk, adding the last touches to the sketch she had made of Grimes. Flandry was seated on the bunk. He was fully clothed.

But. . . .

"Wipe the lipstick off your face, Sir Dominic," said Grimes coldly.

XXIII

Clarisse ignored the exchange. She tore the sheet upon which she had portrayed Grimes off the pad, put it to one side. She started a fresh sketch. The Commodore peered over her smooth, bare shoulder as she worked. The likeness was unmistakable.

"Now!" she whispered intently.

Grimes was almost knocked off his feet as Irene materialized. She exclaimed cheerfully, "Oops, dearie! Fancy meeting *you* here!" And then, to Clarisse, "Hadn't you better put something on, ducks? All these *men*. . . ."

"I work better this way," she was told.

"Ssshh!" hissed Grimes. "This cabin . . . bugged. . . ."

"It was," remarked Flandry, in normal conversational tones. "And very amateurishly, if I may say so."

"So you did, at least, take precautions before. . . ." Grimes began.

"Before *what?*" asked Flandry, smiling reminiscently. "I always take precautions, Commodore."

Clarisse blushed spectacularly, over her entire body. But she went on sketching.

Sonya appeared, looking around her disapprovingly. *What's been going on here?* she asked silently. Then it was Trafford's turn, and finally Metzenther's. The little cabin was uncomfortably crowded. Grimes didn't like the way that his wife was sitting close beside Flandry on the bunk. She, obviously, didn't like the way that he was being pressed between Irene's flamboyance and Clarisse's nudity. Somebody knocked over the tank in which the psionic amplifier was housed. It did not break, but the cover came off it, allowing the stagnant nutrient solution to spill on the deck. It smelled as though something had been dead for a very long time.

Sonya sniffed. "And now what do we do?" she demanded. "I'd suggest that Clarisse get dressed, but I realize that it's almost impossible in these circumstances."

"This is *your* ship, Commodore," said Flandry.

"Mphm . . ." Grimes realized that the operation should have been more thoroughly planned, urgency notwithstanding. "Mphm. When is your next meal due, Clarisse?"

"I . . . my watch . . . with my clothes. On the bunk. . . ."

Flandry rummaged in the little pile of garments and found the timepiece. He announced, "It is 1135 hours, this ship's time."

"Twenty-five minutes," said Clarisse.

"So we wait," said Grimes. "It'll not be for too long. Then we overpower whoever brings the tray and any other guards and take over."

Flandry laughed jeeringly. "Brilliant, Commodore. Really brilliant. And if anybody fires into this dogbox he'll get at least four of us with one shot."

"Have you any better ideas, Captain?"

"Of course," Flandry replied smugly. "If I am not mistaken, those weapons being toted around by Sonya, Captain Trafford and Mr. Metzenther are laser pistols. They are not used much in my continuum, but you people seem to like them. A laser pistol can be used as a tool as well as a handgun. A cutting tool. . . ."

"So we break out, rather than wait to be let out."

"A truly blinding glimpse of the obvious, sir."

Trafford was nearest the door. "Go ahead, please, Captain," said Grimes.

The little man unholstered his weapon. He pulled out a slender screwdriver that had been recessed in the butt of

it. Carefully, not hurrying, he made adjustments to the power settings. He replaced the screwdriver.

Grimes took a pencil from Clarisse. He managed to shove his way through the crowd to stand beside Trafford. He drew a rough circle on the smooth, painted metal panel of the door. He said, "The lock should be there, Captain. If you burn around it. . . ."

"I'll try, Commodore."

The narrow beam of intensely bright light shot from the muzzle of the pistol. Metal became blue white incandescent immediately but was reluctant to melt. The structural components of a starship are designed to withstand almost anything. Trafford removed his finger from the trigger, used the screwdriver to make further adjustments. Then he tried again.

Grimes had foreseen what was going to happen. After all, as Flandry had pointed out, this was *his* ship. Grimes should have warned the others, but this chance to see the silly grin wiped off Sir Dominic's face was not one to be passed over.

The air in the watch room became stiflingly hot, and acrid with the fumes of burning paint and metal. And then. . . .

And then there were bells ringing, some close and some distant, filling the echoing shell of *Faraway Quest* with their clangor. A klaxon added its stridency to the uproar. From the nozzles of the spray system jetted a white foam that blanketed everything and everybody. Flandry cursed, but he could never hope to match Irene's picturesque obscenities and blasphemies.

The door sagged open.

Grimes, pistol in hand, shoved past Trafford, out into the brightly lit alleyway. Sonya, looking like a figure roughly hacked from white foam plastic, was behind him, then Trafford, then Irene. Metzenther staggered out supporting Clarisse, who looked as though she had just emerged from a bubble bath.

"You bloody fool," gasped Flandry, who was last to emerge. "You bloody fool! You should have known. . . ."

"I did know," snapped Grimes. "Pipe down, damn you!"

The fire extinguishing foam was pouring out into the alleyway. Grimes motioned to the others to follow suit, dropped to his knees, let the cool, not unpleasantly acrid

froth almost cover him. How long would it be before the fire fighting party was on the scene? When *Quest's* own crew had been running the ship scant seconds would have elapsed; but Druthen and his scientists and technicians were not spacemen, and at least one of the three officers put aboard from *Adler* would be remaining in the control room.

Somebody, somewhere, switched the alarms off. So they realized that there was a fire. And without that incessant noise it was possible to think, to give orders.

"Keep covered," said Grimes. "They'll not see us until it's too late." He added, in a disgruntled voice, "The bastards are certainly taking their time. Billy Williams and his crowd would have had the fire out half an hour ago!"

"Glumph," replied Sonya through a mouthful of foam.

They were here at last, rounding the curve in the alleyway: a tall figure in a space suit, the spiked helmet of which made it obvious that he was a member of the Waldegren Navy, four men in civilian space armor, pushing a wheeled tank.

"Lasers only," whispered Grimes. "Fire!"

Lasers are silent—but they are dreadfully lethal. Grimes hated to have to do it—but the fire fighters must be given no chance to warn Druthen and von Donderberg in Control. Druthen's men were hijackers, and their lives were already forfeit. The universal penalty for this crime is death. The Waldegrener was acting under orders, but he had no business aboard Grimes' ship. What happened to him was just his bad luck.

Grimes stood up slowly in the waist-high foam. He looked at the five silent figures. They were dead all right, each of them with his armor neatly pierced in half a dozen places. There was no blood, luckily, and luckily nobody had employed the effective slashing technique, so the suits were still reasonably intact.

Five of them, he thought, trying hard to fight down his nausea. *Seven of us. Flandry can wear the Waldegren space suit—it'll fit him. Then myself. And Sonya. Irene? Metzenther? Trafford? Clarisse?*

He said, "Get the armor off them. It's a made-to-order disguise."

Trafford, Flandry and Sonya went to work. The smell of charred meat and burned blood was distressingly evident.

Suddenly, Sonya beckoned to Grimes. He went to look down at the stripped figure. It was a woman. She was, she had been one of the junior technicians. Grimes remembered her. He had referred to her, in his thoughts, as a hard-faced little bitch. Feeling sorry for this would not help her now.

He walked slowly back to where Clarisse was standing, patches of foam slipping slowly down her smooth skin, others still clinging to the salient points of her body. He whispered, pointing, "You know her?"

"Yes."

"Wear her suit. Speak into the suit radio, using her voice. . . . You can do that?"

"Of course."

"Report that the fire is under control. Should Druthen or von Donderberg feel uneasy about anything you, as a telepath, will know the right things to say to put their minds at rest. Say that we are returning topside to report as soon as the fire is out. Get it?"

"Yes."

"Then get suited up."

She obeyed him, assisted by Sonya and Irene. She spurned their suggestion that she should wear the dead woman's long johns. Grimes didn't blame her, although he winced at the thought of the unlined inside of the suit chafing her unprotected skin.

Then Grimes, too, stripped to his skimpy underwear, could not bring himself to put on a dead man's next-to-the-skin union suit. Neither could Sonya. But the corpse robbing worried neither Irene nor Flandry.

The bodies were concealed in the congealing foam, which hid, too, the tools taken from the belt pouches of the fire party. Those same pouches served as holsters for the weapons of Grimes and his people. It was decided that Trafford and Metzenther, who had been unable to disguise themselves, would stay in the watch room. They would be safe enough there, especially since Metzenther should be able to give ample advance warning of the approach of any hostile persons.

Then, speaking in a voice that was not her own, Clarisse said into her helmet microphone, "Sadie Hawkes reporting to Dr. Druthen. The fire's out. Nothing serious. That stupid bitch was burning papers for some reason or other."

"Is she hurt?" Druthen's voice did not betray much, if any, concern.

"Naw, Doc. We just slapped her round a little, is all."

Von Donderberg's voice came through the speakers. "Lieutenant Muller."

"Sorry, Commander," Clarisse told him. "The Lieutenant slipped on the foam an' caught his helmet a crack. His transceiver's on the blink."

"Where is the prisoner now?" inquired Druthen.

"We left her in her bubble batch to cool down. Ha, ha."

"Ha, ha," echoed Dr. Druthen.

Ha, ha, thought Grimes nastily.

XXIV

Grimes led the way into the control room. (After all, this was his ship.) He was followed by Flandry, whose right hand hovered just over the butt of his energy pistol, then by Sonya, then by Irene. Clarisse caught up the rear.

Druthen and von Donderberg swiveled in their chairs to face the returning fire fighting party. The scientist was fatly arrogant. The Waldegrener looked more than a little frayed around the edges. *It's your own fault,* thought Grimes. *If you aren't fussy about the company you keep. . . .*

Grimes and the others stood there. Druthen and von Donderberg sat there. Grimes knew that he should act and act fast, but he was savoring this moment. Druthen, an expression of petulant impatience growing on his face, snarled, "Take your bloody helmets off! Anybody'd think there was a smell in here." His words, although distorted by the suit diaphragms, were distinct enough.

"There is," replied Grimes. "You."

The scientist's face turned a rich purple. He sputtered, "Mutinous swine! Von Donderberg, you heard! *Do* something!"

Von Donderberg shrugged. There was a flicker of amusement in his blue eyes.

Grimes said, "Mutiny, Dr. Druthen? I am arresting *you* for mutiny and piracy." He fumbled for his Minetti, but the little pistol, unlike the heavier weapons carried by the others, was not suitable for use by a man wearing space armor with its clumsy gloves.

But Flandry's odd-looking weapon was out, as were Sonya's and Irene's pistols. Druthen stared at them helplessly, von Donderberg in a coldly calculating manner. "You will note, Herr Doktor," remarked the Waldegren officer, "that there are neat holes in those space suits, holes that could have been made by laser fire at short range." He seemed to be speaking rather louder than was really necessary. "It would seem that our prisoners somehow have escaped and have murdered my Lieutenant Muller and four of your people." He turned to face Grimes. "You will surrender."

"I admire your nerve," Grimes told him.

"That is not one of the prisoners!" exclaimed Druthen. "It's that bastard Grimes! But that's impossible!"

"It's not, Doctor. It's not." The Commodore was really enjoying himself. "You sneered at me—remember—for carrying a practicing witch on my Articles of Agreement. . . ."

The practicing witch screamed, "John! The Carlotti set! It's on! *Adler's* seeing and hearing everything!"

And *Adler's* temporal precession rate was synchronized with that of *Faraway Quest.* No doubt her cannon and projectors were already trained upon their target. No doubt boarding parties were already suited up and hurrying into the warship's airlocks.

Grimes swore. His gloating could easily have ruined everything. He dived for the Mannschenn Drive remote controls. He heard pistol fire as somebody, Irene probably, switched off the Carlotti transceiver in an effective but destructive manner. Von Donderberg got in his way, grappled him. The Waldegrener was a strong man and agile, whereas Grimes was hampered by his armor. His body was a barrier between the Commodore and the Mannschenn Drive control console. Brutally, Grimes flailed at him with his mailed fists, but von Donderberg managed to get a firm grip on both his wrists. Grimes tried to bring his knee up, but he was too slow and the foul blow was easily avoided.

It was Irene who settled matters. (After all, this was not *her* ship.) Her heavy pistols barked deafeningly, the slugs just missing Grimes (intentionally, he hoped) and von Donderberg. The face of the control panel splintered; otherwise the immediate results were unspectacular.

But down in the Mannschenn Drive room the duty technician watched aghast as the great, gleaming rotos ran

wild, precessing faster and faster yet, tumbling down and into the dark dimensions uncontrolled and uncontrollably. Beyond the control room viewports, the image of *Adler* glowed with impossible clarity against the blackness, then flickered out like a snuffed candle flame. Throughout the ship, men and women stared at familiar surroundings and fittings that sagged and fluoresced, that wavered on the very brink of the absolute nothingness. Belatedly, alarm bells started to ring, but their sound was a thin, high shrilling, felt rather than heard.

Abruptly, shockingly, normalcy returned as the Drive shut itself off. Colors, forms and sounds were suddenly . . . drab. The irregular throbbing of the inertial drive was harsh and irritating.

Grimes, still straining against von Donderberg, snapped, "Shut that bloody thing off!" Apart from the Waldegren Commander and his surviving officer—wherever *he* was—there were no spacemen among those who had hijacked the ship. Free fall would not worry Grimes and his boarding party overmuch, but it would be, at the very least, an inconvenience to the planet lubbers.

The annoying vibration ceased. *What next?* Grimes asked himself. It was hard to think clearly. That blasted von Donderberg was still putting up a fight, and Sonya and Clarisse, who had come to the Commodore's aid, were more of a hindrance than a help. "Irene!" he called. "Check the indicator! Are all A/T doors shut?" (The airtight doors should have automatically at the first signs of main drive malfunction.)

"Yes," she replied at last.

"There's a switch by itself in a glass-fronted box. . . . It's labeled LOCK. . . ."

"Got it. . . ."

"Then throw it!"

Grimes heard the little crash of shattering glass, heard Irene say, "Locked."

Sonya had a space suited arm across von Donderberg's throat. The man was starting to choke; his face was turning blue, his eyes were protruding. Suddenly he relinquished his hold on Grimes' wrists. The two women hustled him to an acceleration chair, forced him down into it. They held him there while Irene, using a length of flex that

she had found somewhere, lashed him into the seat. Druthen had already been similarly dealt with by Irene and Flandry.

"Mphm," grunted Grimes. The situation was, for the time being, under control. Slowly he removed his gloves, then took his pipe from one of the pouches at the belt of his space suit. He filled it and lit it, ignoring Sonya's "Not *now!*" He stared at Druthen, demanded, "Where are the prisoners?"

"Find out!" came the snarled reply.

From the intercom speakers came a growing uproar. "Doctor Druthen, what's happened?" "We're shut in, let us out of here!" "Doctor, there's no gravity!"

"We can do without that," said Grimes. Sonya switched off the system. Then, "Where are the prisoners, Druthen?"

Again the scientist snarled, "Find out!"

"And that is just what we intend to do, Herr Doktor," remarked Flandry. He pulled that complicated looking weapon from a makeshift holster at his belt, looked at it thoughtfully, said regretfully, "Not quite subtle enough. . . ." From another pouch he took out a knife, drew it from its sheath. It was only small, but it gleamed evilly. "Perhaps a little judicious whittling . . ." he murmured. "Where shall I start?"

Von Donderberg, who had recovered his voice, croaked, "Remember that you an officer and gentleman are. A civilized man."

"Who says that I'm civilized, Commander? Come to that—who dares say that either you or the learned Herr Doktor are civilized? You, sir, are a pirate. He is either a mutineer or a hijacker or both—but this is no time to discuss legalities. H'm. Your hands are nicely secured to the arms of your chair. Doctor. Perhaps if I pry off your fingernails, one by one. . . ."

"Flandry, you wouldn't!" expostulated Grimes.

"Wouldn't I, Commodore? You may watch."

"But I know where they are," said Clarisse. She added tartly, "What the hell's the good of having a professional telepath around if you don't make use of her?"

"Why must you spoil everything?" asked Flandry plaintively.

Von Donderberg laughed mirthlessly and Druthen fainted.

XXV

Yes, Clarisse knew where they were. It was an obvious enough place anyhow, the empty cargo compartment, right aft, in which Grimes had intended to stow whatever fantastic artifacts could be plundered from the Outsiders' Ship. Sonya, taking with her the electronic master key that would allow her passage through the locked airtight doors, went to release them. She was accompanied by Irene and would pick up Trafford and Metzenther on the way. She assured Grimes that if she encountered any of Druthen's people she would shoot if she had to. Irene growled that *she* would shoot, period. But there was not much risk. Metzenther would be able to give them ample warning of what hostile action, if any, awaited them in any compartment that they were about to enter.

Grimes switched on the second Carlotti transceiver—luckily the ship was fitted with two of the sets—and raised *Faraway Quest II* without any difficulty. She was no longer ahead, relatively speaking. *Adler* had turned, and *Quest II* and *Wanderer* had turned with her, and all three ships were racing back toward The Outsider on a reciprocal of their original trajectory.

"So you've got your ship back, Commodore," commented the other Grimes, looking out from the little screen. "Your Commander Mayhew, and Trialanne aboard *Wanderer*, have been keeping us informed."

"There's a little mopping up yet, Commodore," said Grimes. "But it shouldn't take long. I suggest that you and *Wanderer* slow down to allow me to catch up."

"*Wanderer* can if she likes, Commodore, but I'm not going to. *Adler's* going like a bat out of hell, and has the heels of us. Mayhew tells me that she's using some experimental accelerator, for the first time. Unluckily he's a mechanical and mathematical moron, so he can't get anything but absolute gibberish from the mind of *Adler's* engineer officer. But I know that it's Blumenfeld's intention to race us to The Outsider and then to seize and to hold it against all comers, waiting for reinforcements."

"What about *Vindictive?* Captain Flandry's ship?"

97

"What, indeed?" echoed Flandry.

"We can't warn her," said Grimes II. "That stupid culture she comes from has never developed the Carlotti system, or used telepaths. . . ."

"I resent that," snarled Flandry.

Grimes II seemed to notice him for the first time. "Sorry, Captain. I didn't realize that you were listening. But can *you* warn your ship?"

"No, I can't. But my men have very itchy trigger fingers."

"They'll need 'em. But switch on your other set, Commodore. Mr. Smith in *Wanderer* would like a word with you."

"I can't, Commodore. Will you tell Mr. Smith that his Mrs. Trafford switched off my other set rather permanently? The same applies to the remote control panel of my Mannschenn Drive."

"Then switch over to *Wanderer*. I'll just stick beak."

Grimes made the necessary adjustments, found himself looking at Smith. Tallentire was well in the background.

"Commodore," said Smith, "you realize that neither we nor the other Commodore Grimes can afford to wait until you have effected repairs and adjusted trajectory. *Adler* must be stopped. I, as the charterer, have assumed effective command of *Wanderer*. I do not see either Captain Trafford or Mrs. Trafford in your control room. Could you ask them to speak with me?"

"They're not available at the moment," said Grimes.

"They bloody well are!" Irene contradicted him.

Suddenly the control room had become crowded with people: Sonya, Irene, Trafford, Metzenther, Billy Williams, Carnaby, Hendrikson, Major Dalzell and Daniels. Williams reported to Grimes, "Commander Davis and his juniors have gone straight to the engine room, Skipper. They'll let you know as soon as they can get her started up." He went to where Druthen and von Donderberg were lashed in their chairs. "An' what shall we do with these drongos?"

"Take 'em away and lock 'em up, as soon as we can get round to it."

"Captain Trafford; Mrs. Trafford," came Smith's insistent voice from the Carlotti speaker.

"Yes!" snapped Irene.

"You and Captain Trafford should be aboard this ship.

But you're not. So I had no option but to order Mr. Tallentire to press the chase."

"You . . . *ordered?*"

"Yes. I ordered."

"He is the charterer," pointed out Trafford.

"All right. He's the bloody charterer. And so what?"

"Blumenfeld must be stopped," insisted the little captain. "Waldegren, in any continuum, cannot be allowed to get its hands on The Outsider's secrets."

"You'll never stop us now!" bragged von Donderberg.

"Shut up, you!" growled Billy Williams.

Irene turned back to the Carlotti transceiver. "All right, Smith. Press the chase. But, as owner, I appoint Mr. Tallentire master—until Captain Trafford's return. Mr. Tallentire will act as *he* sees fit. Get it?"

"As you wish." Smith managed to convey the impression of being supremely unconcerned.

"I will talk with Mr. Tallentire now."

Tallentire's face replaced that of Smith in the screen. He looked far from happy. "Yes, ma'am?"

"You are acting captain. Put the interests of the ship before those of Mr. Smith. Press the chase. Make use of your weaponry as requisite. You will revert to your normal rank as soon as we are back on board. That's all."

Somehow a junior engineer had managed to insert himself into the crowded control room. He elbowed his way toward Grimes. "Sir, Commander Davis told me to tell you that you can start inertial and Mannschenn Drives as soon as you like. He's been trying to raise you on the intercom, but the line is dead."

"It's switched off," Grimes admitted. "But we'll get it working again to the engine room. . . ." Daniels had anticipated him, handed Grimes a microphone. "Commodore here, Commander Davis. The remote control panel of the Mannschenn Drive is . . . out of order. You'll just have to get your instructions by telephone. Good." He turned to Carnaby. "Get ready to put the ship on the reciprocal heading—straight for The Outsider. We may be a little late for the start of the party, but we should be there before it's over . . ."

Flandry, Irene and Trafford looked at him with some animosity. "It's all right for *you*," growled the ex-Empress. "You've got a ship now, and we haven't."

"Can you get us back to where we belong?" Flandry asked Clarisse, a little desperately.

"I . . . I don't know . . ." she admitted. "I've never tried *sending* anybody anywhere before."

"You'd better try now," Grimes told her. "Or as soon as we have things sorted out." He didn't want Sonya and Flandry in the same ship.

XXVI

The Commodore's quarters still retained the distasteful traces of Druthen's occupancy, but the cleaning up could wait. Grimes forced himself to ignore the untidiness—no less than his own, but *different*—the scars left by smoldering cigarette ends on table tops; the sticky rings that showed where slopping over glasses had been set down. Sonya had wanted to do something about it at once, if not before, but Grimes had restrained her. "It is essential," he said firmly, "that Sir Dominic, Irene, Captain Trafford and Mr. Metzenther be returned to their own ships as soon as possible. . . ."

"And it is equally essential—to me, anyhow—that Ken be brought back here as soon as possible," Clarisse told him.

"Mphm. I see your point. But first of all both Captain Flandry's *Vindictive* and Captain Trafford's *Wanderer* must be put in a state of full fighting efficiency, so as to be able to cope with *Adler*. I would suggest that you deal with Sir Dominic first."

"Thank you," said Flandry.

"It will be a pleasure, Captain. Well, Clarisse?"

"I don't know how it *can* be done . . ." muttered the girl. "I don't know *if* it can be done. . . ."

"Rubbish!" snorted Irene. "If you can pull, you can push. It's as simple as that."

"Then why don't *you* try it?"

"It's just not my specialty, dearie. I'm just a rough and tough ex-mate out of the Dog Star Line."

"To say nothing of being a rough and tough ex-empress," commented Sonya acidly. "Shut up, unless you have something constructive to contribute."

"What I said *was* constructive."

"Like hell it was."

"Ladies, ladies . . ." murmured Flandry soothingly. Then, to Clarisse. "As I see it, your talent works this way. You're in the right, drug-induced frame of mind. You paint or draw a picture of whatever animal or person you wish to pull into the trap or ambush, concentrate—and the result is instant teleportation. . . ."

"You've oversimplified a little, Dominic, but that's about it."

"All right. Now suppose you sketched, to the best of your ability, the inside of my control room aboard *Vindictive*. . . ."

"I've never been aboard your ship, Dominic."

"But you've been inside my mind."

Oh, thought Grimes. *Have you, indeed? But I suppose that a telepath wants more than mere physical contact. . . .*

"Yes."

"This is what I want you to do. You must order from the ship's doctor whatever hallucinogen it is you need. And then, when you are ready, I'll visualize the control room of my ship, in as exact detail as possible, and you put it down on paper. . . ."

"And what," asked Grimes, "if *Vindictive*'s control room is brought to Captain Flandry, instead of the other way round? I seem to recall a law of physics that I learned as a child: Two solid bodies cannot occupy the same space at the same time."

"Let me finish, Commodore. After she has drawn the control room she will put me in it. . . ."

"Yes, Dominic," whispered Clarisse. "I think it will work. I'm sure it will work."

"As long as somebody's sure about something . . ." grumbled Grimes. "Now, I think that we have some neo-mescalin in our medical stores. It was you who insisted that we carry some. . . ."

"That is correct. If you will have it sent up . . . ?"

Grimes called the doctor on the intercom, and then Billy Williams in Control. "Commander Williams," he said, "unless it is a matter of utmost urgency we are not, repeat not, to be disturbed."

"You won't be, Skipper. We're the also-ran in this race—an' I'm afraid that *Adler*'s the odds on favorite! Of course, *Vindictive* might pip her at the post."

"We're trying to insure that she does," said Grimes, breaking off the conversation.

Slowly, without embarrassment, Clarisse removed her clothing, ignoring Irene's, "Is that necessary?" and Sonya's, "You're only jealous.". She took the small glass of opalescent fluid that Grimes handed her, drained it. In her nudity she was more witch than mere woman. She was . . . untouchable. (But that bastard Flandry hadn't found her so, thought Grimes.) Her face was solemn, her eyes looking at something very far away. And yet it was Sir Dominic at whom she was looking. At whom? Through whom? Beyond whom?

She was stooping slightly over the table upon which a sheet of paper had been spread, upon which the colored pens had been laid out. With her gaze still intent upon Flandry she commenced to draw with swift, sure strokes. The picture was taking shape: acceleration chairs, consoles, screens, the remote controls of machinery and weaponry, all subtly unlike anything that *Quest*'s and *Wander-er*'s people had ever seen before. *Different ships, different long splices,* thought Grimes, recalling an ancient Terran seafaring proverb. *Different universes, different interstellar drives. . . .*

Tension was building up in the Commodore's day cabin as the naked Clarisse stared at Flandry in his glittering uniform; as Flandry stared at Clarisse. As far as he was concerned, as far as she was concerned they were alone. Under her weaving hands the sketch was becoming three dimensional, real. Were the lights dimming? Was the irregular beat of the inertial drive, the thin, high whining of the Manschenn Drive becoming fainter? Was the deathly cold of interstellar space pervading the ship?

There is one law of nature that is never broken—magic notwithstanding: *You can't get something for nothing.* A transfer of a solid body across a vast distance was about to take place. Such a transfer, whether by wheels, wings or witchcraft, involves the use of energy. There was energy in many usable forms available within the hull of *Faraway Quest.* It was being drawn upon.

Grimes stared at the picture on the table. The lights—red, green, blue and amber—on the panels of the consoles were glowing, and some of them were blinking rapidly. The

darkness beyond the viewports was the utter blackness of intergalactic space. Something swam slowly into sight beyond one of the big transparencies—the dome-shaped Shaara derelict.

And then. . . .

And then there was a man there, standing in the middle of the hitherto deserted control room, the details of his face and figure growing under the witch artist's flying fingers. It was unmistakably Flandry, and he was stark naked save for his belt and his holstered pistol.

Grimes looked up from the sketch to stare at the emptiness where Flandry had been standing. He was . . . gone. But not entirely; his uniform, a small bundle of black and gold, of rainbow ribbons, was all that remained of him.

Irene said—was it to Sonya or to Clarisse?—"At least you've something to remember him by, dearie."

Clarisse, her face cold and hard, snatched the sheet with the sketch off the table, screwed it up into a ball, threw it toward the disposal chute. She did not miss. She moved swiftly around the table, picked up the empty uniform, then stuffed it down the chute after the crumpled paper. Grimes made as though to stop her—after all, an analysis of the cloth from which Flandry's clothing had been cut could have told a great deal about the technology of his culture— then decided against it. He would be able to swop information with Sir Dominic after *Adler* had been disposed of. Nonetheless, he was sorry that he had not said goodbye properly to the man, thanked him for all his help. (But Flandry had helped himself, in more ways than one. . . .)

The witch girl was ready to resume operations. A fresh sheet of paper was on the table. She said nothing aloud to Metzenther, but the two telepaths must have been in communication. He came to stand beside her, was obviously feeding into her mind the details of *Wanderer's* control room. Again the detailed picture grew.

Irene asked, "Would you mind if I kept my clothes on, Clarisse? Public nudism never appealed to me."

Sonya said, cattily, "I don't think female nakedness interests her."

Nor did it. When Irene vanished she left nothing behind—and neither did Trafford nor Metzenther.

And now, at last, Clarisse was working for herself. For the last time the lights dimmed, the temperature dropped,

the shipboard sounds were muffled. Grimes looked at the flattering portrait of Mayhew that had appeared, then at Sonya. He said, "I think we'll see what's happening topside, my dear." And, as Mayhew materialized, just as they were leaving, "It's good to have our ship to ourselves again."

XXVII

They had their ship to themselves again, but she was a ship alone. Far ahead of them now were their allies—allies only as long as it was expedient for them to be so—and their enemies. There was communication still with *Faraway Quest II* and with *Wanderer,* by Carlotti radio and through the telepaths. There was no word from *Vindictive;* but as Irene, Trafford and Metzenther were safely back aboard their own vessel, it could be assumed that Flandry was safely back in his.

Grimes, pacing his control room (three steps one way, three steps the other unless he wished to make complicated detours around chairs and banked instruments) was becoming more and more impatient. For many years he had thought of himself as a man of peace—but in his younger days, in the Federation's Survey Service, he had specialized in gunnery. If there was to be a fight he wanted to be in it. Apart from anything else, should he not be present at the moment of victory over *Adler* his prior claim to The Outsider would be laughed at by Irene, by Smith, by Flandry and even by his other self. And his engines were not developing their full capacity.

The emergency shutdown of the Mannschenn Drive had affected the smooth running of that delicate, complex mechanism. It was nothing serious but recalibration was necessary. Recalibration can be carried out only on the surface of a planet. And even if there had been any planets in the vicinity—which, of course, there were not—Grimes could not afford the time.

So *Faraway Quest* limped on, while, at last, the reports started coming in from ahead of her. *Wanderer* thought the *Vindictive* was engaging *Adler.* One of the officers aboard *Faraway Quest II* had broken the code that *Adler*

was using in her Carlotti transmissions to base, and Grimes II reported that Blumenfeld was screaming for reinforcements.

Wanderer and *Faraway Quest II* were now within extreme missile range of the engagement but had not yet opened fire. To do so they would have to revert to normal space/time. Metzenther, aboard *Wanderer*, reported through Clarisse that he and Trialanne were monitoring the involuntary psionic transmissions of the personnel of both ships presently engaged in the fighting, and that Flandry was emanating confidence, and Blumenfeld a growing doubt as to the outcome of the battle. Each ship, however, was finding it difficult to counter the unfamiliar weapons being used by the other, and each ship was making maximum use of the cover of the derelicts in orbit about The Outsider.

Wanderer had emerged into the normal continuum and had launched missiles.

Faraway Quest II was engaging *Adler* with long range laser.

Somebody had scored a direct hit on the Outsiders' Ship itself.

And that was all.

XXVIII

The Carlotti transceiver was dead insofar as *Wanderer*, *Faraway Quest II* and *Adler* were concerned. There were no psionic transmissions from *Wanderer*, no unintentional emanations from the crews of the other ships.

What had happened? Had the allies launched their Sunday punch against *Adler*, and had *Adler*'s retaliatory Sunday punch connected on all three of them? It was possible, Grimes supposed, just barely possible—but wildly improbable.

"Are you sure you can pick up absolutely nothing?" he demanded of Mayhew and Clarisse. (There are usually some survivors, even when a ship is totally destroyed, even though they may not survive for long.)

"Nothing," she replied flatly. And then—"But I'm picking up an emanation. . . . It's more an emotion than actual thought. . . ."

"I get it too," agreed Mayhew. "It's . . . it's a sense of strong disapproval."

"Mphm. I think that I'd disapprove strongly if *my* ship were shot from under me," said Grimes.

"But . . . but it's not *human* . . ." insisted the girl.

"Mr. Carnaby," Grimes barked at his navigator. "What do you get in the MPI? Is the Outsiders' Ship still there?"

"Still there, sir. And, as far as I can make out, only four vessels in orbit about her. . . . There could be a cloud of wreckage."

Possibly a couple of the derelicts, thought Grimes. Possibly *Adler*, or *Wanderer*, or the other *Quest*, or *Vindictive*. Possibly a large hunk blown off the Outsiders' Ship herself. Possibly anything.

He said, "We will stand in cautiously, proceeding under Mannschenn Drive until we are reasonably sure that it is safe to reenter normal space/time. Meanwhile, Mr. Hendrikson, have all weaponry in a state of instant readiness. And you, Major Dalzell, have your men standing by for boarding operations. Commander Williams, see that the boats are all cleared away."

"What is a killer ape?" asked Clarisse suddenly.

"This is hardly the time or place to speculate about our probable ancestry!" snapped Grimes.

"I am not speculating, Commodore. It is just that I picked up a scrap of coherent thought. It was as though a voice—not a human voice—said, 'Nothing but killer apes. . . .' "

"It's a pity we haven't an ethologist along," remarked Grimes. And where was Maggie Lazenby, the Survey Service ethologist whom he had known, years ago, whom he knew, now—but when *was* now?—as the other Grimes, captain of the other *Faraway Quest?* Where was Grimes? Where was Irene? Where was Flandry? He didn't worry about Blumenfeld.

He went to look at the MPI screen. It was a pity that it showed no details. But that large, rapidly expanding blob of luminescence must be The Outsider; those small sparks the derelicts. Carnaby said, in that tone of voice used by junior officers who doubt the wisdom of the procedures of their superiors, "We're *close*, sir."

"Yes, Mr. Carnaby. Mphm." He took his time filling and lighting his pipe. "All right, you may stand by the inter-

com to the engine room. Stop inertial drive. Half-astern. Stop her. Manschenn Drive—stop! Mr. Hendrikson—stand by all weapons!"

And there, plain beyond the viewports, was The Outsider coldly luminescent, unscarred, not so much a ship as a castle out of some fairy tale told when Man was very young: with towers and turrets, cupolas and minarets and gables and buttresses, awe-inspiring rather than grotesque. And drifting by, tumbling over and over, came one of the derelicts, the Shaara vessel aboard which the conference had been held. It had been neatly bisected, so that each of its halves looked like one of those models of passenger liners in booking agents' display windows, cut down the midship line to show every deck, every compartment.

"We will continue to orbit The Outsider," said Grimes. "We will search for survivors."

"Commodore," said Mayhew. "There are no survivors. They are all . . . gone."

"Dead, you mean?"

"No, sir. Just . . . gone."

XXIX

They were . . . gone: *Wanderer* and *Adler, Faraway Quest II* and *Vindictive.* They were gone, without a trace, as though they had never been. (But had they ever been?) There was wreckage in orbit about The Outsider—the shattered and fused remains of the Dring cruiser: a whirling cloud of fragments that could have come only from that weird, archaic and alien ship that had never been investigated, that would never now be investigated. And Grimes' flag, the banner of the Rim Worlds Confederacy that he had planted on the Outsiders' Ship, was gone too. This was a small matter and was not noticed until, at last, Grimes decided to send away his boarding party. Until then the search for survivors had occupied all his attention.

Faraway Quest had the field to herself.

"We will carry on," said Grimes heavily, "with what we came out here to do." And his conscience was nagging him. Surely there was *something* that he could have done for

Flandry, for Irene, for the other Grimes. All of them had helped him. What had he done to help them? What had he done to help Maggie? But space was so vast, and space/time, with its infinitude of dimensions, vaster still; and the lost ships and their people were no more than microscopic needles in a macrocosmic haystack. Too, he told himself, some clue to their fates might be found within that enormous, utterly alien hull.

So it was that Grimes, suited up, stood in the airlock of the *Quest* with Sonya and Williams and Major Dalzell. The Outsider had . . . permitted the ship to approach much closer than she had before; there would be no need to use the boats for the boarding party. The door slowly opened, revealing beyond itself that huge, gleaming construction. It looked neither friendly nor menacing. It was . . . neutral.

Grimes made the little jump required to break magnetic contact between boot soles and deck plating, at the same time actuating his suit propulsion unit. He knew, without turning to watch, that the others were following him. Swiftly he crossed the narrow moat of nothingness, turning himself about his short axis at just the right time, coming in to a landing on an area of The Outsider's hull that was clear of turrets and antennae. He felt rather than heard the muffled clang as his feet hit the flat metal surface. Sonya came down beside him, then Williams, then Dalzell.

The commodore looked up at his ship, hanging there in the absolute blackness, faint light showing from her control room viewports, a circle of brighter light marking the reopened airlock door. He could see four figures jumping from it—the sergeant of marines and three privates. Next would be Mayhew, with Engineer Commander Davis, Brenda Coles, the assistant biochemist and Ruth Macoby, assistant radio officer. It was a pity, thought Grimes, that he had not crewed his ship with more specialist officers; but it had been assumed, of course, that Dr. Druthen and his scientists and technicians would fill this need. But Druthen and his people, together with von Donderberg and his surviving junior officer, were prisoners in the empty cargo hold in which *Faraway Quest*'s crew had been confined.

"We're being watched," whispered Sonya, her voice faint from the helmet transceiver.

They were being watched. Two of the antennae on the

border of the clear area were turning, twisting. They looked unpleasantly like cobras poised to strike.

"Not to worry," Grimes assured her. "Calver mentioned the very same thing in *his* report."

The sergeant and his men were down now. The eight humans were tending to huddle. "Break it up!" Dalzell was barking. "Break it up! We're too good a target like this!"

"So is the ship, Major," Grimes told him.

"Sorry, sir." The young marine did not sound very penitent. "But I think we should take all precautions."

"All right," said Grimes. "Scatter—within reason." But he and Sonya stayed very close together.

Mayhew, Davis, Coles and Macoby came in. The telepath identified Grimes by the badges of rank on his space suit, came to stand with him and Sonya.

"Well, Ken?" asked the Commodore.

"It . . . it knows we're here. It . . . it is deciding. . . ."

"If it doesn't make its mind up soon," said Grimes, "I'll burn my way in."

"*Sir!*" Mayhew sounded horrified.

"Don't worry," Sonya told him. "It's opening up for us."

Smoothly, with no vibrations, a circular door was sliding to one side. Those standing on it had ample time to get clear of the opening, to group themselves about its rim. They looked down into a chamber, lit from no discernible source, that was obviously an airlock. From one of its walls, rungs spaced for the convenience of human beings extruded themselves. (And would those rungs have been differently spaced for other, intelligent, space-faring beings? Almost certainly.)

Grimes reported briefly by his suit radio to Hendrikson who had been left in charge. He knew without asking that Mayhew would be making a similar report to Clarisse. Then he said, "All right. We'll accept the invitation." He lowered himself over the rim, a foot on the first rung of the ladder. The Outsider's artificial gravity field was functioning, and *down* was down.

There was ample room in the chamber for all twelve of them. They stood there silently, watching the door slide back into place over their heads. Dalzell and his marines kept their hands just over the butts of their handguns. Grimes realized that he was doing the same. He was wearing at his belt a pair of laser pistols. He spoke again into

his helmet microphone. His companions could hear him, but it became obvious that they were now cut off from communication with the ship. Captain Calver, he remembered, had reported the same phenomenon. It didn't really matter. Mayhew said that he could still reach Clarisse and that she could reach him.

"Atmosphere, Commodore," said the biochemist, looking at the gauge among the other gauges on her wrist. "Oxygen helium mixture. It would be safe to remove our helmets."

"We keep them on," said Grimes.

Another door in the curving wall was opening. Beyond it was an alleyway, a tunnel that seemed to run for miles and flooded with light. As was the case in the chamber there were no globes or tubes visible. There was nothing but that shadowless illumination and that long, long metallic tube, like the smooth bore of some fantastically huge cannon.

Grimes hesitated only briefly, then began to stride along the alleyway. Sonya stayed at his side. The others followed. Consciously or unconsciously they fell into step. The regular crash of their boots on the metal floor was echoed, reechoed, amplified. They could have been a regiment of the Brigade of Guards, or of Roman legionaries. They marched on and on, along that tunnel with no end. And as they marched the ghosts of those who had been there before them kept pace with them—the spirits of men and of not-men, from only yesterday and from ages before the Terran killer ape realized that an antelope humerus made an effective tool for murder.

It was wrong to march, Grimes dimly realized. It was wrong to tramp into this . . . this temple in military formation, keeping military step. But millennia of martial tradition were too strong for him, were too strong for the others to resist (even if they wanted to do so). They were Men, uniformed men, members of a crew, proud of their uniforms, their weapons and their ability to use them. Before them—unseen, unheard, but almost tangible—marched the phalanxes of Alexander, Napoleon's infantry, Rommel's Afrika Korps. Behind them marched the armies yet to come.

Damn it all! thought Grimes desperately, *we're space-*

men, not soldiers. Even Dalzell and his Pongoes are more spacemen than soldiers.

But a gun doesn't worry about the color of the uniform of the man who fires it.

"Stop!" Mayhew was shouting urgently. "Stop!" He caught Grimes' swinging right arm, dragged on it.

Grimes stopped. Those behind him stopped, in a milling huddle—but the hypnotic spell of marching feet, of phantom drum and fife and bugle, was broken.

"Yes, Commander Mayhew?" asked Grimes.

"It's . . . Clarisse. A message. . . . Important. I couldn't receive until we stopped marching. . . ."

"What is it?" demanded Grimes.

"The . . . ship . . . and Clarisse and Hendrikson and the others. . . . They're prisoners again!"

"Druthen? Von Donderberg?"

"Yes."

Grimes turned to his second-in-command. "You heard that, Commander Williams?"

"Yair. But it ain't possible, Skipper. Nary a tool or a weapon among Druthen an' his mob. We stripped 'em all to their skivvies before we locked 'em up, just to make sure."

"How did it happen'?" Grimes asked Mayhew sharply.

"The . . . the details aren't very clear. But Clarisse thinks that it was a swarm of fragments, from one of the blown up derelicts, on an unpredictable orbit. The *Quest* was holed badly, in several places . . . including the cargo hold. Mr. Hendrikson opened up so the prisoners could escape to an unholed compartment."

"Any of us would have done the same," said Grimes slowly. He seemed to hear Sir Dominic Flandry's mocking laughter. "But what's happening now?"

"Von Donderberg has all the *Quest*'s weapons trained on The Outsider, on the airlock door. If we try to get out we shall be like sitting ducks."

"Stalemate . . ." said the Commodore. "Well, we've a breathable atmosphere in here—I hope. So that's no worry. There may even be water and food suitable for our kind of life. . . ."

"But they're coming after us. The airlock door has opened for them! They're here now!"

"Down!" barked Dalzell, falling prone with a clatter. The

others followed suit. There were dim figures visible at the end of the tunnel, dim and very distant. There was the faraway chatter of some automatic projectile weapon. The Major and his men were firing back, but without apparent success.

And at the back of Grimes' mind a voice—an inhuman voice, mechanical but with a hint of emotion—was saying, *No, no. Not again. They must learn. They must learn.*

Then there was nothingness.

XXX

Grimes sat on the hilltop, watching Clarisse work.

She, clad in the rough, more-or-less cured pelt of a wolf-like beast, looked like a cavewoman, looked as her ancestors on this very world must have looked. Grimes looked like what he was—a castaway. He was wearing the ragged remnants of his long johns. His space suit, together with the suits of the others who had been so armored, was stowed neatly in a cave against the day when it would be required again—if ever. Other members of the party wore what was left of their uniforms. They were all here, all on what Grimes had decided must be Kinsolving's Planet, twenty men and thirteen women.

And, some miles away, were Druthen and von Donderberg and their people. They were still hostile—and in their tribe were only five women, two of them past childbearing age. They had their weapons still—but, like *Faraway Quest's* crew, were conserving cartridges and power packs. None-theless, three nights ago they had approached Grimes' encampment closely enough to bring it within range of their trebuchet and had lobbed a couple of boulders into the mouth of the main cave before they were driven off by Dalzell and his marines.

All of them were on Kinsolving's Planet.

It was Kinsolving's Planet ages before it had been discovered by Commodore Kinsolving, ages before those mysterious cavemen had painted their pictures on the walls of the caves. (Perhaps the ancestors of those cavemen were here now. . . .) The topography was all wrong. But by the time that Man pushed out to the rim of the galaxy,

old mountain ranges would have been eroded, would have sunk, seas would roll where now there were plains, wrinklings of the world's crust would bring new, towering peaks into being.

But that feeling of *oddness* that Grimes had known on his previous visit (previous, but in the far distant future) to this planet still persisted. On Kinsolving *anything* could happen, and most probably would.

Was it some sort of psionic field induced by the Outsiders' Ship? Or had The Outsider been drawn to that one position in space by the field? Come to that—who (or what) were *the Outsiders?* Do-gooders? Missionaries? Beings whose evolution had taken a different course from that of Man, of the other intelligent races of the galaxy?

And we, thought Grimes, *are descendants of the killer ape, children of Cain. . . . What would we have been like if our forebears had been herbivores, if we had not needed to kill for food—and to protect ourselves from other predators? What if our first tools had been tools, peaceful tools, and not weapons? But conflict is essential to the evolution of a species. But it could have been conflict with the harsh forces of Nature herself rather than with other creatures, related and unrelated. Didn't some ethologist once refer to Man as the Bad Weather Animal?*

But They, he thought, as he watched Clarisse, squatting on her hunkers, scratching industriously away with a piece of chalky stone on the flat, slate surface of the rock, *but They have certainly thrown us back to our first beginnings. We didn't pass the test. First of all there was the naval battle—and I wonder what happened to* Wanderer, Vindictive, *the other* Quest *and* Adler. *. . . First of all there was the naval battle, and then the brawl actually within the sacred precincts. Calver and his crew must have been very well behaved to have been accepted, nonetheless. Perhaps, by this time, the stupid pugnacity is being bred out of Man, perhaps Calver was one of the new breed. . . .*

"Stop brooding!" admonished Sonya sharply.

"I'm not brooding. I'm thinking. I'm still trying to work things out."

"You'd be better employed trying to recall every possible, smallest detail of your beloved *Quest.* Clarisse knows damn' all about engineering, and if she's to succeed she must have all the help we can give her."

"*If* she succeeds. . . ."

"John!" Her voice betrayed the strain under which she was living. "I'm not cut out to be an ancestral cavewoman, or any other sort of cavewoman. I was brought up to wear clean clothes, not filthy rags, to bathe in hot water, not a stream straight off the ice, to eat well-cooked food, not greasy meat charred on the outside and raw inside. . . . Perhaps I'm too civilized—but this is no world for me." She paused. "And here we are, all of us, relying on the wild talent of a witch, a teleporteuse, who's been at least half-poisoning herself by chewing various wild fungi which might—or might not—have the proper hallucinogenic effect . . ." She laughed bitterly. "All right—the artists in her ancestry did have the power to pull food animals to them. She has it too, as well we know. But will it work with a complex construction such as a spaceship?"

"It worked," Grimes told her, "with complex constructions such as human beings. And Clarisse is no more an anatomist or a physiologist than she is an engineer."

"Commodore," Mayhew was calling. "Clarisse needs your help again!"

Grimes got to his feet. Before he walked to where the artist was at work he slowly looked from his vantage point around his little kingdom. To the north were the jagged, snowcapped peaks, with their darkly forested foothills. To the south was the sea. To east and west were the rolling plains, with their fur of coarse, yellowish grass, their outcroppings of stony hillocks and boulders. From behind one of the distant hills drifted the blue smoke of Druthen's fires.

"Commodore!" called Mayhew again.

"Oh, all right."

He walked over the rocky hilltop to that slab of slate, to where Davis, Williams, Hendrikson and Carnaby were clustered around Clarisse. The sketch of *Faraway Quest* was taking shape, but it was vague, uncertain in outline. How many attempts had there been to date? Grimes had lost count. Earlier drawings had been obliterated by sudden vicious rain showers, had been rubbed out in fits of tearful anger by the artist herself. Once, and once only, it had seemed that a shimmering ship shape, almost invisible, had hung in the air for a microsecond.

Grimes looked at the faces of his officers, his departmental heads. All showed signs of strain, of overmuch con-

centration. Williams, who was responsible for maintenance, must have been making a mental tally of every rivet, every welded seam in the shell plating. Davis would have been visualizing machinery; Hendrikson, his weapons; Carnaby, his navigational instruments.

But. . . .

But, Grimes suddenly realized, none of them had seen, had *felt* the ship as a smoothly functioning whole.

"Ready?" he asked Clarisse.

"Ready," she replied in a tired, distant voice.

And Grimes remembered. He remembered the first commissioning of *Faraway Quest* and all the work that had gone into her, the maintenance and the modifications. He relived his voyage of exploration to the Galactic East: his landings on Tharn, Grollor, Mellise and Stree. He recalled, vividly, his discovery of the antimatter systems to the Galactic West, and that most peculiar voyage, during which he and Sonya had come together, which was made as part of the research into the Rim Ghost phenomena.

All this he remembered, and more, and his mind was wide open to Clarisse as she scratched busily away with her rough piece of chalk—and hers was open to him. It was all so vivid, too vivid for mere imagination, for memory. He could actually have been standing in his familiar control room. . . .

He was standing in his familiar control room.

But that was impossible.

He opened his eyes, looked around in a slow circle.

He saw the jagged, snowcapped peaks to the north, with their darkly forested foothills. He saw the glimmering sea to the south. To east and west were the rolling plains, with their fur of coarse, yellowish grass, their outcroppings of stony hillocks and boulders. From behind one of the distant hills drifted the blue smoke of Druthen's fires.

But. . . .

But he was seeing all this through the wide viewports of *Faraway Quest*.

He walked, fast, to the screen of the periscope, adjusted the controls of the instrument so that he had an all-round view around the ship. Yes—his people, his crew were there, all of them staring upward. He did not need to increase the magnification to see the wonder on their faces.

"Mphm," he grunted. He went to the panel on which

were the controls for the airlock doors. He punched the necessary buttons. The illuminated indicators came on. OUTER DOOR OPEN. INNER DOOR OPEN. RAMP EXTRUDING—to be replaced by RAMP DOWN.

Meanwhile. . . .

He put his eyes to the huge binoculars on their universal mounting. Druthen and von Donderberg must have seen the sudden appearance of the ship. She would mean a chance of escape for *them*. Yes, there they were, two dozen of them, running. The sun glinted from the weapons they carried—the guns with their hoarded ammunition, their carefully conserved power packs.

It was a hopeless sortie; but desperate men, more than once have achieved miracles.

Grimes sighed, went to the gunner's seat of the bow 40 millimeter cannon. He put the gun on manual control. It would be the best one for the job; a noisy projectile weapon has far greater psychological effect than something silent and much more deadly. He flipped the selector switches for automatic and H.E. He traversed until he had the leaders of the attackers in the telescopic sights. Druthen was one of them, his bulk and his waddling run unmistakable. Von Donderberg was the other.

Grimes sighed again. He was genuinely sorry for the Waldegrener. In many ways he and Grimes were the same breed of cat. Only Druthen then. . . . He shifted his sights slightly. But the explosion of a high explosive shell might kill, would probably injure von Donderberg. Solid shot? Yes. One round should be ample, if Grimes' old skill with firearms still persisted. And it would be a spectacular enough deterrent for the survivors of Druthen's party.

Still Grimes hesitated. The hijackers would be marooned on Kinsolving; nothing would make him change his mind about that. But even if they didn't deserve a chance their children, their descendants did.

And, on a primitive world such as this, the more outstandingly bad bastards contributing to the gene pool the better.

Again he flipped the ammunition selector switch, then lowered his sights. He stitched a neat seam of bursting incendiary shells across the savannah, well ahead of Druthen and von Donderberg. The long grass was highly and satisfactorily flammable. The raiding party retreated in pan-

ic. By the time that those of them who possessed space armor got back to their camp to put it on, no matter how they hurried, *Faraway Quest* would be gone.

"All aboard, Skipper," reported Williams from behind Grimes. "Take her up?"

"Take her up, Commander Williams," ordered the Commodore.

XXXI

"Set trajectory, sir?" asked Carnaby.

Grimes looked out through the viewports, toward the opalescent sphere that was Kinsolving, toward the distant luminosity of the Galactic Lens.

"We have to go *somewhere*, John," said Sonya sharply.

"Or somewhen," murmured Grimes. He said, in a louder voice, "We'd better head for where The Outsider was, or will be, or is. We have unfinished business."

But it didn't really matter. For the time being, nothing really mattered.

He had his ship again.

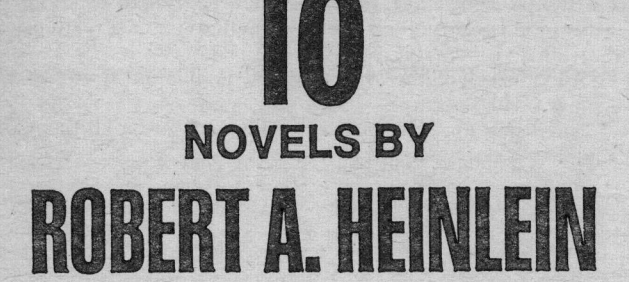

10
NOVELS BY
ROBERT A. HEINLEIN

05500	Between Planets	95c
10600	Citizen of the Galaxy	95c
31800	Have Space Suit—Will Travel	95c
71140	Red Planet	95c
73330	Rocket Ship Galileo	95c
73440	The Rolling Stones	95c
77730	Space Cadet	95c
78000	The Star Beast	95c
82660	Tunnel in the Sky	95c
91501	The Worlds of Robert A. Heinlein	60c

Available wherever paperbacks are sold or use this coupon.

ACE SCIENCE FICTION DOUBLES
Two books back-to-back for just 75c

05595 **Beyond Capella** Rackham
The Electric Sword-Swallowers Bulmer

11182 **Clockwork's Pirate**
Ghost Breaker Goulart

11560 **The Communipaths** Elgin
The Noblest Experiment in the Galaxy
Trimble

13783 **The Dark Dimensions**
Alternate Orbits Chandler

13793 **Dark of the Woods**
Soft Come the Dragons Koontz

13805 **Dark Planet** Rackham
The Herod Men Kamin

51375 **The Mad Goblin**
Lord of the Trees Farmer

58880 **Alice's World**
No Time for Heroes Lundwall

71802 **Recoil** Nunes
Lallia Tubb

76096 **The Ships of Durostorum** Bulmer
Alton's Unguessable Sutton

78400 **The Star Virus** Bayley
Mask of Chaos Jakes

81610 **To Venus! To Venus!** Grinnell
The Wagered World Janifer and Treibich
